PENGUIN BOOKS

THE LYING DAYS

Nadine Gordimer was born and lives in South Africa. She has written ten novels, including *My Son's Story*, *A Sport of Nature*, *Burger's Daughter*, *July's People*, and *The Conservationist* (co-winner of the Booker Prize in England). Her short stories have been collected in nine volumes, including *Jump and Other Stories* and *Something Out There*, and her nonfiction pieces were published together as *The Essential Gesture*. Gordimer has received numerous international prizes, including the 1991 Nobel Prize in Literature. In the United States, she has received the Modern Literature Association Award and the Bennett Award. Her fiction has appeared in many American magazines, including *The New Yorker*, and her essays have appeared in *The New York Times* and *The New York Review of Books*. She has been given honorary degrees by Yale, Harvard, and other universities and has been honored by the French government with the decoration Officier de l'Ordre des Arts et des Lettres. She is a vice president of PEN International and an executive member of the Congress of South African Writers.

D0793078

NADINE GORDIMER

THE LYING DAYS

PENGUIN BOOKS

PENGUIN BOOKS
Published by the Penguin Group
Penguin Books USA Inc., 375 Hudson Street,
New York, New York 10014, U.S.A.
Penguin Books Ltd, 27 Wrights Lane, London W8 5TZ, England
Penguin Books Australia Ltd, Ringwood, Victoria, Australia
Penguin Books Canada Ltd, 10 Alcorn Avenue,
Toronto, Ontario, Canada M4V 3B2
Penguin Books (N.Z.) Ltd, 182–190 Wairau Road,
Auckland 10, New Zealand

Penguin Books Ltd, Registered Offices:
Harmondsworth, Middlesex, England

First published in the United States of America by
Simon and Schuster, Inc., 1953
Published in Penguin Books 1994

1   3   5   7   9   10   8   6   4   2

PUBLISHER'S NOTE
This is a work of fiction. Names, characters, places, and incidents either
are the products of the author's imagination or are used fictitiously, and
any resemblance to actual persons, living or dead, events, or locales is
entirely coincidental.

ISBN 0 14 02.3367 9
(CIP data available)

Printed in the United States of America

FOR ORIANE GAVRON

Though leaves are many, the root is one;
Through all the lying days of my youth
I swayed my leaves and flowers in the sun;
Now I may wither into the truth.

W. B. Yeats

PART ONE

The Mine

I ONE SATURDAY in late August when my friend Olwen Taylor's mother telephoned to say that Olwen would not be able to go to the bioscope because she was going to a wedding, I refused to go with Gloria Dufalette (I heard Mrs. Dufalette's call, out the back door in the next house—Gloriah, Gloriah!) or with Paddy Connolly. —Paddy Connolly's little brother picked his nose, and no member of his family stopped him doing it.—

"What'll she do, then?" asked my father.

My mother was pinning her hair ready for her tennis cap, looking straight back at herself in the mirror. Up-down, went her shoulders. "I don't know. She's not pleased with anything I suggest."

But her indifference was not real. She followed me out into the garden where I stood in the warm still winter afternoon. "Now what are you going to do? Do you want to come with Mommy and Daddy and bring your book?" New powder showed white where the sun shone full on her nose and chin; it seemed to emphasize the fact that she was ready and waiting and yet held back. In a sense of power, I did not answer; my mother's face waited, as if I had spoken and she had not quite heard. "Eh? What are you going to do?"

"Nothing," I said, richly sullen. I saw the bedroom windows jerked in by an unseen hand; my father was ready, too. They were both waiting, their afternoon dependent upon me.

"Where are you going?"

Somewhere away from the houses resting back round the square of the Recreation Hall, beyond the pines in the road and the gums sounding, over the dry veld and in the town, Olwen was putting on a blue crinoline hat. Who could believe it was happening the same time as the doves spread their fat breasts in comfortable dust baths in the garden? Everything was waiting for me to answer. "Helen! You must make up your mind what you want to do. You know I can't leave you on your own, the girl's out." Yes, I knew that, an unwritten law so sternly upheld and generally accepted that it would occur to no child to ask why: a little girl must not be left alone because there were native boys about. That was all. Native boys were harmless and familiar because they were servants, or delivery boys bringing the groceries or the fish by bicycle from town, or Mine boys something to laugh at in their blankets and their clay-spiked hair, but at the same time they spoke and shouted in a language you didn't understand and dressed differently in any old thing, and so were mysterious. Not being left alone because they were about was simply something to do with their mysteriousness.

I squatted, digging the point of my hairslide into the white flakes of dead grass. "Helen?" My mother was not angry yet, still impatient; every moment I went on digging at the grass was riskier and nearer to anger. "Not going anywhere," I mumbled, as if not caring if my mother heard or not. She turned with a skid of her tennis shoe on the gravel and walked into the house. At once she came back again, the key in her hand, my father behind her. It was always strange to see his knees, thin and surprised at their exposure, in shorts; they flickered a suggestion—half recognized, then gone out again—that *he* had mysteriousness somewhere, was someone else, to be seen by other people the way I could see other people. He had little authority with me; believed that, whenever something went wrong, my mother did not quite know how to deal with me, but refrained from interfering much himself. He would look at the two of us with the head-shaking tolerance of a man listening to the quarrels of two women. "What's the trouble?" he said now, though he had been told. It was as if he trusted the tale of one no more than that of the other.

Burning with a new and strange pleasure, I did not answer. I could feel them standing tall, over me. "No, we're just going to leave her here, that's all," said my mother briskly and coldly. Her chin was tightened in offense. "The back door's open and she can just be left to her own devices. If something happens to her it's her own fault. I'm not ruining my afternoon for her."

She had gone too far, and spoiled the effect. We all knew that her afternoon *was* ruined; that she was terrified and convinced that "something" would happen to me; that her stride to the gate was a piece of bravado that cost her more than it was worth. Yet she sat in the car waiting, looking straight before her. "Will you be all right, Nell—? You'll play quietly in the garden, eh?" said my father softly, touching my head as he followed. At the gate he turned back, as if he were about to make a sudden suggestion. But he closed the gate behind him and got into the car.

I heard it shake into life at the push of the starter button, pant obediently until it was put into gear, swish past the tough grasses at the curb and then swell away up the road. When it had gone, I looked up. Sun stroked the pine trees; there was a faint smell of petrol from the empty road where the car had been. I began to walk round and round the lawn balancing on the bricks which outlined it, whispering over and over—Not going anywhere, not going anywhere. I went and climbed on the gate, hanging out over to the road. Far off, along the houses, someone was hammering. Bellingan's old black dog was zigzagging with busy aimlessness in the grounds of the Recreation Hall. He went in, in the shadow, came out in the light, like a fish rising and disappearing in water. A car passed; a reminder.

I came slowly back up the path and to the front door, forgetting it was locked. I tried it a few times and then went slowly round the back—Anna's little room with its padlocked door and shut window protected with homemade tin burglar bars, tight in the quiet—and into the house. In my bedroom I stood before the mirror that was the middle door of the wardrobe, looking at myself. After a long time, steady and unblinking, only the sound of my breath, the face was just a face like other people's faces met in the street. It looked at me a little longer. Suddenly I slammed the door, ran out of the passage which seemed to take up and give out the sound of each of my footsteps as if it were counting them, and through the kitchen which was noting each drip of the tap and the movement of a fly on a potato peeling. I went straight down the garden path and out of the gate into the road.

The sun pressed gently warm down on my shoulders as I walked in the road. Drifts of brown pine needles glistened in a wavering wash; sloping toward the sides, they were bedded down firmly, inches deep, beneath my feet. I stepped on an old orange peel, sucked out and dried so long that it crushed like the shell of a beetle. Tiny gray winter birds bounced on the telephone wires, flicked away. From the long gardens of the staff houses, doves sounded continuously like the even breathing of a sleeper.

Mr. Bellingan sat on a chair on his lawn with his shoes off and his feet up. His head was dropped to one side behind his paper. Next door two little boys hunched up over something they were making, backs to the gate. I left the row behind me.

Along the rippling white corrugated tin fences of the backs of another row, where the tin garages opened out onto a grassy road, some of the Married Quarters people were cleaning their cars. A man and a woman rubbed away in silence; inside the car, a small child was playing, licking the back window, then smearing it with a dirty pink feeder which was tied round its neck. The baby called out something to me that I didn't hear. Farther up, a garage leaned heavily upon by an old bare willow was open and spilled out onto the rough track tools, oilcans and the red, tender-looking intestines of a tire. The two Cluff boys with faces fierce with smears, pale khaki shorts hanging distractedly from their hips and their mother's thick knitted socks sunk into fat rims round their pale legs, were helping someone dismantle a motorcycle. They gave each other technical instructions in terse gasps, as they struggled with the prostrate machine whose handle bars stuck up obstinately in the air.

There was a smell of burning, and the faint intoxication of rotting oranges from the dustbins. I walked closer to the level line of fences, trailing the fingers of my left hand lightly across the corrugations so that they rose and fell in an arpeggio of movement. I thought of water. Of the sea—oh, the surprise, the lift of remembering that there was the sea, that it was there now, somewhere, belonging to last year's and next year's two weeks of holiday at Durban—the sea

which did something the same to your fingers, threading water
through them . . . like the pages of a thick book falling away rapidly
ripply back beneath your fingers to solidity. —The sea could not
be believed in for long, here. Could be smelled for a moment, a
terrible whiff of longing evaporated with the deeper snatch of breath
that tried to seize it. Or remembered by the blood, which now and
then felt itself stirred by a movement caused by something quite
different, setting up reactions purely physically like those in response to the sea.

"Helen? Where you go-ing—?" A child with her hair in curlers
hung over the fence, standing on an old packing case. A tiny kitten
whose eyes were not yet open nosed the air mewing from her tight
hand.

"Somewhere," I said, not looking back.

"Aren't you going to bioscope?"

I had passed. The back of my head shook slow vehement denial.
"Where you go-ing?" the child shouted. "Somewhere!" I shouted,
down the end of the road, now. In the gum plantation that bordered
the Mine property I came to a stop beneath one of the firm trunks
and stood patiently peeling off the curling bark. It was tough, fibrous
and dry to my tugging, and it came away with a crackle and a tear,
leaving a smooth gray surface soothing beneath my palm. The trunk
was hard and cool, like the pillars at the library. I sat down on a
stone that had a secret cold of its own and began to pull off the
scab on my knee. I had been saving that scab for days, resisting
the compelling urge just to put the edge of my nail beneath it, just
to test it. . . . Now it was a tough little seal of dried blood, holding,
but not deeply attached to the new skin hidden beneath it. I did it
very slowly, lifting it all round with my thumbnail and then pinching
the skin between my forefinger and thumb so that the edge of the
scab showed up free of the skin, a sharp ridge. There was the feeling
of it, ready to slough off, unnecessary on my knee; almost an itch.
Then I lifted it off quick and clean and there was no tweak of some
spot not quite healed, but only the pleasure of the break with the
thin tissue that had held it on. Holding the scab carefully, I looked
at the healed place. The new pink shiny pale skin seemed stuck
like a satiny petal on the old; I felt it tenderly. Then I looked at the

scab, held on the ball of my thumb, felt its tough papery uselessness, and the final deadness that had come upon it the moment it was no longer on my leg. Putting it between my front teeth, I bit it in half and looked at the two pieces. Then I took them on the end of my tongue and bit them again and again until they disappeared in my mouth.

The Mine houses had their fences and hedges around them, their spoor of last summer's creepers drawn up about their walls. I went down the dust road through the trees and out onto the main road that shook everything off from it, that stood up alone and straight in the open sun and the veld.

It was different, being down on the road instead of up in the bus or the car, seeing it underneath. A firm tar road, blue colored and good to walk on, like hard rubber. I trotted along, pressing my heels into it. Now and then a car hooted behind me and I stepped onto the stony side where dry khaki weed fastened its seed like a row of pins to the hem of my dress. I liked the feeling of the space, empty about me, the unfamiliarity of being alone. Two Mine boys were coming toward me; passed me, the one wearing his tin underground helmet and khaki trousers drawn in with string around his bare ankles, the other in a raggy loincloth beneath a gray blanket patterned with yellow and cyclamen whorls. They were smoking pipes; one had a little homemade pouch, of some animal skin, in his hand. I looked straight ahead, sternly. When I had gone on a bit, I looked back. But they were a long way off, not caring, laughing as if they were separated from each other by a stretch of veld and wanted to make themselves heard. A delivery boy from the town zigzagged past on his bicycle: a smart boy whistling in black-and-white shoes, brown trousers and a bow tie. A curious feeling prickled round my shoulders. Was there something to be afraid of?

The red dust path turning off to the stores was somewhere I had never been. There were children on the Mine, little children in pushcarts whose mothers let the nursegirls take them anywhere they liked; go down to the filthy kaffir stores to gossip with the boys and let those poor little babies they're supposed to be taking care of breathe in heaven knows what dirt and disease, my mother often condemned. Other children called them the Jew stores, and sometimes bicycled down there to get some stuff to fix bicycle punctures. I slowed. But to turn round and go back to the Mine would be to have been nowhere. Lingering in the puffy dust, I made slowly for the stores huddled wall to wall in a line on the veld up ahead.

There were dozens of natives along the path. Some lay on the burned grass, rolled in their blankets, face down, as if they were dead in the sun. Others squatted and stood about shouting, passed on to pause every few yards and shout back something else. Quite often the exchange lasted for half a mile, bellowed across the veld until one was too far away to do more than wave a stick eloquently at the other. A boy in an old dishcloth walked alone, thrumming a big wooden guitar painted with gilt roses. Orange peels and pith were thrown about, and a persistent fly kept settling on my lip. But I went on rather faster and determined, waving my hand impatiently before my face and watching a white man who stood outside one of the stores with his hands on his hips while a shopboy prized open a big packing case. The Mine boys sauntering and pushing up and down the pavement jostled the man, got in the way. He kept jerking his head back in dismissal, shouting something at them.

He was a short ugly man with a rough gray chin; as I stepped onto the broken cement pavement he looked up at me with screwed-up eyes, irritably, and did not see me. His shirt was open at the neck and black hairs were scribbled on the little patch of dead white skin. "Cam-an!" He grabbed the chisel from the shopboy and creaked it under the wooden lid. The shopboy in his European clothes stood back bored among the Mine boys. I went past feeling very close to the dirty battered pavement, almost as if I were crawling along it like an insect under the noise and the press of natives. The air had a thick smell of sweat and strange pigment and herbs, and as I came to the door of the eating house, a crescendo of heavy, sweet nauseating blood-smell, the clamor of entrails stewing richly, assailed me like a sudden startling noise. I drew in a breath of shock and saw in the dark interior wooden benches and trestles and dark faces and flies; the flash of a tin mug, and a big white man in a striped butcher's apron cutting a chunk of bruised and yellow fat-streaked meat from a huge weight impaled on a hook. Sawdust on the floor showed pocked like sand and spilled out onto the pavement, shaking into the cracks and fissures, mixing with the dust and torn paper, clogged here and there with blood.

Fowls with the quick necks of scavengers darted about between my trembling legs; the smeary windows of the shops were deep and mysterious with jumble that, as I stopped to look, resolved into shirts and shoes and braces and beads, yellow pomade in bottles, mirrors and mauve socks and watch chains, complicated as a mosaic, undisturbed, and always added to—a football jersey here, an enamel tiepin there, until there was not one corner, one single inch of the window which was not rich and complicatedly hung. Written on bits of cardboard, notices said CHEAP, THE LATEST. In the corners drifts of dead flies peaked up. Many others lay, wire legs up, on smooth shirt fronts. From the doorways where blankets somber and splendid with fierce colors hung, gramophones swung out the blare and sudden thrilling cry—the voice of a woman high and minor above the concerted throats of a choir of men—of Bantu music, and the nasal wail of American cowboy songs. Tinseled tin trunks in pink and green glittered in the gloom.

There were people there, shadowy, strange to me as the black men with the soft red inside their mouths showing as they opened in the concentration of spending money. There was even a woman, in a flowered alpaca apron, coming out to throw something into the pavement crowd. There was another woman, sitting on an upturned soapbox pulling at a hangnail on her short, broad thumb. She yawned—her fat ankles, in cotton stockings, settled over her shoes—and looked up puffily. Yes? Yes? she chivied a native who was pointing at something in the window at her side, and grunting. "—Here," she called back into the dark shop, not moving. "He wants a yellow shirt. Here in the winder, with stripes."

I passed her with a deep frown; it was on my face all the time now. My heart ran fast and trembly, like the heart of a kitten I had once held. I held my buttocks stiffly together as I went along, looking, looking. But I felt my eyes were not quick enough, and darted here and there at once, fluttering over everything, unable to see anything singly and long enough. And at the same time I wanted to giggle, to stuff my hand in my mouth so that a squeal, like a long squeeze of excitement, should not wring through me.

Even when I was smaller, fairy tales had never interested me much. To me, brought up into the life of a South African mine, stories of children living the ordinary domestic adventures of the upper-middle-class English family—which was the only one that existed for children's books published in England in the thirties— were weird and exotic enough. Nannies in uniform, governesses and ponies, nurseries and playrooms and snow fights—all these commonplaces of European childhood were as unknown and therefore as immediately enviable as the life of princesses in legendary castles to the English children for whom the books were written. I had never read a book in which I myself was recognizable; in which there was a "girl" like Anna who did the housework and the cooking and called the mother and father Missus and Baas; in which the children ate and lived closely with their parents and played in the lounge and went to the bioscope. So it did not need the bounds of credulity to be stretched to princes who changed into frogs or houses that could be eaten like gingerbread to transport me to an unattainable world of the imagination. The sedate walk of two genteel infant Tories through an English park was other world enough for me.

Yet now as I stood in this unfamiliar part of my own world knowing and flatly accepting it as the real world because it was ugly and did not exist in books (if this was the beginning of disillusion, it was also the beginning of Colonialism: the identification of the unattainable distant with the beautiful, the substitution of "overseas" for "fairyland") I felt for the first time something of the tingling fascination of the gingerbread house before Hansel and Gretel, anonymous, nobody's children, in the woods. Standing before the one small window of the native medicine shop I no longer could be bored before the idea of the beckoning witch and the collection of pumpkins and lamps and mice that shot up into carriages and genii and coachmen or two-headed dogs. Not that these dusty lions' tails, these piles of wizened seeds, these flaking gray roots and strange teeth could be believed to hold tight, like Japanese paper flowers, magic that might suddenly open. Not that the peeled skin of a snake, curling like an apple skin down the window, could suggest a dragon. But the dustiness, the grayness, the scavenged collection of tooth and claw and skin and sluggish potion brought who knows by whom or how far or from where, waiting beneath cobwebs and neglect . . . the shudder of revulsion at finding my finger going out wanting to touch it! It winked suddenly like the eye of a crocodile that waited looking like a harmless dry log: you did not know what you might be looking at, what awfulness inert in withered heaps behind the glass.

It was at this moment that a small boy came skipping down the pavement white and unconcerned with a tin pistol dangling against his navy blue pants, and a bicycle bell tringing importantly in his hand. He walked straight past me with the ease of someone finding his way about his own house, and dodged through the Mine boys as if they were the fowls, making up their minds for them when they did not seem to know whether they wanted to step this way or that. He was dark, but his eyes were big and light beneath childishly rumpled eyebrows: he was gone, into a doorway farther up.

I could not have said why the sight of another child was so startling. He seemed to flash through my mind, tearing mystery, strangeness, as a thick cobweb splits to nothing brushed away by the hand of a man. I was interested now in the native customers inside the medicine shop who were buying roots and charms the way people buy aspirins. I watched one boy who took his money from a yellow tobacco bag and then had a measure of greenish flakes poured into a second tobacco bag. Another was turning a tiny empty tortoise shell over in his hand; I wondered how much such a thing would cost, then remembered that I had no money. It was a charming little mound of brown and amber medallions, so neatly fitted. . . . Perhaps I could come back and get one someday. I felt a longing of affection for the tortoise shell which was to me a creature in itself; I would carry it everywhere with me, look at the light through its stripy shell the way the light looked through a leaf or the stained-glass window that the Millars had put up to the memory of their son, in the church.

The boy did not buy the shell. It went back onto the wooden shelf. I pressed nearer the window and made a spy hole with my hand against the rheumy glass to see in better, and as I did so my eye was caught by another eye. Something was alive in the window: a chameleon, crouched motionless and matching on a bundle of gray-green sticks until then, was making its way slowly up the rib of wood that seamed the corner of the window. Its little soft divided feet, each one like two little slender hands joined and facing outward from the wrist, fluttered for a hold and swayed, feeling the air. One eye in the wrinkled socket looked ahead, the other swiveled back fixed on me. Ah-h! I cried, scratching my finger at the glass and leaning my whole weight against it. I followed the creature all up the window and down again, when it walked across the floor high-stepping over the piles of herbs and objects. Then it stopped, swayed, and a long thin tongue like one of those rude streamers you blow out in people's faces at Christmas shot unrolled and curled back again with a fly coiled within it. The thin mouth was closed, a rim of pale green. Both eyes turned backward looking at me.

I turned away from the medicine shop and went on along the pavement, past a shoemaker's, two more outfitter's and a bicycle shop which had a bicycle cut out of tin and painted red and yellow hanging in the doorway, and sold sewing machines and portable gramophones. Inside the shop the small boy leaned with his stomach against a battered counter. The bottom of his face was heavy with concentration and he had an oilcan and a length of chain in his hands. A baby of about three scuffed the dust on the cement at his feet and said over and over, liking the sound of the words and not expecting an answer, "Let me! Letme, letme, letme." There were only two more stores. Then the bare rubbed dust that had been veld but had worn away beneath ill-fitting mine boots and tough naked toes (the skin of the natives' feet was like bark, the nails like thorn). There native vendors squatted beside braziers offering roasted meal-ies and oranges arranged in pyramids. They sat comfortably, waiting for custom to come to them; they looked levelly out at the Mine boys looking around with money to spend, parcels from the stores under their arms, sometimes a loaf of bread white under the black hot armpit. The gramophones from the stores made music and there was gossip and shouting above the tiny hammering of a man who sat crosslegged beating copper wire into bracelets: —they caught the sharp winter sun like the telephone wires. Fowls hung about the mealie braziers, and just where the stores' pavement crumbled off into the dust, a boy sat with a sewing machine, whirring the handle with his vigorous elbow jutting. Beside him were khaki and white drill trousers, neatly patched over the knees with crisscross strengthening in red and blue. He himself wore a curious loose garment, like a nightshirt.

Even though it was winter there were flies here (one settled lovingly on me again, this time bumbling my ear) and above the gusts of strong sweet putrescence enveloping suddenly from the eating house, the smoke of burned mealies and the rotten sweetness of discarded oranges squashed everywhere underfoot, there was the high, strong, nostril-burning smell of stale urine. It had eaten the grass of the veld away, it had soured the earth with a crude animal foulness. I could not place it (a faint whiff, overlaid with disinfectant, came out of the public cloakroom near the bus terminus where my mother would not let me go); but my lip twitched up in distaste. The shouting seemed part of the smell and the twirl of flies; I felt suddenly that I wanted to bat at my clothes and brush myself down and feel over my hair in case something had settled on me—some horrible dirt, something alive, perhaps. —A child had once crammed a locust down my back at school, and for days afterward I had sudden attacks of shuddering all over the surface of my body so that I had wanted to tear off my clothes and examine every inch of my skin.

I looked at these dark brown faces—the town natives were somehow lighter—dark as teak and dark as mahogany, shining with the warm grease of their own liveness lighting up their skin; wondering, receptive, unthinking, taking in with their eyes as earth takes water; close-eyed, sullen with the defensive sullenness of the defenseless; noisy and merry with the glee of the innocent. And to me, in my kilts and my hand-knitted socks and my hair tied with neat ribbon, they were something to look at with a half-smile, as I had watched the chameleon in the window.

I crunched to the path and the road over burned veld that dissolved crisply in puffs of black dust round my shoes and I passed a Mine boy standing with his back to me and his legs apart. I had vaguely noticed them standing that curious way before, as I whisked past in the car. But as I passed this one—he was singing, and the five or six yards he had put between himself and the vendors was simply a gesture—I saw a little stream of water curving from him. Not shock but a sudden press of knowledge, hot and unwanted, came upon me. A question that had waited inside me but had never risen into words or thoughts because there were no words for it—no words with myself, my mother, with Olwen even. I began to run, very fast, along the tar, the smooth straight road. And presently the run slackened and calmed, and I skipped along, jerking my hair over my ears, one foot catching behind the other.

I did not go back to the house but across the Recreation Hall grounds under the trees and round to the tennis courts where, before I could see the wires sparkling filaments of silver, I heard beyond the pines and the clipped hedge and the deep cooing of doves the pomp! pomp! of the balls.

Round the dark hedge in the clear sun I saw them suddenly as a picture, the white figures with turning pink faces running on the courts, the striped blazers lying on the pale grass, the bare pink legs and white sand shoes sitting in the log house. They were having tea. The young men sat on the grass. Alec Finlay panted, one leg stretched, resting on his elbows. He saw me and waved. Then my mother looked up over a big enamel urn, a little puzzled, as if she had heard a familiar sound. I smiled at her. "Well, young lady?" said Alec, screwing up his eyes and his smile. I walked into the shade, the smell of hot tea, lavender water, and fresh white clothes. "Are you going to join us, Helen?" a pretty grown-up girl asked me. "New blood for the second league!" said someone, and they all laughed, because they had just lost their match. "Just in time for tea, I'd say." My mother was in the grown-up conspiracy of banter, nodding her head mockingly as she smiled. They all laughed again. My mother's hand felt over my damp forehead, lifting the hair back. "D'you want some tea, darling?" Her head was on one side, smiling down into my face, the little springs of red hair escaping. She was pleased to be able to ignore the argument, the vague anxiousness that had ended up satisfactorily in a loneliness that had sent me tailing after her, after all.

I sat beside her, thirstily gulping tea, feet not quite reaching the ground. "No, no, you don't," said a fat fair man, waving back the crumpets. "Do you want to weigh me down and give yourself an advantage?" —They laughed helplessly again; he was the comedian of the crowd, he was always coming out with something. In fact, he had such a reputation for being amusing that they laughed, found their mouths twitching in reflex every time he opened his, no matter what he said. I laughed with them. Soon I was handing round the crumpets, helping with fresh cups of tea. They teased me and talked to me playfully; I blushed when the young men chaffed me in a way that seemed to deepen some secret between them and their girls. But recklessly, I could answer them back, teasing too, I could make *them* laugh. They said: "Listen to her! —Did you hear that—?" I stood bridling with pleasure, looking wide out of my eyes in the face of applause.

I went there often on Saturday afternoons after that, accepted as one of them, but with the distinction of being the only child in the party. It was easy to be one of them because I soon knew their jokes as well as they did themselves and, beside my mother, sat a little forward as they did, waiting for each to come out with his famous remark. Then when they rocked and shook their heads at getting just what they had expected, I would jump up and down, clutching at my mother's arm in delight.

I was quite one of them.

2 THE ROAD ON WHICH I had hesitated before going down to the Concession Stores that Saturday afternoon was the road between Mine and town. I passed along it going to school every morning. I came back along it at two o'clock every afternoon in the bus which had shaken past first the Town Hall in its geometrical setting of flower beds and frostbitten lawn and municipal coat-of-arms grown in tight fleshy cactus; the dirty shopblinds of the main street making a chalky dazzle; the native delivery boys sitting in the gutters, staring at their broken shoes; the buildings, like a familiar tune picked out silently on a keyboard: one, one, two-story, two, one, one-story—then the houses of the township, long rows of corrugated iron roofs behind bullet-headed municipal trees shorn regularly to keep them free of the telephone wires, the Greek shop with its pyramid of crude pink coconut buns and frieze of spotted bananas, the doctor's house with a tiled roof and a tennis court; and out at last, past the last row of houses turning their back yards—a patchwork of washing, a broken dog kennel, the little one-eyed room where the servant lived—to the veld.

Seen from the bus, this stretch of road between town and Mine was featureless with familiarity. A few natives sauntered along, trailing their blankets in the red dust; very occasionally was there a diversion—one day, the figure of a small boy on a bicycle, holding a big live red hen under each arm, and scudding along over the dips and mounds of the dust-deep path from the Concession Stores like a surf rider. And even he had interested no one but me, though as he passed and the yellow scaly legs of the fowls showed sticking out mutely under his elbows, I rose and pressed my forehead against the window, making my gaze felt on the whorl of dark hair on the crown of his head. . . . Mostly there was no focus of attention between the last of the town of Atherton and the point where the bus approached the line of a signboard that widened to spell out ATHERTON PTY. MINES LTD., and the trees separated into gray trunks reaching up in swaths of bark like muscle, and shifting shapes of spilling leaves that, leaves on leaves, moving always, as the sea moves, thinning and thickening as cloud changes, showed and then closed over a flickering of white-painted tin fence, the dim red roofs orderly as tents.

Daily, when the bus put me down here, I was home. Past the first three rows of houses and up alongside the fourth. All built of the same dark brick with low roofs, small windows and porches enclosed with a fine-meshed wire screening which had a tinny dazzle like the sheen off a piece of moire when it was new, but now was tarnished, and darkened each entrance with homely gloom. Even in the middle of the day, little glowing points of orange light showed behind the windows: inside Mine houses it was always dark. The houses of the officials in the fourth row were bigger than the others, set well back from the road with a tall row of pines screening their long narrow gardens. They looked out across the road upon an untidy square park, deeply bordered with great solemn pines which had cast their needles and dark shade so long that beneath them the grass had worn away and died, and the earth was theirs, cut off by them from the sun. Small children fluttered about their nursemaids like butterflies, and in the middle stood the Recreation Hall. Like everything else it had been built by the Mine and it belonged to the Mine; cut-out steel letters spelled ATHERTON RECREATION HALL across the chipped portico, and posters advertising dances and bridge drives long past hung peeling from the pillars.

There our house was; and I lived in it as I lived in my body. I was not aware of the shape of it, of its existence as a building the way the school existed or the houses in the town; nor of its relation to the other houses of the Mine about it and again the town about them: I had begun within it, at the pin point of existence, and hollowed out within it my awareness. When I came home the authority of school—my uniform, the black stockings, the blazer which held the smell of ink and dust and classrooms curiously cold as if they had been steeped in water, of orange peel and curling egg sandwich in my lunch tin—became invalid. There there was no need of an exterior, a way to smile and talk and listen to other people, the little suit of consciousness a child climbs into the very first time he is led in to be shown to someone from outside; there I did not have to put on that to show I was alive, for there was the path, pressing gravel up to my soles, there was the leafless frond of the jasmine bush, touching my ear like my own hair, there was the drift of brown pine needles held in the guttering of the veranda as in the palm of my hand.

Every afternoon, our native girl Anna, eating her lunch: tearing off chunks of bread and washing them down with great gulps of tea from an old jam tin. The voice of my mother, high, questioning, accompanied by an arpeggio of spoons gently striking delicate china; coming out of the house like the voice of the walls: "Helen?" Under the light in the dark little sitting room, the willow pattern tea-things out. Embroidered cloth and tea cozy in the shape of a china doll in a wool crocheted crinoline, crumpets polished with yellow butter, the whole covered with a square of green net weighted with beads. My mother's footsteps in high heels quick and loud down the passage. A little burst of voices: Come in! Hu-llo . . . so I thought we'd just . . . yes, I'm glad you did . . . no, not at all, just right, of course not—and my mother's voice and my mother's sharp heels leading up the passage, past the half-open door behind which I would flatten myself, while the little troop filled my mother's bedroom with movement and gasps and laughter, like the commotion of swimmers rubbing themselves down after cold water.

Past the Eau-de-Cologne presence of my mother, into the room, putting each patent shoe down from toe to heel, smiling, but my lips tucked together as if something might escape. A place made for me at the table, holding their handbags to their laps as they shifted: Here, see what it is I've got for you! Hullo! Was that the tartan my mother had been making up for me one day at the Compound Manager's? —They would smile down at me, as if I were a surprise. And then when my father came home and walked into the bright close sitting room slapping his folded paper in his palm, they stirred and gave little cries, like busily feeding birds startled by a stone.

"So late already!"

"Look, it's almost dark."

The afternoon was their own domain, but the evening belonged to the menfolk. None of them had anything to say to my father; the warm flow of their talk always dried up the instant he walked in. They wanted to pack themselves and the evidence of their close and personal preoccupations—the ridiculous dangle of baby booties, the embroidered crash bags holding tangled silks—out of his way. "A man wants his home to himself," Mrs. Cluff often said.

And then, before dinner, my mother's feet different in her everyday shoes again; lying on the rug, I watched them and the long hard black legs of Anna (without the shine her brown face had— blacker with the cold of the yard, roughened with early mornings and biting nights) bare into shoes hollowed out by someone else's fat ankles, passing and repassing as the table was laid for dinner. . . .

It was this to which the road brought me back always; and it was from this that we set out, my mother and father and I, when we went into the town on Saturday mornings. Then we went by car, and my father parked in the main street outside the department store where dirty ragged little native boys said over and over, like small birds repeating one note, Look after your car, sah? Look after your car, sah? My father would lock the doors and try the handles and threaten: "No! Now get away. Get away from this car." Once one boy had pushed another and said, "Don't take him, sir, that boy's no good," and I had laughed but my father had tightened his nostrils and walked through the native children saying Hamba! Hamba! "Something should be done about it," he often said, "little loafers and thieves, they should chase them off the streets."

Wherever we went to shop in the town we were known, and when my mother bought anything she would simply say, "G. P. Shaw, Atherton"—and that would be enough. The charge slip would go shooting away up the wire in its little brass cage to the office perched above. If by any chance—there might be a new shop assistant—we were asked to give an address, my mother would raise her eyebrows and say in a high, amused voice, lifting the corner of her mouth a little, "Mrs. G. P. Shaw, 138 Staff Officials' Quarters, Atherton Proprietary Mines Limited—but really, Atherton's all that anyone ever wants."

The little town with its one busy street was alive with the mines on a Saturday. The Mine people came from Atherton, Atherton Deep, Platfontein, New Postma, Basilton Levels and the new mines opening up, but not yet in production, to the east of the town. In the three barbershops behind curtained doorways scissors chattered ceaselessly and the crossed feet of waiting men showed tilted up before newspapers in the outer shop. The bright windows held hundreds of small objects, from razor blades and pipe cleaners to watches and brooches, and the smell of sweet violet oil came warmly out to the pavement. I dragged slowly past, afraid to peep in (barbershops were mysterious as bars, and as unapproachable) but wondering if my father were there. I never found him; but later when we met him at the car his neck would be pink and there would be tiny short sharp fragments of hair dusted into the rim of his ear.

There were two big grocers in Atherton, but Mine people didn't go to Golden Supply Stores but to Bond and Son. It took at least half an hour to give an order at Bond's because there Mine women met not only their neighbors from their own property, and women from other properties, but also the surprise of women who had been transferred to some other mine on another part of the chain of gold mines called the Reef, and transferred back again just as unexpectedly. Then Mr. Bond, a short, thick-faced man with many opinions, had known my mother for many years. He liked to lean across the counter on one ham-shaped forearm and, with his eyes darting round the shop as if he didn't want anyone else to guess at what he could possibly be saying, tell her how if it wasn't his bread and butter, he could talk, all right. Cocktail cabinets and radiograms and running up big bills for the food they ate. "I could mention some names," he'd say. "I know. I know." My mother would smile, in a soft voice, pulling her mouth in. "Only if you're in business you dare not talk. Smile and say nothing." "Smile and say nothing," the grocer took up as if it had been just what he was looking for, "that's it all right. Smile and say nothing. But how people can live like that beats me. . . ." "How they can put their heads on the pillow at night. . . ." My mother shook her head. "But it just depends on how you were brought up, Mr. Bond. I couldn't do it if you paid me. . . ."

If Mr. Bond was already serving, it would be Mr. Cronje, the tall thin Afrikaans assistant, who spoke a very careful and peculiar English and had a duodenal ulcer. Before she started to give her order my mother would ask how he was. He would take his pencil from behind his big sad ear and put it back again and say, "Ag, still alive, you know, Mrs. Shaw, still alive." And then looking down the long flat expanse of his white apron he would tell her about the attack he had on Sunday night, or the new diet of kaffir beer or sour milk which his wife's sister had recommended. And my mother would say, "You must take care of yourself, you must look after yourself." He would sigh and his false teeth would move loosely in his wide mouth. "But you know how it is, if you not you own boss. . . ."

While my mother was absorbed at the counter in one way or another, I wandered off round the shop. Near the door there was a sloping glass showcase displaying varieties of biscuits and in the middle of the shop was a pillar with mirrors all round. The oilcloth round the base was stained and often splattered because all the dogs that were brought into the store strained at their leads to get to it.

Occasionally a stray ranged in from the street, wavering bewil-
deredly round the shop and then sniffing up to the pillar; then one
of the assistants would rush out flapping his apron and shout, "Voetsak!" and the startled creature would flatten itself out into the street.
At Christmas and Easter there were big packing cases piled up open
on the floor at the far end of the shop, filled with boxes of elaborate
crackers, or fancy chocolate eggs packed in silver paper and straw,
and there was always the "wedding present" showcase, all the year
round, with flowery tea sets and Dickens character jugs and cut-
crystal violet vases that were to be seen again behind glass in every
sitting-room china cabinet on the Mine. Sometimes there were other
children whom I knew, waiting for their mothers. Together we stood
with our hands and breath pressed against the glass, playing a
game that was a child's earnest and possessive form of window-
shopping. "I dabby the pink tea set and the balloon lady and the
two dogs. . . . And the gold dish" was added in triumph, "And I
dabby the gold dish!" "No you can't—I dabbied it first, I said the
gold dish the first time!"

Then quite suddenly there was the waiting face at the door, the
hand stretched impatiently. "Come on. Come, Helen, I've got a lot
to do, you know."

Out in the street little boys as old as I was or younger were
selling the local paper, which was published every Saturday morning. They were Afrikaans children mostly, with flat businesslike
faces, dull brownish, and cropped brownish hair. Their small dry
dirty fingers fumbled the pennies seriously; sometimes you gave
them a tickey for the tup-penny paper, and the penny was theirs.

The barefoot boys were soft-footed everywhere, at the market,
the railway station, the street corners, outside the bars. And the
yellowish paper with its coarse blotting-paper surface on which the
black print blurred slightly was rolled up under elbows; stuck out
of pockets and baskets; blew at the foot of babies' prams. My mother
would open it in the car, going home, and pass on the news while
my father avoided the zigzag of native errand boys, shouting to one
another as they rode, and the children waiting bent forward on tiptoe
at the curb, ready to run across like startled rabbits at the wrong
moment. The Social and Personal columns had the widest possible

application and filled two whole pages. Twice I had been mentioned: Congratulations to Helen Shaw, who has passed her Junior Pianoforte examination with 78 marks, and dainty little Helen, daughter of Mrs. G. P. Shaw, who made a charming Alice in Wonderland, and won the Mayoress's special prize for the best character costume. Each mine had a column to itself, and often "Atherton Mine Notes," written in a highly playful style by "our special correspondent"— an unidentified but suspected member of the Mine community— mentioned popular or hard-working Mrs. Shaw, wife of our Assistant Secretary. My father's name was usually in the tennis fixtures for the week, too. I liked to read down the list of names and say out loud my father's, just as if it were anyone else's.

Our life was punctuated by the Mine hooter.

It blew at seven in the morning and at noon and at half-past four in the afternoon. The people in the town set their watches by it; the people on the Mine needn't look at their watches because of it. At midnight on New Year's Eve its low, cavernous bellow (there was a lonely, stately creature there, echoing its hollow cry down the deep cave beneath the shaft, all along the dark airless passages hollowed out beneath the crust of the town) announced the New Year. Sometimes it lifted its voice at some unaccustomed odd hour of an ordinary day, and people in the town paused a moment and said: "There must've been an accident underground." To women on the Mine it came like the cry of a beast in distress, and it would be something to ask their men when they came home at lunchtime.

For there were very seldom any serious accidents, and few of those that did happen involved white men. Natives were sometimes trapped by a fall of rock from a hanging, and had to be dug out, dead or alive, while the hooter wailed disaster. When a white man was killed, the papers recorded the tragedy, giving his name and occupation and details of the family he left. If no white man was affected, there was an item headed: "FATAL FALL OF HANGING. There was a fall of hanging at the East Shaft of Basilton Levels, East Rand, at 2 P.M. yesterday. Two natives were killed, and three others escaped with minor injuries."

My father was Assistant Secretary and so never touched the real

working life of the Mine that went on underground the way the real
life of the body and brain goes on under the surface of flesh. He
went down the shaft into the Mine perhaps once or twice a year,
part of an official party conducting visitors from the Group—the
corporation of mining companies to which the Mine belonged.

The "underground" people we knew—shift bosses and Mine
captains and surveyors—had one advantage over us. They were very
much luckier with garden boys than my father was. All had their
own teams of boys working for them underground; they could detail
one, often two or three, to spend a day working in the gardens of
their homes. My father had more difficulty. The clerks and errand
boys at the office could speak English and write, and were rarely
willing to spend their Saturday afternoon off working in our garden,
even for money. And they did not belong, the way the Mine boys
belonged to their white bosses underground, to my father. He could
not send them off to dig a sweet-pea trench or clip a hedge, any
more than he could give them a hiding now and then to keep them
in order. The underground people found that an occasional good
crack, as they put it, knocked any nonsense out of the boys and
kept them attentive and respectful, without any malice on either
side.

But there was one old boy who had started work as a messenger
in the secretary's office when my father had started there as a junior
clerk; now my father was Assistant Secretary and old Paul was still
a messenger, and he came still, as he had done since my parents
had married, to work in our garden two Saturdays a month.

He was one of the old kind, my mother said. A good old thing.
Here you are Paul, she'd say, taking him out a big dish of tea and
some meat between thick bread. And she'd stand with one hand on
her hip and the other shading her eyes, talking to him from the
lawn. They talked about bringing up children, and how Paul managed. He had two sons at school in the Northern Transvaal; it was
hard, and they did not always know that what their father and mother
did for them was best. They wanted to come home to their mother
in the Location. But what was the use of that? —That was the
beginning of loafers and no-goods, she agreed. If they want to get
on nice—Paul's hand round the bowl of strong tea trembled after

the unaccustomed labor of the spade, his small pointed beard held neatly away from the liquid—they must finish Standard Six. —Yes, I know, Paul, but children always think they know better. They must have what they want, and nothing you do is right for them. My wife—he fitted the cold meat carefully between the bread—my wife she say let them come, I mus' see my children while they still small. It's no good they should be away and their mother doesn't know them. —I know, I know, Paul, it's the same with the master and Miss Helen. I say that the child must do this, because it is good for her, he says let her do that. . . .

"You've been talking to Paul again!" I would taunt. It amused me to see my mother talking to the old gardener just as if he were a friend. Yet there was a touch of scorn in my gibe; other women gave orders to their gardeners, why should my mother talk to hers? "—Honestly, he's a lot more sensible than a lot of white people," she would say to my father, as an admittance and a challenge.

Yet I was fond of Paul. I gave him all my discarded games and books for his children, and even my old fairy bicycle, a parting that drew a little string tight inside me, although I did not ride the bicycle any more. He greeted me always as if he were welcoming me back from long absence; a lingering kind of salute, a big smile watching after me as I passed. He fixed things for me, too. And drilled a tiny hole in the shell of a tortoise which, miraculously, he had dug up where it had been hibernating in the dahlia bed, so that I could attach it by a long string to a stake in the lawn. The unexpected discovery of the tortoise was a tremendous excitement, but the pleasure of keeping it as a pet somehow failed to realize. (I had never been back to buy the gold and brown mosaic shell through which I would look at the sun; it had disappeared beneath the overlap of too many impressions of that afternoon, the feeling that something had happened that I didn't know how to think about.) Now this bitter-mouthed, old-eyed, cold-eyed head and these four dry cold legs feeling slowly out of the shell made me hesitate—froze the impulse of the heart. The fact of the creature, living inside, spoiled the tortoise, domed, gold and brown.

One morning after rain only one neat little segment, the one with the hole in it, lay attached like a label to the long string on the lawn. The tortoise was gone. No one could convince me that it must not have been like pulling one's nail out by the roots. I kept trying it, secretly, with my thumbnail, and deep guilt humiliated inside me. I felt that the tortoise was someone I had not got to know until too late; now its reproachful face looked out at me from nowhere in the garden.

3 ON A SUNDAY MORNING when I was eleven the hooter went quite suddenly just before breakfast. It seemed to suck in the quiet leisure of early Sunday and blow it out again in alarm.

"Well, what on earth—" My mother's eyebrows raised in amused indignation. Sunday was the only day she wasn't dressed and busy long before breakfast, and she came in in her dressing gown, looking inquiringly at my father. "Somebody's idea of a joke," he said. He was fixing the plug of the toaster for her. There couldn't be an accident; most unlikely, anyway, because there was no blasting underground on a Sunday, only the pumps kept going. "Somebody at the time office had too much party last night!" My father made a knowing sound.

I went out into the fresh garden. "You mustn't go down near the Compound Manager's," chorused two little Dufalettes, clinging to the fence and peering through the hedge on their side.

"Why not!" They were silly little things; when nobody at home would listen to them, they would call over the fence.

"My daddy says so. My daddy says nobody must go to the Compound Manager's, and Raymond was going but now he's not."

Raymond came bounding round the corner of their house doing something with a cotton reel and an elastic band. "Man, there's a whole lota niggers round Ockerts', all over the garden and in the street and everywhere. Just a lot of munts from the Compound. I was going, but, ag, I don't want to. My dad's up there. —Look, haven't you or your mom got some ole cotton reels you don't want. I'm'na make a whole army of these tanks out of them, I'm'na have hundreds and hundreds, you'll see them covering the whole lawn."

"All right. I'll ask." I ran round and in the kitchen door. "There's a whole crowd of Compound boys in Ockerts' garden."

"Who said so?"

"Raymond just told me."

"Mind you!" My mother stood there lighting upon it. "I thought there was something different this morning—there were no drums! I lay in bed wondering what was different." Every Sunday morning the Mine, and fainter, more distantly, the town, woke to the gentle, steady beat of drums from the Compound: the boys held war dances, decked in checked dishcloths and feathers from domestic dusters now instead of the skins of beasts and war paint, passing time and getting rid of virility the Mine couldn't utilize instead of gathering passion for battle; stamping the dust of a piece of veld provided by the Mine instead of their tribal earth. But this morning there were no drums. Only, now that we listened, expecting something, a distant flare of the human voice; there; then blown the other way by the wind.

My father and I went out into the garden to listen. Then out the gate and along the road which the pines held in deep cool dewy shadow. Mr. Bellingan joined us, raising his hand from his veranda. As we got nearer to the Compound Manager's house, the faint blare grew and separated into the clamor of many voices, high and low, shrill and deep. Now and then, the piercing trill of a whistle shrieked some assertion of its own.

The Compound Manager, by virtue of his position, had a very large garden, laid out with the formality of a park and kept shaved, clipped and pared by bands of Compound boys who were always to be seen squatting like frogs on one lawn or another. Now the gates were open, one facing in toward the house, the other the wrong way, toward the street. About two hundred Mine boys blotted out the green and the color as they sat with their elbows resting on their knees, watching the house, and stood, looking up, packed round the veranda steps. If they had brandished the sticks that most of them carried, now they lay set down beside them; the boys smoked their pipes and stared round in the sun, almost as they did on the veld round the Compound and the stores. Nobody trampled the stars of tight-packed pansies, nobody bent the mound of white lilies that gave out their incense as if convinced they honored a grave. Though some sat beneath scythes of shade cast by the fronds of the palms, none leaned against the monster pineapples of the boles. An immense babble, like a tremendous tea party in full swing, filled the morning.

As I came with my father and Mr. Bellingan a little uncertainly onto the driveway, the way visitors come who are not too certain if they have come at the right time, a few of the boys looked up over their shoulders and then slowly swung their heads back again, like cattle. One was trying to catch a fly that kept flying onto his big mouth as he shouted. Another was not listening at all, quietly exploring his nose. Another one said something about us and laughed.

We saw someone signaling, a beckon and the rather foolish smile of excitement, from the bow window. "Come. It's Mrs. Ockert." My father shepherded us toward the house, through the standing groups who clotted more thickly round the veranda, slapping one another's chests and backs in emphasis of argument, shaking heads and turning this way and that in laughter and disbelief. But they moved aside to let us through, absently. As they moved their blankets stirred the smell of flesh and dust.

Right in the center of the veranda steps a heavy boy in low-slung khaki trousers and an old vest torn down under the arms shouted and moved his big full chest as if that were his form of gesture, curiously expressive, as if it came up out of him without volition. His hair was clipped off bald and showed only as a matt shadow where it would have encroached upon his forehead; beneath the oil of excitement he had a marked, lumpy skin. He was shouting, butting his head at two fat Mine boys who stood about with an air of righteous authority, backed a little away from him, though superior.

We three white people stepped round him onto the veranda. I saw his thick tongue back in his mouth and his big teeth close together and looking strong as he yelled.

Inside in the Ockerts' long serene lounge—there were silky smooth carpets in intricate designs which were the oriental rugs my mother wanted to get someday, and little black tables with thin legs like baby springbok, looking almost alive, ready to leap—tea had been laid on a wide embroidered cloth, and men stood round talking over thin teacups. Mr. Ockert was laughing something confidentially to the Underground Manager, who wore a dotted red silk scarf folded inside his shirt neck. Thin Mr. Mackenzie hadn't shaved; he was taking a scone from Mrs. Ockert. "Come on in," she called to us. "You'll be wanting some tea, I'm sure. We all need our tea after this!" She was laughing a great deal, rather apologetically, as if this was the best she could put up for an impromptu gathering.

Mrs. Ockert is a woman who could carry off any position; she's always a charming hostess—my mother often said. —Now there was no sugar left for Mr. Bellingan in the pot-bellied silver bowl. Mrs. Ockert bit her lip and hunched her shoulders gaily in guilt: "I'm *so* sorry, Mr. Bellingan, I'm so sorry. What a house! What chaos this morning!" And she laughed as if it were all her fault, something naughty she had done. "Richard, more sugar at once, please. —It'll be here in just one moment, Mr. Bellingan—"

"This business of changing the boys' diet—it always does lead to trouble," my father was saying to his neighbor, Dufalette. "—No, thanks—Of course, I wouldn't say it to Ockert, but I've seen it time and again. If you'd been giving them boiled rag for years and you changed it to chicken suddenly, they'd be up in arms asking for the rag back again." Bellingan nodded unsurely in agreement; his eye was on the back of the Underground Manager, standing rather near. He leaned over to put down his cup, taking the opportunity of saying quietly in my father's ear, "All this to-do over mealie-pap." My father laughed tightly inside his chest: "A storm in a porridge pot, a storm in a porridge pot."

"What about another scone? Come on? What about another scone?" Mrs. Ockert was smiling round the room. "These flies! As soon as *they're* anywhere around you can be sure they'll bring millions of flies."

"They soon quietened down when Ockert came out," someone was saying. "I was here early, as soon as I saw them crowding along the road toward the house. —Yes, before eight—they came marching along; I tell you, quite a sight!"

"But why come to the house? They could have complained through the boss-boys?"

"The boss-boys!"

"Oh, the Compound Manager or nothing!"

"Did you hear it all, Mac?"

"Well, there'll be nothing more said now. They won't make any trouble."

"Behind it? I shouldn't say there was, at all."

The Assistant Compound Manager went out, came in again. "Starting to push off now," he said, assuring, belittling, comforting, the way one stands between a child and the undesirable, insistingly smiling, "all on their way."

Soon we left, too, passing the dwindling groups of natives, the emptying garden; my father holding my hand but talking closely to Mr. Bellingan and not knowing I was there.

The boys at the Compound didn't like the food they were given, and so they all came together to Mr. Ockert's house to complain. Now they were going back to the Compound and they were glad because, although they had behaved badly, Mr. Ockert wasn't taking their Sunday ration of kaffir beer away from them. Between the two men talking above my head I heard the word "strike"; "—But it wasn't a strike, was it?" I said quickly. My father smiled down at me. "Well, yes, it was, really. They didn't refuse to work, but they wouldn't eat; that's a strike, too." He had told me often about the 1922 strike of white miners, when there were shots in the streets of Atherton, and my grandmother, his mother, had stayed shut up in her little house for days, until the commando of burghers came riding in to restore order. To me the word "strike" carried with it visions of excitement and danger; something for which, alas, I had been born too late.

Those native boys sitting around making a noise the way they liked to in the garden, and the lovely tea all ready in Mrs. Ockert's beautiful lounge (the scones collapsed into hot butter; I should have liked one more) —*That* couldn't be a strike—?

Hunger was whistling an empty passage right down my throat to my stomach. —I twisted my hand out of my father's and ran on ahead, to bacon and egg put away for me in the oven.

4 MY ADOLESCENCE and the first years of the war were con-
current; both have a haziness in my mind that comes, I suppose, from the indefinite, cocoonlike quality of the one, and the
distant remove from my life of the other.

During that time my life was so much my mother's that it seemed
that the only difference between us was the insignificance of age.
The significance of emotional experience that separates the woman,
mated, her life balanced against the life of a man, that life again
balanced against the life of a child begotten and born, from the girl-
child, was as unrealized by my mother as by me. My mother, with
her slightly raw-featured still-young face—the blood flowed very
near the surface of the thin skin—accepted marriage and mother-
hood as a social rather than a mysterious personal relationship.
Wives and husbands and children and the comfortable small plan
of duties they owed to one another—for her, this was what living
was. I accepted the outward everyday semblance of adult life, the
men father-familiar yet creatures respected and allowed ununder-
standable tastes of their own; ministered to because they were the
providers and entitled to affection from their own families; women
the friends, the co-workers, the companions, busy with one another
in the conduct of every hour of the day. My mother's weeks were
pegged out to street collections and galas and dances and cake sales
and meetings of this committee and that—remote from battlefields
or air raids, with my father's stomach ulcer excluding him from
offering his services to South Africa's volunteer forces, this was what
the war meant in our lives. Outside of school, I too belonged to this
busy to-and-fro that went on above the tunneling of black men and
white in the Mine. I too had my place, the place of the Secretary's
daughter (my father had been promoted at last), in the hierarchy
that divided the Mine Manager and his wife (tall in a clinging skirt,
an exiled Mrs. Dalloway) giving the prizes in a certain order of rigid
gradations from the busy small woman in the flowered apron sta-
tioned at the tea urn—wife of a burly shift boss called Mackie.

I read the books my mother brought home on her adult's ticket
at the library; gentle novels of English family life and, now and

then, stray examples of the proletarian novel to which the dole in England in the thirties had given rise. "It's about the life of the poor in England—but it won't do her any harm if she wants to read it." —My mother was sometimes a little uncertain about these books. "I don't believe a girl should grow up not knowing what life is like."

A young man and a girl went up on a refuse heap above an ugly city and kissed. There was a drunken father who was horrible in an indefinable way—but all drunk people were horrible, I should have died of fear if . . . but it could not even be imagined that my father could dribble at the mouth, vomit without knowing. At the same time I read Captain Marryat, Jane Austen, and to Omar Khayyám in its soft skin-feel cover I had added Rupert Brooke. "She's like us," said my mother, "we're both great readers. Of course, George likes his heavy stuff, medical books and so on—and detective stories! I don't know how he can read them, but I've got to bring them home for him every week end." A book of Churchill's speeches and another of Smuts' found a place on top of the special little bookcase which contained the encyclopedia; my father had bought them. The clean-cut shiny dust covers slowly softened at the edges as Anna dusted them along with the other ornaments every day.

There was a dance, I remember, when I was about sixteen—to raise money for a special comforts-fund that the Mine had inaugurated for ex-employees now in the forces. My mother said, blushing with pleasure, the almost tearful moisture that came to her eyes when she was proud: "Daddy, this'll mean a long dress for your daughter. . . ."

My mother was completely absorbed in the making of that dress; we were up together late every night before the dance, while she sewed and fitted, and I stood on the table with my head near the heat of the light in its beaded shade, turning slowly to show how the hem fell. Then before we went to bed we sat on the kitchen table, drinking tea and talking. I had taken over the care of my mother's fine wiry hair, red, like my own: "You can have it set at the hairdresser's on the Thursday before—then it'll be nice and soft for me to do up for you on Saturday." My mother thought a moment. "But on Thursday afternoon I've promised to bake four-dozen sau-

sage rolls. I don't want to get all steamy in the kitchen after it's
been done." "Tie it up! Why can't you tie it up!" I stacked the cups
in the sink for Anna in the morning.

Up and down the passage, in the bathroom, snatches of our talk
continued until the lights went out.

We dressed for the dance together. My mother had surprised me
with a real florist's corsage—they called it a "spray"—pink car-
nations and pale blue delphinium, and it was pinned to the shoulder
of my dress with its silver paper holder just showing. Every time I
turned my head I could feel it brush my neck.

I danced with Raymond Dufalette in a blue suit with his hair so
oiled that it looked as if he had just come out of the sea, dripping
wet. He went to boarding school and had learned to dance the previous term; he brought me thankfully back to where my mother and
father sat, ready with kindly questions about how he liked school
and what he was going to do when he was finished. Then I sat, my
back very stiff, looking straight before me. I was afraid I was per-
spiring the little organdy balloon that encased the top of each arm.
I was still more afraid that my father might ask me to dance to
save me.

I remember that just as I was getting desperate, a fair boy aston-
ishingly came right across the splintered boards to ask me to dance,
and the dance was a Paul Jones, so that I found myself with a
succession of partners, snatched away when the music broke into a
march and I walked sheepishly round with the other girls—there
was Olwen, but Olwen had come with a partner, and he kept her,
swaying at the side—then replaced by the young man or somebody's
father who found himself opposite me when the march ended. The
evening passed in the stiff hands of thin fair boys whose necks were
too free of stiff collars. Their knees bumped me, hard as table legs.
Their black evening suits and the crackle of shirt front encased
nothingness, like the thin glossy shells, the fine glass wings of beetles which crunch to a puff of dead leaf-powder if you crush them.
When the ice cream was served I ran hand in hand with my mother;
we had promised to help. Over in the corner at the bar, the two
Cluff boys in uniform leaned with one or two other soldiers home

for the week end. They drank beer, and laughter spurted up in their talk, backs to the dancers. "Ice cream?" I held out the tray of saucers, smiling with impartial polite reserve, not knowing whether or not I should recognize them as Alan and Francis Cluff.

"Here boys, ice cream, why not—" Alan began passing the saucers over my head. Francis said in an aside, his eyes lowered for a moment as if to screen him, "Hello, Helen." The smell of war, of young men taken in war, a disturbing mixture and contradiction of the schoolboy smell of soap in khaki, and the smooth scent of shaven skin, the warmth of body that brought out the smell of khaki as the warmth of the iron brings up the odor of a fabric, came from them.

I danced again and again that year at parties with the fair young boys in their formal dress clothes who, like myself, were in their last year at school. Once or twice in the winter holidays, one of them took me to the cinema on a Saturday night; but I was only sixteen, I was busy studying for my matriculation, there was plenty of time. "Time enough when you're working and independent, and school's behind you," said my mother. —Olwen had left school a year ago; she attended what was called a business college, upstairs in a building in the town; the chakker-chakker of typewriters sailed out of the wide-open windows and at lunchtime the girls came down to stroll about the town, not in gym frocks, but their own choice of dresses.

What was the stiffness that congealed in me and in the bodies of the young boys with the spiky-smooth hair beside me in the sinking dark of the cinema; made me sit up straight, my arms arranged along the rests helplessly when the lights went up and the music rose and the colored advertisements flipped one by one on and off the screen, and I waited? Back came the young boy with two little cardboard buckets of ice cream, edging bent, apologetic, along the row. We sat and ate with wooden spoons; the boy kept asking questions: Shall I put that down for you? Can you manage? Is it melted? Did it get on your dress? It seemed that I did nothing but smile, shake my head, assure, no. We spoke of films we had seen, veered back to school, fell back on anecdotes that began: "Well I know, I have an Uncle who told us once . . ." or "—Like my little brother; the other day he was . . ." Sudden bursts of sympathy ignited, like matches struck by mistake, between us; were batted out with the astonishment that instinctively deals with such fires. He had not read the books I had read; I knew that. He talked a great deal about the different models of motorcars. My jaws felt tight and I wanted to yawn.

We sat seriously through the film. Sometimes the young boy's foot would touch mine by mistake—they had such big feet in shoes with thick rubber soles—and there was a ruffle of apologies. The one—the nicer one, actually—had a crenelation of incipient pimples perpetually lying in anger beneath the tender shaven skin along his jaw, to which, in the imagined privacy of the dark, I always saw, out of the corner of my eye, his fingers return feeling along as if reading the bumps in the tender, disgusting language of adolescence; curt, monosyllabic as obscenity, and as searching.

At this time, too, my father was teaching me to play golf. When the hooter went at half-past four I left my books open on the dining-room table and went into my room to put on rubber-soled shoes. My father came home with the air of expectancy of someone who is waiting to go out again immediately, and we were at the first tee just as the sun shifted its day-long gaze and glanced obliquely off the grass. Afterward I sat on the veranda full of Mine officials at the clubhouse, drinking my orange squash at a rickety wicker table, with my father sipping his beer. Our heads were continually turned to talk to people; often two or three men screeched chairs over the cement to sit with us, others would swing a leg against the table while they paused to talk in passing. Even if their talk veered to channels that slowly excluded me, leaving me at some point gently washed upon the limit of my comprehension or interest, I rested there comfortably, hearing their voices rather than what they said, lulled by the warm throbbing coming up in my scarlet, blistered palms. I lolled my head back, put my dusty feet up on the bar of the table; the sky, swept clear of the day, held only radiance, far up above the shade that rose like water steeping the trees and the drop of the grass. Over at the water hole, the whole world was repeated, upside down. It all seemed simple, as if a puzzle had dissolved in my hands. The half-questions would never be asked, dark fins of feeling that could not be verified in the face of my father, my mother, the Mine officials, would not show through the surface that every minute of every day polished. I rested, my foot dancing a little tune; the way the unborn rest between one stage of labor and the next, thinking, perhaps, that they have arrived.

PART TWO

The Sea

5 I HAD A new bathing suit.

It lay on the bed in my room; "Why shouldn't Nell go down to Alice's place?" my father surprised himself by saying. My mother looked from one to the other: "—Well, I don't know, would she like it—?"

I could not conjure up in myself a projection into any single moment—a meal, the sight of the sea, Mrs. Koch smiling from a veranda—ready to exist on a little farm on the South Coast of Natal. We had been invited many times; we had never gone. Alice Koch was my mother's old friend, corresponded with regularly, but materializing only every two or three years, when she would telephone to say that she had arrived in Johannesburg on holiday, and would come out to the Mine to spend a week end or a day. I had always read her letters, and reading them, was easy with her; yet when she got out at the station she was different; a big woman, much older than my mother, with a gentle smile and a faint, refined dew of agitation touching cool from her upper lip as you kissed her. Once —dim with sand castles and a doll that had had its feet trailed in the edge of the water—there was the memory of staying at a place near where Mrs. Koch had lived and Mrs. Koch had come with her two daughters and their children to sit with us on a beach.

"On her own . . . would she . . . ? —I couldn't go." Mother patted the yellow bathing suit.

"Oh, yes." I looked up quickly; it seemed as if there had never been a pause. "I want to go; I'll go."

I was seventeen and I had been a year out of school. The year
had been spent working at a temporary job in my father's office; the
Secretary's daughter in the Secretary's office of Atherton Mine.

The train put me down on the siding paved with coal grit and blew
back a confetti of smuts as it screeched off slowly over the brilliance
of rails. When I took my hand from my eyes I was receding rapidly,
alone on the glittering black dust. With a honk the train was gone.

A double white sign, converging on a V, said, KATEMBI RIVER,
17 ft. above sea level, 57½ miles to Durban. A tin shed, delicately
eroded by rust a foot up from the ground, said, GOODS. It was empty.
At the end of the strip of coal grit, like a short carpet abruptly rolled,
thick bush green and black green and hard with light reached up
and closed in high, singing with hot intimacy far within and dead
still to the eye.

A tremendous heat watched everything.

I was conscious of the feel of the sea on my left cheek, where
it bumped and exploded white below the roll of green that fell away
from that side of the track, but I was still as a lizard, breathing, it
seemed, shallower even than the air, not moving my eyes.

The shaking of a human hand unseen broke the authority of the
bush as it swayed with the passage of human bodies passing down
a grudging pathway I could not see; and the quiet buzzle of two
people talking that suggests to the stranger they are preparing to
meet a side of themselves he will never know, that will have disappeared in hiding by the time they come forward on a smile, gave
a queer misbeat to my heart. I was hot, a little sweat came out and
clung my hair to my forehead as I urged smiling to meet them; Mrs.
Koch pointing and shaking her head beneath a checked parasol, her
feet in men's sandals, and a man with her.

"—My dear! I'm so sorry . . . shame . . . what a way to arrive. . . ."
The soft, damp kiss, the Eau-de-Cologne. I laughed, shaking my
head, hotter, unbearably hot now in the relief of the moment of
greeting over. The man—it was a young man, I now saw, in a sort
of half-uniform, khaki shorts and an army shirt and sandals, but no
cap—wore glasses and stood back looking down at us with the polite
smile of a stranger watching emotion which he does not share. The

smile pulled the corners of his mouth down and in a little. "It was Ludi, he would stop by at the old Plasketts' on the way to say hullo—oh, there was plenty of time. I am *so* sorry. . . . What will your mother think of us?" —Her son, of course; with the German name; the guilty smile of nonrecognition faded comfortably on my face.

In the gaiety of arrival, exchanging questions we did not wait for each other to answer, we trudged up the steep pathway with cinders grinding away under our feet, a hand up to fend off the bush. The young man came up behind, with the luggage. The three of us were packed into the front of an old faded car and he drove away up and down a steep stony road that dipped now between flat-roofed trees where creepers dropped screens over bush secretive with a hidden trickle of stream, now through a cutting—black ooze and wet rock with a bunch of tough grasses stuffed in here and there as if to staunch the wound—rose and turned and discovered the river away below on the left and the sugar cane. As I talked to Mrs. Koch, my elbow crooked on the open window felt the pull of the sun and the sudden warm wet blow of the river. The river was drawn in a brown hank, shiny like the sheath of a muscle, through the soft hills of cane; one against the other they were folded, soft with deep cane, flattened like fur by the wind, down, silver-pale, up, green; sage and brilliant as the sun blew across.

The cane sang on either side of the road. We could not see beyond it. It was tall as a man and thick as tall grass to an ant. "Phew . . . ," said Mrs. Koch at the still heat, as if it were something she could never meet without faint astonishment. She moved her warm bulk to take out a small handkerchief and touch her cheek beneath her eyes, with the movement of wiping away tears. Ludi moved up a little, to give us more room; it was as if, although he did not speak, it was a gesture of having said something, allowing him to remain comfortably silent outside our conversation.

It was extraordinarily easy to talk to Mrs. Koch. She was the woman of the letters, the "Affectionately, my dear, Alice Koch," sitting fat and comfortable with her feet in sandals and the little piece of cambric damply waving Eau-de-Cologne. I got out of the car before the white veranda faintly giddy with journey, smiling the mild happiness of having bridged space. It was all right; unknowing, the decision was made for me, and in my favor; the alternative that waits at all destinations—inescapable, a face in the crowd at the dock or the station you cannot avoid: the desolation of arrival—was not there for me. Unknowing of my escape, innocent even of relief, I stood laughing at my unsteadiness, seeing Black-eyed Susan embroidering the old veranda like gay, crude wool-work, ants trailing down a crumbling step—. I shut my eyes and opened them; two bushes that cast their shape again in pale fallen flowers instead of shade, palms on the breast of lawn cut out against the far-off drop of the river, the cane. Haze and glitter; the river looped through the arched body of a bridge. And there, there was the sea, stretching away, smeared off only into the sky.

In the house Mrs. Koch had prepared my room for me, and left me alone. There was no pressure, no effort demanded of me; I stood at the window in a pause between the open suitcase and the open wardrobe with a misty mirror, feeling the beat of the train in my blood, the cessation of the train's noise in my ears. There was a withdrawal of sound like the tidal silence pulling away at the touch of a spiral shell to one's ear; the sound of the sea.

The next day, the holiday did not begin because it rained. It seemed impossible, in the face of the existence of yesterday, blinding with brightness, that it should be raining. Yesterday nothing could be believed in but sun; today there was nothing but rain. I waited around the house with Mrs. Koch, getting to know the regarding stare of new rooms worn old long before I had ever come to them. I sat on the faded sofa on whose rubbed arms my hands now rested; groping for a hairpin, saw the strip of clear-printed design that lived on untouched down the hidden fold of the seat. I talked in the kitchen with Mrs. Koch while she made a cake, played with a rearrangement of the flowers on the back stoep. There were cats under my feet, dried-up saucers of milk they disdained. Three green budgereegahs chattered foolishly in a little cage with rolled-up blinds.

Ludi was gone all day, fishing in the rain. I stood at the window, watching it come down; if you turned away it did not exist, it was quite soundless. You could only know it was there if you looked, and saw it falling, falling, without the sound of falling. The garden and the sea were a flash, perhaps seen yesterday, no more permanent than scenes turned toward me, then away, along the railway line. The sight had not been grasped sufficiently to exist for me somewhere beneath the rain. "He's only got three weeks, so he'll fish in any weather," said Mrs. Koch, smiling for him. Her voice hung about the most trivial mention of her son with a gentle, unashamed expansion of love. Just as she spoke with emotion over the old photograph albums which she brought out to show to me, waiting for the expected face, the group of her dead husband, some friends, a frowning tall girl who she said was my mother at a picnic; faces shying from a long-set light of the sun.

Mrs. Koch did not attempt to "understand young people"; she did not apologize for her views or preferences. But it also never occurred to her to fear loss of dignity in showing that she felt, that she cared, that she had not the detachment of her years. I was drawn to her because she gave access to herself in a way that I did not know anyone ever did. Tears were embarrassments swallowed back, stalked out of the room, love was private (my parents and I had stopped kissing each other except on birthdays); yet tears were bright in Mrs. Koch's eyes and one could still look at her. That same morning she had moved Ludi's military cap where it lay in the kitchen; "I have been so happy here with him. And it was what he liked." And she smiled and in the middle of the morning, in the middle of peeling fruit, tears had run down her cheeks, taking their place and their moment.

It rained again often, muffling up from the hills over the clear sky suddenly after a blazing morning; but it was no longer a soft restraint holding me back from the holiday. I went about in it, warm, soft, drenching where the ribbon grasses and the stiff lace bracken swept their dripping brushes past my legs, tingling lightly into my cheeks and eyes like tiny bubbles breaking when my face turned against it. Mrs. Koch and I trudged down to the store through the heavy mud that formed so quickly, and broke away in soggy runnels from the mixture of sea sand everywhere in the soil. Somebody stopped and gave us a lift, and in the store, that smelled of mice and millet and tobacco, we had tea with the storekeeper and his wife, a retired British army major with the pointlessly handsome face of a man of sixty left over from his days in uniform.

On the way back we met Ludi coming along the road from Plasketts' without a coat, barefoot, soaked through, and he scolded us for being out. I knew that it was his mother for whom he was concerned, but he was always kind, and the concern was accepted for me, too. Then the rain ceased; suddenly, in a hollow, the grass, the air, the undergrowth steamed. Far behind grayness, the sun showed yellow as a fog lamp. We were steaming inside our clothes; threw off raincoats, the scarves enveloping our heads. Ludi, with his wet shorts clinging strongly to his buttocks, said: "Well, what can I do . . . ?" And smiling wryly, like a father being imposed upon by children, loaded himself with our wraps. A bird called out somewhere as if the day were beginning over; some white, delicate flowers splashed all over common dark bushes let go their sweet breath again.

But mostly the sun shone, only the sun existed. In the mornings just after breakfast, the three of us pottered about the garden and the chicken houses. Ludi and his mother had the endless little consultations, the need to draw each other's attention to this detail or that, the need even merely to remark one to the other what the other already thought or well knew, that people have who have long had a life in common and now live apart. Before Ludi had joined the army, he had been running some sort of little chicken farm; for five or six years after he had left school he had apparently had jobs of various kinds in various places—sometimes Mrs. Koch would say: When you were in Johannesburg . . . but you remember, it was when you were at Klerksdorp—always returning intermittently to the coast and his mother. What he had done during those months, it was difficult to say. Then there had been the idea of the chicken farm, and Mrs. Koch had bought the chickens and the necessary equipment and Ludi had built the runs and the troughs and the perches and the incubation shed by himself, in his own time. Whether the chicken farming was ever a success or not, it was again difficult to say; now Ludi was in the army, and most of the chickens had been sold, or had died, because Mrs. Koch could not look after them by herself.

Yet Ludi spent a great deal of time down at the chicken houses. He was mending the sagging wires, and dismantling and reassembling the incubator, which had deteriorated in some way through lack of use. The few fowls that were left wandered about unscientifically round his squatting figure. The morning sun, testing out its mounting power, frizzled brightness on his bright gold hair, and now and then he paused, frowning, took off his glasses and put them back. He looked strange without his glasses; someone else. Mrs. Koch came to him and went away again, her voice trailing off as she went over to feel the pawpaws pendulous from the finely engraved totem of a young palm but still green, then rising to a question as she returned and stood with her hand on her hip, drawing away from the sun. "But what happens to them, I'd like to know. I have a look at them and they're green. And then when I come back in a day or two when they should be ripe, they're gone. Now there are more green ones getting ready. But I never seem to see them ripen."

"Hey, Matthew, the missus wants to know why the pawpaws don't get ripe—" Ludi screwed his eyes up weak against the sun, calling to the native who was trailing slowly across the grass to an outhouse, carrying a rusty tin bath. "I didn't see it," said the servant, continuing.

Ludi squatted wider, giving his blunt burned hand a steadier grip on the screwdriver. Without lifting his reddened neck, he laughed. "Matthew!"

The native slowly lowered the bath and stopped, regarding us. He stood there in the sun.

The screwdriver slipped; Ludi grunted and tried again. His mother bent over a little, with the anxious grimace of someone who does not know what it is that is being attempted and proving difficult.

"I myself I never see those pawpaw," said Matthew.

"Matthew!" Ludi shook his head.

The native burst into laughter, shaking his head, stopping to gasp, swinging up the bath in a mirror-flash, walking on in a flurry of culpable innocence. He laughed back at Ludi; Ludi laughed after him.

Ludi had gone into the incubation house. There was the sound of something being wrenched away. "Mother, did Plasketts ever take those brackets they asked for? There were two, I think, in the garage. Or in the shed." "Which were they, dear—?" and she was in the dark doorway after him. I went back to the house to write a letter; I had written one when I arrived, had one from home. I went onto the veranda, sat down on the old green-painted chair at the shaky wicker table. I sat pulling at a fraying braid on the table top, my eyes half-closed at the glare that made a bright palpable mist of the space climbing up from the sea. The cane was so live a green that it seemed to be growing visibly; the river a twist of metallic light. Blossoms dropped silently from the frangipani trees. I sat there waving my bare foot.

It was impossible to write the letter; did it exist, a here and there, at this same morning? What could I write to the Mine, to the house with the lights on, the red haze of hair bending over the letter, handing it across the vegetable dishes. For one second I smelled the cold brick of the passage at the Mine offices. But it was not enough to create the existence of the Mine, to make it possible at the other end of a space of which *this* was at one end.

"Are you finding it too quiet? —I hope not. I know there isn't much life for young people there, but the sea and . . ."

An ugly crawling creature (the old house was alive with such creatures, its own and those of the undergrowth) came out the rotting crevice of the table and ran across my mother's letter and the open writing pad. I went slithering my bare soles over the steps down to the grass.

Mrs. Koch did not normally go to the beach except at week ends or to accompany friends, but now she went with me most mornings. Ludi drove us down in the old car and left us to settle ourselves up on the dunes where the bush leaned a little shade and the sand was powder-soft and spiked with bits of leaf and twig; Mrs. Koch liked to sit there, with a sunshade over her legs and her shoes off. Then Ludi took his fishing rod and the stained canvas bag high with bait and was gone away up the beach, the jogging walk smaller and smaller, the old khaki shirt waving some signal of its own as a whip of breeze from the sea animated its loose tails; then gone round the rocks, slid in, it seemed, as if the cool smooth solidities had parted, like a stage-set, and closed behind him. If one could see, of course, there he would be, on the other side of the rocks, a khaki mark like a punctuation, drawing across the sands on the other side, and so on, and round the next bend, and the next, until he reached wherever his fishing ground might be.

The rocks held the scallop of beach. Mrs. Koch brought mending or a piece of knitting for one of the grandchildren; I had a book. We talked, but our words were tiny sounds lost in the space of the beach and the sea and the air; phrases torn fluttering rose to sound, sailed, fell to lost like the occasional birds lifted and dropped in the spaces of the air above the sea. We whispered in a great hall where our voices died away unechoed on the floor. We did not notice that we had stopped talking; Mrs. Koch knitted without looking, a fine sweat cooling her brow, her eyes absently retaining a look of gentle attention, as if she had forgotten that she was not listening to someone. Easily, like a satisfied dog that is so used to the limits of its own garden that it turns at the open gate and automatically goes back up the same path down which it has just trotted, her mind quietly rounded on the beach and the questioning of the silence and went again to examine the small businesses of her daily life.

In silence I got up and wandered down toward the sea. The sand was coarser, yellower; then here, where the tide had smoothed and smoothed it, spreading one layer evenly and firmly down over another, it dazzled with its cleanness, and the hardness of it thudded through my heels to my ears like the beat of my own heart in the heat. A thin film of water spread out to my feet; the sea touched me.

Sometimes I lay, the sharp bones of my hips meeting only the hardness of the sand, the sun puckering my skin. My eyes closed, I lost sense of which side the sea was, which side the land, and seemed to be alive only within my own body, beating with the heat. Water came with the rising tide, gentle and shocking. I jumped up with the pattern of the sand facets like the marks of rough bedclothes on my legs and cheek. Sometimes I went over to the rocks and dipped my hands in the lukewarm pools. Some of the rocks bristled with mussels and barnacles which agonized my feet; others, smooth and black and layered, shone slightly greasy with salt. Red-brown ones were dry and matt, swirled out into curves and hollows by the sea. They were warm and alive, like flesh. I sat back in an armchair of stone, resting the still-white undersides of my arms on the warmth. Sweat softened the hair in my armpits, and suddenly, across the scent of the wind and the sea, I was conscious of the smell of my own body.

I did not talk much to Ludi and yet between the three of us, Mrs. Koch and Ludi and myself, there was a sense of rest and familiarity when we sat together in the living room in the evenings. Perhaps it came partly from a physical tiredness, the tiredness of the muscle, the sun. Ludi in the white shorts and shirt that were his concession to dressing for dinner, still barelegged and wearing old sandshoes, lay on the divan and read, now and then saying something teasing to us, treating us as if we were of an age, seeing in his mother the heart of the young woman which had stayed, like a plant taken from the climate of its growth, static, since the time when his father had left her many years before. He had standards of his own, this Ludi, and the barriers of youth or age were artificial to him because he knew, as easily as the blind know the shape of things beneath the exterior they do not see, the secret contour of the self. Perhaps that was why the human exterior, the faces of the people he knew, interested him so little. He did not seem to know what people looked like; once I had mentioned meeting at the Post Office an old gentleman who I thought might be Dr. Patterson, a friend of the Koches', and I asked Ludi whether Dr. Patterson was a fairish man with a large nose. He hardly seemed to know, and was a little irritated at my incredulity at his lack of observation. Yet places, beaches and rivers and the sea, he saw with all the sensuous intensity with which one might regard a beloved face. All the core of his human intimacy seemed, apart from his mother, to be centered in the large impersonal world of the natural, which in itself surely negates all intimacy; in its space and vastness and terrifying age, shakes off the little tentative human grasp as a leaf is dropped in the wind.

I felt this in the form of a kind of uneasy bewilderment that now and then rose up like a barrier of language between myself and the young man. I could not fit him into the inherited categories of my child's experience, and this made me obscurely anxious. . . . Two days before his leave was up I was alone with him for perhaps only the second or third time since I had arrived. We walked into the village together on a dull afternoon to get our hair cut and he said to me suddenly on the way back: "I suppose you're going to go back and live there? —That life on the Mine is the narrowest, most mechanical, unrewarding existence you could think of in any nightmare."

I was so surprised, shocked, that I stammered as if I had been caught out in some reprehensible act. "Well, Ludi, of course. I mean I live there—!"

He shook his head, walking on.

I felt indignant and unhappy at the same time. "I've always lived on the Mine. —I know you don't like towns, you hated working underground, you like to be at the sea, who wouldn't—" But even as I said it I was aware that no one I knew would dream of wanting to live buried away on the South Coast, not working. Why? It was an existence at once desirable because of its strangeness, yet in some way shameful.

He made a noise of disgust. "Grubbing under the earth in the dark to produce something entirely useless, and coming up after eight hours to take your place in the damned cast-iron sacred hierarchy of the Mine, grinning and bowing all the way up to the godly Manager on top, and being grinned and bowed at by everyone below you—not that there ever was anyone below me, except the blacks and it's no privilege to sit on them since anyone can."

"Oh, *Ludi*." I laughed. He laughed, too, his wry smile with the corners of his mouth turning down.

"You drink in the pubs together and you play tennis on Saturdays together and you go to dances organized by the ladies. You live by courtesy of the Mine, for the Mine, in the Mine. And to hell with Jack so long as I'm all right, so long as my promotion's coming. And I'll grin at the Underground Manager and I'll slap the shift boss on the back—"

"But what are you going to do?" He had admitted me to a plane of adulthood that released the boldness to ask something I had wondered in silence.

For once he turned to look at me, and it was with the patient smile that expects no comprehension, knows that a familiar barrier has been reached. "Look," he said, "I don't want to 'get on.' I'm happy where I am. All I want is the war to end so that I can get back here."

"Shall you start up the chicken farm again?"

"It doesn't much matter. Any sort of job would do so long as it brings in fifteen or twenty pounds a month. Just so's mother and I can manage. She's got a small income of her own."

I was embarrassed by my own reaction. I knew that in my face and my silence I showed a deep sense of shock and a kind of disbelief that timidly tried to temper it. A struggle was set up in me; dimly I felt that the man acted according to some other law I did not know, and yet at the same time the law of my mother, the law of the people among whom I lived and by which I myself was beginning to live, made him outcast, a waster, a loafer, ambitionless; to be sighed over more than blamed, perhaps, like Pat Moodie, the son of one of the officials who had "wasted all his opportunities" and taken to drink. The phrases of failure came to my mind in response to the situation, because I had no others to fit it.

"No, thank you"—his voice was firm and serene—"I don't want it. I don't want the nice little job or the nice little family or the dreary little town or the petty little people. It doesn't interest me" —he was looking at me rather shortsightedly through his glasses; he obviously did not expect or care for an answer or opinion from me—"and I have no desire whatever to get on with anything at all except living down here. —You should see the Pondoland Coast, you know, Helen. You people've no idea. . . . I go down there for a week or so to fish—some tinned stuff and my tackle, and sleep on the beaches. There are coral reefs there, under the deep water . . . you've never seen anything like it. Like some buried city of pink marble. And the fish!"

I looked at him curiously as he pushed a way for me through the wet bracken. Rain brushed off along the bleached hair on his red-brown arms, his bare legs had a curiously impersonal muscular beauty that would have astonished him if anyone had spoken of it: somehow his personal physical attributes existed in spite of him rather than as a conscious part of him, as a plant, being in its function of turning oxygen to sap, does not participate in the beauty of the flower which results and is blooming somewhere on it.

I tried to think of him in one of my father's gray suits, in a shirt with arm bands to hold up the sleeves, like the men wore at the office. It did not seem possible. Suddenly the absurdity of it pleased me very much; I was laughing at the thought of the clerks at the office.

He was scrambling ahead of me up a bank and he half-turned at the sound. His hand went to the bright shaven hair at the nape of his neck. "It's a bit of a mess, I suppose . . . ?" he said, smiling. I shook my head, I was too out of breath to speak. "Mine too," I gasped, catching up with him. The wet, the slither of the grass beneath our feet, and the sudden darkening of the air as the day ended unseen behind a muffling of cloud, filled us both with a kind of intoxication of energy. We tore home, ignoring the paths. I plunged with the child's conscious craziness into every difficulty I could find, madly excited at myself. Sometimes I could not speak at all, but just stood, pointing at him and laughing.

The ten years between us were forgotten.

Ludi left on Saturday morning. In the day and a half between, I had felt rather than thought that he might say he would write to me. I kept out of the way of the mother and son almost unconsciously, leaving them to draw together before the fresh parting or, perhaps as unconsciously, they excluded me; but I felt all the time that the natural moment would arise when the only possible thing to say would be: I shall drop you a line when I get a chance, just to let you know what it's like. Or: But of course you'll tell me that when you write.

And it did seem to me that the moment came again and again, but Ludi smiled into the pause and did not even know that it was *his*. I watched this with the quiet, gradual disappointment of a child who has presumed too far upon the apparent understanding of a grownup for an imaginative game: suddenly, the ageless understanding being becomes simply an adult indulgently regarding rather than participating, and nothing, no dissimulation or protest, can deflect the child's cold steady intuition of the fact. For the first time since I had left home, I felt lonely, but it was not for my mother and father or anything that I had left, but rather for something that I had not yet had, but that I believed was to come: a time of special intimate gaiety and friendship with some vague companion composed purely of an imaginative ideal of youth—an ideal that I would never formulate now, and that only later, when it had gone, would recognize as having existed all the time unnoticed in myself, because it was nothing concrete, but just the dreams, the uncertainty, the aspiration itself.

When Ludi had gone we came back to the house in a gentle companionable mood and sank into a kind of lull of feminine comfortableness; Mrs. Koch took up the curtains she had been making before her son came home, and the tea, set out with the one cracked cup that Matthew never failed to give us, was waiting in the living room. I lay reading with the damp cottony smell of the chintz cushion under my elbows and could not be bothered to go down to the sea. When it got cooler late in the afternoon, we went for a walk, at Mrs. Koch's sedate pace, and on the flattest part of the road. If the obverse side of her son's departure was the sharpness of love and lack, the reverse side was a certain relieved flatness, as if her body protested at the emotional tension of his temporary presence and found resignation more suited to its slowing vitalities.

We were having supper with the radio tuned in over-loudly to the B.B.C. news—the crackling, cultured voice talking of bombs and burning towns was an invariable accompaniment to the evening meal—when I thought I heard the slam of a car door outside, but did not remark upon it or even lift my head because the metallic monologue of the radio, so dehumanized by the great seas and skies that washed between, had the curious effect of making all immediate sounds seem far off and unreal. It was with the most dreamlike astonishment that I looked up from the white of the cloth and saw Ludi. He was closing the door behind himself, sagging from the shoulder with the weight of his kit in the other hand. For a moment I had a ridiculous start of guilt as if I had conjured him up. He smiled at me down his mouth and I saw that his cap, which he normally wore a little too far forward for my standards of attractiveness, was pushed up from his warm-looking forehead. I saw this as suddenly and distinctly as if a light had been turned on in a room that had waited ready in the dark.

All at once Mrs. Koch gave a little exclamation almost of dismay or annoyance, and then she was up and pushed the table away; he had her by the arm. "The bridge is down at Umkomaas. The rains last week, and it's been slipping all the time, I suppose. We hung about and hung about, thinking—"

"You came back! Ludi! But what about your leave, won't you get into trouble? Well, I can't believe it!"

"The bridge is down. So what could I do? The trains aren't running and I thought maybe I'd get a lift—but then it got late and I thought, what's the use?"

They were both laughing, perhaps now because Mrs. Koch had seemed put out, and just to make sure he was really there, his mother had to ask him over again. "I can't believe it." This time he repeated the story with indignation, feeling in some way that although it could not be so in fact, the army, the hated regimentation that defeated itself again and again, was to blame. —After all, if it had not been for the army, he would not have had to be in a particular place at a particular time, and being prevented from getting there would not have mattered to him in the least.

While they were questioning and exclaiming, I stood up quite still in my place at the table, my napkin tight in my hand. Suddenly, like the moment after I had faced an examiner, a light shudder went over my neck and I began to tremble. The tighter I clenched the piece of linen the more my hand shook, and I could not control my bottom jaw. I was terrified they would notice me, and as the fear came so it attracted its object. Ludi gestured his mother's attention toward me: "It's taken away her appetite."

As he spoke the trivial words, not even to me, the trembling lay down immediately inside me and an extraordinary happiness, utterly unspecific and somehow mindless, opened out in me. We gave Ludi supper; I moved about the room with a light confidence that came to me suddenly and for the first time, as if my body had slipped,

between instant and instant, into the ease of balance, never to be
unlearned, as a rider, clinging to the vertical insecurity of his bicycle, suddenly learns how and is easy between the supports of air
and air. There was a family gaiety between the three of us that had
never been between my parents and me; I was delighted with the
timidity of Mrs. Koch's response to the nearest that Ludi's small dry
humor could get to joking. They got quite excited discussing how
long the unofficial extension of his leave could hope to last.

"I'll get the incubator house fixed if I stay three days," he said.

Mrs. Koch, with a conscious bold levity that made me want to
touch her with affection, said: "Oh, to pot with the incubator. Matthew will do something to it."

"You mean he'll give it some thought—until my next leave."

His mother was serious at once; her extraordinary gentleness
toward all human beings made her suspect that the old servant's
feelings could be hurt by implied criticism, even out of his hearing.
"Ludi, his sciatica's got him bent double—"

We laughed at her, and soon she was laughing with us.

Ludi gathered up his kit with a gesture that closed the evening;
always at some unexpected point he withdrew, firmly and without
room for protest, into the preoccupation with a small task or a private
commonplace errand of his own. If you followed him to his room,
you would merely find him lying on his bed, reading, or tinkering
with an improvement to his fishing tackle: yet he was withdrawn into
the dignity of himself in these ordinary occupations as a sculptor or
a scholar who, it is tacitly understood, will leave the company to
rejoin the bright struggle that waits, as always, in the solitude at the
top of the house. Like them, he was only loaned to other people; he
must return to himself. His mother was long accustomed to this, but
now nervousness made her trespass. She called, after a while, to his
bedroom: "Ludi?"

His voice came, muffled as if he were pulling some clothes over
his head. "I'm going for a swim."

"But the tide'll be right out—" she called, not wanting to let
him go without a protest. We heard him padding down the passage
with his steady, soft tread, like the tread of a native who is used to
walking great distances. As he was going down the veranda steps,

his mother suddenly opened the window and called after him, "Ludi! Why don't you take Helen?"

He stood up to the window in the light. "Does she want to come? Of course."

"She hasn't been out all day." Mrs. Koch was periodically seized with the fear that she neglected to entertain her young guest; then it seemed more important that she should arrange something for me to do than consult my wishes. I usually felt a little awkward if the plan involved Ludi, because I was afraid that I intruded on him, and that he felt he must agree out of a sense of duty. And often when he had been persuaded into some little jaunt, I had the feeling, disconcerting in a different way, that he was so little bothered by my presence that to have feared he might be was a piece of presumption, irritating and silly. Now he stood quite patiently in the window, waiting.

This time I was determined to show the decisiveness of an adult. "It'll take me only a minute to change," I questioned him.

Mrs. Koch shook her head. "No, you're not going swimming at night. That's all right for him. He knows how to look after himself in the sea."

One did not argue with gentle Mrs. Koch. "Then I'm ready." I smiled.

"—Then come on!" Ludi put both hands on the window sill.

6 LURCHING DOWN THE HILLS to the beach in the old car, I talked a great deal. The slight sense of adventure in the dark road and the attentive profile of the young man whom, sometimes, as now, I felt I knew very well (I imagined myself saying: Ludi Koch? Of course, he's different when you know him. . . .) brought out in me a tendency to exaggerate and animate. Unconsciously I selected for him those anecdotes of the Mine and the town that presented certain aspects of the life as a little ridiculous, if not quite as reprehensible as he condemned it. There was even one story that showed my father as rather stuffy, rather circumscribed. . . . I could tell it with the child's elderly amusement at the parent.

Then it seemed just as easy not to talk. We left the car and got down onto the dark beach giving short instructions to each other: Look out for that bush; all right now. . . . He disappeared into the dark.

I lay down on my back on the cool sand that held the cool of the night as it held the heat of the sun, deep down, far below the loose billowy surface, cool, cool all through. I kept the palm of my hand under my head to keep my hair free of sand, but soon I took my hand away and let the soft touch of my hair against my neck become indistinguishable from the touch of the sand. At first I was completely sunk in darkness. There was no sea, no earth, no sky. Even the sand I lay on was a tactile concept only. The sound of the sea was the flow of dark itself. Then, as I lay, a breaking wave turned back a glimmer of pale along the dark, and slowly, slowly, I made out a different, moving quality of the dark that was the sea. Flowing over his legs; I saw them undulating in the water dark, like fins that moved like fans. I might be lying on the air with the earth on top of me.

I did not know how long he was away. With nothing but the waves' faint break in the darkness to measure the passing of time, I could not tell if it was ten minutes or half an hour, but suddenly he stepped into the enclosing dark about me and he was there, toweling his hair. A few drops of cold water shook from it onto my cheek. I sat up, and a faint slither of sand ran like a breeze down the back of my dress. I could hardly see him, yet he was there vigorously, his sharp breathing, the smell of damp towel, and as he bent, the fresh smell of khaki.

He said: "Where are you?"

"Here." —I put up my hand, but he could not see it.

"Was it cold?"

"No. There's a lot of seaweed about, tangling up your legs. Come—" he said.

I got up obediently. We began to walk slowly along the beach, quite far from the water, where the sand was dry and coldly heavy to walk in. All my being was concentrated in my left hand, which hung beside him as we walked. My whole body was poured into that hand as I waited for him to take it. It seemed to me that he must take it; I felt us walking up the beach together, with our hands clasped. In my head I listened and heard again him saying: "Come—"; so short, so intimate, and the strange pleasure of my obedience, as if the word itself drew me up out of the sand.

He began to talk, about the men with whom he lived in camp. He talked on and on. I answered yes or no: I was unable to listen, the way one cannot hear when one is preoccupied by distress of anger. He did not seem to notice. Now and then the uneven flow of the sand beneath our feet caused his shirt to brush my shoulder with the faint scratch of material; my hand, numb with the laxity of waiting, felt as if it had been jambed.

We had reached the lagoon, pouring silently down the channel it had cut for itself into the sea. "Shall we get back now?" he said and, with a little groan, lowered himself down to the sand; he squatted with his arms folded on his knees. I stood awkwardly, with what must have been an almost pettish attitude of offense innocently expressed in my stiff body. But as he made no move to get up, I sat down too, facing past the hump of his knees.

"But you know," he said suddenly, as if it were the continuation of something we had discussed, "you're really only a little girl. I wonder. I wonder if you are." He took me by the elbows and drew me round, close against his knees and I saw his teeth, white for a moment, and knew that he had smiled. He enclosed my head and his knees in his arms and rocked them gently once or twice. The most suffocating joy took hold of me; I was terrified that he would stop, suddenly release me. So I kept as still as fear, my hands dangling against his shoes. He gave a curious sigh, as one who consents to something against his will. Then he bent to my face and lifted it with his own and kissed me, opening my tight pressing mouth, the child's hard kiss with which I tried to express my eagerness as a woman. The idea of the kiss completely blocked out for me the physical sensation; I was intoxicated with the idea of Ludi kissing me, so that afterward it was the idea that I remembered, and not the feel of his lips. I buried my face on his knees again and the smell of khaki, of the ironed khaki drill of his trousers, came to me as the smell of love. . . . I remembered the Cluff brothers at the dance . . . the smell of khaki . . . my heart beat up at the excitement of contrasting myself then with myself at this moment.

Ludi was feeling gently down my bare arm, as if to find out how some curious thing was made.

"Well," he said at last, "can't you speak?"

"Ludi," I asked, "do you really like me?"

7 I DO NOT KNOW if I had ever been kissed before. Even if I had, it does not matter; it was as if it had never happened, the prim mouth of a frightened schoolboy dry on my lips, the social good-night kiss on the doorstep that would be smiled upon indulgently by Mine parents, the contact that was an end in itself, like a handshake. Now I lay in my bed in the high little room in Mrs. Koch's house and kept my face away from the pillow because I wanted my lips free of any tactual distraction that might make it difficult for me to keep intact on my mouth the shape and sensation of Ludi's kiss. I thought about it as something precious that had been shown to me; vivid, but withdrawn too quickly for me to be able to re-create every detail as my anxious memory willed. That anxious memory trembling eagerly to forget nothing; perhaps that is the beginning of desire, the end of a childhood? Wanting to remember becomes wanting: the recurring question that has no answer but its own eventual fading out into age, as it faded in from childhood.

Suddenly sleep, arbitrary, uncaring, melted my body away from me. I had just time to recognize myself going; and with only my mind still left to me, the idea of the kiss became complete in itself: I held it warmed in my heart as a child holds the imaginative world in the clasped body of a Teddy bear.

I woke late—by the standards of the Koch household—to a day of such heat that already by the time I had put on my clothes my heart was thumping with effort. Ludi was finishing a second cup of tea, chair half pushed away from the table. He was reading the paper, and on this, as on every other morning, his lifted head excused him from any further talk or attention. There was a whole small pawpaw on my plate instead of the usual segment scooped free of pips. I looked up to Mrs. Koch. "Matthew's conscience offering," she smiled. I cut it open; it was one of those with deep pink flesh and I knew it would have a special flavor, sharper, more perfumed than the yellow ones. The beautiful black pips beaded out under my spoon. I ate the whole fruit, very carefully, and it made me deeply hungry. Mrs. Koch went out to the kitchen to fetch my scrambled eggs and the toast Matthew was making for me.

Now. I turned my eyes slowly, as if their movement might have some equivalent of the creak of footsteps. His raised knee, crossed over the other, was in the line of my lowered vision, the slightly roughened skin of the kneecap, the big taut tendon underneath, the golden hairs over the calf muscle. He moved his toes a little inside the shabby sandshoe.

And now I lifted my head and looked at him, set face at an angle above the newspaper, thick bright lashes crowded round his narrowed eyes as he gave two quick blinks in succession, as though the print hurt them. The clean cheeks of a newly shaven blond man; a faint movement at the nostrils as he breathed deeply against the heat. The mouth. The thin mouth with the little uneven lift to the lip on the left side, the curious rim, like a raised line, outlining his lips which were the same color as his skin.

The same. Exactly the same. Just as he was yesterday, the day I arrived. He had all the mystery of a stranger, unimpaired. Now I looked at his hands. He must have sensed the silent movement of my eyes. Bending the spine of the newspaper, he looked up and said: "Want to go swimming?" I felt his smile rest on me. It seemed to me that the moment was too intimate for speech; whatever he said to me now was intimate to me, nothing could be casual or common-place, because every word, every gesture, I deciphered in the knowl-edge of last night, that lay always in my hand like a key to a code. I only nodded, hard and surely. I could see him running, very fast, through the shallows to the breakers, cutting the water in a wake like mercurial wings at his ankles.

"Too hot for the beach?" said Ludi to his mother. She put down

my egg. "This morning?" Her eyes rested vaguely here and there
upon the table, looking for a decision. "I was supposed to help Mrs.
Plaskett with her re-covering. . . . Certainly too hot to bend about
pinning and sewing. I felt a little dizzy when I got up, as it is." She
was smiling weakly at me, reluctant, ready to be swayed. My heart
beat so fast with anxiety that each mouthful presented an obstacle
to my throat. I cut off great mouthfuls of egg and toast and forced
them into my mouth. A smile of great shame and brightness was
turned to her out of my anxiety. I said, terrified, "At least there'll
be a breeze on the beach." She hesitated still. "You could sit under
the funeral tree." —It was a dark and mournful tree that hung
unexpectedly over a dune—. Trembling with the guilt of my desire
to prevent her, I could have gone on finding reasons for her to come.
Ludi seemed to have lost interest. "Well, then, shall we risk it,
dear?" she assented to him.

The mouthful of food passed from one side of my mouth to the
other. I could not swallow it and did not know what to do with it. I
wished they would go out of the room so that I could spit it out into
my hand, chewed and distasteful. Tears of chagrin came up against
the age of Mrs. Koch; the age and blindness—the waste! Old people
to whom nothing matters anymore, so they do not know how, un-
knowingly and careless, they waste the precious time of the young.
And she was waiting for me, looking at me fondly because it was
settled we were all going to the beach together as we had done
before. I found I was smiling back at her; a smile that came to my
mouth like a blow.

And yet when we got to the beach I was suddenly happy again
as I had been the previous evening at supper. On Ludi and me the
sun flowed, pressed, crawled like the tickling feet of some hair-
legged millipede where the salt water dried. When I lay in the water,
attacked by long rough breakers I wanted the warmth of the sun,
drawing me up through the surface of my streaming skin; when I
lay in the sun, full of the sun as a ripening fruit, I wanted the dowse
of the cool water. And so the whole morning, in and out, the sea
and the sun, dark and glare, with a delight in the energy that pow-
ered me, a pleasure in the firm shudder of the tight burned flesh
above my knees as I ran. I left my bathing cap in the sand and went

into the sea without it. First the tips of my hair got wet and touched
cold fingers on my shoulders. Then the swell, lightly rising up my
back, passed over my head like the cool tongue of a great dog. The
membrane of water split and parted on my knotted hair, running off;
the thickness of it, near my scalp, was still dry. Then I sank myself
head first into a towering breaker and the great cold hands of the
sea thrust in beneath my hair and I came up shocked, gasping,
blinded by the heavy bands of liquid hair that flowed down my face
and clung round my neck.

Ludi said: "You'll never get a comb through that when it's dry."

At once I was afraid he might think I was showing off. I said,
with the self-conscious casualness of a lie, "I've done it often before.
It'll be all right after a shower." Mrs. Koch had lain back with the
paper over her face, and was not awake innocently to contradict me.
A little later Ludi and I went into the sea together, and again I let
my hair into the water, dipping and spreading it in a solitary game.
He swam away out, only his head rising and lost, gone and there,
out where the breakers ended and the sea really began, an element
as solid in depth as the earth, a thick glassy blue earth. I played in
the water and thought of Ludi swimming back to me: it seemed to
me, as I imagined a woman in the complacency of marriage, that it
was wonderful to think of him removed from me, simply because he
would come back. I lay on the sand with my head sheltered in the
darkness of my arms and imagined a life with Ludi, long dialogues
between us, dialogues between myself and others about Ludi; Ludi
talking to someone about me. And whether he was in the sea, beyond
sight, or lying a foot away from me across the silence, and whether
his mother was there, or if she had been left at home, it did not
matter to me. Just as on a distant nod of acknowledgment there are
people who can construct the history of a friendship, so that you are
astonished to hear that so-and-so speaks of you by your Christian
name, so I spun out of Ludi's one gesture of recognition to me as a
woman the entry into the whole adult world of relationships between
men and women, as it existed in my imagination. In this world
unbounded by time, commonplace, and the hazards of human behavior, with, in fact, the scope of innocence, Ludi existed for me in
an exclusive, all-possessive love that made the Ludi suddenly seen

as I opened my eyes—he was blowing the sea water out of his nose and his eyes above the handkerchief glistened with effort—unreal and momentarily unrecognizable, like meeting someone whose photograph you have long been accustomed to.

All day this dreamlike state of mind persisted, and with it a softening that seemed physical, a phenomenon in my warm sea-soaked body that made everything and everyone around me dear and sympathetic. All the angular reticences of adolescence were resolved in the simple fact that cannot be forewarned or explained: the discovery of love. With the irrational changeability of emotions which commanded me and took advantage of my inexperience, I felt a dramatic welling of tenderness toward Mrs. Koch; infinite patience with her elderliness (love was past for her, gone down like a sun that dazzles the eyes no more); the homely face and the curly gray hair, her freckled hands, even, had for me something of the fascination of a neglected shrine: she was Ludi's mother. Excitement at the thought of the three of us, in the car, at table, could bring sudden tears to my eyes; the faint shine of sweat, like the glisten of a dusting of talcum, on the white inner skin of my elbow filled me with the swift, intoxicating thought of my being alive. In my room I studied my face, fixed my hair this way and that with fingers that trembled with eagerness for a result that might change me entirely—with the instinct that gives a flower the bright petals that invite the insect, chose clothes that showed my waist and the small shapes of my breasts. I took off shorts and put on a skirt because in the tight trousers the curve of my belly filled me with disgust. I made my own eyes heavy with the fumes of the perfume that was usually kept for special occasions, I wore a bracelet and painted my nails to please a man who never noticed clothes and intensely disliked the artificial. But he was a man and not a child, as I was, and I believe he saw not the pathetic little artifice of the means, but the complete naturalness of the end, which was the desire to please.

After lunch, Ludi suggested that we drive out to Cruden's Beach for the afternoon—the stare of the sun was completely shut off by thick cloud, but the heat came through, muffled and still.

"You certainly are taking a holiday," Mrs. Koch said, gently teasing, questioning, "How is it you're deserting the fish for us?"

And in a conspiracy of possessiveness that was sweet to me, I allied myself with her in banter. Yet when I went along the passage to get my bathing suit, I could not walk: I wanted to run, jump, my hands were inept with happiness as I assembled my things—Ludi was spending his time with *me*, it was me for whom he stayed. Mrs. Koch's innocent teasing, her "way" as Ludi would call it, gave me the assurance I could have had no other way, independent and un-suspecting testimony of something that could be truly interpreted only by my key. With my delight there was astonishment; I was content to be allowed to be with him, to watch him. My feeling was still so much a cherished compound of the imagination; that the adored object should show signs of wishing to come to life and take part was more than I could imagine.

I sat between Mrs. Koch and Ludi in the old swaying car and it seemed that all the time there was some kind of machine running inside me. It had started up and now it was humming secretly all the time, unbeknown to anyone. I watched fascinated the dance of my lax hands, jolting against my lap with the shake of the car. Sometimes I felt I must keep my head down to hide the excitement of happiness that I could feel in my face. Yet my joy could not be confined; the sight of the sea round a bend, a little native on a calf's back, brought a cry of pleasure I could not hold back. On the great beach there were two or three little gatherings of people, not holiday-makers but residents from the district, stranded in the un-certain boredom of their Sunday afternoon. Of course a hand went up, like a pennant, as we sank from the path to the sand. Mrs. Koch knew somebody: "Why Ludi . . . it's the Leicesters, I think."

Ludi and I lay face down in the sand a yard or two away from the women and children round a thermos flask—the squatting pat-tern, like a party game, that broke up and re-formed round Mrs. Koch sinking majestically to rest. Presently I got up and went back to the car to change into my bathing costume. It was difficult to get into, crouching on the floor, because it was still damp from morning. At last I wriggled and dragged my way into it and came out, feeling as if I were being held by tight clammy hands. From the short distance I could see Ludi, nearer the group now, explaining some-thing with a rotating gesture of his hand as he talked. I walked over

the sand and stood near him. He finished his explanation, saying:
". . . Yes, yes, that's what I was saying. . . . It wouldn't matter which
way you put it on, so long as that axle arrangement was at the right
angle." He paused a moment and closed his teeth on a match, and
I thought he would speak to me, but he had merely paused to ponder
something and suddenly he had it: "Of course you must understand
that a thing like this isn't foolproof . . . not by any means. And I
can't really say unless I see it." And then with a sudden confidence:
"But it should be all right, I don't see any reason why it shouldn't
be perfectly all right." —He had a way of putting his head on one
side and turning one hand up.

I did not even wonder what it was they were talking about. I
simply stood there. Now Ludi lifted his head round to me. "Again?"

The curious inability to speak came over me. I nodded hard,
smiling.

"That child hasn't been out the water the whole day," said Mrs.
Koch, interrupting her conversation with a little thin woman who
was crocheting as she talked.

"Oh, well . . . ," said Ludi, getting out of his shorts. He gave a
shrug and the half-lift of a smile to the man to whom he had been
talking, as one acknowledges the necessity of pleasing a child. He
pulled off his shirt and we went down toward the water together. But
when the cool rill closed over our feet and the breath of the sea
lifted to our faces, we began to walk along the water line. "You can't
go anywhere without mother finding a friend," Ludi said. "Leices-
ter's got about as much mechanical sense as that shell. Stupidity of
his questions—"

He seemed to lose interest in what he was saying. We walked
right away up the beach and over some rocks and to another beach,
a smaller one, where the sand was coarser and bright. I picked up
a handful and saw that it was not sand at all, really, but the fragments of shells, pounded to a kind of meal by the pestle of the sea
on a mortar of rocks. I showed it to Ludi and he looked at it and
then blew it off my hand and dusted my hand and let it fall, in a
gesture that suddenly seemed to me to express him, all that, in him,
was exciting and wonderful to me. And just as the thought was
bursting over me in a curious turmoil of feeling, a physical feeling,

like a kind of blush, that I had never felt before, he put his hand
down on the nape of my neck. It caught my hair back from my head
so that I had to walk stiffly, and, noticing this, seriously and capably
as if he were adjusting something he had made, he slid his hand
under my hair to free it.

Our feet were hurt by the coarse shingle and we wandered to
the rocks and sat with our feet in the pools. We talked about the
sea and the life of the sea around us, and I picked the tiny conical
towers of winkles off the rock with my fingernail and threw them
back into the water. I said: "Let's go in . . . ?" He stretched himself
backward against the rock and for answer, or rather as if he had
forgotten to answer, looked at me slowly, smiling and yet not smiling,
a look of regret, willing reluctance—a look that puzzled me. My
greatest concern was to keep from him anything that might remind
him that I was still a child, and so I did not want him to know that
it puzzled me, that anything he did or said could puzzle me. I smiled
as if in understanding. But the smile must have been too quick, too
bright. He shook his head. I said: "Why do you do that over me?"
—with the anxiousness which came up in me so quickly. He said
with a little beckoning jerk of the chin: "Come here." And very
carefully I slid to my knees in the water, and arranged myself nearer
to him and timidly put my hand, that jumped once, in reaction from
the contact, on his knee. He kissed me as he had done the night
before but this time I held my mouth slightly open though I kept
very still. Then he breathed softly on my cheeks and kissed me
again several times, and between the kisses I waited for him to kiss
me again, while the tepid stagnant water of the pool touched with a
terrible softness against the inner sides of my thighs. I think it was
from the touch of the warm water that I suddenly stood up. Yet I
wanted him to kiss me again, I wanted to prove to myself the reality
of the feel of his lips, smooth and dry, the secret—so it seemed to
me—of the deep, soft pressure of moisture, the astonishing warmth
that, seeing his mouth move in talk, could never be guessed. I waited
but, with the unexpectedness that quickened my pleasure with the
continual threat of small disappointments, we went into the sea instead, though he did not swim away from me, but kept near, so that
I could talk, shout to him, and we would bump against each other,

strangely buoyant with water, each feeling the touch of the other's limbs like the blunt contact of air-filled rubber shapes. There was a joy for me in tumbling about Ludi; I must have jumped around him like a puppy inviting play. But if he was not swimming seriously, he liked to float with his eyes closed, lonely on the water.

We stayed in too long—perhaps I had been in the sea too often altogether, that day—for when I came out and lay on the rough sand I had the feeling of air pressing inside me against my collarbones, and a swinging in my head. Water kept closing over my hearing and as I got up to shake it out of my ear, Ludi lifted my wet hair up on top of my head and pushed me to him with his elbow. He began to kiss me again. This time he took the whole of my mouth into the warm wet membrane of his mouth and his tongue came into my mouth and was looking for something; went everywhere, shockingly, pushing my tongue aside, fighting my cheeks, resisting my teeth. I was afraid and I did not want him to stop. I clung to the flesh behind his shoulder as if I were in danger of slipping down somewhere and as we stood together in the sultry afternoon the cool film of water dried from our bodies, and the warmth of our skin came through, into contact. Against the bare patch between the brassière and the shorts of my bathing suit I felt the steamy wet wool of his trunks and in the hollow of my neck, the slight liveness, as if it was capable of certain limited movement, of the hair on his breastbone. A drop of cold water fell from his hair onto my warm back, and another, and in the soft bed of my belly, as if it were growing there, I became conscious of another warmth, a warmth that grew from Ludi, from a center of warmth that came to life between his thighs. Nobody told me love was warm. Such warmth—I seemed to remember it, it seemed like something forgotten by me since I was born. Nobody told me it was warmth. How can it be understood, accepted, cold? I should have remembered—how? from where?—that it was warmth. All the fires were here, and the warmth of my mother's bed long ago, and the deep heat of the sun.

8 BY MONDAY AFTERNOON a railway bus service was circum-
venting the fallen bridge and carrying passengers to meet the
train at the next station. But Ludi didn't go. I seem to remember
that it appeared to be Mrs. Koch's idea that he should apply for an
extension of leave; perhaps it was the one time in all his devotion
to her that he made use of her gentle blindness of love for him? At
any rate, he stayed. He telegraphed to his Commanding Officer and
was granted an additional week, until the following Monday.

This is a simple statement of fact to relate now, but like all
reports, all accuracy of happenings in terms of comings and goings,
dates and times, its bareness is not the bare truth. The truth about
humans is always inaccurate, never bare; the nearest one can get to
it is to remember its confusion, and complicatedness. It was not a
telegram sent and an answer forthcoming; nor three people waiting.
I only remember that I, alone, not yet eighteen and a novice to
anguish, waited for the granting of that week in a state of longing
anxiety that has never, even in real sorrow, in the fall of bitterness,
in despair, even, been equaled in all my life. Nothing is more serious
than this apparently laughable lack of the sense of proportion in the
young. With the command of emotions like a stock of dangerous
drugs suddenly to hand, there is no knowing from experience how
little or how much will do; one will pitifully scald one's heart, over
nothing. The nothing may be laughable, but the pain is not. For me
those few days, granted or denied, were my share of life. Like a
butterfly, who knows only one day, no other days seemed to exist
for me.

Then the telegram came and I do not know how it was for Ludi
and Mrs. Koch, but for me it was the silence that follows a maddening din. But just as one cannot enjoy the mere negative state of
having no pain in the way in which one believes one shall while
the pain is on, so I did not taste the pure joy of the telegram as the
positive state I had imagined in longing. There was no time. There
was scarcely time to dress, to eat, to sleep even. Certainly no time
to read and no time to write letters. A letter came from my mother,
but though I read it, quickly, line by line, I was vague about what

she had said; it seemed an uninteresting letter. One from a girl on the Mine whom I had begged to remember to write to me, I somehow never did open; I came across it long afterward one day at home, where it lay in an old chocolate box with a perished bathing cap and a broken necklace, and tore it up because it reminded me with a pang of the place and time in which it should have been read. It was not that the days were fuller in the active sense than they had been all through my holiday; it was that they were full of Ludi. If I was in my bedroom, changing a dress, I did not know what he was doing at that moment. Perhaps he was about to go for a walk? Perhaps his mother might be asking him to do an errand for her. He might go without me. I shook myself into the dress, vanity and urgency warred in a moment I saw myself startlingly in the mirror, saw that my hair stood out too much—but flew down the passage pressing it anxiously with the flat of my palm. And there he would be, lying with one leg hanging down from the old sofa.

"Where you off to, miss?"

I would never admit I was tired, never admit I had had enough. It was never too early for me to get up, never so late that I would want to go to bed. At night when Mrs. Koch had gone to her room, Ludi and I went out onto the veranda and talked in the dark. As it got later, the talk got easier, until it seemed to me that if one could go on talking and talking as the night went deeper one would finally get to the other person; just before morning I would find what Ludi really was. . . . But instead I would find myself going quietly past the closed doors of the passage in the settled silence of one o'clock, lying at last in my bed with all the disparate images of him flashing in and out like lights in my mind. Half-sentences that did not connect, this mouth opening to say something I lost . . . ? And then, before sleep, a sudden desire to move, to turn face down on my breasts in the bed. And all night, under my sleep, an alertness for morning.

In my absorption, as if I moved in a trance of excitement, my eyes always on a vision of Ludi, I did not see and so believed that Mrs. Koch did not see any change in the air between Ludi and me. But of course this was not possible. Where for the first part of my stay, he had come and gone with his customary self-sufficiency, now he spent his time at home and wherever he went, took me with him. Yet she accepted this shift of emphasis in the relationship between the three of us with evident placidity; I believe now that she considered it only natural that I should become a disciple of her worship for Ludi, and that, partly out of kindness, partly out of an acceptance of his due, Ludi would let me worship him. She did not fear any woman in what she knew of Ludi, so she certainly feared nothing from so young a girl, a child in comparison with him. I think she was touched by what she saw in me; as someone who has been in the faith a long time is moved by the ecstatic face of the new convert.

"Did you enjoy yourself, Nell?" she would say to me. —We went to the beach in the morning on our own; perhaps because we hadn't asked her, or because she had forestalled this by saying that she could not come. We had walked a long way, past the rocks where no one but Ludi himself came to fish, and he had unfastened the halter of my wet bathing suit and peeled it down from my breasts. Neither he, nor anyone else, had ever touched or seen me before. I let him do this in stillness, looking down at myself as if we made the discovery together. I thought the skin of my breasts too white against the brown of my neck and arms; damp and cold from the sea they turned out away from each other and the left one trembled jerkily with the nervous beat of my heart beneath. Round the nipples tiny fragments of shell and pebble, worn membrane-thin by the water, stuck, shiny, pinkish-pearly to the skin. I lay so still I might have been waiting for a dagger. But Ludi, with a tone of delight that astonished me, smiled, "Look, the sea has been here. . . . You're all gritty."

—Yet I found it perfectly easy to answer Mrs. Koch: "Lovely. It wasn't so windy today. We saw that sister of Mrs. Meintjes' on the road. She expects them sometime on Thursday, because the old father's been ill, and Davey had a cold, and goodness knows what else. . . ." It was only when I took off my bathing suit to dress in my room that I paused, catching sight of myself in the greenish, watery mirror that fronted the old wardrobe, and thought, not with shame but with a sense of unreality, of Mrs. Koch's question that was not a question and my answer that was not an answer. And I understood that almost all of my life at home, on the Mine, had been

like that, conducted on a surface of polite triviality that was insen-
sitive to the real flow of life that was being experienced, underneath,
all the time, by everybody. The fascination of the gap between the
two came to me suddenly; I remembered, even out of childhood,
expressions on faces, the tone of a commonplace sentence spoken
unimportantly, the look of a person's back as he left on some unquestioned excuse. It was not the knowledge of a secret life beneath
so much as the maintenance of the unruffled surface itself that was
exciting. Now it seemed to me that every casual explanation might,
not conceal, but simply float above, like the reflection of the sky
which the water shows rather than its own depths, happenings as
strange and wordless as the time I had just spent with Ludi.

Since he had caressed me, Ludi's physical presence overcame
me like a blast of scent; the smell of his freshly ironed shirt sleeve,
as he leaned across me at the table, made me forget what I was
saying to Mrs. Koch; the pulse beating beneath the warm look of
the skin on his neck where there was no beard held my eyes; the
contact of his bare leg against mine in the car almost choked me as
something opened up inside my body, pressing against my heart and
opening, opening. When somebody spoke to him my heart pounded
slowly, as if the significance of talking to him was something they
could not understand as I did. When Matthew called Master Ludi!
Master Lu-di! across the garden, I smiled alone with warm pleasure.
And I began to watch anxiously every young woman who knew the
Kochs and who came to the house or was visited or merely met with
in the village. I began to be terribly afraid that someone else might
feel Ludi's presence as suffocatingly as I did. I ran over names
anxiously in my mind. I even began to worry about the things he
wore. I noticed that he had two pairs of hand-knitted socks, and
remembered that Mrs. Koch had told me that the one piece of knitting she would never attempt was the knitting of socks. I went to
the trouble of planning and rehearsing a whole dialogue in my mind
that would lead up naturally to the name of the giver of the socks.
When I put it into practice, Mrs. Koch's innocent digressions led
the conversation away from instead of toward the subject of the
socks, and I was left with the question unanswered and suddenly
more urgent than ever. Ludi was putting water in the car. I went

straight out to him. I walked round the car once and then stopped.

"Ludi, who made those socks for you?"

"What socks?"

I faltered—"You know. Your mother's darning them, a sort of light blue pair, and some gray ones."

"Why, what's wrong with them? Mrs. Plaskett made them for old Plaskett and they were too big. What's wrong about them?"

But to my dismay I found that the sense of security is something that is constantly in danger in love. A day later, when Ludi was clearing out an ottoman full of old clothes, he came upon a pull-over that he had evidently believed lost. He came into the kitchen, holding it up. "Look what's here. . . ."

Mrs. Koch left the tap running. "Maud's pull-over! But where was it?"—Then it reminded her, she rubbed her wet hands reproachfully down her apron—"Ludi, you should have gone over there, you know. They would so like to have seen you. You really should. . . ."

"No harm came to it." Ludi was holding the pull-over up to the light, carefully. "Not even a moth. I told you that stuff was jolly good, Mother. Look, it's been in that ottoman mixed up with a lot of rubbish for months, and there's not even a pinhole." Now they went on to argue about the name of the insecticide that had been used to spray the ottoman, and the pull-over was forgotten. Later I said, as if I had just remembered: "What did you do with that pull-over you found, Ludi?" —It was discovered that it was lost all over again, because he'd put it down in the kitchen and left it there. Then Matthew found it in the linen basket.

"How all the old ladies look after you," I said. "Everyone seems to contribute to your wardrobe."

"She's not an old lady."

"But your mother said, 'Maud's pull-over.' "

He gave a little grunt, half-amusement, half-chary. "Maud Harmel made it for a bet. She was wild about horses, never did anything but ride all day. I used to kid her, and she bet me she could do anything I'd name that any woman could do—you know, at home, the kind of thing most women do—. So I said, just like that, make a pull-over—and forgot about it. Anyway, she made it and this is it. But didn't you meet the Harmels from Munster—? Oh, no, of course you couldn't—I was forgetting we haven't been over to see them this time. . . ."

My heart always sank a little at the casualness with which he remembered or forgot the facts of my presence, sometimes not remembering how long I had been staying with them, and vague about the places I had seen and things I had done during the first part of my stay. By contrast, I was almost ashamed of the minuteness of detail with which I remembered everything pertaining to him. Now I was so downcast by the small fact of Ludi's not knowing whether or not I had met a certain group of their friends, that my interest in the maker of the pull-over was eclipsed.

I was too young to want that which I loved to be human. Even in the attraction of Ludi's body, I wanted the ideal rather than the real. My idea of love had come to me through the symbols, the kiss, the vow, the clasped hands, and this child's belief was bewildered even while it enjoyed the realities of heat, membrane, touch and taste. Though tears of ecstasy came to my eyes while I waited for Ludi to touch my breasts and look upon them, naked, the thought that he might want to see the rest of my body filled me with shame. I felt he could not know of the little triangle of springy hair that showed up against my white groins with their pale blue veins. I was terrified that if he saw me, he might be repulsed. I would lie in the bath looking down at myself with distaste, wishing I might be like the women in the romantic paintings I had seen, whose dimpled stomachs simply gave way to the encroaching curve of thighs.

The one time Ludi ever embarrassed me was when I was lying on the beach with my arms above my head and he asked me, tenderly, as one asks a child why she has scratched her knees, why I shaved my armpits. The blood of acute embarrassment fanned over me. That he knew that I grew hair under my arms! I said, muffled: "Everybody does it."

"Women are silly. They're very attractive, those little soft tufts of hair. But of course you shave it, and make it coarse, like an old man's beard."

I was so astonished at this view that I sat up, curious. And it became one of those intimate conversations that make people feel a delicious surrender of inconsequential confidence, very exciting to someone who discovers for the first time this special kind of talk that is released by physical intimacy.

Sometimes when we found ourselves unexpectedly alone but certain to be rejoined by the life of the household at any moment (even the appearance of one of the cats, stalking silently in about its own business, made me start) we would stand together kissing as if at a leave-taking, and he would flatten his hands down my back into the notch of my waist and then cup them round my buttocks. At once I would flinch away, almost crossly put myself out of the way of his hands. But he was not offended. Here in the sweet closeness of intimacy the ten years between us opened up a gulf. I lowered my eyelids, mouth pulled accusingly. But he looked at me gently, with a short catch and release of the breath, smiling comfortingly at me, only wishing to take care not to offend. Clinging to his hard, fast-beating chest, he knew that with my eyes shut tight I could not take that ten-years' dark jump in one leap. With gentle, sensuous selfishness, he only wished to enjoy me as far as I was ready to go, and sometimes, indeed, after a still, absorbed minute of passion when he knew nothing, he would come to himself quite abruptly simply to prevent me from following a blind instinct of desire which later I would not understand and might even disgust me.

On Saturday afternoon Mrs. Koch had to go to a wedding. Ludi was leaving on Monday morning, and she did not want to go, but the obligation of being a very old friend of the bride's mother was something that made an excuse out of the question for her. It was the first week in February and the first day of February heat, and when we had driven her to the MacVies', who were to take her with them to the ceremony at a village twenty miles inland, we drove slowly back to the farm through heat without air, a heat that now burned silent and intense as the heart of a fire after it has seized crackling on all life—trees, grass, flowers. The house was preoccupied with the heat, and as I knelt on the sofa at the window, I saw, outside in the stillness, the very tops of the trees tremble slowly in anticipation of rain. For the first time we lay down together alone in the house. At once I struggled up again, as if I were fussing about

the bed of an invalid. "Wait a minute, let's get the cushion—" Ludi
let his head be arranged with tugs at the cushion which turned it
this way and that. Then I half lay down, but immediately got up to
take off my shoes. Then I lay down beside him, moving my toes and
sighing with my eyes shut. After a moment of sinking pleasure, I
rose to wakefulness and opened them to see him looking at me,
smiling under half-closed lids. I wondered how I looked at that
angle, my cheek pushed by the pillow, and put up my hand to judge
the distortion. But my hand came into contact with his jaw and I
felt the wonderful shock of a burning warmth other than my own
flesh; I rolled over to bury my face in the angle between his neck
and the cushion.

I had a night of my own in there. The warm sweetness of the
skin felt but unseen, breathing out a slight moisture from the afternoon heat, was the essence, the surrender of Ludi himself in darkness. I seemed to sink into it, it lay upon my eyelids and my lips
like warm rain, and I fell through it, falling, falling as one does in
the mazy stratosphere between consciousness and sleep. Then I suddenly became aware of another presence; something else came and
stood beside me in the darkness. The damp, cottony smell of the
cushion in its thin, soft, faded cover beneath my cheek, musty from
the climate and faintly musky with the impress of the cats' round
bodies, was sharp and sad to my nostrils, like the sudden cold blow
across water in a landscape waiting for rain. Tears pricked at my
eyes with strange pleasure. The smell of the cushion was the distillation of the friendly house, of our lives moving about there with the
animals and old Matthew, of our voices lingering about the rooms,
our calls in the garden unanswered by the glitter of the sea, the
whole transience of this time that seemed my life but that would set
me down at some point (although it would be soon, it did not seem
so) and continue, far off and spiced, after I had awoken and gone.

I stirred and lifted my head into the room again, now filled with
the queer presaging yellow light of a storm taking place unheard
somewhere between us and the hidden sun. But Ludi was not looking at me now. His eyes, lids tender-looking from the protection of
glasses, were closed and his whole face was beautiful with the tension of inward concentration. The corner of his mouth relaxed and

then pressed back white against his cheek. He tightened his arms around me but I felt that for him I was not there. And the light, deepening to the greenish gold of wine or pools far down from the sun, lay solemnly on his cheek, but he merely flickered the thin skin of one eyelid, not able to notice what it was that passed over him. He began to kiss me in this concentration and to caress me, and soon I was in it too. It held me and I kissed him and gripped him back and I felt I was trying with all the gathered distress of my body to get somewhere, to reach something. He lay on top of me and he was heavy and that was what I wanted. I wanted him to be more heavy. He could not be heavy enough. I did not know what I wanted, but that I wanted. All at once, an astonishing sensation startled me. As if I had turned my head only in time to see something whipped away, my eyes flew open—. Ludi was gone, lifted away from me; he stood in the shadowy corner by the sofa, shapeless in rumpled clothes, pressing the palms of his hands up behind his ears.

I cried sharply: "Ludi! Come back!"

I lay hysterically rigid, exactly as he had left me.

"Ludi!"

He came slowly over, almost lumbering, and stood at the foot of the sofa. "I can't," he said, gently.

"Ludi," I said, not moving, "it was such a wonderful—so wonderful just now. Come back."

He shook his head. "It's impossible," looking down at me.

I must have him back. I must find out. I must go back and find what I was about to feel. I felt my eyes terribly wide open, fixed on his.

He sat down on the edge of the sofa and gently bent my bare foot in his hand. At the same time I loved him desperately and I resented the lax gentleness expressed in his touch. "It's physically impossible," he explained, gently, reluctantly. He stood up again, smiling at me. "I must go and fix myself up. I'll be back in a minute."

I watched him go out, so untidy, with a curious, disturbed look at the back of his hair, and as I lay, not waiting, but simply lying, my body slowly let go. Now I became conscious of a need to move my leg to another position, and, beyond my slow, deep breathing, heard that it was raining. It must have been raining for some time because the rain had already found its rhythm. All the room was darkened with the shade cast by the rain.

Ludi came back with the air of brightness of people who have just washed their faces and combed their hair, and as he filled the doorway he seemed to be very big and heavy-shouldered and somehow not responsible for, signaling appealingly as a prisoner from, his heavy man's frame. He lay down in the dimness beside me, quietly, hands behind his head. The warmth of his side made me sigh and smile. We lay a long while, perhaps five minutes. I was happy and sad, troubled and serene, bewildered and at rest. And I was thinking, vaguely, in snatches and dashes. And when I spoke, it was not of conscious intention, but like a sentence thrown out loud in sleep, the kind of accurate chance sum of thoughts and ideas not consciously computed in the mind.

"Ludi, have you ever slept with anyone?"

I think he knew what I was asking better than I knew myself. Ignoring the naïveté, the foolishness of the question, which he saw were not the question itself, he said, perfectly gravely, "Yes, miss, I have." —He called me "miss" the way one flatters a little girl; it was his word of endearment for me.

A weak protest of pain flowed over me, as if the protective fluid of a blister somewhere inside me had been released. —Now when I put a finger on the spot it would be raw, unprotected by ignorance. I was silent.

Suddenly it did not seem ridiculous to him to be apologetic. He began to comfort me by excusing himself and I believe he really meant it. For the moment he really believed I had the right to complain of the ten years of life he had had while I dragged a toe in the dust of my childhood, disconsolate, waiting. He said the oldest, comforting words, that were new to me. "Always very perfunctory. It's no good without any real feeling, any other relationship to back it. Honestly" —he was looking at me now, not seeing me properly in the dark of the rain, without his glasses, his close, bristly lashes that I secretly loved so much, showing bright as he narrowed his gaze—"It's no good." He put his arm under my head. I thought, he means it would be different with me. He means he loves me. I was suddenly utterly happy. I turned my head until I could rub my nose on the hairs of his forearm.

He said, with the stiff little preparatory swallow of surrender: "It happens about once a year, with me. One feels—and then afterward—I don't know, I'm disgusted with the woman. Meaningless, really." He thought a while. I wondered if he was remembering this strange act that I had never partnered but that I now understood. I felt a voluptuous tenderness toward him and wanted to take his head in my arms. He got up, slowly disentangling himself as one puts aside boughs, and stood, feet apart against the dizziness of standing upright. Reflectively, dismissing it, he swayed a little. "I assure you it's been a long time, now. Oh, many months." He smiled at me, his sour, confiding smile.

And then, as if he felt at the same instant my sudden desire for air, for the wet air of rain, he padded over to the window and opened it wide. It was sheltered by the veranda so that the rain did not come in, but the fresh, wild air did, rushing in as if the room drew a great breath. Drops like thick curved lenses distorted and magnified the brilliant green of the creeper shaking over the roof's edge. Scent tanged with wet came up from the beaten petals of the frangipani. The veranda with the few unraveling cane chairs and the pot plants breathing the rain they could not feel had the green twilight of a conservatory. We stood with our nostrils lifted like animals, staring out into the falling rain, our arms lightly round each other.

Curiously, this time when he went away and I was not to see him again, I was not lost. Almost before he had gone I had given myself up to the assurance of his letters. The idea of the first letter from him filled me with excitement, so that I half-wished him to go, be gone so that I might get that letter the sooner. And I should be able to write to him; perhaps to make him something. If I thought about home at all, it was to imagine myself sitting making something for Ludi, in absorption, in completeness. Mrs. Koch was mostly silent during these last few days of my stay, speaking of Ludi, at long intervals, as "he" and "him" as if the silences between her remarks were merely times when the conversation continued somewhere in her out of earshot. She would come hurrying from another room to show me something connected with him; a special winder he had made for her wool, a bracket for a bedside lamp that needed only the right kind of screw to complete it.

Once she came in with a snapshot.

"This isn't bad." Her crinkly gray hair hung over her eyes as she peered closely at it. When she had had a good look she passed it to me. Ludi, who, like most shortsighted people, did not photograph well, stood scowling at the sun in the artificial camaraderie of a garden snapshot. Two little boys grinned cross-legged in the foreground, a dog was straining out of the arm of a young woman with a charming, quizzical smile that suggested that she was laughing at herself. A badly cut dress showed the outline of her knees and thighs, and with the arm that was not struggling with the dog, she had just made some checked gesture, probably to push back the strand of curly hair standing out at her temple, which the photograph recorded with a blur in place of her hand. I was instantly drawn to her. "Who's this?" I pointed.

"Let me see— Oh, that's Maud— Oscar—you've heard me talk of Oscar Harmel?—Oscar's second wife. The old fool, we all thought; she's young enough to be his granddaughter, almost. The two boys are his grandchildren, from his first marriage, of course. They love Maud. —Oh, she's a sweet girl, a dear girl, no doubt about that. But of course it doesn't work. She laughs a lot, but she's not happy. She's very dissatisfied with her life. Funny girl. Oscar's not in this"—she lifted her eyebrows to see better, as if she had her glasses on and were peering over the top—"I wonder when it was taken? Oh, I know, last time Ludi was on leave, he went down there and stayed over. One of the little chaps had had a birthday, and got a camera for a present. —He brought me the picture specially, next time his mother—that's Oscar's eldest daughter, Dorrie—brought him to see me. . . ."

Quite suddenly, it came to me that I knew it was she. I looked at the girl half-laughing, half-struggling against the nonsense of having the photograph taken and I knew it had been she. This is the girl, I told the sullen Ludi, not looking at me, not looking at the sun. And in his refusal to meet the eye of the camera, in the obsti-

nate stance of his legs—in the silence of that photograph of him—
he confirmed it to the tingling of my half-pain, my curiosity.

9 BEHIND MY EYES, inside my sleeping body, I sensed the
surface of day. Knew the breath of the warm sea that would
be blowing in the window. The conversation of the fowls with the
dust. Mrs. Koch squeezing oranges in the kitchen. The great brightness of morning that would leap at me, blinding, joyous, as I opened
my eyes.

A dim, cool room. Silence. The call of a dove, curtains with a
known pattern. Silence. High on the wall the lozenge-pattern of light
filtered through the ventilator, the neatly spaced pale yellow crumpets of childhood, that moved round the room through days of sickness. And then my mother, rattling at the stiff lock of the hall
cupboard with her keys. Missus, the butcher he send: Anna. I lay
a minute, looking round the ceiling where every dent, every smudge
was where I knew it to be, and then I got up, went to the wardrobe
for my clothes, pulled the thin curtains back on the dusty, clipped
jasmine bush, the patch of neat grass, the neighbor's hedge.

It was like this for a number of mornings; for an hour I would
be quite dazed with the sense of having mislaid myself in sleep, or
the half-will, half-suspicion that *this* was the dream and the awak-
ening would be other. But soon it no longer happened; I knew before
I woke that I was home on the Mine, in the bed, in the room that
claimed me as their own.

Soon I would wake to myself in the mornings, but I was not
secure for the whole day. I came slowly up the path after the anti-
climax of the post—there was no letter for me—with the dry, wind-
less highveld sun making my hair too hot and electric to touch and
my mother's voice over the preparation of lunch coming from the
kitchen, and I was seized again with the unreliability of my own
eyes, ears, and the utter conviction of my other senses, that made
me smell and feel noon on the veranda above the sea, with the sway
of the sea, from which I had newly arisen, in my blood as I stood.

I waited at the window in the empty house of early evening for my father to come home, and turned to the room to look at, and even to make tentative movements to touch, all the objects, ornaments, carpets, disposition of furniture, photographs, vases, that in their very evidence of reality, and lifelong involvement with me, suddenly could not summon meaning and belonging. Even more strangely, I spent a morning shopping in Atherton with my mother, and the hurrying along the streets gossiping together, the matching of a piece of last year's material, my mother's uncertain look outside a shoeshop where she wanted my confirmation of a decision she had already made to buy a pair of new shoes— all this pleasant, familiar activity came to me as it might come to someone who has been ill, and is filled with the strangeness of standing upright in the sun again. When we stopped to talk to people, I had the smile that invalids summon.

"On Tuesday? Yes, that would be lovely, I think. —Helen, what about Tuesday?" I looked from my mother to the indulgent smile of the matron who was inviting us to tea, as if I had not taken in what my mother was asking. And the sight of the two of them, in their floral dresses and their veiled summer hats, small brown paper parcels from John Orrs' and the Sewing Center and the seed merchant hanging from their white gloved hands, filled me with a kind of creeping dismay.

"Old Mrs. Barrow's so fond of you—" my mother reproached later. "She's always loved to have you, ever since you were a little girl. You can't hurt her feelings—"

I said nothing, but resentment, motiveless and directionless, seemed to crowd out even my sight.

Less disturbing than all this was the habit I got into of disappearing into a re-creation of my time with Ludi whenever I was out with my parents among other people. At the cinema with them, I quickly learned not to see the film, but to use the darkness and the anonymous presence of people about me in the darkness, to create Ludi for myself more vividly than life. This was an intense and emotional experience, highly pleasurable in its longing, its secrecy. When I found myself at a tea party among the women in whose fondness I had basked, I could kill the troubled feelings of rejection and distaste by plunging into myself the fierce thrill of longing for Ludi, which would vibrate an intensity of emotion through me to the exclusion of everything else.

My mother was irritated by me. "In a trance. I don't know what's the matter with her. Alice certainly fattened her up, but she's made her slow."

"Dreaming." My father smiled at me across the table. He had never forgotten his own youth, and mistook the memory of what he had been for an understanding of what I was.

I ignored him kindly; I preferred my mother's irritation; it seemed a temerity for him to pretend to understand a bewilderment of which he was so important a part.

Then I knew what he was going to quote: What is this life, if full of care . . . —But he must have sensed my waiting for it, and he stopped himself this once and only said, with the inclined head of still more certain understanding, "It's the time to dream. Later on she'll be too busy."

The University. Should I go up the shallow gray steps between gray columns like great petrified trees; carry books; wear the blue and yellow blazer? I did not want to talk about it. I wanted to put off talking of it.

"What's happening, Helen?" Nothing stopped my mother. "You've got to make up your mind, you know. There's barely a week left."

"When is the enrollment day?" my father asked.

"Thursday, Mrs. Tatchett tells me. She's going in with Basil."

"Oh—? —That boy'll never do any good. He hasn't a brain. What's he going to do?"

"Something to do with engineering. You know I don't follow the different names of these things. Electro-something."

"I still think a teacher's degree would be the best." My father turned to me. "You needn't necessarily use it as such afterward."

My mother, who saw deflection of purpose in the housewife's sense of waste, immediately took this up. "Why not? What's the sense of wasting four years becoming a teacher if you don't teach?"

"I don't know." My father nodded his head to himself; he believed he had educated himself on the Home University Library, the British Encyclopaedia and "Know Thyself," but that he would have achieved this and his Mine secretaryship ten years earlier had he started off his career as a university graduate instead of a junior clerk. "It's a good general education."

"You've got big ideas," said my mother, "too big for your pocket. Helen must take up something that'll fit her for the world."

I sat through their talk with a growing inner obstinacy. Now that phrase of my mother's that I had heard so often, that had always sounded strong and practical as my mother herself, came to me as a disturbing question. Fit me for what world? So long as there was only my mother's world, so long as I knew no other, the phrase had the ring of order and action. The world of my mother and father, or Ludi's world? And if there were two, there might be more. But my parents wanted to fit me for theirs. My interest, that like a timid, nosing animal edged back and lay down in dim lack of enthusiasm before the advance of their discussion, was again forgotten in a sense of distress and bewilderment.

My mother was tapping her front teeth with her fingernail, as she sometimes did in concern. But when she spoke, it was with her usual vigor. "Perhaps she'd be happier at home? If she didn't go at all—Perhaps you could speak to Stanley Dicks about getting her into the Atherton library. She's so keen about books, and there's a nice type of girl there—"

My father caught her with an accusing look, a kind of concentration of irritation, suspicion and wariness that comes from long observation, if not understanding, of someone's methods and motives. It was as if he did not know what her next move would be, but he knew it should be prevented. He gave a curiously awkward fending gesture of the hand, and said, "Oh, the *library*— What sort of a career, pushing a barrow of heavy books about and stamping people's names on cards! That's no life for her. That's not what I want for her."

And then, with the inconsequence of daily life in the fluid of which are suspended all stresses, the jagged crystals of beauty, the small, sharp, rusted probes of love, the hate that glints and is gone like a coin in water, my mother said without change of tone, "You won't forget about the lawn mower, will you? It's Charlie's day again tomorrow." And with a little glance at his watch to recall him to himself, my father nodded and returned to his office for the afternoon's work.

I went down to the Mine swimming bath. At first there was almost no one there; only the small boys, splashing and squealing hoarsely in their flapping wet rags of costumes. I lay looking at my shining brown legs; a stranger bearing the distinguishing marks of another land. Later some boys and girls of my own age came and dropped to the grass around me, gasping, fanning themselves after their bicycle ride. They exclaimed over me. You were away a long time! How long was it, Helen? My, she's burned—look how she's burned! They giggled and threw sweet-wrappers at one another, and every now and then, without a word, as if at some mysterious sign, a girl would tug at a boy's ankle to trip him as he stood up, or a boy would pull the bow end of the strap that held a girl's bathing suit, and suddenly they would be wrestling, chasing each other, shrieking round the pool, rolling and falling back into the middle of us, the girl screaming between laughter: No! No! Soon the grass around us was strewn with lemonade bottles and broken straws. A bright-haired girl, with the dimples she had had when she was four still showing when she smiled, carefully broke up a packet of chocolate so that it would go round. When I got up to swim, they all came flying, bouncing, chasing into the square tepid tank of water. Lorna Dufalette's head broke through the surface beside me, water beading off her powdered forehead. "It's not fair, those filthy Cunningham kids have got ringworm, and they come into the water. We might all get it." I floated along amid used matches and dead grass. At last I pulled myself out by the shoulders and sat, feet dangling, on the side. One of the boys, at a loss for a moment, swam over to me, a bright challenging grin on his red face. His big teeth in the half-open mouth combed the water like a fish. "Come away to the lagoon with me, Tondelayo!" I had been watching the water streaming over his teeth and was startled when he suddenly appeared beside me. Saliva and water streaked his chin as he grinned, waiting my response. Apparently there was some film I had not seen that would have given it to me. Water poured from him and he laughed toward me. "Come on—" He slipped down into the water again and, at a howl from one of the others, turned his thick scarred neck and bellowed something back, then caught at my ankle. But with a quick slither I snatched my legs back and he was gone, threshing noisily after the jeer that had challenged him. I shifted away from the uneven puddle that marked where he had sat beside me.

In the damp change cubicle I put on my clothes and rolled my bathing suit in my towel. Looking at myself in the post card of mirror that was nailed to the wall brought two tears of loneliness into my eyes.

My mother was sitting behind the fly screen on the veranda when I got home. She was following a knitting pattern from a book, and the tray from her afternoon tea was on the ledge beside her. As I saw her the words seemed to come to me quite suddenly, as if someone had given me a push forward, "Mother, I've made up my mind I'm not going to University." She said, after a pause, not looking up, "All right. I suppose you're old enough to know what you want. Nobody gave me the opportunity." I pulled myself up on the ledge beside the tray and we sat in silence, rather heavily. After a while she said, "It'll disappoint your father,"—and went indoors.

My mother always had had the knack of filling me with apprehension by the meagerness of what she said, and the magnitude of what she left unspoken. Now, as I sat in her chair while the sun went down, the shape that she had hollowed for herself in the cushions, the warmth where she had leaned her back, seemed to speak on for her. I began to feel tense and nervous; in the heat, my hands were cold. I went down into the cooling garden and walked up and down, watching for my father. My heart was beating fast and I wanted to tell him at once. When he saw me hanging about the gate his tired, neat face lifted pleasurably into life and he gave a little signal as if to say, I'll be with you rightaway, but I did not even wait for him to put the car into the garage, but opened the door as he slowed down to enter the gate, and got in beside him. He said: "Give us a kiss," and his cheek was faintly salty from the sweat of the day. "—Daddy, I've made up my mind I don't want to go to University." As I said it we came to a halt in the dusty gloom of the tin garage.

"Well, I won't press you, my dear. It's very important that you should be happy about what you do—no making a success of anything unless you're happy in doing it. I must say I believe that. Not everyone has to go to a university to improve and open their mind, you could do a correspondence course—what about French? Always useful to learn a language. So long as one cultivates one's mind, it doesn't really matter—" He sat on in the car a minute or two and I watched his profile. But I could see he was not unhappy, he was absorbed, he had already set his mind on something else for me.

We strolled into the house together, with him talking sensibly, enthusiastically. I found I was not listening but was thinking of Ludi, seized up increasingly by thoughts of Ludi and what he would have said if I had really thought of going to the University. Getting on, the bright ambitious daughter of the Mine Secretary. I smiled to myself at the idea that I might have lent myself to it. Now I would be able to tell him; I lay in the sun somewhere, caring for nothing, and we refuted the University together. Now that I had decided, it seemed ridiculous that I had ever even considered the place. I felt that Ludi and I were proudly alone, and I was as happy in the knowledge of him as if he had been there. I felt he knew all that passed in me, and that only the things that he and I knew mattered. My tongue shaped his name over and over, an intoxication of Ludi, Ludi, Ludi. I was excited and happy. It overflowed. Suddenly I kissed my father, having heard almost nothing of what he had been saying to me. He said: "Not such an ununderstanding old father, after all, eh?" And stood looking at me with proud tenderness.

I went slowly up the passage to the bedroom, dreaming, hugging my arms, and I heard him in the kitchen: "—Why d'you do it? You know it makes your hair smell, and you grumble—" My mother was frying fish. I lay down on my bed with my eyes closed; I could see Ludi's walk, the startled way his eyes looked without glasses, the way he gave a little snort and his mouth curled up one side before he told me what he thought of something. I could have lain there all evening.

My father was calling me. I let him call three times before I answered: "What?"

"Look—I think this's for you—"

"What?"

"Come here, I can't shout."

To humor him, I got off the bed in mild irritation and wandered into the kitchen, blinking as if from a sleep. He took a letter from out of the folded newspaper he had brought home. "Sent care of the Mine Secretary—it's yours. . . ." I took the blue envelope from him and read my name in a handwriting I had never seen before but that I knew instantly. A wave of blood went through me, my hands shook. It was the simplest thing for me to leave the kitchen and walk back to my room, but all at once I did not know how to do it. I did not know how to walk out of the door, I did not know at whom or what to look. It was not necessary to say anything but suddenly I did not know what to say. "Well," I said, "I'll open it just now—" My father was taking beer bottles out of the refrigerator. "What are you doing that for?" my mother was complaining. "I thought I ordered two dozen? Where're the other six?" "You'll never get them in that way. I've just put them straight and now you're upsetting everything—" I made my escape as if I had been a prisoner momentarily out of surveillance.

And in my room I tore open the envelope, took out the folded letter in that moment of perfect joy that comes just the second before realization; the mouth ready to be kissed, the possession lying ungrasped in the hand, the letter held unread.

Then I unfolded the sheets, saw that there were three, saw the beautiful handwriting, the words "thinking," "knack" . . .

Barberton,
Saturday.

Dear Helen,

It's difficult to find space or quiet to write in a great bedlam of a camp like this one. But it's now close on midnight so I can be fairly certain not to be interrupted by anything worse than snores. I didn't have a bad journey— but you'll know that by the telegram I sent mother—except that it all seemed a bit unreal, the yap of the other men, etc., the usual army nonsense, after the last few days at home. I kept thinking about it, and as usual—only a bit more so this time, the two planes of existence just won't dovetail. Not in me, anyway. Every time I come back to the army I am sickened all over again at the senselessness of the way we live here. Still, you've heard all this from me many times before, so enough.

Fortunately, there have been heavy rains and the dust isn't so bad as it was. That chap Don Macloud I told you about is back in my tent again after all, and we have rigged up fairly comfortable beds for ourselves. As I told you, he's really got a knack of making a home out of a fruit box and a bit of sacking, and is useful to have around. Also pleasant and inoffensive, and as unimpressed as I am by all this so-called army discipline. Also like me, has no wish to get a stripe or a pip up so that he can have a taste of inflicting it on others.

I've had two letters from mother, written since you've gone, and I can see she misses you. You can't imagine what it meant to her to have you around; she really likes you, and you know exactly how to treat her. Particularly just after I'd left. I'm grateful, I can tell you, for the way you stayed on and kept her company. Of course I know you like her too, almost love her, really, and it was no penance to you, but just the same, a real thank you. She's such an extraordinary person, so absolutely right to live with, but not everyone is capable of knowing her and finding that out.

Well, miss? And what about you? Have you settled down again? I hope you've decided what you're going to do and that whatever it is you are happy in it. I don't think we'll be here much longer. All indications are that we shall be moving—soon. In a way, it'll be a relief. I'm sick to death of the child's game we're playing here, even though I've little relish for the real thing. If I can manage a week end before we go, of course it'll be spent in Atherton, if you and your people will have me? But there's a rumor that all leave is to be canceled soon, so by the time my turn comes round, I doubt if there'll be a chance.

Write when you feel like it. When I think of you, in this

place, you don't seem quite true, you know. Figment of the imagination! End of my candle, so I'd better turn in.

Ludi.

P.S. Lost the piece of paper with the house address on it, so am sending this to your dad's office. My regards to him and to your mother. L.

I had not read it so much as flown through the lines, alighting on the word "you." "Well, Miss? And what about you?" —What looked like an island, a beckoning palm top, was as uncertain as a piece of floating vegetation, rootless in the tide. I hovered, went on. And in the last paragraph, there it was. A small island, soon explored, but the place where my heart came down and beaked its feathers. I read it over, and again. "When I think." He thinks about me. But "When" . . . that means it isn't often. Yet it might be. "You don't seem quite true." Oh, the happiness of it! Now I am the woman and the princess and the dream. Now it is like a sign on my forehead. "You don't seem quite true." A dream. Something that's over, then; can't believe it happened. Just forgotten, an incident, like that?

I read the whole letter over again, searching through every word, through the commonplaces, the information of the way he was living, the time, the weather—pushing it all aside like so much rubble. Now I would pick up a word or a phrase, as one fingers a pebble. But no. The repetition of "as I told you" seemed an intimacy, perhaps? Yes. Yes, that I could keep. The bit about his mother. This puzzled me. Of course, it could mean a special kind of confidence in me; of course.

Some sentences I read over to myself a dozen times. Aloud, they sounded different; with another intonation, the meaning changed. Every word of the letter seemed ambiguous; happiness came and went like the color in the bird's wing, showing and going out as it falls through the sun.

I sat on my bed with the three thin sheets and the envelope spread evidence about me. Well, I had a letter, anyway. I rested in that.

But strangely, the mood of exaltation, of closeness to Ludi, was

gone. It was only when I was in bed that night, late and awake,
thinking about him as I remembered him on the farm, as I had done
when I lay dreaming before my father had called me, that it came
back.

10 IT IS AMAZING on how little reality one can live when one
is very young. It is only when one is beginning to approach
maturity that achievement and possession have to be concrete in
the hand to create each day; when you are young a whole livable
present, elastic in its very tenuousness, impervious in its very independence of fact, springs up enveloping from a hint, a memory,
an idea from a book. On this slender connection, like a tube of
oxygen which feeds a man while he moves in an atmosphere not his
own, it is possible to move and breathe as if your feet were on the
ground. Through the autumn and into winter, this was the way I
lived now. The quiet, steeped autumn days passed, as if the sun
turned the earth lovingly as a glass of fine wine, bringing out the
depth of glow, the fine gleam; the banks of wild cosmos opened like
a wake, with the cream and pink and gilt of an early Florentine
painting, on either side of the railway cutting from Atherton to Johannesburg and spattered, intoxicating bees with plenty in the bareness of flat veld and mine dumps, out of ditches and rubbish heaps;
the last rains brought the scent of rot like a confession from leaves
that had fallen and lain lightly as feathers; the cold wind of the
highveld, edged with the cut of snow it had passed on the Drakensberg, blew round the house, blowing bare round the bare Mine,
blowing the yellow cyanide sand into curling miasmas and mistrals
over the road; the Mine boys walked with only their eyes showing
over blankets. I did an afternoon's duty at the soldier's canteen in
Atherton twice a week; I worked for three weeks in my father's office
again as a relief for someone away on leave. There it was chilly in
the mornings; I noticed winter. Dressed in warm clothes, the distance of the summer came to me. I went nowhere, yet I took great
care of my appearance, spending hours before my mirror in the poor

light that always showed me shadowy. Sometimes while my parents were out at tennis (they were proud that they still made the second league) I would spend the whole Saturday afternoon arranging and rearranging my hair. In the evening I would not go out, but sat reading beneath an elaboration of shining whorls and curls, formal as a Gothic cornice. My dresses were chosen each day with hesitation and care, my hands were manicured. All these rites were performed alone in my bedroom, in silence, in a depth of dream that held me, deep, far away, as deafness holds someone still and serene in a room full of talk. Any faint temptation to enjoy the distractions of the Mine—a fete, a party, a concert—was paid for and nullified by the immediate feeling of estranging myself from Ludi, and what Ludi thought. The fact that he was in Italy, that the South Coast was months away, made no difference. Like God, to deny his tenets was to lose him.

The letters I wrote to Ludi became more important to me than those I received from him. In them, I assumed our world in common. His, full of descriptions of places I could not imagine, always written from the moment of the present, seemed to have less and less to do with the Ludi of the South Coast, the bright hair, the shortsighted look, the warm strange breast. In time, the infrequent letters were not the painful thrill, the charged token they had been. I could almost have done without them entirely. . . . For while believing that I was living Ludi's way of life by keeping aloof from that of my home and the Mine, I had all the time been creating a third way of my own, as unconsciously as a spider salivates his thin silver lifeline of survival. The frailty of dreams, imagination and memory was changed and churned by some unsuspected emotional digestion into a vanity and cultivation of myself. Like most finished products, nothing could have resembled less the raw material of emotion from which it was processed. And also, like most survival changes, it was accomplished by personality, unrecognized and unrealized by the conscious mind.

I spent a great deal of time reading, and these were not books about which I would write to Ludi. I began to read poetry, Auden and T.S. Eliot, reading it always for the sound and feel of the words rather than for the meaning, which sometimes I sensed, but seldom

knew with my intellect. Then I took Pepys's diary out of the library,
and Tobias Smollett.—There is a theory that, given the free choice
to hand of various foods, babies who see them only as blurs of color
and shape will instinctively choose those necessary for balanced
sustenance; perhaps the same is true of a hungry mind. One book
led me to another; a quotation from one author by another, a mention
that a character was reading so-and-so, sent me to the source itself,
so that I had Hemingway to thank for John Donne, and D. H.
Lawrence to thank for Chekhov. But in nothing that I read could I
find anything that approximated to my own life; to our life on a gold
mine in South Africa. Our life was not regulated by the seasons and
the elements of weather and emotion, like the life of peasants; nor
was it expressed through movements in art, through music heard,
through the exchange of ideas, like the life of Europeans shaped by
great and ancient cities, so that they were Parisians or Londoners
as identifiably as they were Pierre or James. Nor was it even anything like the life of Africa, the continent, as described in books
about Africa; perhaps further from this than from any. What did the
great rivers, the savage tribes, the jungles and the hunt for huge
palm-eared elephants have to do with the sixty miles of Witwaters-
rand veld that was our Africa? The yellow ridged hills of sand,
thrown up and patted down with the unlovely precision that marked
them manufactured unmistakably as a sand castle; the dams of
chemical-tinted water, more waste matter brought above ground by
man, that stood below them, bringing a false promise of a river—
greenness, cool, peace of dipping fronds and birds—to your nose
as you sat in the train. The wreckage of old motorcar parts, rusting
tin and burst shoes that littered the bald veld in between. The ad-
vertisement hoardings and the growing real-estate schemes, dusty,
treeless, putting out barbed-wire fences on which the little brown
mossies swung and pieces of torn cloth clung, like some forlorn file
that recorded the passing of life in a crude fashion. The patches of
towns, with their flat streets, tin-roofed houses, main street and red-
faced town hall, "Palace" or "Tivoli" showing year-old films from
America. We had no lions and we had no art galleries, we heard no
Bach and the oracle voice of the ancient Africa did not come to us,
was drowned, perhaps, by the records singing of Tennessee in the

Greek cafés and the thump of the Mine stamp batteries which
sounded in our ears as unnoticed as our blood.

Only what was secret in me, did not exist before my mother and
father or the talk and activity that pursued life in our milieu, leaped
to recognition in what I read. The power of love signaled to me like
lightning across mountains of dark naïveté and ignorance; the sense
of wonder at the pin speck of myself in a swirling universe, a creature perpetually surrounded by a perpetual growth, stars and earth-
worm, wind and diamond. Out of poetry and the cabalistic accident
of someone's syntax came the cold touch on my cheek: this. You.
So that when my father pointed at the winter night sky, not the air-
blue infinity of summer, but a roof far off as silence, hard blue as
a mirror looking down on a dark room—when he pointed up and
said: Orion . . . that's the Southern Cross, and over there, on the
left, see, I think it's Saturn—I knew that to know the names is to
know less than to know that there can be no names, are no names.
The bat-squeak of a man's voice in the enormous darkness could
not explain the stars to me.

And so, too, when I lay in the bath looking down at my naked
body, the sight of it suggesting the pleasures of which it was capable,
it was not the touch of Ludi (like the thrilling of a bell that sends
messengers running, doors opening, lights up) that I imagined any
more, but only the pure sensation: the potentialities of loving that
lay there. Constantly relived, Ludi's love-making had worn transparent with recapitulation, so that now his image rubbed off entirely;
but my body was real, and its knowledge.

11 ONE AFTERNOON IN JULY I took a train to Johannesburg.
I went in after an early lunch to book seats for a musical
play which my parents wanted to see, but when I came out of Johannesburg station into the city I took a tram to the University
instead. There I walked about beneath an expression of worried
purpose, slightly amazed at myself. In the foyer of the main block,

where the administrative and inquiry offices were, it was easy to
stand before the boards reading faculty notices and posters advertising student dances and debates. But along the wide sloping passages that led down to common rooms and tearooms, the preoccupied
faces of girls and young men seemed to me to be a continual challenge to produce my right and identity. Each pair of eyes that met
mine seemed to precede a threat of the question: Yes? I stood at
last in front of a boldly painted exhortation to support the Student's
Representative Council in some stand it was taking over the Color
Bar, seeing nothing but a cigarette butt and a piece of crumpled
paper near my left foot, and when a voice behind me spoke my
name I melted in alarm as if an expected heavy hand had come
down on my shoulder. It was Basil Tatchett, from the Mine. "So?
You here too? I haven't seen you before. Don't you travel?—Are
you staying at the hostel? My folks won't let me—"

I did not know what to say—"No, actually I haven't started yet,
I'm just getting fixed up now."

"But that's a waste; they won't let you take credit for half a year,
will they? You're doing Arts, I suppose." He had his mother's long,
spade-shaped jaw and way of feeling it as he spoke, as if he were
privately wondering whether he needed a shave. I do not think he
had ever spoken to me before in his life, in that manly animosity
which schoolboys bear toward schoolgirl daughters of their mother's
friends, but now he believed we shared the distinction of the University against the mediocrity of less fortunate Mine contemporaries.
"John's here—John Eagles—he's with me. And Lester Beckett." He
stood talking for a few minutes of people who were names to me
and then, with a shrug toward his bundle of books, was gone.

When he left me I felt calm, commanding, adventurous. It was
as if all the tortuous calculations of a combination lock had been
resolved accidentally by the careless twiddle of a passing hand. I
did not know him and I had scarcely listened to what he had to say
to me. But a door flew open. I knew exactly why I had come to
Johannesburg on this particular afternoon, I knew that stepping on
the tram had not been an impulse but the decision of the voices
from my mother's tea parties reaching me alone in my room, the

aimless silence of the garden, the bent heads of my mother and father under the red beaded lampshade. I walked straight over to the inquiry office, and I did not need to look busy or purposeful.

There was a little difficulty in getting myself enrolled in the faculty of arts halfway through the academic year, and my father had to go into Johannesburg to interview the Dean, but it was done and I was a student. My mother was reassured that a B.A. graduate could command a number of good jobs and, unexpectedly, made quite a dining-out, or rather "afternoon," tale of the way I had marched into the University without a word after refusing to go earlier in the year, telling the story with a shrug of the amused, victimized indulgence of those mothers who pride themselves in their children by seeming to discredit them. My father, of course, was delighted. He convinced himself that the eighteen-months' break in my education between school and university was an intentional maturing process, a kind of parental system of his own. He told me continually of the advantages I should have over others who had gone straight from school.

Well, perhaps he was right, if not in the way he thought he was. Certainly I did not go now for the blazer or the prestige. I went out of doubt and boredom and a sense of wonder at life: the beginning of all seeking, the muddled start of the journey toward oneself. And I was unaware of this, and excited. I wanted to read and I wanted to talk to people. I wanted to bury myself in the great cool library where no one spoke, and where, on the day I had looked in, people had lifted their heads like deer lifting their heads over water, and in their eyes was the intense blank of concentration; running through them, the endless stream of questions, suggestions from books, a live current from last year or four hundred years back. I was absorbed from minute to minute in the busyness of working out my timetable of lectures, buying prescribed books, and my mother and I suddenly met warmly again in the fittings and discussion of the clothes I would need. Seeing her face hot-looking as she bent over the sewing machine, or anxiously looking up at me as she pinned a hem from the neat row she always kept stuck in the collar of her dress as she sewed, I remembered the smell of her warm from cooking, when I came home from school as a child.

And so in August I began the first of many hundreds of daily journeys from Atherton to Johannesburg by train. When the line left Atherton station, it ran out in the direction of the Mine, and there was a siding just outside the limits of the Mine property. Here the train stopped for a minute or two and here I boarded it, every morning, waiting with a handful of other people, poised like starters at a race for its screeching arrival, and getting off in the early winter dark in the evening, dropped from the day with a soft thud to the dust of the platform. The siding was a bare place of deep red dust and coal grit, where the wind fought torn newspapers and the tin ticket office seemed perpetually to be closed, the man in charge sat so far inside it, and the little bleary window had such a look of ignoring everything, like a closed eyelid. Where the platform ended, man-high khaki weed began. In the summer it was lurid khaki-green and bitter-smelling, and in autumn it bristled with seeds like black pins that fastened to anything that brushed by, and blew and seeded and found their way to every inch of bare soil, but now it stood in black, dead stooks, scratching through the wind. That was all there was to hear on winter mornings. A few natives, swathed in blankets as in the silence of a cocoon, waited around the ticket office. Sometimes it did not open at all before the train came in, and so they missed the train, but other times the little window would snatch up and I would see the face of the man behind it, hating the natives for the winter morning and the tin shed, hypnotizing them into fumbling timidity with his silence and his sudden shout: Yes? Yes?

Sometimes there was a native who sat on the ground, shrouded like a Mexican in his poncho, and from his hidden mouth beneath the blanket came the thin grandeur of a mouth organ, being played to himself. Around him two or three white men in business suits turned the morning paper awkwardly with gloved hands, a shopgirl clutched her knitting in a chiffon scarf. Basil Tatchett and his friends, who had just bought themselves pipes, stood comparing boles and tobacco pouches.

At night the siding was very dark. Only one lamp, high up, lifted the steel rails like streaks of water out of the dark, and often a stone was thrown at it and for a few days there would be no lamp at all. There were more natives about, sometimes a great many, and they shouted, carrying trunks on their heads, balancing their bicycles in and out. Plunging down through the khaki weed to get to the road, the evil smell of it was like the smell of a swamp, and the dark figures with their strong body-smell and their great knobkerries passed silently. Down in the ditch in the khaki weed the body of a Mine boy had once been found, with a knife in his back. He had lain there for a whole day before someone had tried him with a foot and found that he was not simply lying asleep and close to the ground in the sun, the way the Mine boys did.

My father was always there to meet me in the evenings; I would see the rim of light on his glasses turned to the carriages as the train drew in in the pale dusty radiance of its windows. Then with our coats drawn round us we would huddle off to the car parked at the roadside, walking quickly through the dark and the shouts of the black men for whom we were not there, so that they stumbled and bumped into us as if they stepped through the bodies of pale ghosts. Thinly and quickly the few white people dispersed, leaving the cries that in the dark and in a strange language sounded savage and the whiteness of eyes that in their dumbness seemed like the eyes of slow beasts in the darkness, beasts who are dreaming or preparing to charge, one cannot tell. And within a few hundred yards we were all home, in houses that smelled of food cooking, the radio was on, and the telephone kept up its regular spaced ring for the friends who choose mealtimes to make plans.

The same people traveled on the train every day. Most of them got in at Atherton and by the time I climbed into the carriage they were settled in what were their places rather than their seats: for everyone returned day after day to the carriage originally boarded by chance and made familiar by habit, and everyone disposed himself automatically in the seat, in the relation to the other occupants of the carriage, in which timidity, a taste for reading in solitude, looking out of a window, or the desire to sit where the view of the head of a particular girl—long since disappeared or forgotten—had dictated. When a new traveler, like myself, got into the train for the first time, certain circumstances and forces set to work immediately making a place for him too, though he might believe he had simply sat himself down in the nearest seat. I walked through the first carriage because that, I saw, was where Basil Tatchett and his friends gathered and, hesitating at the next, I passed through that one too because an old man with a thickly clouding pipe sat beside a determinedly closed window. In the second coach of the third carriage, I sat down. Eyes turned with a pretense of no curiosity on me, and later, when they were looking elsewhere, I turned mine on them. A pretty girl with sternly ridged blond hair bit her nails and read an Afrikaans novel beside me, two others knitted, the one hunched over the ceaseless bite of needles, the other talking low and confidentially in her ear, while her own knitting rested often in her lap. A young man stared into his window, a lunch tin dangling between his knees. A woman's legs were crossed beneath a paper; the hands that showed holding it had long red nails, a beautiful ring that slipped round on a thin finger. Opposite me was another pipe-smoker; but he was young, with a pleasant bulldog face over a yellow muffler, and he was reading Anthony Trollope beside an open window.

Soon getting into the carriage every morning was like coming down to breakfast at a hotel where you have been staying for some time. Were they all there? Yes. There is the pattern of the Colonel eating his kipper, only the wife down at the young couple's table, the six commercial travelers smoking expansively over coffee. And with an approving eye they all note you dropping into your place.

I had a great deal of reading to do in order to find the lectures I was attending intelligible, since I had missed the first half of the year, and so I had time each morning for only this quick glance of reassurance before disappearing into my book. The pipe-smoker and I now and then touched each other's shoes by mistake, as we stirred over our reading, and we smiled and sometimes exchanged a comment. Another young man, whom I had seen getting in ahead of me one morning and whom I thought a casual traveler, strayed in for a single journey, was greeted aloud by the pipe-smoker and silently by the others, and was, I discovered as the make-up of our carriage became clear to me in the initiation of day by day, also one of us, although he caught the train only on alternate mornings, and sometimes did not appear for several days. When he was present, he sat beside the pipe-smoker with one stubby shoe crossed over the other and read from large brown-paper-covered books that were evidently borrowed, judging from the care with which he handled them. Nearly always he had a very sharp pencil in his hand, and he seemed to be making little drawings or sketches on the thin sheets he kept as a bookmark; sketches that sometimes he crumpled and stuffed in his pocket, other times folded and put in his case. He was evidently a student, too, for I used to see him disappearing upstairs in the tram as well, and then flying through the gates of the University far ahead of me, the belt of an old blue raincoat that he wore instead of a greatcoat trailing beside his shoe.

The second or third morning I dropped into my seat opposite him, I greeted him as I did any other of the carriage occupants whose eyes I happened to meet. But instead of the lip-service smile and murmur that one gives and gets from strangers, he lifted his head and looked at me, a slow smile lifting round his eyes and no answer—a curious smile, the smile of remembrance and recollection that you meet on the face of someone whom you yourself fail to remember. And as this look sets you searching yourself for the place, the year, where this face belongs, perhaps now even imagining some familiarity in the features, so for a moment or two I vaguely tried to find this face. . . . But now with a finger following the bone of his nose as he read, or his head turned toward the window as he lifted it to take in something, as a bird lifts its head to let each sip of water go down, there was obviously no place for it. And I did not think of it again, for he became familiar in any case, and this present recognition overlaid any shadow recollection that might have come to me. Every day I was exploring further into my own ignorance. What I did not know, what I had not heard of—this the University was teaching me. I was slightly dazed, the way one is from days of sight-seeing. Brought up on gossip and discussion of the mechanics of living, I had never heard talk that did not have an immediate bearing on the circumstances of our daily life on the Mine. Words were like kitchen utensils. "Ideas" were synonymous with "fancies." "She's getting ideas" was a phrase of scorn for a neighbor who bought a Persian carpet or invited the Mine Manager to dinner too often. Now I found myself with the daily evidence of semantics, philosophy, psychology; hearing the history of art and music when

I had never seen a picture other than the water colors by a local
schoolteacher which were up for sale in the tearoom at Atherton,
never heard any music other than the combined pupils' yearly concert of the Atherton piano teachers. I had dabbled in books like a
child playing in the ripples at the water's edge; now a wave of ideas
threw me, gurgling in my ears, half-drowning and exhilarating. The
place where I was washed up, alien, astonished, was as far from the
daily talk of my parents as theirs was from that of Anna, sitting over
her paraffin-tin brazier in the back yard.

I began to look at other students covertly, as the member of an
underground political movement might watch for signs that would
discover to him others of the same conviction. These mouths pursed
round straws over pink ice-cream foam, these heads bent over notes
on the grass, these eyes faraway with overheard talk of tennis or
dresses for the Engineers' Ball—were they feeling that they were
living inside a half-inflated balloon which had suddenly been blown
up to twice its size? Surely there must be someone for whom, too,
it had slowly to shrink again every day as the train door slammed
behind, the porch door waited, the mouths of home opened to speak.
Yet as we talked of lecturers and grumbles and advice, of timetables
and clothes, it did not seem so. Or I forgot to look. And it was only
afterward, sitting in the train, that I would examine the said and
unsaid, and find nothing.

But whether I knew it or not, I never ceased to be looking. This
I found one day when I was in the cloakroom, excusing myself
toward the washbasins past a knot of girls who hovered concentri-
cally, like insects, attracted by the mirror. It bewildered me afresh
to see them powdering and fluffing out their hair, eying themselves
and looking without interest at the images of one another. And as I
came through I saw on the other side of the washbasins an African
girl drying her hands. She stood there in her nurse-girl's beret and
little dark dress looking at me quietly, half as if she expected a
challenge of her right to be there, for the University was the one
place in all Johannesburg and one of the few places in all South
Africa where a black girl could wash her hands in the same place
as a white girl, and this fact, so much more tellingly than the pro-
nouncement that there was no color bar, took some getting used to

for both the African students and the white. Yet as she saw me—
perhaps it was something in my face, perhaps in my walk—the look
changed. And I had the curious certainty, that one sometimes gets
from the face of another, that what I saw on her face now was what
was on my own. I recognized it; it was the sign I had been watching
for, not knowing what it would be.

We both left the cloakroom at the same time, and in silence,
without embarrassment, she stood back to let me go through the
door first.

In the train in the mornings, the faces, the presence of the two
students opposite were closed to me. The bulldog-faced one, smoking his pipe as if he were enjoyably cutting a tooth over it; the other,
his eyes running a race with the printed page, sometimes meeting
my eye with the slight smile that tells a child comfortingly that the
grownup is there—there was no secret response from either of them
to what was in me. Probably both came from places where university
was merely a formal extension of an atmosphere in which they had
learned to talk; I returned to my book.

In time I learned that the bulldog-faced one was in fact not a
student at all. Sometimes, on the days when the other was not there,
the empty seat beside him would seem to make him expansive, eager
to talk, and in between deep draws at his pipe—as if he were coaxing a furnace—talk and smoke poured out together. No, he wasn't
a university student, though, like Aaron there—he gestured his head
to the space beside him—he was an ex-serviceman. Who? I asked.
Young Aaron, he told me, you know, who sits here usually.

His own name (I.P. on his briefcase) was Ian Petrie and he was
a Londoner who had emigrated, fought with South Africans in Ab-
yssinia and Egypt, and married an Atherton girl.

"D'you read him at all—" He indicated his Trollope.

I hadn't yet. He talked about Trollope as people do of some
delightful crank of a friend they would like you to meet. He smiled
on the clenched pipe, an attractive smile showing uneven, smoke-
tinted teeth. Even though I hadn't read Trollope, I was prepared to
like this man because he had. He said: "You've awed me with your
George Eliot every morning," and we laughed. (Meeting me on the
siding Basil Tatchett had picked the book out of my hand, opened

it, said, "Who's he?" and not even waited for a reply.) When we had talked about books several mornings, he said to me: "I believe you might know my wife? Lindsay Theunissen?" I looked at him uncertainly. I did know her, but I felt there must be a mistake; there had been a wild-eyed girl at school, Lindsay Theunissen, very backward, as if the stammer of her excited voice kept her in too much agitation to be able to learn. One of those vague troubling rumors, half understood by children, said that her mother had "tried to get rid of her" and she had been born with some slight injury to the brain.

"Then you do know her?" He seemed satisfied and confidential.

"Long ago. At school. Then they went away, lived somewhere else, I think."

He waved out a match. "You'd be surprised how she's turned out. She's really pretty, you know. Still got that wild look—" He smiled, liking it.

"I don't think I'd know her—"

"Oh, yes you would." He sat back, frankly, not letting me evade, smiling at me. "It's not so surprising as you think. Of course I can't talk to her, you know what I mean. She's not interested in what I read, and I tell her a few snippets from the newspaper that she can use for conversation. But she's got a kind of instinct for sport; I can't explain it. She simply can't help playing everything extraordinarily well, almost the way a hunting dog can't help pointing at a scent. And I have an admiration for that sort of thing; I play a lot myself, with more calculation and less success, I can tell you. Lindsay's really quite amazing that way. She's got what one might call a physical intelligence. And let me tell you—" He leaned his elbows on his knees, dropped his voice. He had the air of giving advice rather than a confession, and I found myself listening as if I were accepting advice. "—It's very important. I enjoy making love to her and I enjoy playing games with her. What is married life, really? You're away at work eight hours a day. Half of what's left you spend in bed, one way or another, and the other half you spend looking for some sort of recreation. —I can talk to other people, I can read on my own."

I laughed and shook my head to myself; there was something

about this man that set one at ease, as if a tight button had popped. He returned to Trollope, I to George Eliot, until he said, "Damn, we're here just as I get comfortable, always . . . ," and I looked up and saw him stretching for his briefcase as the sooty, antiseptic scent of the city came in at the window.

"What time d'you say it leaves?"

"Half-past seven."

"Well, it's nothing. Only twenty minutes earlier than the one you usually get. I'm up at a quarter-to, anyway." My mother was decorating a cake with candied violets. As I had always done, I put a petal on my tongue, let the sugar melt off, and stuck the tiny dab of bruised silk on my palm. "Don't be a baby, Helen. I'll be short."

But I winced at the idea of getting up still earlier to get to a lecture which had altered my timetable. "You see, here's the disadvantage of staying out of town. Anyone else can get up at eight o'clock." I saw by my mother's precision and arched neck that it would be better not to pursue this reasoning, so I said, as I remembered: "Oh . . . ! I shall miss my early morning talk."

She was not listening: "Who's that?"

"You remember I told you about the student with the pipe opposite me? D'you know who he is? He's married to the Theunissen girl,—Lindsay. I think she's lucky. We're quite friendly."

"That awful man Petrie who was Belle Theunissen's fancy man that she married off to her daughter—? I don't know how you can talk to him." She was making a green bow with strips of candied peel; the loops were exactly the same size, the ends were cut exactly level. I stood watching this. But she knew when she had annoyed or offended me, and she could say to my silence with the laugh of pretended innocence: "Huffed? Well, I can't help it—I must say you have the most peculiar taste."

The early train was crowded. Like huddled cattle holding their horns motionlessly clear, men balanced their papers above the press. Yet out of habit I pushed through to stand in the third carriage. "Come and sit down." Among the strangers, the other young man was there; he got up slowly, waited while I climbed over legs to his seat. "—No protests necessary," he said.

"Still, it's very nice of you."

Holding on to the window frame, he smiled down at me the same way again, the resting smile of long acquaintance. Suddenly I was going to ask him . . . what, I did not know. But the conductor came struggling down the corridor, drowning hand appearing in an appeal for tickets. When ours had been passed from hand to hand and returned, the young man bent to me and said: "Petrie and Trollope are left entirely to themselves now." I smiled with the quick pleasure one feels when someone unexpectedly confirms something one has felt and been doubted for. "He's pleasant company, isn't he? The journey passes quickly with him."

"He's one of those people"—he was searching for exactly what he wanted to say—"one of those men whose presence makes— makes the air comfortable. It's the only way I can put it. All those people rocking from here to there in the train every day; rocking back: he sits there like a sensible hand over the questions you'd pester yourself with."

I wanted to interrupt with eagerness to agree. That was it. But the young man with the biblical name returned to his reading. When two or three stations had drawn off their workers and the level of heads in the carriage sank to normal, he sat down opposite me, arranging his legs carefully so that his shoes would not scuff mine. I leaned forward and said: "Thank you all the same for giving me the seat," and he smiled and slid down in his seat spreading his knees comfortably with a faint air of puzzled surprise, as some close member of one's family, used to the silent acceptance of intimacy, might be surprised by formal politeness.

I sat back gathering my own silence for a breath or two. But I would not let the moment glide by; in defiance to my mother, in response to the stirring that opposed her in me, I wanted to say something real, a short arrangement of words that would open up instead of gloss over. It came to me like the need to push through a pane and let in the air. I leaned forward. "Why do you treat me as if you know me?"

He looked up; there was that quick change of focus in his eyes: from print to a face. He said patiently: "Because I do." And now it was easy and my boldness made me laugh. He was laughing too. "I've known you ever since I can remember. You used to wear a yellow tartan skirt with a big pin thing in it—I used to think you must have a pretty bad mother, if she wouldn't even sew up your dresses properly."

"But it was supposed to be like that!"

"So I found out. Not for years though—" He shook his head. "I'd never seen anything like that."

"But where? I don't know how it was you could have seen me, known me, if I don't know you."

"In the bioscope, the town with your mother, passing in your father's car—for years. Ever since I can remember."

I sat there, smiling, doubting. He nodded his head slowly at me, as if to say, yes, yes, it's true. "You used to have a little pale blond friend and you both used to carry white handbags. Like grown-up women."

"Olwen. Olwen Taylor and I! But you've got an astonishing memory." My deep interest in myself made the fact of a stranger's recollections of me remarkable; it was like being shown an old photograph, taken when one was not looking, a photograph of which one did not even know the existence until this moment. And yet there it is, the face one has sometimes caught unawares in a mirror.

"But I used to see you so often in the bus, too. Coming from school."

"You were never in the bus—I should have remembered you. I can remember any child who traveled on that bus." At once I was dubious.

"Not in it. I used to cycle home from school at about the same time, and we used to pass the bus—two or three other boys and I, it was a great thing to race it."

I was filled with the delight of interest in myself. I asked a dozen questions. "I had a fringe? Did you know me when I had a fringe —awful, it was always too long, into my eyebrows. Or was it later, when I had plaits?"—I stopped in amazement again. "I remember all the phases," he said.

In the pause an impulse of regret grew in me at not remembering him; I could turn back to so many faces, some I had never known, watched and never spoken to, and all the time the one that had been fixed on me had gone unnoticed. His look questioned me, dark, water-colored eyes, mottled and traced with an intricacy of lines and flecks, like markings of successive geological ages on the piece of polished quartz my father kept. "I was trying to imagine you seeing me, and I not knowing you were." He laughed. I was curious again: "But what were you doing that way? You certainly didn't live on the Mine, that I'm sure."

"At that time we were living out at the store—my father's store. Not in the town"—he anticipated the association—"The Concession stores just outside your property." He went on explaining but now it was himself my attention was taking in and not what he was saying. Of course this was a different face. There was no place, no feature, no bone one could point to and say: Here, this is where it is; yet the face was different. The faces that had looked in at me when I was an infant, the faces I had fondled, the faces that had been around me all my life had differences, one from the other, but they were differences of style. This face was built on some other last.

I said: "Your name's Aaron?" not meaning it to sound, as it did, a conclusion.

But he said with that sweet reasonableness that he seemed to keep inside him the way some people keep strength, or touchiness: "Joel. My surname's Aaron."

"I thought Ian Petrie said it was Aaron, that's why."—Smiling, but I was thinking of a tortoise shell, a confused memory that brought up with it the faded camphor of a defiance, my mother, angry with me, in white tennis clothes. "There was one time I'll never forget." He was laughing, with the relish of a story. "I was riding into Atherton to have two of my mother's hens killed—one under each arm, and balancing furiously—you were sitting at the back of a half-empty bus and you stood right up and watched me go by with such an expression on your face! I kept my head down and rode like hell."

"D'you know I've only been down there once in my life . . . to

the stores. I couldn't have been more than ten. I was angry with my
mother, so I went down all by myself one Saturday afternoon." The
tone of my voice showed that it was still an adventure to me.

"Was it forbidden, then?" he asked.

"Oh yes. Quite forbidden; the natives, and unhealthy . . ." I did
not think to pretend otherwise my mother's distaste for the stores.

I was right; I did not need to. "We survived very well," he
laughed, as if he knew my mother, too. Perhaps, knowing me, shaped
by my mother, he did.

"You certainly have," I said with a little gesture of my face
toward his books; I did not know why.

"Yes." Now he was thoughtful.

I remembered something, seriously—"By the way, perhaps I
should have said, but you seem to know so much—"

He smiled at me again, that expressive smile that had an almost
nasal curve to it, gently. "Yes I know; it's Helen. Helen of Atherton."

It was a title. Perfectly sincerely, I could hear it was a title. And
although the obvious reference that came to mind was ridiculous, it
made me blush. Entirely without coquetry I suddenly wished I were
better looking, beautiful. It was something I felt I should have had,
like the dignity of an office.

12 THE AARONS did not live behind the Concession Store
any more, but in a little suburban house in the town. There
was a short red granolithic path from the front door to the gate, and
the first time I went there a fowl was jerking cautiously along a row
of dahlias. Joel said, opening the gate for me, the sun laying angles
of shadow on his face: "I often thought about going into your house,
but I never imagined bringing you to mine."

It was a Saturday morning, and I had met him coming out of the
stationer's in the main street of Atherton, carrying a paper bag from
which the head of a paintbrush protruded. "My builder's supplies."
He waved the bag. I knew all about the model hospital he was

making as part of his year's work as an architectural student. He
had explained the sketches for it to me in the train.

"Did you remember the ambulance for the front door?"

"—Come with me to buy it."

The town had taken spring like a deep breath; it showed only
in the bright pale brushes of grass that pushed up newly where there
were cracks in the paving, the young leaves on the dark dry limbs
of the trees round the Town Hall, but we felt it on our faces and I
on my bare arms. There was a feeling of waking; as if a cover had
been whipped off the glass shop fronts and the faded blinds. When
we had been to the bazaar, he said: "You've wanted to see my
hospital and you've heard so much about it—why don't you come
home with me now? If you're doing nothing, it's not far—" So we
walked slowly to his home in the light glancing sun, talking past
the bits of gardens where children scratched in the dust, women
knitted on their verandas, a native girl beat a rug over a wire fence.

It was only when he spoke at the gate that our interested talk
dropped lightly and suddenly. The faint sense of intrusion that
quietens one when one is about to walk in on someone else's most
familiar witnesses came to me. It was suddenly between us that we
really knew each other well; oddly, it seemed that a matter for
laughter—Joel's eyes silently on me from a distance—really had
secreted a friendship that it had only been necessary for us to speak
to discover. Since that morning on the train we had been companions
on every journey, and with an ease that comes to relationships most
often as a compensation for the dulling of years, very rarely with
the immediacy of a streak of talent.

Yes, we knew each other well, the young to the young, a matching of the desire for laughter, meaning and discovery which boils
up identically, clear of the different ties, tensions, habits and mem-
ories that separately brewed it. But this brown front door with the
brush hairs held in the paint, an elephant-ear plant in a paraffin-
tin pot below the bell, watched Joel Aaron every day. Inside; the
walls, the people who made him what he was as the unseen powers
of climate shape a landscape; force flowers, thick green, or a pale
monotony of sand.

He lifted the mat made of rolled tire strips, looking for the key, and dropped it back. "Ma's home, then." He smiled, and the door gave way to his hand.

It was not spring inside the Aarons' house. The air of a matured distilled indoor season, an air that had been folded away in cupboards with old newsprint and heavy linen, cooked in ten-years' pots of favorite foods, burned with the candles of ten-years' Friday nights, rested in the room with its own sure permeance, reaching every corner of the ceiling, passing into the dimness of passages with the persistence of a faint, perpetual smoke.

Joel was not aware of it as one cannot be aware of the skin-scent of one's own body; he picked up some circulars that the postman had pushed under the door and threw them onto a chair. The house opened directly into the living room where there was a large dark table with a crocheted lace cloth, high-backed chairs set back against the wall, a great dark sideboard with two oval, convex-glassed pictures above it. A pair of stern, stupid eyes looked out from the smoky beard of an old photograph; the face of a foolish man in the guise of a patriarch. But next to him the high bosom, the high nose that seemed to tighten the whole face, slant the black eyes, came with real presence through a print that seemed to have evaporated from the paper: a woman presided over the room.

Past a green leatherette sofa with shiny portholes for ash trays in the arms, Joel led me through the white archway into the passage. A refrigerator stood against the wall as if in a place of honor; our footsteps were noisy on thin checkered linoleum that outlined the uneven spines of the floor boards beneath it like a shiny skin. In his room, Joel showed the self-conscious busyness that comes upon one in one's own home. He put out the little rough dog that had been sleeping on the bed, kicked a pair of shoes out of sight, cleared one or two rolls of plans off the table that held his model.

To me the model was a cunning and delightful toy and I exclaimed over it with pleasure. I made him take the miniature ambulance out of its packet and place it under the portico.

"What I'm worried about, you see, is this—" He knew I could not detect the functional pitfalls of his design, yet he hoped for reassurance in itself, even the reassurance of ignorance. I tried to separate my intelligence from my fascination with the perfect little windows, the flower boxes made of cork. "I see. I see . . ."

He had a way of looking up penetratingly to see if the face of the person to whom he was speaking confirmed his words. It was quick, earnest, almost a request. "I'll show you, here on the plan— somewhere here—" His long olive-skinned hands unrolled the paper on the bed, we knelt on it together, rumpling the blue taffeta cover that smelled of dog. The plan shot up again like a released blind. He picked it up, blew down it. He said calmly, as if the thing had dwindled to its proper small importance; "Well, there'll be no problem getting it back again after it's seen. I'll take five minutes to break it up." I protested, but he only smiled at me, swinging a leg. "You might want to look at this," he said, "and these"—he was pulling books out of an old high case that stood by his bed—"Corbusier, Frank Lloyd Wright—the high priests—"

I bounced his bed. "It's very soft." I laughed, looking round. He shrugged, deprecating it. "Feather bed; from Russia. Look, Helen, what do you think about this?" And he brought a book of Danish furniture design to my lap.

I wandered slowly, curiously round his small room as if in a museum. The glossy books on modern architecture and the poetry of Ezra Pound, Yeats and Huxley, paper-backed John Stuart Mill and Renan's *Life of Jesus* were stacked on the hand-crocheted mats which were spread on the chest of drawers, the bedside table and the top of the bookcase. A photograph of a school group hung on a brass wire, and a framed address in what looked like oriental characters and must be Hebrew hung at a lower level beside it. On the other wall a modern print had a frame that had evidently belonged to something else, and did not fit it. The only modern painter I had ever heard of was Van Gogh, from a novelized version of his life which I had taken from the Atherton library. "That's not a Van Gogh, is it?"

"Seurat."

"Oh."

A Treasury of Folk Tales for Jewish Boys and Girls, How to Make It, The Wonder Adventure Book—and on top of this battered pile an army cap. It was easy to forget that Joel had been in the army.

"Joel, you've never told me, why were you discharged?"

"I got a mastoid and it did something queer to my middle ear. For about a year I couldn't hear at all."

I was curious. "Show me how you looked in uniform?—Oh, come on, you must have a picture somewhere?"

He was kneeling next to his model, adjusting something with precision, and the light of the window behind him glowed through his ears and made his teeth shine in contrast to the darkness that blurred the rest of his face. "You laughing in anticipation?"

"It's the light through your ears—all red.—But put it on, then, if you won't show me your picture."

He came forward laughing, with the air of a good-natured dog that allows a ribbon to be put on its collar. "Wait—wait—" I was knighting him with the cap, and his hand, with the short movements of someone searching by touch, was feeling to arrange it, when a hoarse little voice said softly, like a reluctant question: "Joel . . ."

I turned round.

"No, sit down—you'll excuse me—I just want to ask something, Joel, d'you know if Daddy's coming home to lunch or he's going straight to Colley? He's coming?" A short round woman stood in the doorway; she held her hands in front of her in the attitude of someone coming for instructions. They were puffy hands with hardened flesh growing up round small, clean but unkempt nails, the ragged-cuticle nails of domestic workers or children. Her body in a cheap silk dress that had the remains of an elaboration of black cotton lace and fagoted trimming round the neck was the incredibly small-hipped, thickened body of Jewish women from certain parts of Europe, the swollen doll's body from which it seems impossible that tall sons and daughters can, and do, come. The floral pattern of the apron she wore was rubbed away over the bulge of her breasts and her stomach. She looked at me from under the straggling, rather beautiful eyebrows you sometimes see on the faces of eagle-eyed old men, and beneath arches of fine, mauvish, shadowy skin, her lids remained level, half-shuttered. But the eyes were bright, liquid, water-colored.

I knew she must be Joel's mother and I felt acutely the fact that I was sitting casually on the bed, in the house of strangers. This I felt in relation to her, and to Joel, the embarrassment he must feel at her accent, her whole foreignness before me.

But he answered her: "Colley?—Why should he go there first —Of course he's coming home."

At once I was alone and they were both strangers. Something in the way he spoke to her, something he took from her own voice, as one takes a key in music, put me outside of them. I sat very consciously on the bed; what had been unnoticeably comfortable was now precarious: I had to brace my legs to prevent myself from slipping off the coverlet.

I smiled at Mrs. Aaron timidly as if to excuse her to herself. But she did not feel the need to be forgiven; she gave herself time to look at me with frank curiosity, as one might stop to finger a piece of material in a shop. "Joel," she bridled, "why don't you bring the young lady into the lounge? Must she sit in the bedroom?—You must excuse him, he doesn't think." She drooped her head at him in an appraising, irritated smile. He made a little noise of smiling impatience. "No, it's not nice she should be stuck in this room— It's not so beautiful, believe me—" Suddenly she and I were both laughing; as usual, I had deserted, in a desire to be liked had aligned myself in a sudden swift turn with what embarrassed or frightened me. We were led back to the living room, his mother talking on as if he were absent: "It's always like that. Anybody comes, he hides them away in his room.—Come sit down. Take a comfortable chair—"

"No, really, I'm quite all right—"

"Come on—" She made me move. All her own movements were slow, heavy and insistent as her voice, the movements of someone who has been on her feet a long time, like a horse who keeps up the plod of pulling a load even when he is set free in the field.

She went over to the sideboard with a kind of formal dignity, as if in spite of her wrinkled stockings and her feet which defied the shape of her shoes, her slip showing beneath the old afternoon dress as she bent, there was a grace of behavior that existed independently, as a tradition, no matter who performed it or how. Next to three packs of cards was a pink glass sweet dish filled with clusters of toffee-covered biscuit. "You'll have something? Come on." I took one, but when she saw it in my hand uncertainty came to her. "Perhaps she'll rather have a sweet, Joel—Take my keys, and in the bedroom cupboard—" I protested and bit into the sticky biscuit. "—Go on, I've got some nice chocolates."

I sat there eating my biscuit like a child who is being anxiously fattened.

"A bunch of grapes, perhaps? I got lovely grapes today from the market."

Joel assured his mother that we did not want tea, lemonade or fruit.

She sat down near the door on a straight-backed chair and her swollen ankles settled on her shoes. We had been introduced, and after she had sat breathing heavily, thoughtfully, over her resting bosom for a moment (neither of us spoke; we could hear her) she said with polite, cautious inquiry, as if the reply would really give her an answer to something else: "Your father he's something on the Atherton Mine—and mummy? Your mummy's still alive?"

"Yes." In an awkward burst I made some attempt to make my life real to her. "We've always lived there. My father's Secretary.— I hate the Mine."

She stirred slowly in her chair. "So? It's your home, we all got to like our home."

There was a pause. I was overcome with the theatrical way I had burst out ridiculously: I hate the Mine—and the even acceptance of this old woman's reply. She got up slowly, stood looking round the room as if to make sure she had forgotten nothing. "Well, you'll excuse me—" she said, as if I were not there, an air of apology that seemed to throw the onus of my presence on me, and went out slowly and suddenly both withdrawing and yet taking the field at the same time.

"Would you like to wash?" said Joel, getting up. "They leave you rather sticky, though my mother really does make them very well." He put the dish of sweet biscuits away carefully in the sideboard.

I don't know why he surprised me; Joel was continually surprising me by ease when there might have been strain, a word where there might have been a vacuum. He said what he thought and somehow it was never what I thought he was thinking: his nature had for mine the peculiar charm of the courage to be itself without defiance; I had always to be opposing myself in order to test the validity of my reactions, a moral "Who goes there?" to which my real feelings as well as those imposed from without and vaguely held suspect must be submitted in a confusion of doubt. And when I answered myself and acted, anxiousness sometimes made me mistake bravado for honesty.

Now I had been ready to make it easy for Joel; to show him that so far as I was concerned, he need not mind about his mother. This was quite a different thing from finding that he did not mind about his mother; that far from being apologetic of the peculiar sweetmeat which politeness had forced me to eat, he seriously commended her skill in preparing it.

Yet, as so often happened with him, what put me out momentarily, set me free as the expected reaction from him could not have done; it was not necessary to pretend anything, even understanding. I could be curious about the old portraits looking down on us. They were his father's parents: "The old chap was supposed to be a Talmudic scholar. I don't quite know what the Christian equivalent of that would be. . . . The Talmud—it's a kind of book of religious philosophy. Somewhere in every Jewish family they've got a Talmudic scholar preserved, it's a distinction none of us can afford to be without. Like ours, he's usually dead, but there are stories about how during his life time he spent his days and nights poring over books of wisdom—you know, the Talmud's rather like Shakespeare or *Finnegans Wake* now—hundreds of different interpretations of the text and scholastic arguments which die unsolved with their protagonists.—He doesn't look much of a scholar, does he?"

We looked the old man in the eye.

I laughed. "*She* looks the brainy one."

"She was the go-getter. These Talmudic scholars are nice for prestige, but mostly they don't make a living. With him I really think it must just have been an excuse to get out of working and hang around the synagogue with his pals."

"You make it sound like the men's commonroom."

He pulled his nose down sardonically, laughing. "Now you see where I get it from. The family glories in the education I'm getting myself, while really all I'm doing is learning to play a devastating hand at bridge.—But seriously, as soon as any member of a Jewish family shows any inclination even vaguely connected with learning —it could be stamp-collecting or pornography—everybody starts wagging their heads: he's just like old Uncle so-and-so, so studious. . . . *She* took in dressmaking to keep the family." Under her eyes, we wandered back to Joel's room; she had the imagined power of the dead and alien to fasten her look far beyond the frame or carved limits of their presence; like the face of the idol whose symbolism you do not understand—is he to bring rain, corn or protection?— but whose jeweled eye you feel long after you have left the temple.

I left the house just before lunch with two of Joel's books under my arm—one was always taking something from him, he was one of those people who give out of a sufficiency in themselves, welling up beautifully to a constant level no matter how often dipped into, and quite independent of material possession or the condescension of generosity. His father had come home but I did not see him, although I could hear, in the back of the house, a heavy tread and a moody voice speaking another language. Joel hung on the gate making a ridge of his brows against the sun. There was a fascination about the way he looked in the full sun; the fascination I had felt in the faces of Indian waiters serving food in Durban hotels. That steely darkness of black curly hair—perhaps it was just that his hair was like theirs. But their faces came up in the sun as his did. The quiet-colored faces and neutral hair among which I had grown up had a way of almost disappearing in bright sunlight, only a sear of gleam here and there traced their light-flattened contours, and they blinked laughter, as if the brightness were a hand pushed in their faces. Ludi was something else again; his brightness took on brightness, like metal.

One could not know whether it was the sun or thought that was making Joel frown. His hesitation made me wait. When we had already said good-by, he asked: "Shall I come to you, now?"

I felt I understood what he meant. One could have a friendship in a train that could exist for years outside one's life as an entity, but once one met and talked at home instead of between here and

there, one part of one's life and another, the friend of the train moved
in to one's life. "Yes, what about one evening? Tuesday—no, that's
the night I get back late. Wednesday, then?"

But he said, as if it suddenly didn't matter: "Oh, we don't have
to fix it now." Then he smiled on an inner comment. "Right," he
said, dismissing it, very friendly, and with a little wave, turned up
the path. When I looked back as I turned the corner, to take in a
last curious impact of that little house, I saw he had not gone in but
was still standing there, on the veranda steps, watching me go or
staring at some object of his own.

Joel came to the Mine several times and my mother received him
without remark. She spoke to him for a few minutes with the usual
slightly arch pleasantness which she showed toward my contemporaries—her whole manner on a higher, soprano key, like an ac-
tress helping across some lines whose meaning she feels may not
be clear—and then left us on the fly-screened porch that was full
of the flowered cotton chair covers and embroidered cushions she
had made, the sawdust-stuffed stocking cat that held the door open.
At four o'clock she came out with a tea tray laid with fresh linen
and, not the best cups, but a little twosome breakfast set that was
not in common use. I recognized in Joel's serious, careful manner
that she was even pretty, with her thin, dry-skinned face and her
red hair only slightly faded by the curls that the hairdresser steamed
into it once a week, now that it was cut, and the almost antiseptic
scent of lavender water that waved out of the flounces of her dress.
She was even well dressed, in what I was now beginning to recognize
was the Mine style: the flower-patterned, unobtrusive blues and
pinks of English royalty.

My father spoke to Joel about "your people" and "the customs
of your people" with the same air he used to surprise the Portuguese
market gardener with a few words of Portuguese, or, when once we
drove through Zululand, a Zulu tribesman with a brisk question in
his own language. But though I sat in awkward silence, Joel answered with patient explanation, as the cultured native of a country
ignores the visitor's proud clumsy mouthing of a few words of vulgar
patois, and returns patronage with the compliment of pretending to

mistake it for real interest. "That's a well-mannered boy," my father informed me. "They know how to bring their children up to respect older people. And of course they're clever, it goes without saying."

Some weeks later I told my mother that Joel had asked me to go with him to a faculty dance. She put down an armful of clean laundry in alarm. "You wouldn't go when Basil asked you! And the Blake boy."

"So?"

She stood there looking at me. Her face had the fixed, sham steadiness of someone who does not know how to say the unexpected. The impact of her thoughts left a sort of stinging blankness on her cheeks. As usual, she took refuge in an unspecified umbrage, her suffering of a complaint against me for which I must bear the burden of guilt without knowing its cause. She buried herself in the counting of shirts, left my pile of underclothing and handkerchiefs abandoned on the kitchen chair and swept away with the rest of the bundle to the linen cupboard.

I went after her. "Why don't you want me to go?"

Her tactics were common ones, and always the same: she went about a succession of household tasks with swift effort as if you were merely a distraction on the perimeter of her concentration of duty. When, as a child, I had wanted to be forgiven for some piece of naughtiness, I had had to follow her about the house like this, watching her hard, slender hands ignoring me. I asked her again:

"Why shouldn't I go?"

She hated to answer. By withholding her complaints, her accusations, her arguments, she withheld also the risk of their refutation and kept for herself the cold power of the wronged.

So now she said tightly: "You wouldn't go with Basil or the other one."

I laughed. "Because I didn't want to."

"They're not your type." It was a quotation.

"No, they're not. It doesn't mean that because we happen to come from the Mine we've got to stick to one another at University. Basil's never ever been a friend of mine—we've nothing in common."

"And you have," she stated, meaning Joel and me.

"We get on well. He's intelligent, and well—nice, that's all. . . ." It was almost an appeal; my tightening of irritation unwound into a desire to have my mother agree with me, to accept her. A feeling of tears coming in a longing for her approval, even if she was wrong, even if we were different.

She ignored it off the hard back of her understanding; it slid, harmless. . . .

"As I say, you certainly do have the queerest taste." There was something indescribably insulting in the casualness with which she dissociated herself by this callow, mild cliché; she would not even give me the blunt words of her real objections, trouble herself with an examination of what she felt. The Petrie man and now the Jewish storekeeper's son: Well, it's so, isn't it? her back turned on me said.

I believe that was the only dance Joel took me to; he had little money, many things he wanted to do, and as he was two or three years older than I was it was only the interruption of the war that made him an undergraduate when, in himself, the stage had already passed. And curiously, I did not mind. The one dance had somehow not been an entire success; Joel and I could not hold hands, dance with my cheek raised and his lowered like love-stalking birds. We could talk endlessly, spend more and more time together, meet each other's faces above other people's chatter with the sudden comfort of each other's understanding; but this we could not do. Perhaps for dances something in me wanted the tall, fair-haired boys who could clown over beer bottles and flirt with me in the permissive code of gentlemen of my own blood. With one of them I did not have to meet the purposefully unremarking smiles of my classmates (we think nothing of it!) nor did I feel, as I did when Joel stopped to speak to a group of friends, the sudden insipidity of the blue organza dress my mother had made me, the locket on a chain round my neck, in contrast to the interesting dramatic clothes of the friendly Jewesses, bold in their ugliness, bold in their beauty, outdistancing me either way.

This need of mine existed not only outside but also in contradiction to the expansion of my confiding intimacy with Joel Aaron. Out of the silences that followed some minor confession—the silence that is really the rise of sudden floodwaters of words, blocking by pressure the trickling release of speech—came the real unburdening. I told him of my gradual suspension from the life of the Mine . . . my voice tailed off in what seemed tame and not quite the truth. We were silent, or spoke of something else. Then all of a sudden it came: I told him about Ludi. He himself seemed to impose the limitation of what I should tell him. "It's a pity to give it away," he said, combining, as usual in his manner, the immediate sympathy of a contemporary with the comforting, dispassionate remove of a much older person. "When you tell someone else about someone you have loved, you always have the misgiving afterward that you've given that much of it away."

"You sound like a romantic."—For him, at this time, it was a term of scorn and like a simple object that has been handled by the great, I was fascinated to be able to use it, for it belonged to the vocabulary of that group with the sense of self-ordainment to a sharper, warmer, ruthlessly honest life which exists in every university, and whom, through Joel, I was beginning to hear around me.

He spread out his dark hands stiffly in the pleasure of yawning. "Only in love. Which is the right place."

One subject that often brought us to near-argument was my mother. A curious kind of struggle seemed to go on between us at the alert of her name, a battle in the larger air above our heads, the clamor of which reached us only faintly in the reasonable sound of our two voices. She and I had argued again one evening about my going to live in Johannesburg, and after dinner I had heard her in the kitchen, behind the muffle of the door, discussing me with Anna. When Joel arrived to see me with a book he had found for me, I was withdrawn into irritation.

"—She's been shut in the kitchen since dinner, discussing me over the dishes with the native servant." We were sitting on the porch; moths and rose beetles from out the summer night beat a tattoo against the wire gauze that enclosed us in light. Joel sat, looking at but not seeing his hands hanging between his knees.

"*Her* opinion's so valuable, you know—Naturally, she's been absorbing my mother's personal homespun philosophy for fifteen years—she's the one person calculated never ever to disagree with a single word; and that's how my mother likes it. It's a wonder she doesn't buy herself a parrot. That would be more dignified, anyway, than discussing me with a servant."

Joel's silence annoyed me because its questioning suggested the fear that somehow I might be in the wrong. I stared at him for answer, but he merely widened his nostrils as if he were stifling a sigh as one stifles a yawn. The blood trapped in his forgotten hands showed veins crossed and wound like tendrils of a creeper that has come to life round the fingers of a broken stone hand in a garden. Something in the heaviness of his look, a look passing like a river beneath the dark arches of his eyes, reminded me of his mother; of the way she sank, sometimes, out of the family talk; was her, despite her white shoes that were never cleaned, the big hairpins that fell out of her thin hair and smelled, when you picked them up, of the greenish tinge of metal and old frying. Suddenly I wanted to make him move; I said: "Joel?"—to do that, rather than to urge him to speak.

He said: "You discuss Professor Quail's shortcomings with Mary Seswayo." Mary Seswayo was the African girl I had seen in the cloakroom when first I went to the University, and to whom I had begun to speak lately.

I was angry. "Ah, you know it's not that!—It wouldn't matter if Anna were white, yellow—whatever she was—she's a servant, an illiterate. It's humiliating for a woman to discuss her private family affairs with a servant, someone who isn't even capable of forming a judgment—"

"You don't like the way your mother speaks about natives. You told me only the other day that it 'made your blood boil' when you heard her describe someone's way of living as 'worse than a native.' To prove your enlightenment as opposed to her darkness, you pursue a poor frightened little native girl who happens to have passed English I, or whatever it is, round the Arts block, offering a rare tidbit of white acquaintanceship—"

"I want to talk to her as I might want to talk to any other student. I don't see why I should be debarred by my white skin? Why, it's from you yourself—"

"—And then when your mother puts aside considerations of

status and color and talks—as one woman to another, mind—to Anna, your blood boils just as hard again."

"You're deliberately choosing to misconstrue. You know that's just what I cannot stand about my mother's attitude: making use of Anna as a friend and conveniently ignorant yes-woman, elevating her to the status of a confidante, and at the same time pushing her, along with her whole race, into a categorical sloth—of moral, spiritual—everything—inferiority. It's a variation on the same old theme—you know; of course, you're different, you're my friend, it suits me to like you, even though you're a Jew. Isn't it the same, isn't it?"

"Yes, it is. And so is your attitude, neatly inverted. Your mother succeeds in the personal relationship; she fails in words, in the theory. Your theory's sound all right, but you betray it in the heat of personal involvement; your blood lets you down. In fact, it boils when it shouldn't. You can't recognize that your mother's heart-to-heart talks with Anna are the real thing, the thing we're all piously rolling our eyes to heaven for—a contact between a white and a black simply as human beings—nothing else."

I felt moody. "Simply, nothing—it's simply the Trusted Black Mammy situation, that's all. And you know how much good *that* sort of good will has done for race relations."

He gave a little patient smile at the term, hearing it new on my tongue, as one hears someone use the vogue-word of a particular set, and so knows where his affinities, like antennae, are taking him. He shrugged. "None at all. About as much good as those militant liberals who love humanity but can't stand men and women."

I was still young enough to lose my temper and be a little ridiculous when I felt I was losing ground. "I'm going to be one of them, I suppose?"

"Don't be a coy bluestocking," he said aside, smiling. "—I hope not—" he commented, as if he feared it was something he might be responsible for.

Somehow one of the hard, round-backed beetles had got in. It hit the reflections of light wavering like smoke rings on the ceiling, slithered down the brittle burning surface of the globe itself, and dropped onto Joel's head. With the calmness of the male, who distinguishes between the biters and the harmless hateful, he scooped it absently into his hand and threw it onto the floor. I put my heel down on it; like crunching a nut. We were in the unsatisfactory listless state of people who have argued about something other than the argument's cause. I had the sudden impatient feeling that all this talk that I sought after and felt was so important at the time of talking was nothing, was of no interest to me: all that I really cared about was what happened directly to myself; there was nothing and no one in the world beyond the urgent importance of me, of a burning, selfish grasp of what would happen to me, alone. This feeling held me glowering, like a fit of sulks.

After a few minutes Joel began to tell me of a mix-up on the telephone in which he had been involved with his married sister, Colley, but though I accepted the amusing way he told the story, I ignored the change of mood, and flung out, like a challenge and an excuse for a return to disagreeableness: "Joel, why do you always side with my mother against me?" It was spoken as pettishly as it was phrased.

He looked as if he had been expecting it. Again he became heavy, wary. "Do I?"

I waved it aside. "You know what I mean. If I tell you anything about her—not disparaging, exactly, but anything to which one might expect you would agree was unreasonable on her part—you shut up like a clam. I don't understand it."

"Look, Helen, I don't side with her—"

"But so often she's wrong, quite wrong, and you'll never give me the satisfaction of admitting it!"

"Of course I know she's wrong; difficult, anyway. But it doesn't matter. You can't do anything about it, so it doesn't matter. You can't change them, her or your father, you can't make them over the way you think—we think—they ought to be or the way we believe we'd like to have them."

He saw the dissatisfaction in my eyes. "But you can't get rid of them, either."

I was shocked, at myself rather than his words. "—What a way to put it."

"Making them over would be getting rid of them as they are.

Well, you can't do it. You can't do it by going to live somewhere else, either. You can't even do it by never seeing them again for the rest of your life. There is that in you that is them, and it's that unkillable fiber of you that will hurt you and pull you off balance wherever you run to—unless you accept it. Accept them in you, accept them as they are, even if you yourself choose to live differently, and you'll be all right. Funnily enough, that's the only way to be free of them. You'll see—really, I know."

I protested. "But I tell you I don't want to 'get away' in that sense. I don't want to change them, really. . . . I just want them to be a little more understanding . . . to let me think my way. To have some respect for the things I want to do, the things I think are important." I was amazed to have put these reasons to Joel, with whom I had discovered the extent of the gulf between the life of my parents and the life I wanted for myself. Joel, with whom I was hearing live music for the first time in my life; who said, Come on, I've got something to show you—and, between lectures, pushed me before him onto a tram to town to see exhibitions of painting and sculpture, showed me the inside of the municipal art gallery that all my life till now had been a gray stone exterior from which one might take one's bearings, like the magistrates' courts, or a fire station. Joel, from whose books and whose talk I was even beginning to see that the houses we lived in in Atherton and on the Mine did not make use of space and brightness and air, but, like a woman with bad features and a poor complexion who seeks to distract with curls and paint, had their defects smothered in lace curtains and their dark corners filled with stands of straggling plants which existed for these awkward angles between wall and wall, as one evil exists simply for another.

"Still in the Second League. Been in the Second League, every year for twelve years. My mother tells everybody who comes. Soon it'll be awful; the way all the Mine people repeat to one another with awe: the Compound Manager's *wonderful* old mother! That *wonderful* old Mrs. Ockert! And why is she wonderful? Because she's eighty-two. . . ."

Joel smiled.

I said: "I suppose I make them seem . . ." He nodded. I looked at his hands with their sensitive-tipped fingers that always moved a little on the surface on which they rested, as the nose of a sensitive animal responds constantly to the mere fact of being alive; his broad, European peasant body, the curious, patient, implied shrug of his people: he had eyes that one could never imagine closed, like a light that is never put out.

It was as if I had blundered into the fact of his parents; I felt as if I had suddenly said, aloud, There!—and produced them, bewildered, ignorant, embarrassing, blinking like moles brought up into the unaccustomed light of Joel's world of books and music and houses clean, sharp as beautiful paper shapes. He had said: I know. I sat staring at my own silence hardening around me; a person who suddenly remembers that the illness of which he has been talking with unsparing clinical thoroughness is the very one from which his companion must be suffering.

13 GETTING TO KNOW Mary Seswayo was like gently coaxing a little shy animal to edge forward to your hand.

There was, as Joel had inferred, something of a collector's suppressed eagerness in the trembling bait I held out to her from time to time; and we were afraid of each other, she of the lion-mask of white mastery that she saw superimposed on my face, I of the mouse-mask of black submission with which I obscured hers. Yet there was the moment in the cloakroom; a meeting of inherited enemies in the dark in which they mistake one another for friends. And it is never forgotten: not the fact that enemy could be mistaken for friend, but the shared bewilderment of the darkness each recognized in the other's eye. That is a moment of fusion that cannot be taken back and discussed with one's own side, for it is a moment for which they too are the enemy. It has none of the sentiment of the armed truce, the soldiers of warring armies drinking beer together on Christmas Day and going back to killing one another on Boxing Day, but is more in the nature of an uncomfortable secret.

When after almost six months at the University I started my first year proper, I found myself in an English tutorial group that included two Africans. One was a fat, pompous teacher-priest "continuing his studies," the other was Mary Seswayo. When she came in, walking with her head down to the back of Room 325, we knew each other, though I did not look up as she passed the desk at which I was already seated. The native girl from across the washbasin that day. ("African" was an acquired word, preferred by non-Europeans and liberals not only because it was a more accurate designation, but rather because it was as yet clean of the degrading contexts in which the other had been dyed more deeply than with color—in the unself-conscious privacy of my thoughts I still used the old inherited word.) I felt that now and then she looked at me; felt the gentle, curious glance of her recognition touching my back.

She never spoke in class discussions, but the priest did. He used his old manner of the preacher to the layman for the new purpose of the black man to the white man: hearty, hand-rubbing, bright. We are all God's children; let's make the best of it. Sometimes there was the suspicion that he half-clowned his unctuous jolliness, wood-touching for the temerity of his equality, that he snatched with a conjurer's patter and glee while his white audience was being amused, and his own people, in the know, demonstrated his superiority to them in their inability to follow his sleight of hand. So he apologized beforehand for any offense your whiteness might, with its awesome sensitivity, take from the innocuous, like litmus paper mysteriously turning red with immersion. And it seemed to him he got away with it; a trick kind of equality, in a trick kind of way, but still, an equality. "How are we this morning, how are we? —And is our Dr. East not 'on time'?" He would swing round the door and pile his books on a desk in the front row, beaming at the class through polishing gestures with which he swept his hot face with a handkerchief as someone cleans a pair of spectacles preparatory to settling to work.

He did wear spectacles, but these were permanently misted by the heat of his hands, and he took them on and off as he sat, face poised beneath Dr. East like a seal waiting for the keeper's fish to land in his mouth. The instant Dr. East paused to invite discussion, the preacher rose to it. (The subject of discussion, on one occasion I remember, was Thackeray's discursive muse.) "Sir, well, I should like to say—in my humble opinion that is—I don't know how my fellow students are feeling about it—but this bad habit of Thackeray's, it makes it very difficult for the student. It is hard for him to know what is the story, if you know what I mean, and in examination it may be that you are asked a question about the story, and you know the book too well and put in what is not the story?" He smiled round the class with a slowly widening gesture, as a conductor acknowledges applause by taking it for his whole orchestra.

Dr. East had faded ginger hair and colorless eyes that had the cold snap of a pair of scissors, impatiently cutting off irrelevancies and idiocies with a look, before they could rise to articulation. After giving the preacher two or three commentless hearings, with the allowance of attention in the face of irritation which would be accorded to any foreigner, he refused any further concession. Yet he was not quite so hard on the African as he would have been on a European student: the viper-flicker of his sarcasm he kept in his mouth. "Just a moment, Mr. Thabo—" He would signal him down and raise his eyes at some other student who was struggling with the desire to speak.

The girl, as I have said, did not speak at all. She listened with the painful intentness of someone who is always balanced on the edge of noncomprehension, and she wrote things down when one could not imagine what had been said that was worth noting. Dr. East had a peculiar affection for those who did not offer dissent or opinion; probably he was grateful to be spared the risk of hearing more banalities. Yet at the same time he had the endearing quality of literary men—those in the exact sciences are much less hopeful—the belief that perhaps something fresh and intelligent is being muffled by timidity. Particularly in the unexplored country— jungle profusion? sweet grassland? silence of rock?—of the other race's intellectual innocence. His compressed lips that twitched at the fly of impatience suddenly opened in his surprising smile; a friendly smile on big even false teeth that altered the whole set of his face and seemed to flatten his ears and his forehead with the look of pleasure that comes to the head of an animal when you stroke it. "Miss Seswayo, wouldn't you perhaps like to say something about this?" He lifted his head courteously to the back of the room.

She would get up slowly, moving her notebook, putting down the pencil, resting her palms on the desk ledge. She shook her head carefully as she spoke, after a pause in which everyone was silent, "No. . . . No, thank you."—Dr. East made a small noise of regret —"Yes, now what is it, Mr. Alder?"—and talk broke again upon the room.

Once or twice, when I happened to sit at the back of the room in line with her, I tried to see what it was that she wrote down so purposefully. But I only caught a glimpse of lines of copybook hand-writing, a child's at its most careful, with great round stops and hooked commas. One of these times a paper with the text of a literary-appreciation test was handed out round the room, one for every two students, and as she was my neighbor I moved to share mine with her. Sitting over the same printed sheet, I could see the brown, shiny plate of her breast, moving a little fast with her breathing beneath a necklace of white china beads that she always wore. I could see the very texture of her skin, sliding over the ridge of her collarbone as she lifted her arms. The top of her arm, in a brown coat sleeve, slowly sent its warmth through to where my arm touched against it.

It must have been fifteen years since I had been in such close contact with an African; not since that other breast, longer ago than I could remember, the breast of my native nanny, had I casually felt human warmth, life, coming to me from a black body.

The following afternoon I stopped to speak to her where she sat in a window embrasure in one of the wide corridors, reading a key to Chaucer whose edges were worn round as a stone. I made the usual banal overtures about our work and she answered in the faint, stilted English of the European-educated African woman, out of whom all the buoyancy, music and spontaneity that is in the voices of nursemaids and servants seem to have been hushed by respon-sibility.

An obstinacy of shyness made it very difficult to talk to her, but the reassurance of repeated casual meetings slowly thawed her silent, wide-eyed greeting as she hurried past into a smile. We met again in the cloakroom. Alone, this time, in the litter of lip-stick-streaked tissues and balls of crumpled paper like cabbages, she was repacking her things on the floor—she always carried about with her a complication of coats, books, notes that she watched and counted with the poor peasant's anxiety for his pos-sessions. The tap frothed out over my dirty hands and I said: "You are loaded up. . . ."

It was not easy for her to speak lightly. "Sometimes I cannot seem to get it all in. It seems to get bigger and heavier as the day goes on."

To anyone else I could have said: "But why on earth do you carry all that stuff about, anyway—but with her I could not. "You know, you frighten me with the notes you take; every time my mind's wandering at a lecture, I see you writing away and I get an awful feeling that I've just missed hearing something very important."

She smiled, and this time it was the sudden, quick, surrendering smile of the piccanin caddies at the golf course. It seemed ridiculous that here was I, talking to a little native girl about lecture notes at a University.

"Well, it *is* a lot . . . ," she admitted with the shy acceptance of a commendation, "especially with Dr. East. Everyone in the class always has so much to argue about.—The expense of all the paper is something, too."

She takes down everything that anyone says. She struggles to get down the commonplace inaccuracies, the embarrassed critical shots in the dark, the puerile fumblings toward an opinion.—I was so appalled that I looked at her with the polite daze of someone who has not quite heard, really listened. . . .

"Do you—do you live here, I mean in Johannesburg itself?" It was not a question I had meant to ask, but I snatched it up as the first thing to hand.

She answered dutifully. "I have a room with a family in Sophia-town. I was at the hostel and then at Alexandra, but I moved."

"Oh, I live at home—that is, in Atherton, on the Mine." Questioning her about where she lived suddenly seemed too much like a mistress expecting to be decently answered by a servant, and I looked for some way to put it right.

"It's a long way," she said.

"An hour by train every morning." I always said it with some sort of distasteful pride in the hardness of it.

But to her, living in a native township where people got up at five o'clock to queue for busses in order to get to work by eight, it was nothing to commiserate about. She nodded politely.

"I have to go." She smiled, with her bundles on her arm, as if she did not want to. She stood like a neat schoolgirl, feet together.

I said: "Bye now. . . ."—But no airiness could take from that quiet, serious little figure the consciousness of privilege that sent it, alone, down the corridors and down the flanking steps and through the gardens out into the street; into Johannesburg, to be swept aside with errand boys and cooks and street cleaners, still alone.

A susurration of voices—now and then a phrase would land, shrill on our table: "tastes like soap!" . . . "his FINAL YEAR, I said"—the warmed-over humidity of canteen foods, and the grinding, bursting effort of a box apoplectic with colored lights to release the snarling of a swing band—stood between Joel and his friend, and me.

"Big attraction of this tearoom, now." The light-haired young man indicated the juke box.

"Big attraction of the other one is no juke box," said Joel. "Let's go."

There nothing moved but a lethargic tearoom fly, feeling over the sugar bowl. "What happened to you?" said Joel in the hush, referring to my lateness.

"Joel, I was talking to that girl, the African girl. I discovered she takes down *everything that is said*. She sits at tuts taking down miles of notes. All the rubbish that everyone talks." I sat back in my chair, looking at him.

He pursed his lips. "Just a minute—" He went up to the counter and came back with our lunch balanced; the steady, heavy approach of his legs, a thoughtful, nervous walk that I watched for assurance.

"Did you tell her, though?"

"Well, no—it was so difficult to know where to begin. If I knew her a bit better . . . I don't know how not to be officious about it."

"Showing the poor savage the ropes."

"Yes, that's just it."

Joel took a long drink of cold water that made him gasp. He looked as if he had just come up from a swim under water, and somewhere, parenthetically, there was a smile in me that did not reach my face. "Still, it's a damned shame, someone should tell her. The confusion behind it—"

"You mean it's not the waste of effort so much, it's that it means she doesn't know what to take and what to leave?"

"That's the whole thing. That's the whole unwieldy thing." He looked from one hand to the other as if he saw it, did not know what to do with it, lying amorphous on the table, in the air, between us. "We see only one little corner of it—this native girl needs to be told that one abstracts from lectures, discussions, what-have-you, only what is useful, relevant, illuminating. So then you find that you've solved nothing for her; you've simply twitched up and caught hold of one corner of a dilemma that shifts continually beneath everything she does here. It's the most difficult thing in the world for her to discern simply because she has no comparative values. It's the African's problem all the way up through all struggles with a white man's world. On a higher level, it's the problem of Colley's servant girl, who gives the cat milk out of a saucer from the best tea set, or the old kitchen one, quite impartially. She doesn't know it *is* a best tea set; she simply never has known such a sufficiency of utensils that there could be gradations of use—"

"What's this? The evils of property?" Rupert Sack, whom we had lost between one tearoom and the other, rejoined us. He had dark, theatrical eyebrows that confirmed the suspicion that the bleached streaks of his hair were dyed: perhaps his one gesture of allegiance, if a rather misplaced one, to the art of architecture, since he was sure to leave before completing his course, in favor of his father's business, pleasantly knowledgeable about cantilevers and clear-story lighting for the rest of his life. He was intelligent but his mind wandered. He sat looking elaborately at me, one eyebrow raised in his own convention of idiotic admiration.

"And *she's* never known a sufficiency of ideas?"

"From where?" Joel answered me with a question. "The life of an African—especially of her generation, pressed into a sort of ghetto vacuum between the tribal life that is forgotten and the white man's life that is guessed at—it's the practical narrow life of poverty. All the kinds of poverty there are: money, privacy, ideas. Even suppose she didn't grow up in a two-room shack in a fenced location where her father couldn't go out without a pass from his baas—she probably went to a mission school, at best. In some ways, at worst. Because in a location, in a room in somebody's back yard, she might get some sort of idea of white people's context. But in a mission, shut away in some peaceful white-walled place in the hills, God, her idea of the white world would be the Standard Six reader and Galilee nearly two thousand years ago."

"Hell, that's true, you know, Joel—" Rupert was suddenly attracted into the conversation. "It's funny, I was talking about the same thing last night—at my sister's place. With that chap Goddard, a pathologist I think he is; he'd been taking some medicals for some oral examinations—"

"A viva."

"Yes—He was saying that it's bloody difficult with these natives. Bloody difficult for them. No matter how clever they are, there's just that lack of common background knowledge—you know, there's nothing to back up what they've learned out of books. So some white fellow who messes around half the time playing poker has a better chance of bluffing his way through than the poor devil of a native who's worked—well—like a black. . . ." He laughed at the lameness of his own joke.

"And that's a purely scientific collection of subjects, medicine. Imagine how much more difficult where nothing is certain, everything's a matter of opinion, judgment—" My voice lost itself in the prospect of the rich ambiguity of language and the vast choices of literature.

"Look, if you're a native," Joel was saying, "you have to be exceptional to do ordinary things. You have to be one of four in ten who go to school at all, in the first place. You have to be able to concentrate on an empty stomach because you haven't had any breakfast, you have to resist the temptation to nip off and do a bit of caddying for pocket money you never get given to you, you have to persuade your parents, who can't afford to keep you, to go on keeping you after you're twelve or thirteen and could be a houseboy or a nanny and keep yourself. And that's only the beginning. That's what you've got to do to get to the point at which white kids only start off making an effort. Just to get through an ordinary schooling you've got to be a very exceptional kid. And from then on you've just got to be more and more exceptional, although in your school life you've used up enough determination and effort to put a white boy right through to qualification in a profession. That's how it is." He sat back, looking at us.

"Okay-okay," said Rupert, staring at his coffee. He had listened with the subdued attention that comes over a shady character in the presence of a person of authority.

Joel began to eat. "Butter, please—Helen and I, here, we never had a chance to hear any music when we were small. You don't, in a little mining place like Atherton. Or you might, if your parents knew about it. But my folks were poor, and in any case they haven't had any education at all—neither of them can even write English. And Helen's—well, they like a bit of musical comedy, but that's all. So now when Helen and I go to a concert we like everything, good, bad, indifferent. We like the noise. The suits the orchestra wear. . . . You see?" He laughed.

I knew it wasn't true of Joel, but it pleased me not to have to bear my ignorance on my own. "We do not! I don't even have to be stopped from clapping between movements any more!"

"You should hold her hand," said Rupert. "That's the way to teach her."

"I should do just that," said Joel, seriously.

We ate in silence for a few moments, lapsing into that abstracted service to necessity that breaks up the surface of attention. We burrowed away off into our separate thoughts.

I shook my head without knowing.

"What?" said Joel, apologetic, as if he thought I had spoken and he had not listened.

"Nothing—" Suddenly I was embarrassed to speak. "She said

something about the expense of the paper——" The little fact, so bald
and paltry, a matter of sixpence or a shilling, was silencing in a
different way. It seemed to grow in the dignity, the reality, the harsh-
ness of a need, something felt instead of thought, experienced instead of spoken.

"Of course," said Joel. "Nothing's happened. Just talk. You're
right."

14 MY PARENTS HAD GONE to a braaivleis on a West Rand
mine, fifteen miles the other side of Johannesburg. My excuse was work. "That's all very well," said my mother, fastening her
pearls. "But you don't get out and meet people."

"Isn't she meeting people all the time at the University?" My
father patronized her a little, smiling at me.

My mother settled the pearls on her neck. She looked herself
over in the mirror, shook out her gloves, looked again, herself and
her mirror self challenging each other for correctness. "I mean her
own kind of people."

They would be standing under the trees, the corseted women,
the thin, gracious women who always dressed as if for a garden party,
the satellite young daughters in pastel frocks. Where the drinks
were, the men would be, faces red from golf and bowls, voices loud,
laughing and expansive in departmental allusions as cosy as family
jokes; the older men spry or corpulent with position, the up-and-
coming younger men showing here a hinted thickness of neck, there
a knee peaking up bony that assured that when the first lot died off,
the second would be ready to replace them identically. As the darkness tangled with the trees, and the boys "borrowed" from the office
or Compound brought the braziers to the right stage of glow, the
daughters and the young sons would stand well away to avoid splashing their light frocks and blue suits and patent-leather shoes while
they roasted lamb chops stuck on long forks. The smell of hair oil
and lavender water would come out in the heat, mixed with the
smoke and acridity of burning fat. They would giggle and lick their

fingers, eating with the small bites of mice. And run over the lawns
back to the house to wash their hands and come back, waving handkerchiefs freshly charged with lavender water. I had been there
many times. I knew what it was like; a small child in white party
shoes that made my feet big and noisy, tearing in and out among
the grownups, wild with the excitement of the fire and the smoky
dark; and then grown-up myself, standing first on one foot, then the
other, drawing patterns with my toe on the ground, feebly part of
the feebleness of it all, the mawkish attempts of the boys to entertain, the inane response of the girls: the roasting of meat to be torn
apart by hands and teeth made as feeble as a garden party. That
was what these people did to everything in life; enfeebled it. Wed-
dings were the appearance of dear little girls dressed up to strew
rose petals, rather than matings; death was the speculation about
who would step up to the dead man's position; dignity was the chain
of baubles the mayor wore round his neck.

"Anna'll stay in the yard. I've told her. She'll take Wednesday
off instead. But if you go out at all lock up the front in any case. A
drunk boy came over from the stores last week right up to Mrs.
Ockert's dining-room window; she got the fright of her life.—It's
terrible, you're no safer on the Mine than in the town, anymore—"
my mother complained to my father.

"I've told you, you should let me get out my Browning."

"No, no, there are too many accidents with those things. Only
the other day, I saw in the paper—little boy of five lost his arm."

"Yes, but where there are no small children."

"I wish they'd do away with those stores.—All the flies come
from there, too. . . . —George, you've got hair on your collar, wait
a minute—Don't forget, Helen?"

With one of those curious looks that mothers give their children—the same look, whether they are babies or grown men and
women—half-abstracted, mind on the outing, half-smitten with the
pang that is all that is left of remembrance of a time when the child
was in the body and an accompaniment of all ventures, sleeping and
waking—they were gone. I wished I could have gone with them;
wished I could have wanted to go. My other life, my life at the
University, turned me loose at week ends. And I wandered about,

wondering what I had been sent back for, for everything that I picked up seemed a relic, sometimes pleasant and loved, but outside the direction of my life, washed up on the bank. The face of our house, of our whole row of houses following every bend and bush of my memory behind the pines, reproached me like the gentle expression of some forgotten person whom you have come back to see but find you have nothing to say to. I opened my mother's accounts drawer, which as a child had been my safekeeping place, and found at the back some gilt transfers that had been saved for some occasion that had never come, and the little crocheted hat, a thimble cover, that I remembered Mrs. Mitcham giving me when I was about ten. In the front of the drawer was Ludi's Christmas card of many months back. "Are you married yet, miss?" his beautiful handwriting said on the inside corner.

No, I hadn't written. At the end of the war, the Kochs had bought a little store in the village, I had heard through my mother; lending library one side, fishing tackle and hardware the other. I thought, with love and guilt of neglect which both would come to nothing, of Mrs. Koch. And sitting on the cool floor where I could see beneath the dresser the stencil of quiet dust with which Anna defeated my mother, of Ludi. Again the dumb pressure of his breast, that was driven, and the informed pressure of his thighs, rose to the surface in my body. More than eighteen months ago. My body was ready, mistook signals, was deluded into stillness. I thought again, with a catch of deep pleasure that was like a hook, buried deep in my entrails and forgotten, now pulled, so that it moved queerly, disturbingly all the secret inertia of flesh gathered about it, how his tongue reached into my throat and the wetness on our mouths seemed to come neither from him nor from me. . . . —This capacity for feeling had become buried under so much; like leaves, the days, little and big, fluttered down upon it. Yet though they were piled so high, like leaves, there was no substance to them: lean on them heavily and sharply once, and the whole pile flattened lightly away—there it was, alive.

My eyes must have closed as I hunched there, for when the telephone began to ring through the house, I shot up startled and bumped into a chair, rocked my own photograph off the dresser. I had the sudden guilty fear that it might be anybody; anybody. But it was Joel. Joel's voice, as unsuspected, as reassuring—Would I do him a favor? Would I take a parcel of working drawings to University for him tomorrow morning?—He wouldn't be going in as he had to drive his father to the Free State on business.

When we had concluded the arrangement there was a little pause, in which there seemed nothing to say; when we spoke to each other from our two separate homes, across the mile of veld that held the Mine apart from the town, there was always slight constraint. One did not know in what atmosphere the other stood: who was talking around, what sort of things they were saying. When I thought about the Aarons privately, alone in their own family, they became two curious wooden dolls whom I could not make speak the casual exchange of Mine intelligence, the mild gossip, the reiterated opinions that occupied us round our table. Whenever I met Joel's parents they seemed to lapse into a kind of heaviness, sitting about as if they did not know where to put themselves. I could not imagine them more at ease, any more than I could imagine the demeanor of the lion I saw blinking behind bars, back in its own jungle.

"So?"

"Nothing."

"What are you doing with yourself?" In his voice there was the suggestion of an afternoon being passed, pleasantly enough, out of his sphere.

"I mean nothing. All on my own . . . my people went off to a braaivleis."

He was genuinely surprised. "Well then come out into the country. Really. I've got my brother-in-law's car for tomorrow. Will you? We'll go out into the veld—" We laughed.

"All right. Come and fetch me. . . . I said I was going to work."

When Joel came he looked different. He slammed the car door and bounded up the path, rat-tatting knuckles in a summons on the porch. He wore an old pair of gray flannels and an old-fashioned fugi silk shirt, washed thin, open at the neck. There were drops of water on the shining ends of his hair, where he had pulled a wet comb quickly through it; still it was glossy as a black horse's flank. His face was newly burned, with the slick of health that the South

African sun dabs on in an hour. He had the delighted look of someone who surprises.

"Bernie said to me at lunchtime, you can have the car this afternoon. Most amazing thing! You know how often I get an offer like
that. And I said there was nowhere I wanted to go, so we'd decided
to go to Cloete's Farm."

I went about locking the front of the house, as I had been told.
"What's that?"

"Not a tea place. It's a training farm for young Jews who want
to go to Palestine—or at least it used to be; now we're at war they
secretly train them to use guns."

I nodded. The way he had said "we're at war" drew from me the
momentary silence of respect for one who is involved by allegiance:
it seemed odd to hear him say it; to me, the war between the Jews
and the Arabs and the war in Indonesia were pieces of deplorable-
ness equally remote. "—I must go and tell Anna." He followed me
to the back yard, where, despite the rich autumn warmth with which
the sun brimmed the enclosure of grass and bright, thinning fruit
trees, Anna sat formally in her dim little room with an old black
man in vaguely clerical garb and two fat women who wore shoes
and stockings for Sunday. She ducked out of the dimness, a bossy
figure in the dirty jersey and overalls worn colorless across the behind and frayed over the breasts, in which she would never have
dared appear before my mother. My mother had seen to it that she
had proper false teeth made, and written a note to the dentist so
that she would be fitted with the same care as a white person, but
Anna never wore the bottom plate and had developed the busybody
jaw of a very old man. "Miss Helen?"

When I told her I was going out she looked at Joel as one eyes
an enemy to whom one has not been introduced, and said: "Where
you going?"

"Out with the young master—" I gestured.

"And when you'll be back?" She was shrill; she gave me up,
grumbling. "If the missus she comes, what I'm going to tell her? She
tell me I must stay in, you'll be here—" She ignored the presence
of Joel, hostile in proxy for her mistress. It came to me that perhaps
my mother really did disapprove of and dislike Joel; I had not until

then believed that her uncommunicativeness about him meant anything more than her usual distrust of the unfamiliar.

We left Anna grumbling and went back through the house to the car, Joel stopping a moment in the dark passage to look at an old photograph of a blazered team with my father cross-legged near the trophy. "I thought it was some school thing of yours," said Joel. And added, interested, "Is your father there?" I pointed him out, ashamed, and said: "Come on—" closing the front door finally behind us.

When we were settled in the car, I could see his mood of enthusiasm lying upon him. "Really." He smiled, shaking his head at the dashboard. "It's the strangest way it happened—"

"You look different today," I said. "You look like an Indian, you know."

"Yes, I know I'm black."

"No, an Indian in a hotel we used to go to in Durban. He used to bend over the menu, a really lovely head, such black hair, and a skin that looked liquid, like some kind of metal that had just been poured smoothly over the bones—"

"Right. I'm greasy, too."

"No, I don't mean *that*—" We laughed at the impossibility of getting it clear, and as we turned the corner past the Recreation Hall, I saw a group of young men and girls from the Mine office walking along in their tennis clothes, and waved so warmly that they turned in the road to see whom I was with and I saw the curiosity and blankness with which people recognize, however fleetingly, the set of a stranger's head.

We drove a long way, to where one end of the Reef of gold mines and their attendant towns petered out. Here a low range of hills that lifted your eyes like mountains after the flatness of veld broken only by shaft heads and dumps of yellow sand, hid a deep, gradual ravine. It was as if the earth, ugly, drab, concealing great riches for sixty miles, suddenly regained innocence where it no longer had anything to conceal, and flowered to the surface. All down the inner sides of the ravine low trees and bushes were curly green. At the bottom, where perhaps once a great river had spread, the municipality of the near-by village—it was a real village, not a

Reef town, a village with a peaked church raising a finger, little bridges interrupting the roadway where willows closed over
streams—had built a swimming pool and fenced it in with wire.
This gave the place a name: Macdonald's Kloof, named by Afri-
kaans-speaking farmers after a Scotsman who was connected with it
in some way by local legend. Lorries were parked in the dusty
cleared earth round the fence, and children ran about in makeshift
bathing costumes, shouting in Afrikaans; as usual, there was a
Sunday-school picnic or orphanage treat clustered there.

But the sides of the Kloof remained uncultivated, and people
could climb up leisurely and lose themselves in the scraggly foliage
and the rusty-looking boulders, finding a level to sit in the sun where
it was quiet with the quiet of high places, and the occasional human
voice floating up from below in a scarf of wind sounded more like
the cry of a bird. It was not a beautiful place, but the broken planes
and rather tame wildness that it offered our eyes forever resting on
the level and the treeless, made it seem so to us, or gave us pleasure
by reminding, in its poor way, how beautiful the country could be.
Joel said: "I wouldn't mind being at the Cape, now."

We left the car at the bottom and clung and slithered up. The
dry season was beginning, and although the leaves were still fleshy
and bright, the barks of the trees were scaly as the lichened rocks,
and warm dust fluffed round our feet and seemed part of the sunlight. It was a dust that smelled of eucalyptus and now and then of
some mauvish herb-bush that reverberated with bees. We grunted
as we pulled each other up, breathing earnestly. "What are you
looking for?" he asked. "No flowers," I said, disappointed. "—You
should know the Transvaal."

But there was a big lizard, moving off as if a streak of the rock
had liquefied. We stopped and felt disinclined to go on. Lifting our
heads after the concentration on footholds, we came out clear above
the lorries and the children and the valley, clear above half the fall
of treetops. "Ah—hh." Joel was satisfied to sit down on the lizard's
rock, and I sank down, too. He unrolled himself onto his back after
a moment or two and had on his face the strange smile of people
who look up at the sun. Everything seemed to sheer off into the
space, the emptiness; my mind drained clear. The steady winter sun

hunched my shoulders the way the warmth of a low-burning fire does. Then thoughts began to trickle back, unconnected by logic, but by links that I did not inquire or bother to understand. Mary Seswayo at the washbasin: a tingle of feeling toward her; what?— She is a girl, the discovery came, like me. It was not the rather ridiculous statement of an obvious fact, but a real discovery, a kind of momentary dissolving of obvious facts, when the timid, grasping, protesting life of my own organism spoke out, and I recognized its counterpart in her, beneath the beret and my kindness and her acceptance. Then my mother. She would say, "Helen had such a pile of studying to do;—yes, very hard," proud as she could never feel in my presence, with its reminder of all I was not. For a fanciful second I saw her at the braaivleis, tried to turn her face toward me and could not. You are a very clean people, of course. Who said that? Daddy to Joel, the first time. A clean little woman, clean little place, my mother would say seriously; it came before godliness with her. Of course, all Jews are circumcised; but my father hadn't meant that. How embarrassing for Joel if he thought it. . . . But that was months ago. . . .

"Did you ever speak to the girl about her notes?" He spoke suddenly.

"D'y'know, I was just thinking about her!"

"Did you, though?"

"I thought I told you? On Friday. I showed her some other notes—not mine, they're too scrappy—but someone else's I borrowed."

After a moment I said: "She was horribly grateful. I felt like a bossy missionary presenting a Bible to a little savage who has no shoes and chronic hookworm."

"She's going to teach?"

"Of course."

"Helen, what are you going to do?" He knew I planned a librarianship or perhaps some job of vaguely imagined interest in a consulate, but the question cut past that.

"I don't know . . . I sometimes wonder what I'm doing it all for—Other people want to teach . . . and it's not as if I write. All this reading; just for pleasure and curiosity, really."

"Not that. You really have the honest itch to know."

I lay back, too; we spoke dreamily, the kind of parenthetic exchange people have on the edge of sleep. The rock offered us to the sky, Joel Aaron and me, side by side, but not touching. "But what?"

"That's it." He turned the question into an answer, as if it were satisfactory.

"Sometimes I think I should have done social science. . . ."

"You'll take too much in from other people," he said to the sky. "That'll be your trouble. You'll bolt it all. . . ."

I wanted an answer: "I think I should have done social science. I could still do it."

"Helen, perhaps you should get married, I mean sometimes there are women with a kind of—how can I put it—vivid feeling for life. They push it into things that waste it; activities that could run on something colder. So it's lost; they change. Because it's something for between men and women." He became vague: "If you cut it up, parcel it out . . ." He shook his head at himself.

I felt queerly hurt, indignant. It was as if I discovered in the expression of someone's face some defect in myself that I was not aware of. "So that's all you think I'm good for. Married. But I'll marry as well . . ." There was a silence. I said, still half-offended, "Joel, I don't understand you. You've done more than anyone to get me out of my rut—I've always felt we were escaping Atherton together; you understood because you were stuck in it, too, and when I talked to you I found someone who was struggling out of a kind of comfortable mediocrity that I was dimly aware of wanting to break—and that made it possible for me to put my finger on it. I've learned to look, to hear. . . . Now you say a thing like that."

Whatever he had been thinking, he had put it aside, out of my sight. He lifted his head from the rock, straining his neck to smile at me. "It's just the way Jews are. There, it comes out in me, too; we really only want girls to marry.—It's like my Indian hair—You don't lack the brains, my girl, it's not that."

I smiled, as I always did, apologetically, when he became aware of his Jewishness.

"Helen," he said after a pause, "do you mind my being a Jew?"

I sat up, with the smile again. "Why? You know—"

"No." His hand twitched where it lay on the rock. "I mean really. And your people. Does your mother say anything?"

I lay down again. The rock had the comfort of spareness, resisting the spine firmly, like lying on the floor. I said, timidly, "No. Sometimes you make me feel—ginger. Just because you're dark."

"No, even if I were ginger, too, it'd be just the same."

"My mother never says anything. Daddy neither."

There was no answer, and when I twisted my head to look at him, I saw that his eyes were closed.

I was still looking at him when he opened them after quite a long while, and I could see them, veined with the gray and green of stones under water, slowly bringing me into focus after the dark of his eyelids. I had the curious feeling that he saw me as nobody else had ever seen me; like when he had said "Helen of Atherton" on the train that day. We lay a moment, looking at each other, and nothing moved but the very corners of his eyes, where his eyelashes lifted together as if they smiled on their own.

A great bird waved across the sky. The sinking sun spread up a fan of radiance; light sprang about the high air like singing spray.

Still we lay there. I sat up, with my cheek on my knees, and Joel rolled round onto his elbow. With his finger he was tracing out something on the surface of the rock, gently absent. I looked, too. Weather had layered the ancient surface away in a wavering relief. The sidelong glance of the sun caught along the edges, showing them up dark, but within the outline, the warmth of other suns, the wash of rains fallen and sucked up, fallen and sucked up, endlessly, was fixed with delicate, smudged color: ocher into green, rose into gray.

"A map," Joel was saying. He spoke out of the sky, yet his voice was human; it was lost to the dust, the rocks, the dusty bushes with their little pebbles of animal droppings, like an offering, left under the leaves, but it came to me. I should have heard it even if he had not spoken: the way creatures of the same kind instinctively communicate their identity of presence when they are lost in the enormousness of landscape and sky.

"Here's a continent, and provinces—the biggest river. There the mountain range, and the sea. An ocean. Some islands . . . And a

long way"—his finger traveled the seas—"another country. This is
a small one, latitude due north, a cold one. Snow and seals on this
rocky coast, but down here—just about here, the dolphins begin.
Here's a whole group of islands, with a warm current wrapped round
them, so they're the coconut-palm kind. The people sing (you would
find out that they've got hookworm) and they sail about—all over
here—in the hollowed-out barks of trees, with figureheads like ugly
sea monsters. Over this side is a huge, rich country, an Africa and
America rolled into one, with a bit of Italy thrown in for charm—"

He made up the world, and threw into it all the contradictions,
the gradations and clashes of race and face and geography, rear-
ranged to suit ourselves; but it seemed that the physical plan of it,
a trial universe idly scratched down by season and chemical in a
time before time when the world was actually taking shape, sinking
and rising from the sea, exploding volcanically, shifting in land-
slides, really was preserved there on the rock: an abandoned cosmos,
the idle thought of a god. . . .

Joel paid me the tribute of making a game out of it for me, but
there was a tinge of wonder to it. We played with the discovering
pleasure of children, ignored and watched by the Kloof and the sky.
Quite suddenly, but with authority, the Kloof's own shadow fell upon
us. Enough, it decreed. It had closed like an eyelid over the sun.
The rock faded; we felt our elbows and hipbones sore. Under the
shadow, that was a little chill, but missed the treetops so that they
remained alight in the sun, we came down. Joel's warm brown hand
helped me; below every rock he waited, the hand, palm up, receiving
me. Its warmth in my own had the comfort of a renewed contact; yet
we had not touched each other up on the rock. I felt a vague sadness
that was not unhappy. I did not know why. . . . We were coming
down the side of the hill like two people who have kissed and held
each other. The elderly Afrikaner packing rugs and empty beer bottles into the boot of his car looked up and saw us that way. We
walked past the bitten-out rinds of watermelon, the eggshells and
torn paper, back to the car.

Something had stuck to my shoe—"Just a minute—" I held on
to the door handle of the car, balancing on one leg, laughing.

"Here"—Joel snapped off a twig and pried at the mess on my heel. It fell away and it was a rubber contraceptive, perished and dust-trodden, relic of some hurried encounter behind the trees, inconsequent and shabby testimony. But between us at this moment it was like a crude word, suddenly spoken aloud. In dismay more than embarrassment, we ignored the happening, jumped quickly into the car. Joel, encouraging the reluctant kick-over of the engine, his hand over the gear knob, the frown with which men pay attention to engines drawing down his eyebrows, was my reassurance. The finger of disgust had hovered, but could not make its smudge on us. Again, I did not know why.

Joel began talking of his plans with the cut-and-dried assessment of the future with which people eye their lives after some decision has been made, something has become clear. It was as if he said: Ah, well—and deliberately turned to what remained to be maneuvered, what was malleable, obedient. "If I could get a job in London for say a year—" He was talking of post-graduation. "Then I could walk, hitchhike back, over Europe, down Italy . . ." —Yet I had the feeling he was thinking of something else.

"You'd want to come back?"

"Yes . . . Sooner or later, everyone gets the feeling he wants to come back. I don't know why it should be, for people like us, really: no roots in the real Africa—you can't belong to the commercial crust thrown up by the gold mines. If you look at it honestly, my roots in the land must be away somewhere in a place I've never seen or known, where my parents come from. In Latvia. Or somewhere else, even further back. That's where they must be"—he smiled—"though I can't say I feel them. I was born here, right. But on the surface, on the superimposed Africa, this rickety thing, everybody's makeshift Europe. These Reef towns are hardly more than putting up a shack and making it look like home in some other country. And then the temporary dwelling becomes permanent, is thirty or forty years old (Atherton must be about that? When did the coal mines open up—1900?) and never loses its makeshift character. Our little six-story skyscrapers in Atherton, our little bit of makeshift

America—they're made of reinforced concrete but they look like shoe boxes. It's hardened into the character of the place—contemporary makeshift."

"I belong to it, too; I'm only a second-generation South African.—You mean people who're descended from the 1820 settlers—people whose great-grandfathers trekked, and so on . . . ?"

He nodded as he drove. "Anyone who's lived directly out of the land; even one generation. If my people had come out here and farmed; if I'd been born on the land that'd be different."

I had never thought of it: "Never occurred to me that I might not belong in that way."

He smiled. "I think about it often. It comes up whenever I think of going away, and coming back to Africa. . . . I correct myself; not Africa, 129 Fourth Street, Atherton."

"You won't go on living here, that's certain," I said, thinking of myself.

"Well, not quite Atherton, I don't suppose. Helen, come and have supper with us? Your people won't be back till late." Again there was something disconnected, smothered, about the way he spoke, though the words came out ordinary enough; it was as if he had suddenly swerved back through the distraction of his own talk. Yet the look in which he held me seemed to stay any response, keeping me in that sad-happy mood, a kind of self-hypnosis, that falls like a trick of the light on people who are young, sensual, and still in the state where life is imagined and apprehended rather than lived. I smiled, that was all.

"Are you sure?" I questioned inconvenience, but had already taken my acceptance for granted.

"Better get some milk on the way," said Joel, remembering a chronic Sunday-night shortage. He stopped at the first corner Greek shop when we reached Atherton, and smiled at me through the plate glass as he stood inside waiting to be served. Even in the car, there was a companionable silence that seemed to be of his making; I waited for him to come back. The blinds were down over the pavements: Garter's THE Tobacconist, Wedding Gifts and Novelties for all Occasions; B.B. Bazaar, 3d. 6d. 1/–; Suliman Ismail Patel, Grocery, Provisions, Fancy Goods; Paris Modes for Latest in High-Class

Ladies Wear. And in the empty sawdust arena of the butcher's shop, a striped fat cat sat like an owl in the window. A woman with an arm about each of two little girls whose skinny legs gave them the look of walking on tiptoe moved slowly along the shop fronts; a way behind, the father in the miner's Sunday white shirt and blazer came along without interest. One of the little girls broke away. "Oooh, Pappie, ek hou van daardie—" She skipped between the mother and father, in love with something she had seen in a window. "That's the one I want—" She used a mixture of English and Afrikaans to express the delight of her desire. The mother and father turned their heads blankly above her, neither responding nor refusing, as if her pleasure were something complete and dependent upon them or circumstance neither for denial nor gratification. It was something she would grow out of, as they had grown out of all expectation; they were placid in that.

"—D'you know what's wrong with Atherton?" I grumbled to Joel as he came back. "Not one splendid thing about it. Every place should have one splendid thing—a fountain, one building, a wide street, even. We haven't even got a real tree."

"Poor old Atherton," he said affectionately.

As soon as I walked into the Aarons' house I saw that Sunday-night supper was an occasion with them. They were all already at table, under the bright yellow lights that were used in every room, high up on the ceiling, glittering on the shabbiness, the peeled, stained, worn or tawdry. Joel's sister Colley and her husband were there, with their nine-year-old girl, and an old relation who looked like Mr. Aaron and was given the courtesy title of Auntie. There was another relation, a very thin old man whose flesh was knotted and twisted stringily over his features and his hands, and who, as he stared at us when we came into the room, looked as if he were going to whistle, because his mouth had sucked in over toothlessness.

"I told Helen we'd have enough supper for her," said Joel, flourishing me in.

But no one took up his tone. Mrs. Aaron got up in some bewilderment, pushing the others along, urging them to make room (she snatched up the cutlery in front of the thin old man and moved it

for him) and began apologizing dubiously: "Will you eat a piece of
nice brisket? I'm sorry, I haven't got something . . . A piece of
chicken, if I had . . . —Joel, what's about I make a piece of had-
dock . . . ?"

The father, who had been talking animatedly over a mouthful,
died out and, not taking much notice, nodded at me, looked about
as if he thought he should move, but left it to the others. While the
adjustments were being made he hunched sullenly over his plate,
now and then grunting for pickles or salt. The sister, Colley, smiled,
signaling to establish the ease of contemporaneity in the old-
fashioned parental atmosphere, and her husband, not quite happy
in the fat that begins to build up round many young Jewish men
when they are thirty-five and in business, nodded a conventional
acknowledgment, more for Joel than for me: I was young once myself, with an eye for Gentile girls. . . . Joel and I were seated between
him and the aunt. The table was spread with an untidy abundance
of delicatessen foods, mostly things I had seen in shops, but never
eaten: my parents had a horror of what they called "made-up" foods
and we always ate simple, fresh things, home-cooked; on Sunday
evenings we had ham-and-tomato sandwiches, eaten with milk (beer
for my father) on the veranda in summer, or with cocoa before the
fire in winter. Mrs. Aaron did not seem to sit down again at all,
although everyone kept urging her: "What'sa matter with you, why
do you keep running about?" "For goodness' sake, Mommie—"
"What *is* it"—and was now out in the passage at the refrigerator,
now pushing past the backs of our chairs with some new offering.
Horse-radish sauce and fish paste filled up the few empty spaces
on the tablecloth. Not all the attention was for me; she pressed a
confusion of tastes on her grandchild, and when the little girl accepted something, bent over and pressed the child's round cheek to
her side: "Oh, she's a lovely girl! Oh, bless her!"

The aunt showed the formal overtures of the intensely curious.
If Joel's mother and father drew away into a shell at the sight of me,
she was the kind that bristled out. There were touches of worldliness
about her; her body, of the homely shape of Mrs. Aaron, was corseted, and she wore an American teen-ager's brooch that was something between a mouse and a rabbit, where I would have expected

to find a cameo. "Go on——" She offered sardines, still holding the mold of the tin. Her eyes were carefully turned away from me, giving a pained look to her weighty cheek. She gestured with her mouth full; when she had swallowed she said to Joel, drawing back from me: "The young lady, your . . . perhaps she wants a tomato? Lily, haven't you got such a thing as a tomato?"

"But you had——?"

"Well, it's finished. Five or six people, y'know; it doesn't go so far." There was the inference that she knew how to do things. "The young lady—you must excuse me, I didn't catch the name. . . ." It was true I had not been introduced to those who had not already met me before; there was the feeling that I was known indirectly, through discussion.

Joel waved it away, as though he were clearing a troublesome fly from my plate. "All right. We'll have beetroot instead. Colley, ask Ma for the beetroot——"

The awkwardness of my being there did not melt; it became accepted. The table re-formed itself, irresistibly, over me, the room itself took up again the sounds and gestures of people talking and eating that belonged there with Sunday night. There was the feeling that perhaps they should not talk in front of me—not that there was anything said too personal for me to hear, but out of half-shyness, half-irritation. Between them and me was uncertain ground; they did not know what would be familiar and normal to me, and what strange; among more sophisticated and less genuine people, there would have been little joking remarks made to me about the food, and one or two unusual habits, such as the old relative's way of sweetening his tea by sucking it up through a spoonful of jam, might have been explained, forcing me into the position of a tourist. But as it was, their naturalness came in gusts that swept over me and made them forget all these considerations. I remained, ignored but intact. Now and then in a drop in the talk, I would appear, like a stranger in the parting of a crowd; their forgetful, vivacious exchange of food and talk faltered—and then someone would ask a question that set them off again.

Only the thin old man, receding from all that was immediate except the food before him on his plate, was as vague about my presence as about that of anyone who had not belonged to the clear hard times of the Russian village he had left forty years before; when he saw the faces of Mrs. Aaron or her husband, brightness came into his small eyes (they were two tears on his face) like recognition in the face of an old dog. But I was no more alien to him than all the other sons and daughters whom he was supposed to know.

At last Mrs. Aaron had wedged herself back into the circle and was spreading a mess of gray wet fish (it was marinated herring) on a roll. Sometimes her uncertain eye fell upon me, not hostile, but with an uneasy appraisement in passing: Do you really want to be here? The family evidently had been to a party that afternoon, and she called out to Joel with real pleasure: "What a lovely affair. Really very nice."

"Did you stay late?"

"They wouldn't let us go. I'm telling you, we still could have been there."

Her daughter reproached her: "Why didn't you stay? Couldn't we have eaten at home for once?"

The old woman smiled and shrugged at the unthinkable. "Joel, what does it mean, an F.R.C . . . ? After the wedding, the young couple's going to England, he's going to study something else there . . . I don't know."

"F.R.C.S., Fellow of the Royal College of Surgeons. Is Maurice's girl nice?"

"Pretty girl," said the aunt. "No question."

Mr. Aaron roused from his food. "Maurice's a fine boy." He shook his head in fatherly pride that such a person could exist, no blood of his own, but a matter for pride that he, closely confined to interest in the welfare of his own family, only knew how to show as a fatherly reaction.

No, it was not merely that. They were proud of this boy, whoever he might be, because he was one of themselves: they all broke in, in a hesitant enthusiasm that at once generated its own spontaneity.

"Already he's got a partnership. Mrs. Marks, you know, his mother's sister—she was sitting next to me and she was telling me. . . ."

"No, it's the promise of a partnership when he comes back. Now

he's just working with Dr. Bailey, but even then, it's very good—
he's only twenty-two. . . ." —Joel's sister offered facts that seemed
corrective but were actually the wonder which she could not allow
herself to express with the simple awe of the old and ignorant, but
could not altogether forbear. "He was always a clever boy." The
father brushed aside aggressively. He had a hoarse, coarse voice,
as if the words caught on invisible snags.

"No question, no question." The aunt's throat trembled with
praise. "And didn't they work hard enough to give it to him? Mrs.
Berman built up that business. I remember when the children were
little things, she used to be there, running between the shop and
the house."

Mr. Aaron ignored her, particularly when she agreed with him.
To Mrs. Aaron's face there came, quickly, slightly, a smile like the
drop of a pause. "Well," she excused in a low voice, as if covering
over some breach of taste with weary sympathy, "it's nothing, everyone knows Meyer got no brains. It's all right, what she did, she
did. Plenty others the same."

The aunt whipped the talk back to enthusiasm again. "Anyway,
today they've got pleasure from their children, thank God."

Mrs. Aaron smiled. "Really, a wonderful boy," she said, as if
she were in love.

"The fiancée's a research chemist—I think she's from Capetown," Colley was telling Joel.

"I don't know what. But they'll go everywhere, they'll be in Europe, they'll do what they like. . . ." Mrs. Aaron, sawing off another
slice of bread in answer to some unintelligible sounds from the old
relative, was defiant with the freedom of the two young people. Her
body woke up to the swiftness it might have had. "Here." She gestured the bread on the point of her fork. "Anybody else wants?"

"Joel," said the aunt, with the coy smile of someone venturing
a question she pretends not to remember having asked several times
before. "I wonder why you didn't study doctor. You know, I often say—"

"He could have done it. Just the same as Maurice." Mr. Aaron
—he reminded me of some heavy, thick-skinned animal, a rhinoc-
eros or boar, rising reluctantly and powerfully to the prick of

words—flew into an aggressive assurance, staring at Joel. "You could have been like Maurice?"

"Of course. I know." Joel spoke to him with assurance of another kind. "You let me do what I wanted. I'm not sorry."

"There you are! It just shows you," said the aunt, not saying what.

"He'll also go to Europe, to America," Mrs. Aaron said. "No, no, sit down—" She gestured her daughter, going round to gather the dirty plates herself.

"Was Hilda Marks at the party, Ma?" Colley wiped her child's mouth with the firm, hard movements of a cat's tongue.

"No, I told you, only her mother."

"I hear they've got a stand near ours, they've started building already."

"Is that so?"

"You're going to build a house?" Again I had the feeling that the aunt's surprise was feigned; she was one of those women who so intensely enjoy the affairs of others that they can savor being told a dozen times and versions, by a dozen different people. I felt quite sure she already knew the answer to her query. "Where?"

Colley's irritated smile confirmed my suspicion. "But surely you knew? I mean we bought the ground from Dave . . . and I'm sure he would be the first to run and tell you."

"My dear, unless you tell me yourself, it's not for me to say I know." She turned to Mrs. Aaron, more at ease. "Where's it, here in the township?"

Mrs. Aaron drew her mouth up and shook her head. "Here? What for? Who lives here now? It's in a lovely neighborhood, you know there by the dam, open—"

Her daughter supplied the name of the new suburb, an English county name that the estate agent had taken from an overseas magazine.

"But it's so near the mine dump, there, isn't it? Mrs. Friedman would have bought there, only she told me the dump's stuck in middle . . ."

So they bridled and argued, their voices rose and fell, cutting one across the other, and tea came round, already poured out into the cups in the kitchen and slopping over into the saucers. It reminded me of my mother, for whom this served as a standard for hotels and people; if she got her tea served in her own teapot, then the hotel was a real hotel and not a glorified boardinghouse, the woman whom she was visiting was at least a social equal by personal habit—the most reassuring and revealing gauge. Telepathically, Joel said to me: "Aren't you going to phone? They might be home by now, and wondering." I excused myself—nobody heard me—and went to the telephone, which was in the passage, fixed to the wall, as in a public call box. I had not put the light on, and only the wash from the light room where they all sat made watermarks along the nobbly linoleum. I could hear their voices and the click and clatter of the table, while down the telephone, I heard the bell ringing in my mother's house; heard it as I did from my own room. It stopped. My mother's voice said challengingly, faint: "Hullo?"

"Mummy—"

"Daddy was getting worried. Where are you?"

"Have you been back long? I'm sorry. Didn't Anna tell you?"

"Something about you'd gone out with a young man, but it's half-past nine—" Her voice became muffled, she had turned away from the mouthpiece; then came clear again. "No, that was Daddy.—What? I don't know.—He says did you take the key."

"No, it's under the sword fern on the stoep."

"All right. The big one or the new one?"

"The old one."

"I've put away something for you. We didn't feel like having any more to eat."

"It's all right, I'm having supper here."

"Supper? Where?"

"At Joel's. With the Aarons."

"With the *Aarons*?" There was a pause.

"Did you enjoy the braaivleis? How are the Mackenzies?"

"Very nice," she said, without attention. "How will you get in when you come home—?" It was a voice ignoring a profession of taste that simply could not be understood; not condemned, but quite incomprehensible.

"Leave the key for me where I put it before."

"All right, then——"

"I won't be late," I weakened. But our voices had crossed; she said good-by and hung up.

I stood there a moment. On a small table under the telephone was the outline of a vase of paper flowers, crazily angular with the look of lifeless things, even in the half-dark. I touched one out of curiosity or compassion for the ugliness I could not see, and a smell of dust came away with my hand. The refrigerator shook away at the top of the passage. There was a different smell about the narrow place, like the passage outside the bedrooms of an old country hotel where you have stopped for one night.

I went back into the living room and nodded to Joel under the talk. "Rubbish! Rubbish!" Colley's husband was shouting. "They couldn't do without us here, and they know it. Think Malan doesn't know it?"

"Nothing's indispensable in South Africa but the Chamber of Mines and native labor." Joel smiled.

They ignored him. "Look at medicine, law—even the farmers. The whole economy would collapse."

"But that's what they say, Max, that's what they say. The Jews in everything, they don't want it. . . ."

The women were clearing the table, and when it was done the older people remained sitting round it, arms resting on the scratched and ringed surface, under the beat of the light. The mother and father sat with their hands loosely in front of them, the way people do who do not read or amuse themselves in their leisure, but take it as inactivity between labor and labor. Joel was kneeling with the little girl over her collection of sample breakfast foods and patent medicines, spread on the carpet.

The business of eating, which in common with a crisis or danger brings heterogenous incompatibles comfortably together, was over and now suddenly we were all fallen apart. The heaviness, the sense of patiently waiting for me to be gone so that they could resume their life, came over the old Aarons again as I had noticed it when I had been in their house at other times. No one seemed to have anything to say. Mrs. Aaron got up and fetched a dish of preserves from the sideboard; but everyone turned his head away. Even Joel

was silent, stretched on the floor with his head against a little stool
with a broken riem seat; it seemed that sometimes he was aware of
me, and sometimes he was aware of them, but never was he present
to all of us together.

I sat alone on the sofa, smiling when someone smiled at me.

Soon he got up suddenly, and raised his eyebrows at me. I said
my good-bys and thanks and in an atmosphere of sterile politeness,
we left, our footsteps very loud on the boards behind us.

Joel drove me home. It seemed to me it was because I was tired,
with that sense of tiredness that keeps one floating just above the
surface of reality, but we did not speak. In place of communication
there was between us a speechless ease that I have never forgotten.
It was as if we had ducked through a crowd and found ourselves
alone in a small quiet place.

When the car died out quiet at our gate under the pines, he sat
a moment. I said, "Good night . . . ," gently, to rouse him, and he
looked up slowly, coming awake.

"Don't come in," I said. And then: "I'll be all right."

He nodded. Smiled, waiting for me to go.

I got out, but a curious sensation overcame me, a physical sensation of distress prickling over my skin. I stood with a kind of
helplessness on the muffled feel of thick pine needles. I felt with
distress that there was something that I must say now; no, that there
was something that had passed unsaid, and that now was too late.
. . . A great bird waves across the sky: look!—but you have not
seen it; when you lifted your head it was gone. Something in me
clutched: What is it? What is it?

It was dark; Joel could not see my face. There was a moment
when we both waited.

I said: "I've got the drawings . . . ," held them up.

The feeble commonplace flung across a bridge. "Good night,"
we said, warmly, gently. And by the time I reached the porch door
I heard the car, gone.

As I took the key from under the fern and let myself into our
house, with the silence and scents and disposition of furniture that
flowed into me with the sense of an animal feeling its way back into
its own nest, the urgency that had cut me off in pain began to melt,

to flow away in my blood like a clot that dissolves. Yet I was weak, empty with the relief. It had been, I thought suddenly, as I took off my clothes, put on a nightgown that slid loosely over my body, as if I had been told without warning that I was never going to see someone again. A hollow premonition of loss.

And how ridiculous, since I should see Joel on Tuesday morning, and in any case, he would be the sort of friend one would have all one's life.

15 I DID SEE HIM AGAIN on Tuesday, and for many other Tuesdays.

A whole year passed, unremarkable, one of those periods of consolidation in change when one is growing and filling out into the spaces of a life the shape of which has been set but not yet seen: the time will come to stop short, and look, up and around at the walls, the ceilings, the staircases leading from here to there, that one has built around oneself out of daily dabs of mud. Or the year was like a ship; inside it seems much the same town you have always lived in—restaurants, shops, the hairdresser, the cocktail bar and the library. But beneath the patterned carpet oceans are moving past your feet; and you yourself have determined this with a ticket you bought months back.

I continued to travel in and out of Johannesburg to the University. I did my work with pleasure, if a certain lack of conviction. The vague, luring promise of childhood persisted, like a whiff of smoke on the horizon, become now the uninvestigated idea that, since the need was there, something would come to coil up my energies like a spring. I should find the people and the life where all that was in me would be released into action. Joel still said to me sometimes: Any ideas? Thought about what you're going to do? But now I always replied, rather tartly: You remember—I'm going to get married.

Through him I continually met people who seemed to me to put a finger of confirmation on my vague sense of promise. A girl and her husband, both medical students, who talked proudly, with what was almost a sense of adventure, about the clinic they were going to set up in one of the squatters' townships of African workers outside Johannesburg; another girl who talked of nothing but the literacy campaign on which she was working among the thousands of "wash-Annies" and cookboys and houseboys who had never been to school at all; the young man who was a journalist on a conservative paper but spent most of his leisure helping the gentle, revolutionary-minded wife of a University professor to bring out a liberal weekly that didn't pay.

And, of course, Joel himself. But Joel's commitment was not so easily nor so satisfactorily defined. Joel's raison d'être eluded one. To borrow the definitions of faith, if the others were monotheistic in their grasp of life, he was pantheistic. He worked at his architecture with enthusiasm and a detached seriousness—there were plans about that: an experiment in mass-produced cottages for Africans he was working on privately with the progressive Town Engineer of one of the Reef towns, and that might come to something. The tentative offer of a particularly interesting job with an architect (a friend of his who had been with UNRRA in Europe and now wanted to go back and take Joel walking with him through France and Italy) in Rhodesia. And, most tempting, the chance he might get to work under one of England's most original and brilliant men on a reconstruction project in London.

All these things he kept calmly in consideration. And yet at the same time he sometimes spoke, with the practical evaluation of plans and not the dash and sweep of dreams, of joining his mother's brother on a recently acquired citrus farm, or working only part time as an architect when he qualified, so that he could go back to the University to do a course on soil conservation. Looking back on it now, I can see that he could have done any of these, or perhaps several at different times in his life, and that if one had failed he would not, like so many other people, have been lost, because his sense of his own potentialities was so broadly based, and his aliveness was not confined to any narrow aspect, but to the whole of aliveness itself: with everything that grew, that inquired, that illuminated instead of merely perpetuating the human state.

Of course, this did not seem so to me then. I only saw that Joel stood in many rooms, talked or lapsed into the silence of familiar understanding with many different people, but belonged, somehow, not with one group or the other, but with them all. This amounted in the end to belonging only to himself; a puzzling position that was quite the opposite of loneliness. Often he introduced me to a little circle by which I was taken up so that a friendship was formed from which he was excluded and they became my friends rather than his. Yet he did not seem to mind. He almost literally stood at the door of interest, diversion, stimulation, and watched me go in: quietly, inwardly ablaze with pleasure and curiosity.

Most of these people moved in or about the fringe of the life of the University, though many had never been students there. Whatever the diversity of their true interests, or the variation of their sincerity, they had one common condition: all were young people who had overflowed the group, race or class to which they belonged. The sons of Jewish merchants who wanted to paint instead of make money, the daughter of a Nationalist farmer who worked for the establishment of native trade-unions, the boy who incurred all the scorn of a country of tough pioneer stock turned tougher business-men because he wanted to dance in the ballet, the fiercely intellectual young Afrikaans poets who had more in common with Baudelaire than Paul Kruger—they formed the only society where all the compartments of South African life ran into one another. Even the barbed wire of wealth was down; the sons of the poor found that a certain lack of money was honorable, the sons of the rich escaped the confines of luxury. Loosely attached to the arts and learning at one end, and to politics and social reform at the other, this society is a common phenomenon all over the world. The important difference was that in South Africa, a young, fanatically materialist country with virtually no tradition of literature or art, and, in the problem position of a white minority predominant over a black majority, a socio-political preoccupation that is closer to obsession than to mild academic discussion, this society had far greater responsibility than its counterparts in older countries. Lopsided—tethered to a thin line of culture from Europe on one side, dragged down toward an enormous, weighty racial tangle on the other—they had only the tantalization of recorded music, imported books, reproductions of pictures; but ate, slept, worked and breathed in the presence of the black man, like the child's monster of inherited guilt always at his back. The desires to which these facts gave rise consequently tended to be even more confused than those of young people in other countries, so that a young man's passionate eagerness to win the music he was denied hearing in the comfortable torpidity of his home jumped like a little flame from a grass stalk to a great, dry crackling mass of a whole nation of black people denied so much that *he* had taken for granted. So, if his social conscience was not pure, if in some other country where his parents' money and cultural standards would have been more equitable he would not have concerned himself with the cry of the dispossessed, in South Africa a quick sympathy from his own small struggle struck out and identified itself with the vast one. There were many others like him, who, wanting something for themselves, suddenly found understanding for the yawning want of the Africans—not the clamor of the few leaders and rebellious papers who were articulate for them, but the plain, unremarked want of food, of clothes, of houses, of recognition and friendship that was silently in the thousands of ordinary black people who went about the life of the city.

Of course, this society which excited me much and quite impartially was made up to a large extent of people for whom it was only a stage in the process of becoming placid, conventional citizens. As you have to be fish before fetus, so for a time they were liberal before conformist. They flirted a little with the vague stirrings of a sense of beauty, just as the fetus remembers a prehuman life in the sea, and then put away the Bach *Chaconne* and the Mozart *Mass* like toys outgrown, and turned to the real business of having babies and bridge afternoons. They put Balzac and Dante and Martin Buber where they looked impressive in the bookcase, and became family men concentrated on the fluctuations of the stock exchange and the relative merits of Buicks and Cadillacs. Men and women, when they reached forty-five, they would sometimes like to mention that they had gone in for that sort of thing once; they had also had measles or mumps and had at one time thought of going on the stage—this with a kind of helpless, satisfied smile at the children produced and the elegant house apparently grown up round them as unavoidably as a tortoise grows its shell.

They were unimportant. So were a great many others, who would never be writers, never be painters, never bring the legitimate stage to South Africa, or dance at Sadler's Wells, although they lived, talked and worked in what they believed was the manner of people who did these things. In fact, this set of eager, intense, earnest and gay people consisted mainly of the intelligent pseudo, the hangers-on who at the time were quite indistinguishable from the few who were something: the few who were of them and in their midst and were in reality to become the writers, the painters, the actors, the dancers and even the leaders all believed themselves to be.

I do not think there was anything at the time to suggest that Leo Castle, the dark boy with the spotty forehead (he was working as a window dresser in a department store then, and ate the wrong food irregularly), had any more chance of becoming a ballet dancer instead of a window dresser who danced in the chorus of visiting musical-comedy shows once a year than his friend John Frederic, who did the same. Yet a year or two later he was dancing *Comus* in London, and *The Rake's Progress* in New York, and in time a little book about him came out, showing him invested with all the satyr-like beauty of the male dancer at his best, in the company of people like Balanchine and Fonteyn. And Isa Welsh, always talking to some young man, with the tip of her tongue touching the corners of her mouth now and then as if she were a bashful adolescent.—Who would have believed that the book she was supposed to be writing would get finished and that she would divorce Tom and become one of the four or five important writers, writing intensely indigenous South African books from the self-imposed exile of England, America or Italy. Or Phil Hersh, wearing the same rather fluffy beard and haggard slouch as André, William Otter, or Hugo Uys; who would have marked him out for the painter of an epic of Africa as shocking and famous as Picasso's "Guernica"?

I have said that all the barriers were down, and so saying have slipped into a South African habit of thought more national than any ideology; more difficult to outgrow than love or loyalty.

—I spoke as if European society were all of Africa. I spoke with

the subconscious sense of the whole overwhelming Bantu race, waiting in submission outside the concepts of the white man. I spoke
from our house on Atherton Mine, with Anna in her room in the
back yard.

Among these people with whom I moved, the last great barrier
was not down in the practical sense. How could it be? But it was
coming down in their heads, an expansion in them was bursting
through it. And even when it was achieved in the mind, in the moral
sense and the sense of dignity, there remained the confusing pull
of habit and use as well as the actual legal confines.

We were all like sleepers, coming awake from a long lull of
acceptance. I know that I, who for all my childhood had lived surrounded by natives who simply attended our lives in one function
or another—Anna, the gardenboys, above all, the stream of bare-.
breasted underground workers between the Compound and the shaft
of the Mine—found with a real consciousness of strangeness and
wonderment that I was beginning to think of them as individually
human. They had passed before me almost as remote if not as interesting as animals in a zoo. I would not have been physically
unkind to them because it was part of the strict pride of my up-
bringing that civilized people—what my parents would call "nice"
people—were smug in their horror of squashing so much as a bug.
If a hungry native came to our door, he was given food or even a
sixpence. "At least *they* can't go and spend it in a bar," my mother,
who would not give money to white tramps for this reason, would
say. Anna, who by qualification of long years of working for us, was
known as being "almost like a white person," might be granted some
concern over her family, but as a general rule, emotion was denied
them and personal relationships were suspect. They have half-a-
dozen husbands; every girl off the street's a "sister."—So they were
casually denied love, jealousy, concern; everything that made us
human. They were also denied entertainment (no swimming pools,
libraries, radios), friendship—"I won't have *my* back yard made into
a location," Atherton women boasted. "I've told her, no friends hanging about the room, you can meet them outside if you want them"
—and personal pride: we children would be called out to be amused
by the sight of the servant going out dressed up in her Sunday

best.—In fact, everything that made our human state pleasant. And
we white children had grown up innocently accepting and perpetuating this until now, when slowly we began to turn on ourselves,
slowly we began to unravel what was tightly knit in us, to change
the capacity of our hearts, the cast of our sense of humor, the limits
of our respect. It was as painful and confusing as the attempt to
change what has grown up with the flesh always is. And unlike the
analyst, prizing down for the significant incident on which the com-
plex and the cure are based, we could not triumph and say: There
—it was everywhere, in the memory and the eye, the hand and the
laugh.

It had begun for me with Joel and Mary Seswayo; I did not know
which. Now when, the second or third time I went to the Welshs'
flat, Isa said, "Would that African girl of yours like to come along
next time, d'you think?" I felt as I did so often in the slightly uncomfortable, impermanent-looking homes of these young people, a
sudden sense of my own climate blowing upon me. The way someone
from an American city or a Scandinavian seaport comes in the
course of a summer cruise to some unimportant little foreign island
he has never heard of before and suddenly recognizes the warm
breath off the beach more deeply than the streets of Chicago or
Copenhagen. "Or do you think music'd be a bit much for her?"

The high English laugh of Jenny Marcus sailed out, a girl commanding attention in the pinkness and assertion of shape and flesh
that sometimes precedes the ugly stage of pregnancy quite daz-
zlingly. "It's all right for you, Isa, you haven't got a servant. Whenever John wants to bring Nathoo Ram home for dinner I have to let
Hilda go off. And he's only an Indian, that's not so bad. But the
next day I always feel her looking at me in contempt; she knows
he's been there. Nothing infuriates your own servant more than the
idea that you've lowered yourself to eat with a non-European."

"And Nathoo Ram, too." Her husband turned his head from his
own talk. "I always see him look anxiously into the kitchen and see
with relief old Jen battling there. . . ."

"Well, I'll ask her—" I said to Isa.

A little man of twenty-four behind curly balding hair and glasses
thick as bottle ends, said: "It's a confusion of social and color bar-

riers, surely? To Africans, if you entertain an African, you're entertaining a houseboy or a cook. You see? Nathoo Ram's not a lawyer,
he's the vegetable hawker known by the generic of 'Sammy.'" But
the young man was someone whom Isa "allowed" to be in her flat,
one of those persons who fail to catch the imagination and so to
whom no one listens. They ignored from him suggestions that, coming from someone else, would have provoked an evening's wrangling.
Now they were already talking of something else. He was left, as
often, with the subject on his hands, discarded just when he had
something to say on it. I should have liked to have heard him further,
because what he had begun to say was a change of focus of the kind
that interested me. But he was not interested in carrying on for me;
already he was sitting silent and following the zigzag swerve of their
new discussion with the quick eyes of a fan at a tennis match.

"Aren't we going to hear the Couperin?" John Marcus was asking
from among the records. Only his wife seemed to hear him, and
pulled a face at him across the room. With a tremendous shrug he
put the record down and squatted at her side. She bent, hanging
her hair over their faces, and they whispered and laughed into each
other's ears and necks. Her mouth changing and her eyes crinkling
with the look of someone being tickled, she looked out into the room
but took no notice of it while he cupped his hand round her ear and
she kept screwing up her face and saying, What? *What?*

I was still being talked about by two people behind me. Or rather
my acquaintance with Mary Seswayo was being used by the re-
sourcefulness of Edna Schiller to illustrate her Communist argument. She was a good-looking Jewess with an intensely reasonable
manner and eyebrows that raised up a little at their inner limits,
inquiringly, like the puffy eyebrows of a puppy. Her attractive
clothes and the large collection of earrings that she wore seemed an
abstraction; you could not imagine her among hairpins and lipstick,
choosing which she would wear, before a mirror. There was the
feeling that somebody else dressed her. It was the same with the
young man she had with her, a handsome young American who
despite a yellow pull-over and a pair of veldschoen had his big head
and neck set with the dummylike perfection of Hollywood. Some
other Edna must find time for him, too.

Now she was talking of me as if I were not in the room at all. "She befriends this girl, but what does it mean?—Like you and your sports grounds and recreation centers and sewing classes. A waste of effort on charity. That's all it is, a useless palliative charity, useless in the historical sense. It's damaging, even. The simple African who is not yet politically conscious is lulled into another year or so of accepting things as they are—"

"But this native girl probably is politically conscious. She's seeking education, and the two go together. She may be one of the potential leaders you people are always looking for."

Edna, once she had discovered the shortest distance from any subject to her own—and she had only one—was not to be deflected. "Unlikely. She will become a teacher and a bourgeoise and feel herself a little nearer to the whites instead of closer to the blacks. African leaders will come from the people."

"Funny, in practice I thought that revolutionary leaders had usually come from the middle class?"

There was a groan from a young man lying on the divan near them. "For Christ's sake, don't start that. . . ."

"What it amounts to, then, is that you don't approve of ordinary, nonpolitical friendship between black and white individuals?"

"Approve, nothing," said Edna, coming forward in her seat. "It's quite immaterial who your friends are, or what color. What I'm saying is, that even if they're black, it's unimportant to the struggle of the blacks against white supremacy."

The young man sat up suddenly, with the dazed look of someone changing too quickly from the horizontal. "Christ, must *everything* be important to the struggle! Can't I sleep with a girl, get drunk . . ." He fell back and muffled his face in the cushion.

Edna used the same degree of intensity to bring home a small point in a casual discussion as she did faced with the defense of a whole doctrine before the snap of a dozen shrewd dissenters. Her zeal released her like liquor and she did not seem to know the rise of her own voice or the persistence of her vehemence. "If people would take a look at what is to be done. The work that a handful of us have to do. You can't tackle it in terms of soup kitchens. But, of course, I suppose people are afraid; can't blame them. But you get used to it, it's amazing. I know my telephone's tapped. Twice last week there was a man asking questions in our building, some excuse about a survey, but we're so used to it now. As Hester Claasen says (Hester Claasen was a trade-union leader of great courage and the cachet of toughness), you can smell a dick a mile off."

Isa, who was easily bored, and so had a reputation for sharpness, came wheeling a tea wagon from the kitchen. "Edna," she asked, bending down to pick up a spoon, "exactly what is it you *do?* I mean, I know you hold meetings and so forth." She stood up looking at Edna with a rather childish expression of simple inquiry.

"*Do,*" said Edna, "how do you mean? One can't answer a question like that offhand. It's difficult to know where to start. Assuming you know what we want to do—"

"Ah, yes," Isa interrupted as if she had suddenly remembered the answer for herself, "I thought so. You sell three dozen copies of the *Guardian* in a native township once a week. Yes, Mike told me, you are pretty good as a newspaperboy, you sell at least three dozen. . . ." And she proceeded to hand round coffee in an assortment of containers from beer mugs to nursery beakers. I got a tarnished silver-plated one, inscribed DOWELL MACLOUD BETTER BALL FOUR-SOME ROYAL JOHANNESBURG CLUB 1926, with an unprintable comment scratched by pin underneath.

"She's intelligent, but she has no grasp whatever of politics, and that infuriates her."—Edna was stirring her coffee and, with a flicker smile at her American, was now asking her companion if she was aware of what was really happening in China, and in the Indies? Like all Edna's questions, it was rhetorical.

"Who's got my dirty mug?" Laurie Humphrey accused Isa.

"What mug?"

"I think I have." I waved it at him.

"Oh, Laurie." Isa held it up, twisting her head to read and slopping the coffee over. "It was the pride of my aunt's mantelpiece."

"You have no Aunt Macloud."

"Well it was the pride of somebody's aunt. We got it in that Claim Street junk shop, near the apfel-strudel place, you know. It was in a job lot that Gerda wanted because of an old straw-covered bottle. Isn't it nice? Everytime I used it I used to see Dowell on his big day, beaming on the green in plus fours with freckles coming out on top of a shiny bald head. Now it looks like an Oscar designed for Henry Miller."

I laughed along with the others, but I could see by the face of the young man on the divan that he knew I didn't know who Henry Miller was. He used it as a small blackmail between us. "Come and share my couch, Titian," he said, "come on." I sat on the end, near his feet, and he studied me. He was the kind who says, Don't tell me—and, appraising you, proceeds to answer his questions for himself. "You're Scotch, hey. Scotch red." He indicated my hair. "When something rough touches your neck your skin gets all patchy and annoyed. And you're prim. Scotch prim." He smiled at how right he was.

And curiously enough, I felt hypocritically prim. I seemed labeled, sitting there on the edge of the divan with my hands holding the sides of the cushion. "Half Scotch. Mostly on my mother's side. There's English and a dash of Welsh to water it down."

We went on like this all through coffee. It was something like going to a fortuneteller, with the added titillation that this was a young man. The slightly scornful and detached summing-up extended to most other subjects; it is an attitude common to doctors and in particular to those who have specialized in some minutiae of the body—brain cells, or blood cells, or lymph glands—and accept their own and other people's knowledge in any other sphere with an amused reservation, like the antics of a clockwork toy to which they hold the key. This tinge of patronage sometimes extends even to the performance of life itself, so that there are some rather pathetically brilliant men who feel slightly superior to their own human desires.

But I only noticed the pleasing insolence of this person, and I could easily place that. "You're a medical student, of course."

"Of course," he agreed without interest. John Marcus was busy with the records again, and he stood, tense as if he had made the recording himself, until the voice of the oboe, a voice out of the marshes taking up an ancient tale, lifted and silenced.

And music fell upon the room. It seemed to fall like lava upon these people, making another Pompeii of their attitudes stayed wherever they sat or stood or leaned. For twenty minutes they were returned deeper and deeper into themselves, and all the movement and speech that had blurred them, the exchange that made them shift and overlap in living, died out cold. Each now was contained in his own outline and none had anything to do with the other. Even that English girl, with her husband's baby somewhere in her body; she sat with her legs slightly spread at the knee and her feet flat on the floor, the attitude of a peasant or a pregnant woman, her eyes light, surface blue, her upper lip lifted a little to listen. With his back to her at the other end of the room, the husband had his arms on his humped knees, staring into the floor: as if the music had caught him looking into some campfire of his own. Backs of heads, and arms, and hands and shoes; all took on the sealed importance of limits; here, with these drooping fingers, with these small crooked toes with their painted nails showing through sandals, these heavy unhuman brown brogues, the person ends. He is shut up in there; she is shut up in there: you see them looking out at their eyes. But not at you, not at the room.

Laurie Humphrey, just across from me, slumped inside a loose gross body that made a rumpled rag of his collar and swallowed the division between his shirt and his trousers. His eyes closed in that big, coarse-textured face, the sagging ears and thick mouth (I could see the patches of dry skin, scaling on the lips) that he wore through his life like a disguise. And Joel's throat, near Isa. Sitting on the floor with his head hung back over some great book he had pulled down, so that there was his throat, like all that an animal offers of himself to the curious, the muscles spread, the end of the beard line, the beat of his blood widening and closing, widening and closing.

A harmlessness about the sitting Edna; the innocence of the ordinary suitcase from which the dangerous documents have been taken out. Her thighs crossed, a small soft rounded stomach let out under her dress. Isa with a broken look about her limbs, and her face become small. Dug up, dusted of ashes and put in a museum, not Isa the writer preserved, not gusto and wit and intellect, but a creature of sensual conflict, every little sticklike bone twisted in passion, the balked, lovewise curl to the mouth. Only the young man sharing the divan with me winked once, like a sardonic sphinx.

The concerto ended and at once movement and talk obscured them in a flickering gnat-dance zigzagging a tingling blur before the separateness of these, scribbling away the outlines of those. The English girl was shaking out her dress as if the music might have left crumbs. "Herby can get a lift with us," her husband shouted over to the door. But Isa had suddenly put her arm round the old young man, with the blatant advance a woman can only show toward a man whom everyone can see is quite impossible for her. "No," she said protectively, "he's staying here. I'm all alone and you know this is no country for a white woman."

"How is it you never even get offered a beer here, any more," Laurie yawned.

"Well you can all come on to my place," someone offered, but no one took it up.

"—For the simple reason we're flat. Right out of everything. When Tom brought Ronny and Ben home on Sunday he had to go to the emergency dispensary and wheedle a bottle of invalid wine out of the chap."

"Are you coming with tomorrow, John? Bring some food."

"No. Not in your car, Laurie—hey, look out! I've got a baby in there!"

The room had broken up in the push to go home. I signaled good night to Joel across the room; he was spending the night with Laurie. I was going to sleep over at the house of an old friend of my mother's, the usual arrangement when I went out in Johannesburg at night. The house was on the north side of town, while Laurie lived on the east, so I had arranged a lift with someone going in my direction. But as I was getting into my coat the young man of the divan appeared and said: "Which way do you go?"

"Parkview, but the Arnolds are taking me."

"That's my way, too. You come with me." And he dragged me off, picking hairs from my coat collar. "Either don't wear a black coat, or buy yourself a clothesbrush. You're a sloppy kid, you know." "But you said I was prim." "That was the first time I looked. Anyway, I know that primness. You use it because you don't want to give yourself away. Not even to yourself. But you're there all right, just underneath, and don't think you can forget it." I suddenly felt that he saw me on the beach with Ludi, two years ago, looking at my own breasts against the sand. I laughed with embarrassment and misgiving. "Oh, yes," he said. As I got into his small object-crowded car, Joel and Laurie came out of the building and I put up my hands and smiled to Joel. But the light of the foyer caged him in, and though he was looking right at me, he could not see beyond it.

I did ask Mary Seswayo to come to hear some music at the Welshs' flat, but somehow she never came. When I spoke of it to her she sat very seriously for a moment and then said as if she were replying to the question of an examiner: "The difficulty is how can I get home afterward."

I said: "Oh, someone will take you." Like a rope tied to one's ankle, the limits of their recognition in the ordinary life of the city constantly tripped one up in even the most casual attempt at a normal relationship with an African. Because I was white I continually forgot that Mary was not allowed here, could not use that entrance, must not sit on this bench. Like all urban Africans she had learned to walk warily between taboos as a child keeping on the squares and off the lines of paving. But everywhere had been mine to walk in, and out of sheer habit of freedom I found it difficult to restrict my steps to hers. I remember once going into town with her to buy some textbooks, and when I wanted to go to a cloakroom, realizing for the first time in my life that because she was black she couldn't even go to the lavatory if she wanted to. There simply was no public cloakroom for native men or women in the whole shopping center of Johannesburg. Now if she came to the Welshs' someone would have to take her home by car to the native township seven or eight miles out of town where she lived; their flat was nowhere near a native bus route, she could not travel on a European bus, and if she went home by train (even then someone would have to get her to the main station—there was no suburban underground in Johannesburg), there would be a dangerous walk between the halt and her home at the other end. These details were irksome and tedious and because I found them so I felt irritated with her for thinking of them first. It was not the music or the invitation that her inward eye looked to, but the business of getting from here to there.

So we drank our coffee and she kept turning back her sheaf of papers and reading a line or two, slowly. She was continually preoccupied with her work as I, in my work, was preoccupied with other things. She had now a friend who worked in a city bookshop (an enlightened tradition seemed to go with the books and it was one of the very few businesses where an African could be something more than an errand boy; he did what was known as "white man's work" in the stockrooms). Today she had another handbook with her, this time called *Effective English*, that I guessed he had lent her.

Watching her opening it the hesitant, expectant way she opened a lecture-room door or the door of the library, and her eyes unraveling its mystery of print as if they were unwrapping a parcel that just might contain something miraculous, final, I suddenly wished for her that she was less harassed and flattened. And that she would not keep hoping for this miracle, finality. As usual, there was nothing I could say. I went on sipping the sweet coffee and her face hung transfixed over the book like a pool in which she would never see herself. She was very dark skinned—there is a theory, probably originating with the Africans themselves, that when they are well fed and fat they are lightest, and it was certain that she was not particularly well fed—and she had the small, good and also slightly projecting teeth of many African girls. Also the lovely round smooth forehead. She took a gulp out of her cup and as she put it down I wondered, Would I drink out of that cup? At home, as in most households, the Africans had eating utensils kept separate from the common family pool. Don't take that—it's the girl's cup. My mother had often stopped some stranger, fetching himself a drink of water.

But it was a stupid thought I had caught myself out in, and I was learning to recognize them. I was beginning to find that in friendship with an African, a white person is inclined to submit his sincerity to tests by which he would not dream of measuring good will or affection toward another white person. Would I particularly like drinking out of anyone's cup, for that matter?

She went off to the library, and I wandered down to the grassy amphitheater in which the swimming pool lay, still and cold with winter, although the sun was hot. It was one of those immense high-

veld days when the buildings and trees of Johannesburg are all
mountaintops, lifting up into a dazzling colorless sky, distanceless,
dazing as air that has shaken itself free of the earth and rises just
out of reach of the last aspiring finger of rock. It is impossible to
look into such a sky. I struggled a little with some Italian. Then lay
back on the dead grass. A native gardenboy silently looped strands
out of the pool with a long hook; then he stretched out with an old
torn stained hat over his face. The hoarse voices of two students in
shorts and rugby boots were gruff near me. It was the afternoon the
young man of the divan was to take me to tea before I caught my
train home. The suggestion had interested me enough at the time it
was made, on the impetus of the evening at Isa's, but the days that
had elapsed in between had returned the young man to the haziness
of a stranger, and I wondered, as I had before about such enthusi-
asms gone cold on me, why I had agreed.

But at four when the shadows of the buildings made chasms of
chill I dutifully came out of the cloakrooms with my lips freshly
drawn and my hair smoothed with water at the temples, and he was
waiting in his black car. At once the inside of it was familiar, the
assortment of odd shapes in the darkness appearing in the frankness
of afternoon as ampule boxes, a couple of battered instrument cases,
and piles of theater programs, empty cigarette boxes and dusty pamphlets put out by drug manufacturers. When he turned to talk to
me, he breathed ether like a dragon breathing fire. "Exotic," he said,
"and it's cheaper than standing a round of drinks." I saw with a
sense of justification that he was attractive, after all, and my mood
lifted. We were going down the hill in the gaiety that sometimes
springs up between people who are attracted but know each other
very slightly when he swerved to avoid a native girl carrying a large
brown paper parcel, and I interrupted—"Just a moment"—and
turned to make sure.

I thought I had recognized the coat and beret. It was Mary, even
more burdened than usual, so that she could only smile and had no
free hand to wave. Charles had pulled to the curb. "Oh, I didn't
mean you to stop," I said unconvincingly. "Well? What's wrong?
You practically flung yourself out the window."

"It's a girl—an African I'm friendly with. We nearly knocked her over. There she is, just behind—"

"Nonsense, we didn't nearly knock anyone down. Where is she?"

I turned to look through the rear window at Mary coming hesitantly toward us, unsure if we had stopped on her account, and she should approach, or for some other reason, when she would have the embarrassment of answering a signal that was not for her. I nodded my head vigorously at her.

But Charles suddenly reversed the car with a rush that brought us level with her and almost knocked her down again.

"Are you mad?"

"Well, it's quicker for us to go backward than for her to go forward."

Mary stood at the window, smiling at his air of impulsive calm. Before her, I immediately felt a kind of pride in this young man; my indignation took on the purpose of showing him off. "I hope you don't always drive like this. Really! —Mary, why are you walking with all those parcels?"

"It's the dry cleaning for the people where I stay. I went down to the shop to get it, and when I got back I couldn't find my bus money." She was smiling in apology.

"So what'd'you think you're going to do? Walk home?"

"I'm going into town to see if I can find my cousin at the factory where he works. He will lend me bus fare."

"Where is this place?" said Charles. He had the patient, practical, uninterested tone of the white person willing to help a native with money or authority, so long as he is not expected to listen to any human details of the predicament.

"But I'll give you the money," I said, and at once became flustered because I felt I should have said "lend." "I mean, it's silly to go into town—He may not be there . . . ? Charles—"

"Where does she live?" he asked again.

"Oh, in Mariastad—"

"Well, come on then. Hop in."

"It's seven miles," Mary told him first, quite simply, not getting into the car because she expected the distance would change his mind.

"I know where it is. Get in."

And now I began to urge her too, feeling a mild intoxication of possession of the young man and his car.

We went off with another roar, and she settled herself, very quietly as if anxious not to disturb, among the dust and rubbish in the back, clearing a space for herself carefully, and bending down to pick up a pile of pamphlets that had slid to the floor. We drove along one of the big highways that lead out of the city to the north and south, hemmed in with thousands of other cars, the faces of people drawing level behind glass, then snatched away as the lights changed. On the left hundreds of bicycles skidded through, Africans riding home with the yells and something of the exhilaration of skiers, and along every second or third block native bus queues lay like grayish caterpillars. Then there were villas on either side, the cars thinned, a roadhouse took some of them, and we passed our escort of bicycles, panting and riding hard now on the long stretch.

Many South Africans have never been inside a native location, but I had been with my mother to the Atherton one as a child, when the Mine held its yearly jumble sale of old clothes there, and I had also been with Joel to see the shantytown at Moroka and the experimental housing scheme near by, where the houses looked like sections of outsize concrete pipe and smelled cold as tunnels. One native location is much like another. Mariastad was one of those which are not fenced, but the approach to the place was the familiar one: a jolt off the smooth tarmac onto a dirt road that swerved across the veld; orange peel and rags, newspaper and bits of old cars like battered tin plates, knock-kneed donkeys staring from tethers. All around the veld had been burned and spread like a black stain. And all above the crust of vague, close, low houses, smoke hung, quite still as if it had been there forever; and shouts rose, and it seemed that the shout had been there forever, too, many voices lifted at different times and for different reasons that became simply a shout, that never began and never ended.

It was something I had known before and yet this time, with Mary Seswayo in the back of the car, it came to me as if the other times I had not seen it. As we bumped down into the township Charles and I stopped talking, as people do when they feel they may have lost their way; animation died into awkwardness. Along the road, he had talked to me but not to Mary (I had turned every now and then to draw her into our chatter) but now he began to try and speak naturally to her, as you do when there is something you do not want a person to notice. The effort was not much of a success, and everytime he got an answer from her he seemed not to know what to do with it.

The car went slowly through the streets. It seemed to descend into noise that sealed us up inside it. Children changed the outline of the street, grouping in the gutters, skittering over the road, running alongside the car in a fluttering pennant of rags. When there are so many of them, they lose human value; you could have put out your arm and brushed them off, back into the road.

First we passed the administrative offices, orthodox and red brick in official decency beneath the shabbiness that had washed against them from all around, weathering them to the corrosion of poverty. Chipped brick, dirt and litter disguised the solidity and professional proportions of the place like the ivy a villa pulls over its glaring newness in a stately suburb. A flag clung round a pole, and two fat native policemen stood arguing with an angry man on a bicycle. Then the usual small street of shops, homemade and pushed tightly one against the other so that you felt that if the first were taken away, the whole lot would slowly keel over and collapse. Most were one-eyed, and the pocked whitewash was covered with signs, advertisements and exhortations, but one or two had crooked verandas—mud or homemade brick under the whitewash—and the shoemaker sat outside. The fish-and-chip shop had a proper shop front, and young natives hung about it, city hats pushed back on their heads, drinking Coca-Cola. After the shops there was an empty space covered with ashes, mealie cobs, dogs and children, and at the far end, a tiny church that was the utter simplification of all that has accreted round the architectural idea of a church through the ages: a peaked tin roof, a rounded wooden door, a horizontal bar across two poles with a piece of old railway sleeper suspended from it, and a smaller piece of iron dangling to clang it with.

We followed Mary's directions past decent little houses, each as big as a tool shed with a tin chimney throbbing out the life of the house in smoke. In many of them the door was open and a sideboard or a real dining table in varnished wood showed. Outside their bare walls were ballasted with lean-tos made of beaten-out paraffin tins, homemade verandas like the shoemaker's and porches made of box-wood, chicken wire and runner beans. Each had two or three yards of ground in front, fenced with a variety of ingenuity, and inside mealies hung their silk tassels from the pattern of straight stalk and bent leaf. Some grew flowers instead; as it was winter, rings and oblongs of white stones marked out like graves the place where they would come up again. And some grew only children, crawling and huddling in the dust with only eyes looking out of dust.

Every third or fourth house there was a communal tap from which everyone fetched his water, and which no one troubled to turn off properly. A muddy stream trickled from the tap's soggy perimeter out into the street, and we felt it squelch beneath the tires.

Mary said: "Here it is—" and with quiet and insistent thanks was gone into one of these houses and the car was taking us past again before I had realized that this was the place in which she lived, the house that was individual because one of its components touched my own life. I looked with confusion at the other houses of the row, passing; all alike in the limitations of their humble differ-entiation. Into a house like this she disappeared: there was a chair on the veranda, I had at least seen, and a sword fern growing in half an old tire, painted silver and hanging from a wire. Inside there might be four chairs round a table on a piece of clean linoleum, pressed for space against a high bed with a white crocheted cover —like this house. Or this one—a kitchen dresser, one or two chairs, something tall and dark with a flash of white—could it be a piano? It might be, without incongruity, for there were not enough of these rooms for each to serve one designation: dining room, bedroom, kitchen—they were all simply living rooms in the plainest sense, whether you must work or cook or sleep or make love. I had sud-denly a great regret and curiosity for the room of Mary Seswayo that I had not seen; I wanted to make it up for myself out of the raw material which I saw in flashes in the other houses all about me. Essentially, it could not be any different from my imagining, because there was nothing else, in a place like Mariastad, of which it could have been composed. All else it could contain could be the little pile of books and notes from the University; and those I could supply, too. Just at this point we turned the corner and passed another tap, and there was a neat girl with an ordinary white enamel jug, fetching some water for herself. And at this the grasp of my imagination—that was really more like the entrance into another life through a re-creation of atmosphere, like an archaeologist restoring the arms, trinkets and drinking vessels to the excavated city, so that all that is needed is his own human step through the streets, and it will be as it was again—let go. She, too, came with a jug for water to a tap in the mud. So in how many other commonplaces that I take for granted in my own life shall I be wrong in hers? The thousand differences in the way she is compelled to dress, wash, eat—they piled up between us and I could scarcely see her, over the top. Sitting in the car I was conscious of a kind of helplessness, as if it were taking me away, further and further away, not only in distance. The car that at night must occupy a garage as big as these houses. The house Mary lives in. The bench she can't sit on, the water that must be fetched from the tap in the street, the physical closeness of her life to the lives of others; these differences in the everyday living out of our lives—could they end there? Or out of them did we love, want and believe, and so could the formula of our loving, wanting, believing, be the same? Further and further. I thought of her eyes into which I seemed not to have looked hard enough. I tried to remember them so that I could try again.

The young man Charles said: "I'm damned if I know how to get out." And certainly, although he had turned and turned again, we were not leaving Mariastad the way we came in. We were now rocking and bumping through the rutted streets of what must have been the oldest part of the location. The closeness of the place, the breath-to-breath, wall-to-wall crowding, had become so strained that it had overflowed and all bounds had disappeared. The walls of the houses pressed on the pavement, the pavement trampled into the street, there were no fences and few windows. Fires in old paraffin tins burned everywhere, and women stood over them among the screaming children, cooking and shouting. I was accustomed to seeing Africans in ill-fitting clothes that had belonged to white people first, but these people were in rags. These were clothes that had been made of the patches of other clothes, and then those patches had been replaced by yet others. They must have been discarded by a dozen owners, each poorer than the last, and now, without color or semblance of what they had been, they hung without warmth, fraying in the fierce flicker of flames that seemed greedy to eat them up, return them at last to the nothing their frailty had almost reached. The children were naked beneath one garment cast off by a grownup; streaming noses and gray bellies to show that under the old army jacket there was something alive instead of a cross of sticks to frighten birds.

All movement seemed violent here. The lift of a woman's elbow, stirring a pot. Their red eyes when they looked up. Their enormous, yelling laughter above the smoke. The grip of their bare feet on earth worn thin as the rags they wore. The men went about as if they were drunk, and perhaps some of them were; the strong, fermented smell of kaffir beer fought with the smoke.

"Christ, what a place," said the young man, annoyed with himself for losing his way. Some of the people stared curiously through the smoky confusion as we passed, and children yelled, Penny! Penny! jeeringly. Behind the crooked outline of their mean roofs held down with stones and pumpkins a magnificent winter sky turned green and bejeweled, and as it arched away from their gathering darkness the hovels seemed to crawl closer to the earth beneath it, and their tins of fire became the crooked eyes of beasts showing. I was afraid. There was nothing to be afraid of in the people, no menace in their shouts or their looks: like their shacks, their bodies, they were simply stripped of gentleness, of reserve, all their bounds were trampled down, and they only moved or cried out in one need or another, like beasts. Yet I was afraid. The awfulness of their life filled me with fear.

He said: "What a noisy lot of devils they are, eh?"

But I did not answer and he was so busy peering his way through the unlighted streets that he did not notice. On the banks of a trickle of stream that smelled of soda and rotting vegetables, and that, in the light of the car, showed the earth caked with dried soap scum, Mariastad petered out. We followed a man on a swaying bicycle over a bridge and drove up a rise to the main road.

"Light me a cigarette," he said. I found the packet and some matches and lit the cigarette in my mouth. As I handed it to him I looked back over my shoulder and saw Mariastad, a mile away. It rose in smoke and the pale changing light of fire like a city sacked and deserted behind us.

Presently he put his hand lightly on my thigh, just above the knee, and squeezed it gently once or twice as if he were trying a fruit. Then with an air of calm decision he stopped the car at the side of the road, right under a street light, and kissed me with deliberate passion. I felt, as I always did when someone kissed me for the first time, what a stranger he was, and how far, in our mingled lips and saliva, we were from each other. We sat back in our own corners of the car and he said: "Can't you stay over in town tonight? It's so late as it is."

I looked uncertain; I did not know what I wanted to do.

"Let's go and have dinner and we could see a show."

"—Well, I suppose I could. I could phone home. But I'll have to find out if the woman I usually stay with can have me."

So we drove quickly into town and when I had done my telephoning I found him already seated at the bright little table of the hotel restaurant. For the first time, he looked young and nervous. As I passed the bowing maître d'hôtel and the pianist who played as if she were asleep and her music was a sentimental dream, and the buffet where the turkey wore frills, the ham was the delicate pink of petals, and the lobsters lay ornate in silky bouquets of lettuce, I felt a kind of voluptuous thrill at the chanciness and irreconcilable contrasts thrown up to me in Johannesburg. The guilt, the desire to assume my part of the human responsibility for it all, sharpened the assertion of my self opposing greedy claims for pleasure, love and admiration. I ate whatever looked prettiest and drank some sour white wine that made me feel so full that I had to unfasten the hook of my skirt. We sat through the cinema holding hands, with our knees and calves touching, and afterward struggled together in the car. I was shocked and fascinatedly excited by the way his stranger's hand went firmly under my clothes as if it were a live thing in itself, an animal finding its burrowing way. And the hand was cold, from the steering wheel and the winter night air, on my warm sheltered skin. I had never believed love-making could be such a casual thing for me. When I went into the house and crept into the room where I was to sleep, I found that beneath my coat all my clothes were unbuttoned, unfastened, ready to take off. But I did not feel ashamed and instead laughed, suppressing the laugh with my hand, and flung the coat to a chair in a kind of independent satisfaction.

16 DURING ALL THIS time my position at home was slowly changing. What had at first been clashes of opinion, the quick flare of defiance and disapproval that springs from the very closeness of parents and children beneath the difference of age, became something colder, silent and unexpressed. My mother and father and I now lived in the intimacy of estrangement that exists between married couples who have nothing left in common but their incompatibility.

"Helen lives her own life," my mother told people briskly, as if it were something she and my father had decreed out of a superior and enlightened judgment. It was curious, in fact, how in her relations with other people she now often expressed views and even acted in accordance with ideas that were mine, though these same ideas were part of the way of life that was taking me away from her, and to which, in me, she was bitterly hostile. Suddenly she had begun to grumble about the backwardness of Atherton; of course, here we never get the chance to see a decent play or hear a concert, she would say with a curl of the lip, as if in some other life somewhere else she had been accustomed to these things. She would sneer, too, at some of the innocent diversions she had once enjoyed so much. You can go, she would say to my father, who was a little put out by her lack of enthusiasm over the Pioneers' Dinner to be given by the mayor of Atherton; I don't want to be among all those old fossils, thank you. And she had even begun to take a brandy and soda if they went out or had friends to visit in the evening.— It's ridiculous to be old-fashioned, she said. These days girls of Helen's age take a drink.

But her casual, almost boastful acceptance of me before strangers had too much determination behind it. At home long despairing silences fell between us when she knitted and looked away when our eyes met, because she was thinking about me, and I read down the page of my book and did not know what I had read. She wandered alone into this strange tract of country with a gun, vague about what she might find while looking for me; and, at a word, there we were seized with the confrontation of each other, I motionless, self-conscious beside a palm tree, she feeling a little foolish at the gun.

"Would you like a peach?" she would ask suddenly. "I went to the market with Mrs. Cluff this afternoon and we shared a box. They're Cape peaches, big as a soup plate. When I think that I pay Sammy sixpence each for those hard sour little things. Really, I feel I should go more often." And we would talk politely about the price and quality of fruit for a few minutes, while her interest quickened and mine flagged until she noticed it and the subject died. We were silent again. I thought of how, when I was a little girl, we used to go to the market together on Saturday mornings, I holding on to her arm and carrying the basket, excited among the slippery vegetable leaves and the pushing crowd and the smell of earth. Now she was counting stitches, her lips moving as if she were telling beads. I began to read, starting from the top of the page again. Soon she got up, rolled the knitting neatly away and said brusquely, "Helen, please clear your papers and things away now. Your father's bringing Mr. Mackenzie from the Group home." And so, from long habit, I collected my notes and books and helped to make our living room look as if no one had ever done any living there. My mother did not like living to show; all evidence of the casual, straggling warmth of human activity was put out of sight before the advent of visitors as if it were peculiar and private to us, and did not exist in their lives, their homes as well. I noticed now how we were presented to visitors in our own home as creatures without continuity, without a life put down and ready to take up again, like actors placed in a stage-set.

And I thought with relief and longing of the way in which one entered into, but did not interrupt, the life of people like Isa Welsh; there were no preparations for your coming, you drank out of the same cups as your hosts did every day, and if they were cleaning their shoes or eating dinner, or having an argument, for the time that you were there, you were part of their stream of activity. My mother, again, liked to have "everything nice" for visitors, and was greatly put out and irritated if someone dropped in unexpectedly or at a time unusual for callers. She could not enjoy their company if my father had his old slippers on and there was only a piece of stale cake in the house.

One of the greatest sources of pain and contention between us was the fact that I did not "bring my friends home." My father suggested often: "Why don't you let Helen have a little party, Jess?—You could have some of your friends from the University out one Saturday evening, and you could dance if you wanted to . . . mother would prepare you some sandwiches, and you could have beer. . . ."

My mother shrugged as if she didn't care. "She doesn't want it. We're not good enough for these friends of hers, my dear. Don't you know that? Her head's turned by fine houses in Johannesburg."

How could I explain that what was the matter was that everything would be *too* good for my friends? That they would leave wet rings on the furniture and put their feet up on the sofa, and perhaps use somebody else's towel in the bathroom (towels were sacred personal possessions in our house). I could imagine exactly the kind of evening my father visualized; I had been to them in the houses of other sons and daughters of Mine people. My mother would work all day preparing homemade sausage rolls and round water biscuits spread with cheese and potted relish, and when the evening came would have everything set out on a table in the living room, under an embroidered net. A dozen bottles of lemonade and a dozen bottles of beer would be stacked in one corner. All the lights would be on, the two silver vases filled with flowers, and not a piece of thread, a newspaper or a used ash tray would betray the fact that the room had ever been used before. Into this overawing atmosphere of preparedness the guests would come, clattering over the bared expanse of floor which instantly killed the spontaneity of the desire to dance, and very soon, quite unable to keep away, my mother would appear as if by accident at the door, dressed in her best frock and smiling confusedly, and in no time my father would have set himself up jocularly in shirt sleeves to act as barman. And they would both hang about, like parents at a children's birthday party, protesting all the while that they "did not want to disturb the young people." An inverted snobbery made me burn with shame at the idea. I could not face the picture of the people I knew with their uncluttered lives in flats and rooms, suddenly finding themselves in this church tea-party atmosphere.

The same kind of situation arose over the men who took me out. Charles Bessemer was a good example. My mother and father were vaguely disquieted when, as I did the night he took Mary Seswayo to Mariastad, I telephoned unexpectedly from Johannesburg to say that I would not be coming home. Because I went to places they did not know and with people whom they had not met, I think it was as if, when I put down the telephone, they felt me swallowed up into an anonymity of city streets. Though they would have been astounded at the suggestion, the principles of their code of behavior toward young men were entirely sexual, the elders of the tribe measuring the daughter's choice of mates against the background of her own home, the young male assessing the worth of the family and consequently the girl whom he was considering. This was the way it was always done on the Mine and in Atherton in general, where as soon as a young man became interested in a girl, and long before there was any talk of marriage, he was taken about everywhere with the family, to cinemas and social gatherings, so that if and by the time marriage resulted, he was already inculcated in the kind of life the girl's family had led and which, without question, he would be expected to lead with her, trooping off as ants go to set up another ant heap exactly like the one they have left.

Joel came to the house, of course, but the fact that he was a Jew gave him a position of peculiar if wary privilege, like a eunuch. But this young man Charles Bessemer affected them conventionally. I had made a point of mentioning him to them although I had not spoken of others, unconsciously, I believe, as a kind of compensation: he was a Protestant Gentile, like themselves, and in addition, a doctor.—This I had discovered from Isa; it was typical of him that he should have preferred to let me go on thinking he was a medical student.—I offered him as the only thing I had that might please. He must have roused hopes in them that my withdrawal from the life and opportunities of the Mine was not a deviation after all, or if it had been, was merely the clever short cut to a life on the same safe pattern, but a higher level. A doctor from Johannesburg. I could see that the possibilities of this pleased them. And for the first time I saw a similarity between them and Joel's parents, whom I had long ago resigned myself to accept as irreconcilable strangers to everything in my mother and father. But now I saw that the idea of a doctor in the family pleased them in exactly the same way as it would have done the Aarons. I recognized in their questions the tone of the discussion when it had been suggested, that night at Aarons', that Joel might have studied medicine.

Now there was no cold pretended lack of interest expressing disapproval when I said I was going here with Charles, or there with Charles. "Did you have a good time?" my father would beam, as if there could be no doubt about it. (I often wondered what he visualized when he said this—the Masonic dances of his youth, I am sure, with young ladies dangling silk-tasseled pencils from their little programs.) "I'd give you my pendant," said my mother, "but I know you wouldn't wear it. . . ."—The women I knew longed for the strange, monolithic rings and heavy beaten silver jewelry made in the style of Berlin in the thirties by a German refugee, and because they could not afford his work, wore Zulu beadwork that in its primitive gaiety gave them the look of peasants.

My excuse for not bringing Charles home was the demands of his job. How he would have thrown his head back and laughed his explosive laugh if he had known. And how horrified he would have been at their picture of him as a rising suburban G.P. in a blue suit; Charles who wanted so much to be free (of quite what, he did not know) that the moment his good work—and he was good at his work—brought him promotion or the chance of permanency in a hospital, he resigned and went somewhere else. "What does he do, is he in private practice . . . ?" my father asked. I told them that

he was assistant medical officer at the big tuberculosis hospital outside Johannesburg. My mother got the look on her face she had had
when there had been a whooping-cough outbreak at school. "Well,
I hope he's careful," she said, "but I don't suppose you could get
it, just going about with him."

I felt suddenly forlorn. I had a sudden flash of this young man
and me, lost in each other's mouths, utterly mindlessly mixed in the
drunken secretions of love-making, our faces faintly sweaty and
smeared with passion like a bee mazed and messed with pollen.
And as I looked at my mother and father I seemed to see them as
if they were actually receding from me, in the blur and strain of
irrevocable distance. It was a floating, drifting feeling, with the pow-
erlessness of dreams.

Our life at home went on, touching at fewer and fewer points.
Charles Bessemer, like the hope of a sail, passed. They regretted
him more than I did, I am sure. After a few weeks he moved on,
whether because of a new job or a new girl I no longer remember,
or perhaps never knew. I think he must have tired of me because
the promise of my passion in our encounters in his car came to
nothing; when he began to consider where we might go to conclude
our love-making, he saw me brought up short, like an animal gal-
loping toward an abyss. In my eyes he saw the contradiction between
my headlong passion and a prohibitive fear that survived the moral
code of my parents which I believed I had rejected. To satisfy both
sides of my nature, I contrived to cheat them both. By denying
myself the final act of love, I kept to the letter of the moral prohi-
bition, and by allowing myself all intimacies short of the act itself,
gave a kind of freedom to my natural self. He was probably disgusted
with me. In any case it did not matter; there were others. The important thing was the knowledge of being desired that brought me
to a consciousness of myself as a woman among the women I knew,
that looking around me among my friends, made me feel myself
received into the fullness of life, the revealed, and the hidden.

More and more I longed to leave the Mine and live in Johannesburg. The very comfort and safeness of home irked me. I felt I
was muffled off from real life. I wanted the possibility of loneliness
and the slight fear of the impersonality of living in a strange place

and a city; the Mine oppressed my restlessness like a hand pressed over a scream. Often I wanted to call out to my mother: Let me go and you will keep me! But it would have been no use; would only have started another cold argument of offense and hurt. Now my parents were planning a visit to England and Europe, the visit of a lifetime which every Mine official waits for, and it was assumed that we should all be going together. When I suggested that they should go, and that I should perhaps like to go alone, or with a student tour, less elaborately, later, gloom fell like a blow on our house. The pleasure had drained out of anticipation, for them. I became guiltily distressed at what I had done, and began to pretend that I wanted to go with them, after all; and all the time resentment that they should force me to feel guilty toward them grew to match my desire to show them love.

The simultaneous experience of a longing for warmth and closeness and a wild kicking irritation to be free bewildered me and made me moody. I seemed to have nowhere to lay my bundle of contradictions, and so I stood a kind of touchy guard over them. To my mother and father I seemed more and more withdrawn and self-willed. They pressed to themselves the sharp belief that I no longer needed them; my mother retaliated with the pretense that she no longer needed me, my father with a gentle sadness of self-blame, a kind of timidity at my distance, as if conceding me a right to it.

Yet with the peculiar power of the inadvertent, the innocent, it was to be Mary Seswayo who blew up this no man's land between my parents and me. Like a stray dog she ran across it and set off a mine field that threwe up depths and plowed chasms which would be there forever.

17 IT WAS TOWARD the end of the year, when the heat and examinations came together. We all grumbled about the strain but I believe that in a way, I enjoyed it. It caught me up at least temporarily in a sense of urgency and purpose that discounted the strain, and it meant that at home I could shut myself up with

my books and, living apart from the household, be respected for it. I do not think there was a home anywhere that did not invest its student with a sense of importance and special consideration at this time.

That was why I said to Mary Seswayo one afternoon, "Why do you hang on here? I like to get home and get down to some real work as early as I can."—There were no more lectures once examinations were about to start, and we simply came to University to use the library or discuss something with our tutors. But the African girl seemed always to be sitting over a desk somewhere, in the library or a deserted lecture theater, while everyone else was hurrying to get away.

She looked up with the dulled expression that, contradictorily, comes from concentration. "I'd rather work here."

"Oh, would you?" I said in the polite tone of disagreement.

"The woman I stay with's got her children at home and you can't expect them to stay outside all the time. Then she takes in sewing and the books and papers get all mixed up. . . ." She smiled.

And then I remembered. I stood there looking at her with a kind of appeal of concern on my face and she smiled back at me with the reassurance of resignation. "So I'd rather work here."

For once I forgot the tacit pretense I kept up in an attempt to spare her feelings, to make her feel less different from me. "It must be like hell. How do you manage at night? Can you get anything done?"

Suddenly we really were intimates at last. "How can I? I sleep in a room with the children. In the other room the man and woman sit and talk, there are always people. So I try early in the morning. But the children are up at dawn." She laughed at the hopelessness of it.

I shook my head, not knowing what to say. "You couldn't go home to Natal?"

"No."

We both knew there was no money for it.

"Isn't there anywhere else you could stay for a bit?"

She shrugged and moved her brown expressive eyes with their

bright whites, lingeringly from one side of the room to the other, as if to say, Where?

But then she said, to remind herself how privileged she was to be at the University at all. "But I can get a lot done here, you know, in the daytime."

I made a little noise of impatient dismissal; conscious at the same time that this in itself was a luxury only a white person could afford.

And I went home. The train had been standing in the full sun of three o'clock in the afternoon before it left Johannesburg station, and the leather seats were searingly hot to the touch. My clothes stuck to the leather and my body stuck to my clothes, and, with my legs crossed, tears of sweat ran helplessly from my thighs down the backs of my bare knees. The green blinds were down and the thick dusty light brought out the varnish smell of hot leather. I closed my eyes and sank into the sweat and staleness of myself (five wet prints showed where my hand had clutched my books), and the train seemed to pamper me in it, shaking yes, yes, lazily as a fat woman breathing. I saw the old motorcar tire with the fern straggling out of it; the children shouting; the flatness, the dust, the noise. I imagined the woman with the sewing machine stuttering and the bits of material everywhere. Probably she chattered while she sewed. No, probably that was wrong, too; native women are always far more gay or far more serious than white women, so one mustn't try to visualize their moods from one's experience of Europeans. They sing and shout in the street over nothing, and they are solemn under the weight of some task we shouldn't even feel. There was no way of knowing, no way of knowing. And sitting in the physical reality of the heat that tacked my mind down to consciousness of every part of my body, sweating or touching in discomfort against the encumbrance of cloth, I had an almost physical sensation of being a stranger in what I had always taken unthinkingly as the familiarity of home. I felt myself among strangers; I had grown up, all my life among strangers: the Africans, whose language in my ears had been like the barking of dogs or the cries of birds.

And this feeling seemed to transmute itself (perhaps by a trick

of the heat, altering the very sensibility of my skin) to the feeling
Mary must have, trying to oppose the abstract concepts of her books
against the overwhelming physical life crowding against her. What
a stranger it must make of her. A stranger to herself. And then again
how slight, how stupid, how useless it must all seem, how impossible
to grasp, the structure of the English novel, the meaning of meaning,
the elegance of exchanges between Beatrice and Benedict—with the
woman making mealie porridge over the fire, the man carefully pre-
serving the dirty bit of paper that is his pass, the children playing
for a few years before they become nursegirls and houseboys.

When I got down from the train at the siding the Mine property
lay like an encampment, dead in the heat. Atherton, just seen over
the veld in a watery haze, was another. The horror of full light
showed it for what it was. Inside there might be coolness, the illusion
of shelter and color, the depth of books, the dignity of enclosed
space in rooms, the symbols of fruitfulness in flowers and grapes;
but the sun looked down on the bare, stolid huddle of tents that
expressed nothing more than complacent survival. And all around,
like a child's revenge of muddy footprints and dirty words scratched
on a wall, the natives had fouled the niggling benefits of the white
people's civilization. The siding was littered with bitten-out hunks
of stale bread swarming with ants, filthy torn papers and rags clung
to the boles of the gum trees, and the smell of stale urine, which
had been there as long as I could remember, came up from the
weeds along the road.

Inside our house, the dimness was overcome with heat. But it
was absolutely quiet. In the vacuum of heat and quiet the work that
I had to do had space to fill my mind entirely.

The heat and quiet and torpor of the Mine irritated me like the
uselessness of a person who lies snoring in the sun. Why shouldn't
Mary Seswayo come and work here for a week or ten days? No one
would disturb her, she would bother no one. And there was the
playroom—the little whitewashed lean-to built on the back of the
house as a "cooler" before the days of electric refrigerators—that
had been used to store my toys and was now a place for things that
had no place. She could sleep there; it was neither inside the house
nor out. I could clear it up and put a bed in.

The idea was so simple and practical that it gave me the particular satisfaction of an easy solution which has been overlooked. I vaguely thought my mother might raise some objections, but I felt that the "cooler" was the answer to those; I had the cooler all ready to produce, and there was all the rightness of it, for my mother, self-evident: neither inside the house, nor out in the yard with Anna, but something in between. And what would it matter to Mary how my mother looked at it; she would have peace and a place to herself.

My mother was secretary to some Mine charity committee that year, and just before supper she was sitting at the dining-room table addressing envelopes. She looked from the telephone directory to the writing under her hand with the air of determination and distaste with which she efficiently tackled tasks of this nature, and when she heard someone come in, said without looking up: "You must wait another few minutes, my girl." She thought it was Anna, wanting to lay the table.

"Oh, it's you. I've promised to get these wretched things out by tomorrow. I sent them all out last week, and now at this afternoon's meeting they want something added. I've got to do it over again."

I felt suddenly shy of her, I didn't know why. Instead of saying quite simply what I wanted to say, I wandered around the table for a moment or two, picking up and reading an envelope here and there. Mrs. W. J. Corbett, President, L.S.C., P.O. Box 127, Atherton. Mrs. J. Dale-Smith, c/o Manager's House, Basilton Levels . . . And when I did speak, I began in a roundabout way almost as if I were making a charity appeal. "Mother, I was thinking just now—working in my room I can get such a lot done, nobody to bother me. . . . Really, if one can't get through under conditions like this . . . But I was thinking, there's a young African girl in my group, she's really a bright girl and it's so important for her to pass. She lives in this awful location place, with people milling around all the time. She was telling me, she doesn't get a chance to work at all. And so I thought, at least I thought just now, couldn't she come home here for a while? Just for, say, ten days. Until we start writing."

"A native girl?"

"Yes, an educated native girl, of course." Every time I spoke my voice came out with more humility. I felt I stood there like a beggar.

"But where would she sleep?" my mother brought out at last, as if she had found what she wanted in the pause: the unanswerable.

I had it ready: "In the cooler. It'd be quite all right. I'll fix it up for her."

I began to make light of it, sensing that if I spoke of Mary as an inferior my mother might be edged to a position where it would seem that she herself and I stood together. "She's as clean as a white person and she'd do her own room and so on. It's just to give her somewhere to work."

"Yes . . . ," said my mother. "Where will she wash? And where's she going to have her meals? That's something. I don't fancy her using my bath."

"Oh, she'll wash outside. She'll eat in her room. Or she and I'll eat together."

"You'll eat . . ."

I made a gesture of quick dismissal. "She won't care where she eats."

Anna came in from the kitchen with the tablecloth over her arm and a faggot of knives and forks in her hand. "I'm sorry, missus," she said determinedly. "All right, all right, I'm off," said my mother, scooping up her things. She put them on the sideboard. "Look, Anna, don't use those mats Miss Julie gave me. The old ones are good enough for under the meat dishes."

I did not say anything but stood and watched her. She could not ignore me as she left the room. "Well, I don't know," she said. "I'll have to speak to your father."

That was what she always said when she did not know whether or not she wanted to do something. I had heard her say it in shops hundreds of times, when she suspected that she might get what she wanted elsewhere, or that she was being overcharged: "I'll have to speak to my husband." Yet I knew that she had never sought my father's advice in her whole life, and he had never cared to have any authority over her, or questioned any decision of hers. It was her way of playing for time to go into consultation with herself.

Now I accepted the lie with a show of respect. I sat on the veranda letting the insipid music of the radio flow over me, and soon my father came home and let himself down into one of the creaking chairs to read the paper. As he grew older the sprightliness of small, thin men was intensified in him and his face grew smaller behind his glasses. Fits of dizziness and weakness had been diagnosed as anemia, and he was no longer allowed to discipline himself with the dietary fads that he had adopted from time to time. So he had gone from the stomach to the psyche. Now he had a little shelf of books of popular psychiatry, and adopted the theory of psychosomasis as wholly as he had once believed in the doctrine of Christian Science or the Hay Diet. He was also one of the many people who confuse eccentricity with culture, and he saw my modest and hopeful attempts to expand myself as on a level with his blind belief in the elixir of the moment or, rather, the latest book of the month for hypochondriacs. "This'll interest you, Helen!" He held up a new one. *The Subconscious You.* A popular, concise explanation for laymen written by an eminent American psychiatrist. Two million copies sold. "It seems it's all up here," he said, putting a finger to his forehead. "No matter where you feel it, it's all up here. Look somewhere toward the middle, there—there's a chapter on how to study, that's something for you now, eh?"

I paged through the book and caught one chapter head as it flipped by: "How you think with your blood: The problem of prejudice." I smiled.

I went back to my room to look over my work, but spent one of those timelessly vague half-hours that young women fall into now and then, combing and recombing my hair, looking at my figure in the mirror, moving about among the clothes in my wardrobe. Anna came to call me to dinner and my mother was already carving the leg of lamb. As soon as she saw me she said, carelessly and finally, like the inevitable dismissal of something quite ridiculous. "I don't think it's a good idea to have that native girl here. Best cut it out." Obviously she had made up her mind, and simply told my father that I had made the suggestion and she had repudiated it.

I don't know whether it was the result of the kind of self-hypnosis induced by my passionate absorption with myself in my room just before, but an intense arrogant irritation shot into me. "I knew it. I knew it." I gave her a look of summing up, smiling, unpleasant.

"How do you mean you knew it?" she said, rising to it. Nothing angered her more than suspected patronage because she believed that in some obscure way I had some advantage from which to patronize her. The knife squeaked through the thin slices of meat; she carved excellently.

"I just knew it."

She countered her fear of patronage with a kind of smugness. Calmly helping my father and me to cauliflower, she said with a little warning laugh, "When you've got a home of your own, you can do what you like. But while you live in my house . . . I don't see why your father and I should pander to one of your fads. It's just another idea you've got into your head, like all the others."

I cannot explain how her tone affected me. Perhaps it was because I was so uncertain of the validity of much that attracted me and that I believed in, and this small help that I wanted to give was one of the few things that had come so spontaneously and simply to me that there was no possibility that it was part of a pose or an attitude, something within the context of what I wanted to be rather than what I really was. To question it, to lump it with all the rest was like doubting my own reality. That the questioning should come from my mother was painful and frightening. It was as if she had said: Have I really got a child? Is she *there*? And in the end, no authority could speak above hers.

She had no idea of the enormous power to hurt that she retained. I could not have told her, I could not have explained. She would only have laughed again, missing the point: Of course, my opinion matters so much to you!

I felt sick with the impossibility of getting her, anyone, to understand what she did to me. I sat there trembling with a frustration like suppressed desire. And my voice went on, irrelevant and out of control. "You let Anna have her cousin here while she was looking for work."

"Look, I've said no and that's the finish of it."

"You haven't really thought about it at all," I said, sitting back slowly from my plate. "You're simply terrified of anything I ask you, no matter what it is, if it's something I ask, you must say no on principle. Because it's bound to be wicked, crackpot, not respectable. You wouldn't really mind having the girl here at all. But I ask it, so, no, no—it must be suspect."

My mother said, noticing my agitation: "That's right, you were always good at turning on the drama."

"Look," said my father, "must we argue at the table?" Of course, he was thinking of one of the tenets of his latest theory: Digestion is impaired by emotion.

My mother climbed slowly and mightily into her anger like a knight putting on his vestments before mounting for battle. "Of course, you let her do as she likes. And grumble to me afterward. Well I won't have it. I've had enough. I don't know her friends and their ways and I don't want to. Nobody's good enough for my daughter here. How do you think it looks, her keeping herself aloof from the Mine, never wanting to do the things other young people do? I'm ashamed, always making excuses—" She stopped, breathing hard at us. But once it was released, all that she had not said for months, all the preserve of her cold silences, her purposeful ignoring, could not be checked.

It pushed up against her throat and she had to say it; it seized her and poured out of her with something of the uncontrolled violence of the emotional babble that comes out of a person under gas. "What do you think people think of you? The girls you went to school with, you won't look at. Of course not. They're content with their jobs and the decent people they've known since they were children. And I have to have Mrs. Tatchett saying to me, What's wrong with Basil?—Yes, I'm telling you, she came to me the other day and asked me straight out, and I admire her for it. What's wrong with my Basil, she said, that Helen stayed at home rather than go to the Halloween dance with him and she never came to the cocktail party we had for his graduation? After all, he goes to the University the same as she does, why doesn't she consider him good enough?"

"Good enough," I flashed out. "That's all they ever think of, the petty snobs. The only reason why one should be friendly with anyone is because they're good enough."

My mother turned on me. "No, you like to roll in the mud. Anything so long as it's not what any other reasonable person likes. You'd rather be seen running about with the son of a Jew from the native stores, that's much nicer, someone brought up among all the dirt and the kaffirs. *He* must be a finer person, of course, than anyone decently brought up by people of our own standing."

A kind of thrill of getting to grips with real issues went through me. "Ah, I thought that would come. You've had that on your chest a long time. And you've always pretended to be so polite to Joel. And all the time you're as bigoted as the rest. Worried because all the old crows of the Mine saw your daughter out with a Jew. Well, you can tell them to mind their own damn business, I'll be friendly with whom I choose. And I'm not interested in their standards or who they think would be suitable for me. You can tell them."

"We've got nothing against the boy," said my father. "No one's saying anything against the boy. But why him, rather than anyone else?"

"Why?"—I was almost laughing with excitement. "Because he's alive, that's why. Because he's a real, live, thinking human being who's making his own life instead of taking it ready-made like all your precious little darlings of sons on the Mine."

"Have him," said my mother shrilly. The venom between us seemed like a race that we were shouting on. "Why don't you marry him? That would be nice. You can sit on a soapbox outside the store and shout at the natives. That'll be nice for your father, after he's worked himself up to a decent position to give you a background."

I looked at her. "It would kill you, wouldn't it? It would kill you to have the Manager ask after your daughter, who married the Jew from the Concession store. Well, don't worry. He wouldn't have me. He can find something better than the half-baked daughter of a petty official on a gold mine. He'll want a richer life than a person with my background can give him." I did not know where this came from in me, but all at once it was there, and it seemed to become true in the saying.

"After all, Helen, be reasonable," my father was insisting, on the perimeter of this. "How can you have a native staying in the house? I've got to think of my position too, you know. It's our bread and butter. What does it look like? I can't do things like that. I've got a responsibility, my girl. Next thing is it will be going round the Group that I'm a Communist."

"You disgust me. You both disgust me," I said fiercely, half-weeping, half-laughing in shame at the shrill crescendo of pettiness of the scene that, inescapably, caught us all up for what we were. Like a certain shape of nose or tone of skin it showed in all of us. I had it, too. I burned for the dignity and control my blood betrayed: "Do you hear? You disgust me."

"That's all right," said my mother. Her anger seemed to tremble meltingly through her, like a fire lambently consuming a bush. "That's all right." It was as if I had handed my words to her like a knife. The danger of them seized us both, but it was done. She would not give it back to me; I could not take it from her.

At that moment Anna walked in with the sweet, and her detached and servile presence, a kind of innocence of ignorance, showed up by contrast the peculiar horror that was in the room. She came in on her sloppy, shuffling slippers, and went out again, looking at no one. In the sudden, mid-air silencing of her presence, the intensity of the room was like that of a room enclosed by a hurricane. And all the stolid evidence of ordinary things, the familiar furniture, the food on our plates, the crocheted cover with the shells over the water jug, took on the awful quality of unknowing objects in a room where violence has been done.

When she had gone the silence remained.

My mother began to ladle stewed fruit into the three bowls. Suddenly she burst into weeping and ran from the room.

She cried like a man; it had always been hard for her to cry.

18 I WENT TO JOEL. I had not seen much of him lately, but I went to him with an instinctive selection of the one person I needed to counter the situation at home. I telephoned him in the morning and we arranged to meet for lunch at Atherton's one tearoom. Over breakfast and the business of dressing our household went about in silence, a kind of shame which made everything se-

cretive and perfunctory, like the trembling hand and dizzy air that
harks back from a hang-over to the excess that reeled behind it. My
mother did not speak to me. But as I made ready to leave the house
I heard her complaining to Anna behind the closed kitchen door,
the familiar plaint of the mother who has "done all she can" for a
callously wrong-headed child. The door was closed to exclude me,
but her voice was as heedless of my being able to hear it as if I had
been a child too small to understand anything except the tone. I
could also hear the murmur of agreement from Anna like the hum
of responses from a chapel congregation.

The tearoom was not a good place to meet because it was always
full of Atherton women and women from the Mine, dropping in for
tea between shopping. At eleven o'clock, too, the lawyers came over
for the recess from the courthouse near by, and sat at two large
tables to themselves, their heads together, very conscious of their
serious purpose as compared with that of the women. Now it was
school holidays in addition, and many women whom I knew gave
me the smile of patronizing frankness used by married women toward young girls, as they trailed children in like strings of sausages,
holding hands and straggling behind. I sat and waited for Joel in
the atmosphere that smelled of warm scones and lavender water.
The waitress said: "How's your mother?" and dusted crumbs importantly off the table before me. Other women came up and spoke
to me. Say hello to Helen, dear.—Won't you? Oh, the cat's got away
with her tongue. That's it, you know. Helen, the cat's got away with
her tongue. Laughter from the woman and myself. Well, remember
me to your mother, dear? Daddy all right?

In between I sat in a kind of listless daze, as if I were not there
at all. I kept thinking: I want to go away. But there was no indignation, no strength in the idea any more. I did not want to be at
home, but there was nowhere else I wanted to be, either. Often since
then I have known the same grogginess of the spirit, that comes from
emotional excess and, like any other bankruptcy, has no choice but
to be passive. Sitting in the Atherton tearoom that hot day in No-
vember, I knew for the first time the distaste of no-feeling, the incredible conviction one hasn't the strength to discover with anything
more than a listless horror like nausea that not to care about the

love that agonized you is more agonizing than the agony itself; to
have lost the motive of anger is worse than living anger was.

When Joel came I did not say anything to him of what had
happened, after all. My express intention seemed suddenly not to
matter and I found myself saying: "I don't seem to have seen you
properly for such a long time. I thought it would be nice to get away
from work and talk." And we did. We discussed the people we knew
and the things we had seen and done with all the space of the ground
that was always so easy between us, and by the time the "pot of tea,
6d." had been reached, I found that my numbness was coming alive,
with a rush of gratitude I felt I was being taken back into human
life again. The pain of the house on the Mine shrank to one pin
point in a whole world; outside, other airs existed. So I was able to
say quite easily: "There's been a terrible row at home. It's no good."

When I told him, he said: "Did I crop up at all?"

"No," I said, pouring his tea. And added because the shortness
of my reply left a pause for doubt, "Why should you?"

"I don't know—I've always felt I should, some day.—Of course
the row wasn't really about Mary Seswayo."

"No, I know."

"—So you'll get away after all. You'll get what you wanted."

For a moment I had a return of the feeling that there was nothing
that I wanted. "But I didn't want it *this* way—" I appealed.

"Things keep on happening that way.—Did you want to see me
to tell me?"

I smiled.

He drank slowly, deliberately, his eyes moving about the room.
"No, it wouldn't be much good letting it blow over and waiting for
next time. Because it's obvious there's going to be a next time." He
shook his head with a half-smile to himself. "It's a pity for them."

"And what about me?" I felt impatiently it was something Jewish
in him, this softening he had toward my parents.

"For you, too," he said, not retracting the other.

"All this fuss about a girl going to live somewhere else. Hundreds of people never live at home after they're grown up. The way
we talk about it, you'd think—"

"Ah, but if they'd let you go while they still had you—" he said.

As he got up to go over to the little counter of cakes to pay, I laughed. "—You talk as if I'm leaving for ever."

A week later I telephoned him to tell him that Isa had promised to find me somewhere to live in Johannesburg.

There was a pause. "Well, if that's the case you might as well go to Jenny and John. The Marcuses."

"Why?" I was intrigued at the suggestion.

"Yes, they're a bit hard up and they want someone to help out with the rent of the flat."

"But why didn't you tell me before? I think that'd be a wonderful idea. Can I phone them?" The Marcuses had attracted me immediately the few times I had met them, and I was at once excited by the coincidence by which they wanted someone to share their flat, and I wanted somewhere to live. I badgered Joel with questions. "The flat's very small—" he said dubiously.

"I shan't be kept in the manner to which I'm accustomed—shame!"

"Well, you wait and see. The best thing will be for me to take you there. I have to see John on Thursday. I'll have Max's car so I'll pick you up after four."

After I had rung off I sat a moment or two on the little telephone stool, in the restless inertia of eagerness that must be curbed. Suddenly I wanted to telephone Joel again to tell him to be sure the Marcuses made no arrangement with anyone else in the meantime. I was trembling with excited urgency to have it all decided at once. For at the mention of the Marcuses, something lifted in me; I felt that here I might be about to come out free at last; free of the staleness and hypocrisy of a narrow, stiflingly conventional life. I would get out of it as palpably as an overelaborate dress that had pampered me too long.

19 WHEN I WENT TO THE FLAT for the first time that Thursday Jenny Marcus sat up very straight on a divan with her bare breasts white and heavy and startling. Like some strange fruit unpeeled they stood out on her body below the brown limit of a summer tan. She wore a skirt and a gay cotton shirt was hung round her shoulders, and face-down over her knees a baby squirmed feebly. As we came in behind her husband the baby belched, and, smiling brilliantly, calling out to us, she turned it over and wiped its mouth.

They lived on the sixth floor of a building on the first ridge that lifts back from the city itself. The building took the look of a tower from the immense washes of summer light, luminous with a pollen of dust, that filled up the chasms and angles of the city as the blinding eye of the sun was lowered; like eyelids, first this building then that was drawn over it; its red glare struck out again fiercely; came; went; was gone. As I got out of the car I had looked round me like a traveler set down in a foreign square; prepared to be pleased with everything he sees.

Inside, the building put aside the slippery marbled pretensions of the foyer and there was the indigenous smell, that I was soon to know so well, of fried onions and soot, and behind the door on which Joel and I rapped and walked in, Jenny in an unexpected splendor.

What is meant by love at the first sight is really a capture of the imagination; and I do not think that it is confined to love. It happens in other circumstances, too, and it happened to me then. My imagination was captured; something which existed in my mind took a leap into life. I saw the bright, half-bare room, the books all round, the open piano and some knitted thing of the baby's on a pile of music, a charcoal drawing tacked on the wall, a pineapple on a wooden dish and the girl with her bare breasts over the baby. Something of it remains with me to this day, in spite of everything; just as in love, after years of marriage that was nothing like one expected it to be, the moment of the first capture of the imagination can be recalled intact, though the face of the person who is now wife or husband has become the face of an enchanting stranger one never came to know. It was a room subordinate to the force of its occupants; the first of its kind that I was to live in.

"We really wanted a *man*," Jenny explained, while her husband wandered about the room looking tousled and vague, pushing his shirt into his trousers. "They're less trouble, we thought."

"Ah, it doesn't matter," he said. "She'll be able to sit with the baby. You'll see, Jen, she'll be useful to you." And we all laughed.

"Of course I'll move all the baby's things out of here."—She drubbed her stiff dark nipple at the little creature's nose and with a blind movement of frenzy it snatched it into its mouth. I was fascinated by the look of her breasts; the skin with the silky shine of a muscle sheath over the whiteness of flesh, and the intricate communication of prominent blue veins. They did not seem recognizable as a familiar feature of my own body, so changed were they from the decorative softness of my own sentient breasts. As she moved about settling the baby when he had fed, they swung buoyantly with the strong movements of her arms; she was a big girl with the slight look of rawness about the tops of her arms you sometimes see in English women. Still talking rather breathlessly—that was her way—she wriggled into a brassière and buttoned the blouse. "We must take the other room, John? Because of the porch.—We've rigged up a kind of little room for the baby on the porch, and the door leads from the other room—We're going to start putting him out there to sleep. It's not healthy to have him in with us. And you'll have this divan—the only thing is the cupboard." She caught her lip and laughed, waving toward the door of a built-in cupboard. "That's why we wanted a man—they take up less space somehow."

"Oh, I see—you mean my clothes. Yes, I'd have to have somewhere to hang—"

She nodded. "Exactly. Well, I'll have to take the groceries out of the bathroom one and put the junk out of this one in there." "If the worst comes to the worst . . ," said John, hands on his hips, speaking slowly, "I could move those maps and other stuff of mine over to my father's place."

His wife giggled at him carelessly fondly: "Oh, no you couldn't. Your mother's acid about the stuff of ours they've got already—"

He had a way of raising his eyebrows exaggeratedly. "Is that so? We-e-ll. When, Jen? Did my father say anything—" And they got caught up in one of the wrangling personal exchanges that were always easily parenthetic to their participation in general conversation. Joel had his head in the cupboard, which John had opened while he was talking, and he called out: "You've still got that archaeological data! Good Lord—" And started pulling out colored cardboard files. John dropped his discussion with his wife and went over to encourage him. Soon the floor was littered, and they sat in the middle of it. "It didn't come to anything," said John mildly. "I heard it was you, Jenny," said Joel, with innuendo. "They tell me you put a stop to it."

"Well, I like that!" she said. "Mickey backed out, and they didn't have the money without him. All I did was say that I knew something like that would happen, that's all."

John pointed at her. "But she was pregnant and she couldn't have gone!"

The two men laughed at her. I went over and sat down on the floor among the papers and photographs; they had the fascination of the practical details of something that had always been impressively remote: an archaeological expedition. While John and Joel explained and argued, she went about attending to the baby, dipping in and out the talk, competently. Once or twice the husband got up to help her with something; they laughed and pushed each other aside officiously over the child, like two people over a newfangled machine whose workings they do not quite get the hang of. "Look, put it this way—" "No, you idiot, they're always supposed to be put down on the *opposite* side to the one they were lying on before." The baby was like something they had bought for their own use and pleasure; a casual, forthright attitude quite different from the awe and flurry and worshipful subordination of normal life to a little sleeping mummy that I had known in homes on the Mine where babies were born. I had never cared for babies and I did not feel constrained to admire this one; even this small freedom appealed to me.

It was just as casually accepted that I should come and live with them. We had discussed little of what my mother would call the "details," but when Joel and I were leaving, John said as if he had just remembered: "Well, look, when is she going to come?"—I noticed he had a way of addressing remarks to people in the third person, through his wife, as if he and she interpreted the world to each other, and again I felt drawn to them for their evidence of solidarity, what seemed to me an intimacy as simple as breathing. This was what had appealed to me in them the very first time I had seen them, at Isa's flat. I felt in some obscure way that what they had was the basis of all the good things in life; from it like casements their minds opened naturally on beauty, compassion, and a clear honest acceptance. Now as we said good-by to them at the door, he leaning an arm on her shoulder, I felt a pang something like jealousy, but without bitterness, as for something which was still possible for me.

In the car I said to Joel: "I like them."

The intensity of the way I spoke must have struck him, and he said quickly: "Why . . . ?"

"They love each other."

I kept my head down in a kind of shyness for what I had said. He did not answer, but later, in the silence of a long, straight stretch of road on the way to Atherton, he did something he had never done before; I was gazing at the green summer veld threading past when I felt his hand on the nape of my neck, which was turned away from him. I turned back in confusion and surprise, as at a summons; Ludi's hand had come down upon me once just like that. And Joel was looking at me with the look of a smile in his deep, cool eyes, wondering in understanding, moved and questioning.

The little thread of continuity showing against a relationship so far removed in time, in experience, seemed part of the sense of disturbance and unreality that the upheaval at home had cast like a glare: a milk jug becomes an urn from another age; the feeling of fear, resentment and longing that I hold against the angry voice of my mother somehow becomes the feeling I had, pressed against the door of my room after a hiding. With my mind only half there, I watched the profile of the man sitting beside me; the hand that had rested on my neck relaxed on the steering wheel. Joel will never handle me with love, not even that love of the moment, like Charles', that deeply desired, faintly insulting recognition of the pure female, discounting me, making of me a creature of no name. Yet I said to myself, Why? And I saw him then for a moment not as Joel, but a young man alive and strange beside me, the curve of his ear, the full muscle of his neck, the indentation at the corner of his closed mouth, his thighs with the unconscious lordliness of any young male's legs. A faint ripple of sensation went over me. And instantly I was ashamed, I felt I had lost Joel for that instant. That was why it could never be; if I get him to touch me he will never be Joel again, he will never look at me the way he did just now, but with the concupiscence of lovers.

This peculiar afternoon light of my upheaval lay upon everywhere I went, everything I did, during that time. I did not see Mary Seswayo to speak to until after I had been to the Marcuses. She had smiled at me, or rather conveyed with the expressive quick movements of her intense eyes the sympathy of strain across the examination room, where we had sat together writing, but in the abnormal, distracted atmosphere which disorganized the normal life of the University at examination time, we had continually missed meeting. When we did meet, we were both exhausted by a three-hour paper rather pompously headed "Classical Life and Thought." We sat on the low stone balustrade feeling the lightness of the sunny air with the indolence of invalids.

I said to her: "I tried to get you somewhere decent to work. I wanted you to come home with me."

She looked at me quickly.

"Yes. I suggested to my mother that I should bring you home for a week or so. I had it all planned out. We've got a room that isn't inside and isn't out. But they were afraid to have you, even there."

Her face, that always waited, open, to receive the impress of what I was saying rather than to impose on me what she felt and thought, took on, for the first time since I had known her, something set. Set against me. Her eyes searched me, shocked, and her nostrils widened, her mouth settled in a kind of distressed annoyance. It was the expression that comes to the face of an older person when a young person does something the other had feared he might.

I gave a short uncomfortable laugh against it. But she continued to look at me. The palms of her hands went down firmly to lean against the stone. She seemed to be waiting for an explanation from me; I could feel the pressure of it as if I were being shaken to speak. Just as suspicion makes an innocent person falter like the guilty, so I was queerly upset by this displeasure I felt in her.

"I shouldn't have told you. Perhaps it's hurtful, after all. But I

thought we'd got to the stage where it was better not to pretend.
Then between us, between you and me, *at least,* you would
know . . ."

But I saw it was not that. There was nothing in her of the person
who has been slighted. She was not humiliated; in fact I had never
seen her so confident, so forgetful of *herself,* of what she inherited
in disabilities before the fact of me.

At last she spoke. "Your mother was angry," she said.

A spasm of annoyance caught me. "You mind? You expect it?
And you think it's right?"

"You made trouble for nothing," she said.

"*I* don't care about the trouble. It's more important to me than
the fear of offending. Even in my mother, what's false is false. I
won't accept it. But you will. Where's your self-respect?—Come to
think of it, you *should* be hurt. Yes, you should. . . . —Or is it even
worse—some sort of tribal nonsense coming up in you—what my
father would call 'the good old type from the kraal,' full of 'honor
thy father and mother' no matter how they think or what they do?"

She listened to me calmly. "I can see," she said, "you're upset.
There was trouble. And for nothing. For nothing, Helen—" She
made an appeal of it, shaking her head.

"Well, I don't understand you. Either you think that because
you're black you're not good enough to be a guest in my parents'
house, or you're distressed at the idea of my disagreeing with my
mother."

She said dully: "That's talk." Her eyes moved in her brown face
looking for fluency. "The fact that I'm good enough doesn't mean
that she's got to want me. If I were a white girl she could say no, if
she felt like it. But because I'm black she's got to say yes. Don't
you see, if I am good enough, I'm good enough not to go where I'm
not wanted?"

"You mean you wouldn't have wanted to come?"

"No. How could I come? All the time I would have had to feel
that they were letting me be there because of your—ideas—"

I said impatiently: "Yes, of course, I know that—"

"Never your friend staying with you. I would be forced on

them. And how would it have been for them with their friends? And the native girl who works for you?—It would have been hard for her. How was she to speak to me? Call me 'Miss' like you? Bring me tea?"

"Yes, why not? Anna's a domestic servant, you're not. There's no indignity in her bringing you tea. The fact that you're both black is irrelevant."

She thought a minute. "But there are so few of me. We're still exceptions, not a class. To your mother and Anna, I belong with Anna."

"So, must that always be considered first? Mustn't I think of you as a girl and a human being because that will upset the very thing that *must be* upset, my mother's and Anna's prejudices?"

She gave me her big, quiet, serious smile. "You want to give a nice plump person to practicing cannibals and tell them they mustn't eat him because it's like eating themselves. But they're used to eating people. They haven't had their ideas of diet changed yet, like you have."

I couldn't help smiling at her choice of analogy, the memory of some Bantu folk tale, cast in the form of the Department of English. She smiled back at me gently, expansively, a patient smile. But the moment of ease went out again.

"I'm so sorry . . . ," she said after a silence.

I was sharp. "You don't have to be. I'm not." I wanted her to say: I hate your saintliness. Don't be saintly. But we were not equal enough for that; for all my striving to rid myself of what was between us, I did not respect her, accept her enough to be able to quarrel with her. I still made a special consideration of her for that.

"You are quick," she said, with a flourish of the head, the way Anna might have said it, "quick, quick."

She leaned toward me, distressed, wanting me to understand. "If it had been your own house," she said, "but you can't expect to do it with the house of your mother. . . ."

"Mary," I said, "that's what *she* said. That's just exactly what *she* said. No—No—" and I would not let her talk. I laughed angrily, shook off what she wanted to say, protesting. I felt in myself the brightness, the edge that is very near to tears. And so to change the subject and save myself I told her that I was going to live in Johannesburg.

She did not know then or ever that this had anything to do with of what we had been speaking. She rubbed her neat straight hands together to relieve the stiffness of leaning on them. "Oh, that will be better for you!" She was shyly pleased. "But you'll miss them at home. I know. Like I miss mine."

PART THREE

The City

20 I USED TO WAKE UP for the first time very early at the baby's one strange sad cry for food. The night had just drained out of the room, and in the pale, hollowed space, a cave dimly gleaming after the tide, I lay with my body in sleep. In the next room, the soft dull sounds of Jenny moving about. Round the curtains that did not fit well, white edges of light; and quietly, deathly still, the books came out round me on the walls, a silent arpeggio of gleam ran across the case of the piano. Somebody's coat rose on a chair. A beer bottle answered from a corner. The white curl of Jenny's sketch propped against the wall; my dead roses black in the hanging vase.

I oared soundlessly away.

When I woke again in the noise and brightness of morning all the life of the night before was about me, where we had flung it down. I took it up again as I put on my clothes, dropped here and there on books, sheets of music, letters, a half-sewn romper for the baby. The flat was so small and the lives of Jenny and John so expansive that our possessions and our movements were hopelessly interlaced. The cupboard which had been cleared for me soon attracted back many of the objects which had been housed there before; John would forget and throw in a concert program he vaguely wanted to keep, the exposure meter for his camera would be put for safety on top of my silk blouses. As there was no mirror in the room, it was more convenient for me to keep my cosmetics in their room, where I could use Jenny's mirror. Then the piano was in my room

—or rather I was in the room where the piano was—so that meant that my shoes had to share space with John's music. This elastic exchange went on all the time, and was managed with a thoughtless ease that at first, out of my mother's conviction that life outside the facilities of a particular order was utterly unworkable, almost surprised me, in spite of myself. We were clean enough, fed enough, and it seemed to me a lot more comfortable, without making these necessities the whole business of living.

I moved in with the Marcuses after the Christmas vacation, at the beginning of my third academic year. John was a structural engineer and, like me, was out all day, but now, since the birth of the baby, Jenny was at home. In England, where she came from and where he had met her, she had been a designer of stage-sets attached to some repertory group, but although she had come out to South Africa with ideas of bringing professional creative competence to what was a semi-amateur field, where dress designers and students experimented happily, nothing much seemed to have come of her crusade since she had done the décor for a play I had seen before I knew her, and that had been unremarkable in its conventional startling unconventionality and literally rather shaky in execution, so that in one scene it did not hold together as it should. Still, there was a cardboard box of programs with the imprint of one of those particularly English-sounding names of a repertory company, crediting her with sets for Shaw, and Restoration comedy and Clifford Odets, and every week when the *New Statesman* came she would have something to say as she read down the column advertising experimental theater and lectures: "John, they're doing some Italian thing!" or "I see they're trying Lorca again—God, I'd give something to do that set for *Yerma*—" So it was accepted that the opportunities for her work were ridiculously limited in Johannesburg, and she must simply look on and mark time, smiling at the efforts of the dress designers and the technical college students. Before the birth of the baby she had done window dressing for a firm of commercial artists, and now she still managed an occasional free-lance job, for which the preparation could be made at home.

Their friends were all people whom I knew; a kind of distillation of the acquaintances I had been meeting over and over again for some time. Like a school of fish these people appeared at Isa Welsh's, at Laurie Humphrey's, disappearing into the confused stream of the city again, and then reappearing, quite unmistakably, known at once by the bond of specie which showed them unlike any other fish and like one another, although they were big fish and little, tame fish and savage, as if they had all worn a pale stripe round the tail or a special kind of dorsal fin. Now I was permitted to see what went on when they had whisked out of sight round the deep shelter of a dark rock; in this home water they swam more slowly and clustered, two or three, in a favorite shade.

I called them, along with John and Jenny, "our kind of people"; and certainly I felt myself more closely identified with them than I had with any others who had looked in upon my solitude.—First Ludi, then Joel, in their different ways, had stepped within its circle and been with me there, but this had not broken its transparent compass. It still had thrown me back like a sheet of glass that smashes a bird's head with the illusion of freedom. Now, quite un-dramatically, it melted, was suddenly simply not there: the way of life that I wanted seemed to be lived by these people with the acceptance of commonplace. Nothing could have been more reassuring. I felt as a man must who finds himself in a country where the subversive doctrine he has believed in for years is actually the dignified practice of government. An almost physical expansion took place in me; I began to wear bolder clothes, I even sat and moved with an ease and assurance of my own. And the timidity fell away from my opinions; in the intoxication of company I spoke them, ill-considered or not, in emulation of the outspokenness of Isa. At University, too, a new alertness, a consciousness of belonging to a certain attitude, made me more critical and less ready to accept as superior judgments the valuations of my professors.

"My, but it's become a keen little scout . . . ," Isa broke in on an argument I had been having, one evening. Her eyes, nimble as caged rodents, were too alive in the narrow pale freckled face that seemed to tighten and shrink when she was tired. On this night she was in a bad mood, which had the same effect. I blushed burningly before her tone, her look, rather than what she said, the implication of which was a little vague to me, anyway. But I was not really annoyed because I was confident in my new emergence, and the very fact that she should cross her sharp tongue with mine, even in derision, was evidence of it. And still over and above that, there was the thought that here, among "people our own kind," a bad mood was accepted along with the other facts of life, publicly. Some-one might growl at Isa: "Stop bitching," but no one would seriously suggest that she should pretend to be other than she felt.

The next morning, a Sunday, when we slept late, I wandered into John and Jenny's room and lay across the foot of their bed talking lazily. "Paul's the one for her." John was touching a mole on his wife's shoulder, covering it with his finger, then looking at it again. Jenny laughed.

"Kittie Paul?" I asked. There was a man we knew who for some forgotten reason was nicknamed "Kittie."

"No, Paul—Paul Clark."

"Oh, the one from Rhodesia." They often spoke of this Paul Clark, though I had not met him. Now, as so often happened with them, they had become absorbed in a little private tussle, a thing of protests and stifled monosyllables and laughter. I rescued the baby from between them—it started out the night in its own cub-byhole, but as soon as it cried one or the other brought it into their bed—and said, "Really? Why him?"

John looked vague, then remembered whom we had been talking about. "He would've shut her up," he said knowingly to Jenny. She began to laugh and they would have set about each other again but I put the baby into his arms. "Here—I'm going to get my cigarettes."

"Put some music on? While you're there—there's a good girl?" he yelled after me. "—And the kettle?" called Jenny. And so on this, as on most Sundays, we sat about in pajamas until twelve o'clock, Mozart or Bach flowing majestically through the flat, the energetic breath of coffee coming from an untidy kitchen. The Af-rican servant girl did not come in on Sundays, and Jenny and I did not trouble to clean up beyond emptying the ash trays and making the divans. She went leisurely about tending the baby, with his complication of sponges and cotton wool and his incense of talcum powder, her hair hanging and her pink English skin shining pleas-antly. But I always have been one of those women who look pale and desperate in the morning, who drown in sleep and must be brought back to semblance of life again, and so I used to slip into the bathroom and wash my face with cold water and put on some lipstick. Then they would laugh at me and Jenny would say, as from some superior knowledge: "You ought to get married, Helen."

Sometimes on fine Sundays we would go out into the country for the day—not the elaborate folding banquet of jellied tongue, sliced chicken and ice cream that I had known at home as a picnic, but a sudden enthusiasm at the sight of the sun clean and light on the pavement trees below the balcony, and a quick trip to the delicatessen shop in the old Jewish quarter which was the only food shop open in Johannesburg on a Sunday, and then out of the town to some farm where Jenny could ride a horse. She was given to moods of yearning craving for a kind of life that astonished me; a sudden assertion of her big fresh country-girl's body that belonged a generation or two back to a small squire's daughter in an English hunting county. Then she would whine and sulk and cajole to be taken where she could ride, while John, Jewish and deeply city-bred, seemed in the bewildered muscular inertia of his sedentary body, something completely removed and eternally stranger to her. I would hurry to help make plans that would make it easy for her to go, not, as it seemed, out of real sympathy or unselfish concern for someone else's whims, but because I did not want to see even the lightest crack running down the surface of their relationship. Their closeness—he practicing the piano intently, having about him that fascination of the person whose absorption in what he is doing is pure interest, while she, more practically and closer to the world, yet also with a decent relish for the performance of her hands, worked on a design; the knowledge that often, discounting my existence entirely, they were making love in the next room; even the swift anticipation of each other's wants (like breathless trapeze artists who know when this must be slapped into the palm of the other, that must be quickly swung past) with which they got through the business of dressing and breakfast on a working morning—was some sort of important proof to me. They were my beliefs, all miraculously coalesced into the lives of two people—or rather the indivisible life of two people: that was an essential part of the belief.

In the same way, I took a secret pride in the frugality of their living. Ever since I had begun to see the natives all around not as furniture, trees, or the casual landmarks of a road through which my life was passing, but as faces; the faces of old men, of girls, of children; ever since they had stepped up all around me, as they do, silently, at some point in the life of every white person who lives in South Africa, something had been working in me. The slow corrosive guilt, a guilt personal and inherited, amorphous as the air and particular as the tone of your own voice, which, admitted or denied, is in all white South Africans. The Nationalist farmers who kicked and beat their convict African laborers had it and it was in me. Like an obscure pain we can't confess we clutch to it this counterirritant, or that. One pretense is kinder than another, that is all. With kicks and curses you may keep the guilt at a distance, with a show of the tenderness of my own skin, I may clasp it like a hair shirt.

The Marcuses had little choice to live otherwise, since they had little money, but they made it clear that they regarded it as only decent to keep one's wants as few and simple as possible. They had a kind of amused detachment toward wants which exceeded their own, making friends at whose house a servant waited white-aproned at table feel somehow ridiculous, and raising their eyebrows at Laurie when he brought to the flat a girl innocently wearing a rather cheap fur coat. While they scorned a superfluity of possessions, they believed that almost any sacrifice was worth the possession of one or two really beautiful things, and their Japanese-cum-Swedish aesthetic of utility answered perfectly my own reaction against the overgrown knickknackery of the Mine.

But my response to the austerity of their living went deeper than that. It assuaged something in me which was nameless, which I scarcely consciously knew; that something working in me, eating at me, since the realization of those faces. It put me that much less of a remove from them, playing in the gutter when I had played in the garden; going to work in the silent dark while I slept; looking on at the armor of my white skin.

Of course, I realized that my participation in the Marcuses' way of life was that of the privileged amateur. My father paid my University fees and my share of expenses at the flat, although I no longer

took a dress or spending allowance from him. During the long summer vacation, when I still had been living at home, I had taken a
job in a bookshop, and I determined that the money I had earned
then should last me until the next vacation, when I would get another
temporary job. I had fewer clothes, if more ingenious ones, than I
ever had had before, and even then, when I was going out, I felt a
little ashamed to parade my choice before Jenny, whose entire wardrobe, she was always eager to admit, took up four hangers. I found,
however, that I was spending money on things I had never bought
before. Toward the end of the month, when funds were low and we
were all a little tired of subsisting on thin stews consisting mainly
of green peppers, I sometimes brought home a small smelly box of
frozen crayfish tails that, as they boiled, sent a tantalizing scent of
the sea through the flat, or a punnet of strawberries and some cream.
I also contributed heavily to our liquor stock—the two or three
bottles of brandy and gin and the case of beer that seemed no sooner
delivered than they went to join the dusty collection of empties on
top of the kitchen dresser. Although they shrugged at the delicate,
high-heeled American shoes I brought home with a defiance born
of vanity (Jen couldn't wear things like that, said John, she's got the
strong, heavily modeled feet of peasant women, feet made to dance
and walk), they were not affronted by these other signs of my social
dilettantism; when there was something good to eat, and a bottle of
Nederburg Riesling I had picked up at the bottle store on the corner,
we ate and drank together with gusto.

One Saturday morning something happened that surprised me.
It was trivial and so overshadowed by the meeting that followed it
that I did not really try to interpret it, yet its oddness, like something
small, sharp and bright that is obviously part of a larger design,
made me automatically put it away in my less immediate consciousness even while I forgot it.

I had been to town early and, on coming back, had thrown my
parcels and coat and hat on John and Jenny's bed. I went into the
bathroom and when I came out and passed down the passage, I
thought I saw, in the liquid flash of the mirror through the door,
Jenny looking at herself. When I had been in the other room for the
length of time it takes to smoke a cigarette, her silence in the room

next door roused a faint curiosity. I got up lazily and wandered in on her. She was sitting on the edge of the bed with my hat on. With her back to me, she saw me first in the mirror, and in the mirror, smiled, and with a little noise of embarrassment pulled off the hat as she turned round.

"It suits you better than me," I said ruefully. "But it shouldn't be so straight." And I put it on her again, at more of an angle. We both looked at her, a pretty girl in the red hat. She put up her hand and touched at the side. "The velvet's so soft," she said. "I saw a green one, not the same, but something like it, a dear, in town. So cheap, too. I'm dying to buy myself one, but John'd kill me."

And she quickly pulled the hat off again and held it out to me, with a little shake, as if she wanted me to take it from her quickly. With that smile of guilty pleasure warming her face, I suddenly had the feeling that this was not Jenny; I had not been talking to her the way I would talk to Jenny.

She stood looking at the hat. "I wish I could persuade him. But I know he won't." She actually had lowered her voice, longingly.

"What about the money you got for the Graham display?"

She gave a little laugh and I really thought I saw her look at the door. "It's not just that—he says—you know . . . only bourgeoise women wear hats." She ran her first finger over the pile of my hat.

"He won't"—I was going to say "allow" but stopped myself at what was quite an unthinkable word between John and Jenny—"he won't let you wear a hat? Oh nonsense—" I had to laugh to convince myself it was some kind of loverlike game between them. And I stood there forcing her with the laughter of unbelief. This was not John, either. For a second it was as if I caught a glimpse of two people who seemed very like, but were not them, could not be them.

Before she could answer, the quiet of the flat was caught up with the creak and bang of the front door flung open in the assault that meant John was home. His voice was mingled with that of another man as he called along the passage: "Anyone home? Jenny, hi, look what I've brought—" At once he was in the doorway, a bag of eggs under one arm, a bunch of bananas in newspaper under the other, looking, as he always did when he had shopped, like a triumphant looter.

What he had brought was Paul Clark, standing behind him look-ing at us over the gasping, disjointed, excited monologue. He wore a pale green waistcoat and I remember I wondered what the Mar-cuses would have to say about that. In his small, slim, energetic hand with the watch just above the wristbone and the veins ner-vously enlacing the knuckles, he held a toy rabbit by the ears, and a bottle of wine by the neck. Jenny rushed up and kissed him.

—I stuffed away the curious glimpse of a moment or two before, like a scrap of paper with the address of the place where I had seen two faces and must return sometime to verify or refute the resemblance.

In the confusion of greetings that followed, the stranger said, looking at me, "It's grown up awfully quickly . . . I thought it was only six months?"

"That's not it, that's Helen." John was always a little wild when he brought friends home. "Here the thing is in its pram, you idiot."

21 THE STRANGER. Paul the stranger. I have looked at that face as I shall never look upon another. There was a light in it for me that put something out; dazzled into black silence. So I shall never again answer with the vivid compulsion that made me watch the face of Paul, spelling it out feature by feature with my eyes, as if my finger traced it in the air and my lips moved about a name without sound.

So much has been written about the curious compelling fasci-nation of the faces of some women, but I do not remember reading anywhere anything that would testify to the same innocent deadli-ness in the face of a man: a face such as Paul's. Yet just as they do in women, these faces exist in men. It is as if a chance disposition of features, pleasant and ordinary enough in themselves, creates a proportion that is the magic cipher of power. The owners of these faces have only to look. They themselves cannot escape the power which is upon them; indeed some of them, a few men as well as many women, live their whole lives off it, making the world pay for a divine and lucky accident. Others, for whom it is not the only asset, are sometimes unaware of it, and even mistake the advantages it draws as due to some more responsible cause.

Paul was an enchanting talker. When he talked his body became a puppet animated by his mind; he mimicked, he made emotion graphic with his hands, his voice turned his anecdote this way and that in quick pleasure. From that first day, when we sat over the lunch which Jenny and I had opened out of tins, I felt that he took up attention in a special way: I found that while he talked I must watch him intently, and believed that this was because what he said and the way that he said it were so interesting. But in time I came to know that it was his face itself that held me, that face at which I could look and look so that sometimes the fascination would take me away entirely, and I would lose whole passages of what he was saying.

This angered me with myself then, and does still. My lip curls when I must admit that even had Paul not been what he was, had he been trivial, passionless and commonplace, I might still have loved him. The look of him never lost its power over me; even in anger and hurt it retained a higher authority that my whole self as a woman, deaf, dumb, blind, never failed to answer.

As it was, Paul was quick. Quick as opposed to dead in the most accurate sense, for in no one I have known could one have more clearly the sense of blood running, heart beating, impatient intelligence alight, even the attraction of his sex upon him like the gloss on the plumes of a male bird—a creature becoming rather than merely being. And all this he took as carelessly as if it were as common an evidence of life as the first gulp of breath we all draw with the same eagerness at the sharp moment of birth. In him, it seemed to me, most of the things the rest of us talked about or hazily aspired to, came to life. He had spent a magnificent childhood on the farm in Natal which had belonged to his father's family since the middle of the nineteenth century, running wild with no consciousness of the lordliness of the life, riding horses and playing with young native boys of his own age and prowess. He spoke the two main Bantu languages, Zulu and Sesuto, with the colloquial familiarity among their formal difficulties that comes only when you have learned a language as you have learned to speak, and so, unlike the rest of us, he did not move half his life like a deaf man, among people whose speech and thought and laughter were closed to him. The almost feudal character of his life as a child included his parents' odd English tradition of courtesy toward any difference that became evident as he grew up, between their ideas and his. His rejection of the farm for the study of law, and then his rejection of law in favor of social science, and a job in the offices of the Native Affairs Department in Johannesburg, they gently regarded as a matter of taste. When Paul spoke about them, you could not fail to feel the charm of the way in which they saw what Edna might have called a revulsion against a capitalist-imperialist outlook and way of life—the putting aside, in fact, of everything they had to offer—as a young person's whim, in which it was parental and polite to show mild interest. So, unlike my parents and me, whose differences, like our lives, were on a closer, more suburban scale, Paul and the Clarks remained on affectionate terms.

When he came to the flat for the first time that day, he had just been home on a visit, and before that he had been in Rhodesia for four months. This was part of the six-months' study leave he had been granted by the Department to write his Ph.D. thesis on "African Family Adjustments to Urban Environment."

He was moving into a very small flat where the edge of the city raveled out into shabby suburbia—among the whores and the hoboes and the motor-spares business, he put it—and for a week was busy painting the one room and rearranging the intricacies of the cupboard-kitchen.—A dehydrated affair, he told us, open the doors, turn on the faucet and sprinkle—up comes the stove and the refrigerator. John and Jenny were amused but not particularly interested by his activity with the flat; I understood that he moved frequently, and they had gone through the whole reorganization process with him before.

He spent a great deal of time at the Marcuses' flat and I gathered that he always had. He was also an intimate of most of their friends, and was almost always on his way from or to people we knew. Over lunch the first day there had been much talk of common friends, questions asked, news related. "Seen Isa yet?" John had said keenly.—Later I saw that there seemed to be a vying for the attention and company of Paul among his friends. Often Jenny would say severely, almost jealously, "Now don't forget I expect you tonight. I'm making a pilaff and I don't want you to turn up at eight full of Laurie's beer and sardines." Since we seldom made any special preparation for anybody, and certainly not for anyone who came as often as Paul, it was not the waste of dinner but the idea that he might prefer to eat with others which prompted her.

"Has she gone back to her book?" Paul asked. "There was a letter of hers supposed to be sent on to me from Luanshya, but it hasn't come yet."

John shrugged his lack of interest. "She wouldn't be discussing it with me, anyway."

"You should have heard her the other night," said Jenny, warming to gossip, with an eager smile. "She simply snapped Helen up in one bite. One of her charming moods."

When he had heard the story, Paul said, supplying the answer to a problem that didn't puzzle him at all: "You were having an argument? A political argument with a man, and keeping your end up? Of course; Isa can't stand intelligence in other women, don't you know? She has the greatest respect for the views of an intelligent man, but she can't listen to another woman talking sense. Oh, she'll defend the equality of men and women all right, but God help the woman who's equal to her."

"Well, apparently she doesn't think me intelligent enough," said Jenny tartly, "because I've never had any trouble with her."

In the laughter that followed, John hooked an arm round her neck, pulling her over to him, and said, "Never mind, Jen, Isa's just sex and a brain and nothing in between."

"John said that you would have been the one to deal with her," I laughed to Paul. "He seemed to think you could defend the rights of women before the ardent feminist."

But he only smiled slightly, politely in answer and lifted his

eyes once to John, who was not looking at him, before giving his
attention to choosing a ripe tomato from Jenny's untidy bowl of salad.

"He likes her, eh?" said John to Jenny one evening after Paul had
left us. He looked at me with the warning, smiling approval of the
madam who sees one of her girls favored by a special client.

I looked from one to the other.

"You'll see," said John. "She'll be the next."

"Oh, John, you're awful," smiled Jenny in what we called her
"hush" voice; the awed, slightly arch reaction that belonged somewhere back in her English nursery. The two of them had the habit
of discussing the personal lives of their friends as if they were en-
tomologists observing the mating patterns of beetles; it did not seem
to occur to them that the bald facts of who went to bed with whom
might have the same meaning and emotional commitment as their
own prized relationship, which they held jealously and privately
apart. At first I had seen this attitude as part of a desirable frankness
and acceptance of people the way they were, life the way it was,
part, in fact, of their honesty. But when I had noticed that they
excluded themselves from this clinical valuation, I had begun to
think that the manner in which they discussed their friends' love
affairs was unfair—I would not allow myself to consider that they
were capable of the breach of human feeling that is bad taste.

But now that their cold and gleeful surveillance was turned on
me, annoyance rose. I was still unsure and admiring enough of their
grasp of life to wish to conceal it, and so only my tone belied the
carelessness of my words when I said: "Do they go in strict rotation?
Are there so many?"

They laughed. "One or two. There have been one or two, believe
me. Women!" And John put on the face of knowing, reluctant bewilderment, contemplating the way they were attracted to Paul.

Jenny said suddenly: "I wish you'd offer to type his thesis for
him, Helen—" And added: "Otherwise Isa will." She looked at my
face as if she were entreating me out of some threat to herself.

"Oh, yes." John's voice jumped to the eagerness of hers. "Go
on, Helen.—Because she will, she will."

My annoyance rose a spurt higher at what I saw as an obvious acceptance that I wished to bait Paul Clark's interest, and that they, tickling the beetles along with a blade of grass, wanted to connive and watch. "Damn it, why should I? What an idea! I haven't the slightest intention of spending my evenings over a typewriter for Paul or anybody else. . . ."

Yet I was baiting Paul's interest, and I knew it. On some other level than speech or conscious connivance, and toward some other end than the social and sexual titillation of a new combination within our group, I was beckoning him with all the thunderous silence of the deep attraction between us. Every time he or I walked into the room where the other was, coming into relation with each other and others like figures in a group of sculpture, there was a tightening of this. Every time we talked, ate together, trooped off to a cinema or a concert, the design of the company shifted a little, re-formed with him and me closer, more apart from them and significant.

I felt a consciousness of my physical self—the attractiveness of my face as I turned my head and looked along my cheekline, the color of my loose red hair against a lilac-colored dress that created for me in combination a light of my own, fixed, like the light in which a painter has seen his picture—that I had not known since the time of the South Coast with Ludi. And as it had been with Ludi, the warm smell of Paul's hair as he bent down in front of me to pick up something in the sun, the look of the skin of his arm as he rolled up a shirt sleeve, the damp look of his forehead when he had been running, had for me a pure fascination that needed only touch to become desire. It was difficult to believe that I had felt this before, for some other particular combination of flesh and spirit that makes every man a creature never to be matched, never to be repeated. . . . Yet it gave me a kind of simple sensual pride to understand out of experience the flow of this current. To wait, till it should take me up again; till I should lay myself down Ophelialike, and be carried by it.

There the comparison with Ludi ended. As a human being, Ludi was remote: no one could have been more involved with life than Paul. And with him, for those first few weeks, my relationship with the Marcuses was lifted into a new meaning, blazed briefly into something approaching the free, gay, competent intimacy which had

been my illusion of adult life when I was an adolescent. My presence
with the Marcuses was now balanced out; as a young woman, I had
my opposite number, a young man, and the sexual attraction between us lightly underscoring the heavier emotional threat in our
own private air corresponded to the sexual ease between John and
his wife. We were four friends, and two pairs; also two men friends
and two women friends. So I felt myself an equal in the Marcuses'
participation in life both public and personal. If there was a point
in understanding at which by gesture or implication John and Jenny
ducked beneath the surface to some life of their own out of sight,
so I, too, had, in the certain instinct of Paul's attraction to me, a
place they could only guess at.

And they said no more about the chances of affection or an affair
between us. I was sure that they speculated about it in private—
was vain enough to wonder, when I heard the murmur of their voices
in their room at night, whether they were discussing it—but the
confrontation of us, in all the mystery and delicacy with which,
though we used the stereotyped gestures of modern sophistication,
the irony, the cool banter, the love of argument, we circled round
each other in approach, made open comment impossible in spite of
themselves.

When Paul had been back in Johannesburg for nearly three
weeks, we spent a dull evening without him. He had had to go to
the Welshs' for dinner, and we had Herby and a friend coming. The
friend proved to be a girl in a taffeta dress with a string of pearls
round her neck of the graded kind that small girls are given on their
ninth or tenth birthday, along with their first bottle of scent, and a
lace-bordered handkerchief which she kept clutched in her hand all
through dinner. By the time dinner was over it was obvious that
conversation with this girl was not only impossible (she replied with
yes or no, and dropped her eyes quickly) but that she was as inhibiting to conversation excluding her as a child who listens with round
eyes to what she cannot understand but cannot help hearing. Jenny
and I, going into the kitchen to help Hilda with the coffee, impro-
vised a seemingly spontaneous dialogue that would bring up the idea
of going to a cinema. John was quick to take the cue, and we went
into town and saw an indifferent film which I, for one, had seen

before. Herby was essentially a useful person; tolerated for this
rather than his rather dull manner of presenting his sound ideas,
and so, as his friends, we could not help feeling rather impatient at
having been used ourselves, by him—for obviously he had been
obliged in some way to take this girl out, and had shifted the impossibility of entertaining her onto us. So we felt as if it were only
what was due to us, the least, in fact, he could do, to suggest, as he
did when we came out of the cinema, this particular night to take
us to Marcel's Cellar.

Marcel's Cellar was, as the name implies, the nostalgia of a group
of restless young people for the Left Bank Paris of the brief experience of one or two and the imagination of the others. In the idea
of the place there met, vaguely as could only happen thousands of
miles away from the actuality, the garret of Mimi and Rudolph in
the eighties and one of the cafés where Sartre characters talked.
Even the name of the "owner" was in character, if out of date—but
this was pure fortunate coincidence that Marcel du Toit's name, common among Afrikaans South Africans with their mixed Huguenot-
Dutch antecedents as Smith or Robinson among people of English
descent, should be so appropriately romantic. He himself was a
willowy, shady character, who with less pretensions would have been
running a side show in a traveling fun fair, and, indeed, he presided
over his cellar with an air of extreme languid dissipation that was
clearly his underworldly bohemian version of the robust flourish he
would have used for The Greatest Show on Earth.

How he had come by the place, no one seemed to know. As I
have said, it was the idea of seven or eight young people who decided to find some cheap convenient place in town where they could
be private from any but their own kind and sit talking and perhaps
drinking a little cheap wine until one o'clock in the morning. Each
would pay a share of the rent, and this levy would serve as a sub-
scription, so that the whole thing would be a kind of club. They
dragged in some old mattresses, lit up the cobwebs with a few candles in bottles, and were probably as cosy as children playing be-
sieged Indians. Unfortunately, they enjoyed themselves so much that
they told their friends, and their friends began to come along, too,

and bring their friends' friends, and in no time the original group
found their mattresses and their Jeripigo taken over by medical students who had picked up with vaguely arty girls, young men who
worked as window dressers or clerks and wanted to paint or write
—the whole shoal of restless, vaguely Leftist, mostly innocent Johannesburg youth which escaped to another unreality from the neon
and air-conditioned unreality of the cinemas and the shops of their
daily lives. It must have been then that Marcel saw his opportunity,
and, like the Wolf dressed up as the Grandmother, put on his velvet
jacket and relieved the bewildered group of the responsibility for
the rent.

The great thing about the place was that it really was a cellar.
This was an inestimable advantage that Marcel must have been
quick to see. Instead of driving out to a roadhouse or going to a
shiny Greek tearoom or a plush-insulated hotel where a trio played
blearily from *Showboat*, we drove down to the area of darkened
warehouses. There, where the cement and the paving rang like iron
beneath the street lights, almost opposite the central police station
which was only a name or a vaguely disquieting joke to us in our
white skins and middle-class security, was the old building which
once had housed a wholesale liquor business. We went in through
the old-fashioned door of an empty shop whose windows were hung
with hessian and then down a rickety wooden stair for which a hole
had been made in the rotting wooden floor, into the cellar.

It looked and smelled like the workshop of a garage, and we
stood looking round with the suppressed giggles of curiosity while
Herby was engaged in some sort of argument with an official-looking
blonde sitting at a kitchen table. She was flanked by a couple of
very young men who established their status as habitués by the
extreme casual untidiness of their clothes—no one could be so hap-
hazardly rumpled anywhere but at home. As the place had no li-
cense, no charge could be made for admission, but apparently this
snag was circumvented by the rule that patrons had to pay a "sub-
scription" which varied on the blonde's assessment of what they
looked as if they might pay. Even when Herby had put down a note
and we were officially in, one of the young men sauntered up to the
women of our party and said: "Wouldn't any of you like to give us

a donation—? Anything—a piece of your jewelry?" The girl froze terrified as if it had been suggested that she leave her virginity at the door, and Jenny and I burst out laughing at the idea of gravely presenting our "jewelry"—a Zulu bead collar she had bought for 5/6, and a pair of cheap oxidized silver earrings that I wore. "— She'll leave her wedding ring with you on her way out—" said John, ushering Jenny past.

"Where're we going to sit ourselves . . . ?" Herby was looking briskly out over the dark, bare place where here and there a candle threw huge shadows on the rough whitewashed walls and the huddles of people with their voices lowered to the dark as if he were entering a restaurant where an obsequious maître d'hôtel would come up to lead us to a white-covered table. All the mattresses on the floor were fully occupied with murmurous burdens and the few wooden forms round the walls were clustered with people sitting and standing, so we all laughed at him. "It's exactly like an air-raid shelter," Jenny was saying. "If they'd ever lived in England it wouldn't be their idea of pleasure. Exactly like a shelter, even the mattresses." Herby had dashed on ahead and, the perfect host, found a vacant mattress for us, or rather an almost vacant mattress— someone's coat claimed a corner of it but the owner was not there. As we settled ourselves down, the group around the radiogram near the stair broke away like a football scrum, and a French tango, scratchy, passionate, the musical equivalent of the breath of sweet wine and garlic, swung out.

At once I liked the place; it was ridiculous, self-conscious, pathetic in its attempt to be dramatically sordid, but it was fun: an amusing parody of a kind of life which did not exist in Johannesburg. I was watching the couples who were getting up all around us to dance on the part of the cracked concrete floor that was kept clear, and the tall figure that Herby had pointed out as Marcel, moving about with a way of arresting his head, lifted momentarily in the advantage of a flicker of light, so that you could see his pointed golden-colored beard and the curl of smoke round his head from the long holder in his mouth and the nimbus of his golden-brown velvet jacket. I saw that, rather pointlessly and harmlessly, since the place was so dark, people of diverse talents had been allowed to contribute

some wall decorations—just behind our heads there was a horrify-
ingly emaciated Christ, represented as an African, with the half-
finished background of the hovels of Shantytown, and over above
the bunch of dancers, where a candle in a tin holder was hung on
a nail, a tremendous female figure, bulbous in the magazine manner,
covered half the wall. The radiogram, too, was magnificently vulgar
and incongruous; a great thing of shiny veneered woods, zebra-
striped in imitation of fancy grains—the kind of machine that can
only be bought on hire purchase.

But Jenny and John were regarding the place perfectly seriously;
I could see that. They were looking around just as they did when
by some chance they found themselves in a typical "nice" middle-
class home in one of Johannesburg's fashionable northern suburbs.
"It's hardly the sort of thing to interest progressive people—I mean,
I should think that if they have any politics at all they're likely to
be anarchist and antisocial." Jenny bent her head to me in the
confidential deprecating tone with which she would point out a built-
in cocktail cabinet or a baby crib hung with lace and ribbons.
". . . The obverse side of this is, of course, Houghton," John was
saying to Herby. As a Jew who, by marrying a Gentile girl from
England, had completed his assimilation in a society that held as
one of its basic tenets a complete absence of race-consciousness,
he made his Jewish origin a guarantee of good faith which allowed
him to speak of the Jews in a manner which would not have been
considered acceptable in a Gentile with the "right ideas." "These
are the children of Market Street merchants, I'll bet. Papa makes a
hundred thousand in soft goods, there's a swimming pool and a
tennis court and two Buicks, and the kids start up this sort of thing.
Petit Trianon of the bourgeois. But you'll notice it's not the rousing
drinking songs, the lively dancing and the open-air eating places
they try to re-create. Those are in their racial memory, too, but they
want to forget them. Their fathers want to forget those; they've spent
thirty or forty years piling up money to put them at a distance from
everything that was in their lives when they were simple oppressed
people in Europe. But their suppression of their working-class origin
creates a guilt feeling in the kids which goes the usual way—it
manifests itself somewhere else. Here it poisons their healthy fan-

tasy; when they want to play at being poor it's not the vigorous, hopeful proletariat they ape, it's the miserable, nihilistic café life of the dispossessed exile. Forgetting one bad memory, they 'remember' a worse one: they want the darkness, the instinct to hide away, to meet secretly and talk in whispers, of their brothers who survived concentration camps. —The concentration camps for which our Houghton friends have a certain moral responsibility because they were the product of a Fascist-Capitalist society much like the one in which *they* are making their money. . . ."

The girl whose coat had been lying on the mattress we had taken apparently noticed we had commandeered her place, and came flying up to see if her coat was still there. She was a bright-haired girl unfashionably dressed in a print frock, and her rounded breasts, not divided and pressed into a uniform pointedness by the American brassière that was accepted as a decree of desirability by Johannesburg women of all classes, suggested a farm girl. She was panting and warm from the dance and the twist and pressure of her body against her rumpled belt and the seams of her sleeves as she caught up the coat had something of the sensuous emanation of the bodies of children sweaty with hard play. She seemed to make nonsense of what John was saying. Not because she was Afrikaans, obviously poor, and neither suffering from nor even sufficiently burdened with sophistication to know that there was such a thing as a guilt feeling, but because she was in a moment of completely unthinking living, and he, a young, good-looking man, was capable only of dry observation.

I felt again the sense of drift, of alienation from the abstractions coming out of people's mouths—my own and others—that came to me sometimes at the highest point of a discussion. It would seem to me that the creaking ropes that attached talk to living raveled out with a thin snap and what I was listening to and saying with such intensity floated away as unconnected with my living being as a kite to the earth from which its string has been cut. Now I felt myself living and aware as part of the dank, dusty dark where contact with other men and women was the brush of a hand or the momentary warmth of a thigh bumped against you, rather than speech. The way they managed to dance on the rough floor, cavorting breathlessly, or pressed together, the girl's head limp on the man's shoulder, the man's face turned to her hair, in the spell of concentration desire puts suddenly upon people, gave the tomblike place a contrast of warm-blooded life, a sort of human impudence which made the air sensual. I felt closer to the young Afrikaans girl than to the friends with whom I lived.

Herby, too, seemed slightly excited by the Cellar, and gave only a distracted half-attention to John. He had managed to get some wine. There were no glasses so we had to gulp it out of the bottle, and it became clear from the teasing way he pressed it upon me and kept asking me what I thought of the place, that he intended to neglect the girl friend and attach himself to me. When he pulled me up to dance I found myself looking at the line of his jowl, the thick skin uneven with shallow shining holes like the bubble holes in a slice of cheese, and noting without pity or regret his complete lack of attraction and the way my body automatically held well away from his and even my hand, loosely in his, kept a withdrawn formality of its own. He would think that we were dancing like this out of respect for me because I was not an "easy" girl and he would not believe that I would dance pressed close with my legs interlaced with a man's like the people around us. He would go on for years thinking this about all the girls of his own world, all the girls who were proud and good-looking and able to talk on his own level of intelligence: that casual love-making was only to be had where he got it, from girls who were inferior and did not interest him outside the relief of sex.

While I was thinking this about him and we were dancing he was talking to me and I was answering with a certain exertion of charm which was a little unkind, but which the atmosphere brought out in me almost without my volition. Every time we danced near the stair he would crane his neck to see the people still coming in although the place was already crowded, and when this had happened several times he explained: "Isa's having some friends and she said she might come along. I promised I'd keep a look out so's I could get them in."

It seemed a very long time before they came.

They won't come, I kept telling myself, make up your mind

they're not coming. I never took my eyes off the stair, through the well of which people appeared feet first, so that sometimes they paused with only the bottom half of their bodies visible and I had to wait to make sure that those were not the thin calves of Isa, the brogues of Paul. Jenny said: "Oh good! Do keep a watch out, Herby? They may not see us in this dingy hole." But I did not know whether I wanted them to come or not: in case Paul should be with another girl; in case he should see me in the context of dancing with Herby. Yet the fact that he might be coming was hardly the surprise of something unimagined, to me. He had been in my mind in the power of his absence all the evening; my sympathetic pleasure in the atmosphere of the place, my warmth toward the odd-looking young men and the cheap, yearning girls, was the softening toward all human frailty that comes from one's own sudden involvement in wanting and loving. Even the cold appraisement of the accepted for the outsider which I had given poor Herby had been really a measure of Paul's irresistibility, of the eagerness of my response to Paul rather than the nonexistence of my response to Herby.

When they did come it must have been at a moment when politeness had forced me to look away from the stair to answer someone, for suddenly the American boy whom I had seen once with Edna Schiller caught Herby by the shoulder and said exasperatingly: "Good God. —You're a bloody fool, Herb? We been battling half an hour to get in without your fraternity pin." Herby broke out in fusses and apologies like a hen flying up off the nest but before he could convince the American that we had been watching, the rest of the party pushed their way up headed by an Isa stimulated by the argument at the door and glinting sharply, in the dimness and her dark dress, with earrings and some kind of broad metal belt. Her quick eyes and the whiteness of her small face and hands caught the light in the same way as her jewelry; darkness did not put her out, make her a vague shape and scent like the other women. The whole force of her personality was defined against the softness, a little knife showing steely and keen in a wicked ripple on dark ground. With her was Paul and a big, beautiful blonde girl.

We looked at each other for a moment like people who look

across the water between the deck of a ship and the quayside and then he came over to me and sat down next to me. I had made some sort of conventional laughing greeting to him as well as to the others, but though he had answered the rest with his usual fluent gaiety, he had said nothing to me. He leaned across me to speak to them and his hand pressed down firmly on my thigh as he did so. The gesture was not expedience. The grip of his thumb and his four fingers on my flesh made that clear.

When the music started again he got up and held out his hand for me. He edged a way for us through the groups of men who stood laughing, arguing for attention around slowly smiling girls, and neither resisted nor moved as you pushed past, and as we went through a gauze of thin light I saw a girl turn her head swiftly to look at him; a look that opened her lips and showed a glint of teeth, like the hidden pistil in the softness of a flower. We were buffeted by the soft, blind shapes on the floor; now and then a voice said lightly—sorry! All the ugly, mysterious place turned slowly round us; Christ, the bulbous nude, the candles in their tin holders, the vents high up on the wall that, as you passed beneath them, breathed the fresh night like a queer reminder. Men without girls stood watching the dancers, their hands hanging as if something had just fallen from them.

My one hand lightly touched against the texture of Paul's jacket and the other held his, a warm hand, not thin, in which you felt the bones. He said: "I saw a friend of yours today. Joel Aaron."

"Oh, where?" I asked with pleasure, hardly knowing what he said.

"Bumped him in town." When he wanted to talk, he had to press his chin back and down away from me, looking at me along his small nose with the beautifully curved nostrils. "I didn't know you knew him. But he seems to know all about you."

I said: "He's the best friend I've ever had—" It sounded lame and almost insincere. I arched back from Paul a little to give what I had put so poorly the emphasis of my look.

But he was looking at me, smiling, ignoring my look. "Is he, is he. . . ." he murmured, and drew me back to him.

"Yes . . . ," I said, and it no longer seemed to matter what we had been talking about. Under the flow of cold air from the vents he dropped his head and kissed me delicately and passionately.

We moved round and round, slowly, among the others. I was sunk in the voluptuous relief of leaning against his body: ah, how I wanted this, I kept saying to myself, how I waited for this from you. A kind of midnight frenzy was on the place now. Smoke made the dark mist and the candlelight radiance, and the lonely young men were a little drunk. Two traffic policemen had wandered in and, with some hazy notion of keeping in with the law, were being made much of. Marcel carried a demijohn of wine above the crush; the one policeman put his foot, with the calf gleaming militarily in its fine high boot, up on a bench. The other man stood jeering amorously with a girl who had put his peaked cap on her huge head of curls that danced like springs as she moved. As we passed we heard his deep voice speaking a coy Afrikaans, egging, insinuating.

Everyone looked at two girls who had begun to sway before each other, each holding the gaze of the other like cocks about to fight. A woman danced with her whole body droopingly suspended from her arms about a man's neck, her face sunk and eyes closed.

I smiled to Paul in the dark half-jokingly: "We're just like the rest."

He said: "Of course." And I was suddenly pleased; I felt a kind of loyal partisanship with the crude advances of the traffic policemen, the lonely determination for gaiety with which men without girls passed the metallic-tasting wine, the hoarse, sentimental voice of the gramophone—the whole half-pathetic, half-greedy demand of the place. It seemed to me that all we wanted was music, someone to hold, a little talk. It made all human beings seem so simple; it was the touch of love that sounded so impossible in books and speeches. The one touch of love, of regret for barriers erected, misunderstanding, sneers and indifference, without which all intentions came to nothing. But although it was needed there so badly, it was not a thing that always attended or even, paradoxically, survived the conscious efforts of human beings to reach one another. Look at Mary, I thought; I tried hard with Mary. They try with justice, with declarations of human rights, with the self-abnegation of Christ.

Love one another. —It becomes nonsense when you decree it. An absolute, like black and white, that has no corresponding reality in the merging, changing outlines of living.

When it does come, it comes irrelevantly; out of the unworthy cheap atmosphere of a place like this; out of the deep receptivity of a personal emotion. But it doesn't matter where it comes from. Gods come like that, not in the places prepared for them, but appearing suddenly among the rabble. I only wished it would last, that I could take it with me away from the warmth of Paul and these faces pitiful with the strange strength of the desire to assert life in pleasure.

We went up the stairs and into the quiet street. We could not even hear the music. The night was clear but the blue light of the police station showed as if it burned through a fog. His short, self-possessed profile fascinated me with its detachment. When he had kissed me he said: "I wanted to do that properly," and we both swayed a little, like people who have just stepped out of some unfamiliar motion, a swing or a boat. I drew his head down and, in the street, kissed him again, pulling the flesh of his lower lip through my mouth with soft ferociousness. When I let him go he gripped my arms with a little shake of pride and gratification, smiling at me. And all his gaiety and restlessness swept back to him with a boast. "Let's get them some hot dogs," he cried. "Come, there's a stand about two blocks away." We ran as if the air were nipping our heels.

Back in the Cellar again, the warm exhausted air burned against our cool cheeks. The others were hungry and exaggeratedly delighted with the hot dogs. Isa held hers away from her dress as if its steamy heat were dripping and called to me: "You shouldn't let Paul drag you around the streets. He could have gone on his own." But I only said, with the swagger in my voice of the child who has been tumbling out in the cold to the grownup who huddles at the fire: "But it's a beautiful night, really—I could have walked miles."

Later I smelled her perfume and found she was beside me. I said: "Do you want another? There's a half left here—" I felt her looking at me appraisingly in the dark. "Yes," she said to me, "you're the kind. You're a giver. You'll pile everything on the bonfire. But don't marry him." She was a little drunk, but I felt also that she had caught from the atmosphere of the place, as I had, a sympathy and a softening toward the pain and danger of being human. So I was not annoyed or offended at her presumption. I merely mumbled something foolish about a gypsy's warning. "Cassandra," she said irritably, on a rising note, "Cassandra tipping it straight from the horse's mouth. . . ."

Herby had his head on the big blonde's shoulder; he had to sit up very straight to get it there, because he was much shorter than she. Jenny was begging John in a low, insistent, reasonable voice to come home. And Paul was offering some wine to a straggling group of burly young men who had hailed him and now drew him admiringly into their midst with the air of showing off in the flesh someone about whom they often spoke among themselves. They were heavily built, and the two blond ones had beards on their broad faces. They listened with smiles of anticipatory pleasure while he spoke: he was repeating some anecdote, apparently at their request; now he was mimicking someone; he shook his head and gave a quick twist to his shoulders, tossing the plaudits of their laughter away like the butt of a cigarette.

I watched him and suddenly Isa's idea of me excited me; the warning, if that was what it was, aroused in me in the desire to stake my whole life, gather up from myself everything I had stored against such a moment, and expend it all on Paul. Everything on the bonfire. I stood up. Our heads were still in the smoke, the music and the voices, but a stiffening cold was coming up from the cement floor of Marcel's Cellar, the cold of the earth that comes with the early hours of morning.

22 IT WAS ON A Sunday afternoon that we made love for the first time. I remember the deserted silence coming up from the streets where we had forgotten to pull the curtains; dawning on me slowly as I opened my eyes and saw, past the corner of the old eiderdown that covered us and the piece of feather that flattened every time I breathed, Paul's room. I could see his shirt on the floor; one shoe. My skirt and the light heap of my stockings thrown down

as only a man would handle them, irritated with their clinging sub-
stancelessness, snagging them on the wood of the chair. My sweater
I had so often worn in our house in Atherton. Perhaps the last time
I had had it on was there.

Paul's head was buried in the heat of my neck beneath my hair
as if he did not need to breathe. His arm lay across me like a spar.
He might have been lying dead if it had not been for the little line
of wetness that I felt him draw now and then with his tongue on my
skin. I looked on his exhaustion with wonder; how far it was from
the frenzy in which I had seen him snatched up—ten minutes ago,
was it? And the squash racket behind the door, the alabaster ash
tray—it was the kind of thing his mother must have given him—
the three tomatoes ripening on the window sill, the calendar, the
telephone: the casual disorder of our dropped clothes, lying there,
provided the only link that related that unspeakable intensity, to
these witnesses out of ordinary life. I remembered how when I was
a child I had wondered how people could make love and then walk
calmly in the streets, fit into rooms naturally among people and
objects, with no revealing mark. . . .

I said to him: "I almost thought you were in pain." He did not
seem to hear. He lifted his heavy arm and put his hand up to draw
my head down into the warmth, groping as if it were dark. I found
with delight that his ears and his temples were still burning. "You
seemed just as if you were in great pain. The way you arched your
neck—" Now he smiled at the wonderment in my voice. I could not
explain to him the blast of tender anguish that had come upon me,
quite maddening and unbearable, at the astonishing onslaught of his
passionate release. I could not believe myself, my body, the mesh
against which he struggled like a creature meeting death: I once
had seen a bird die wildly, like that, its wings magnificently caught
up in some net you could not see. How often again I was to say that
to him! Are you in pain? To grip him and beg him with a kind of
savage insistent tenderness, even tears. What is it? What is it?

Now he opened his eyes dazedly with the slow smile of someone
who hears something about himself he cannot know, and while I
traced the soft brush of his mustache (it was younger and lighter
than his hair, bleached, like the short hair at his temples, brighter

than brown) he said with almost an element of curiosity in his voice:
"This is nothing. You understand? It will be better for you next
time. I promise you, it will be wonderful for you. I want to make it
wonderful for you."

I said: "You thought I'd made love before."

"Well, yes, of course."

I was silent. He kissed me.

"I was so ashamed. I wanted to invent lovers I'd had. But that
would have been all right only so long as you didn't make love to
me. . . . Was I all right?" I suddenly felt that perhaps I had not
pleased, that in my inexperience I was not a good lover.

He kept on kissing me. What I had said seemed to fill him with
an anxiety of delight. "Oh, I adore you, adore you." He stopped and
looked at me with exasperation. "My little demi-vièrge."

His words sent an afterglow of passive sensuality through me,
his bright, tousled, roused face above me, the blood pulsing against
the angle at which he held his neck, seemed to bring me to a mar-
velously full consciousness of being alive. Those empty moments of
falling terror when the wings of life suddenly cease and drop and
all the props of one's effort cave in meaninglessness—not because
they may fail, but because the end itself seems nothing—seemed
secured against at last in this. This was the answer of reality to a
phantom: perhaps the mystery of the end to which life is directed
is simply the miracle of the means. With my arms about this other
young human whom I had just taken symbolically and strangely into
my body, I felt myself secure against the void of infinity.

So I, who had inherited no God, made my mystery and my reassurance out of human love; as if the worship of love in some aspect
is something without which the human condition is intolerable and
terrifying, and humans will fashion it for their protection out of whatever is in their lives as birds will use string and bits of wool to
make a nest in the city where there are no reeds.

When it was nearly five and the city afternoon began to darken
with winter outside, we sat at the bright-barred heater drinking coffee that Paul had made. I was dressed again, a little self-conscious
in the identical order of my clothes with the way I had been before.
I felt suddenly like a visitor, looking round at the cheap, yellowish-

walled room that had the public look of rooms where people never live for long, like the eyes of restaurant cashiers who continually watch comings and goings. Paul's few things, so eloquent of him as a separate entity, filled me with curiosity. My eyes wandered over the desk with its files and piles of paper, the bottles of green and red ink and the open typewriter, the snapshot of two shy native babies, the good old tapestry chair with the sagging arm where some-one made a habit of sitting with his legs slung over, even the rum-pled divan where we had lately lain, with its faded blue eiderdown quilt that belonged to an unknown childhood. Here he lived and moved among things when I was not with him and before I had known him: that old quilt must have followed him to boarding school in his mother's winter parcel and covered him on cold nights in the antiseptic, serge-redolent atmosphere of a boy's dormitory, his little boy's rough hands clenched under the cold sheet years away from the softness of my breasts.

He put off the old coat he had used as a dressing gown and got into his clothes, and I watched this strong tender body, so different from my own, take on, like a public manner, the anonymity of men's clothing. Those thighs with their dark warm hair, that other hair that drew a crucifix on his breast and belly, the bare-looking triangle of bony white at the base of his spine; all this which was withdrawn and secret from his outward appearance to the world made me con-scious with a kind of solemnity of what else must be hidden; behind his voice and his impulses, the life he chose and the men and women with whom he chose to live it: even me, and what he believed he had found in me—all the unknown forces of memory, conviction and desire from which his personality glanced off, like a light. And I think I started then that strangest of journeys which is never com-pleted, the desire to understand another in his deepest being. And I knew already, even then, that love is only the little boat that beaches you over the jagged rocks; for the interior something more will be needed.

When we got back to the Marcuses' flat I was somehow a little irritated to find that they were waiting supper for us. We had not said, when we went out, at what time we should be back, and there was the echo of something irksome in the way Jenny came to the

door of the kitchen as we came through the front door: "Well, now
I can heat the spaghetti—at last! What happened to you?" It seemed
to me that although she was young, she too had forgotten already
the liberation from time, the privileged suspension from all the practical mechanics of life into which it is really a device for plunging
men and women deeper than ever, with which love begins. Momentarily there had already dropped across her young, passionate eye
the film of the matron, who in suckling children has forgotten the
other urgency. We went into the living room and Joel was there,
with Laurie Humphrey and John.

"Was she putting grated cheese on it?" Laurie asked. "Did you
tell her to put cheese on it?" and I said in a queerly put-out, startled
voice: "When did you come? I didn't know you were coming." Joel
seemed to know that the nervousness of this meaningless compulsion
to say something was directed at him, and he lifted his familiar head
(what a big, heavy head he had in comparison with Paul!) from the
paper over which he and John were bent and said with a mock air
of relief at finding someone who would be bound to know: "Now
come on, Helen—who's going to win in Calvinia—?" And because
I was still in the startled moment of taking in the changed relationships with which the room was innocently charged, and so merely
registered the convention of a question requiring thought instead of
realizing what he had said, my expression of weighing consideration
was unintentionally comic. The three men roared with laughter; John
with a childlike, expansive delight in someone making a fool of
himself, Joel with the gentle human amusement of sharing an absent
moment with someone, Paul with a proprietary pleasure in the idi-
osyncrasy of someone over whom one has the ascendancy of possession in love. The Sunday paper was holding a competition in
connection with the national election which was to take place in the
coming week: a list was printed with the names of constituencies,
the candidates and parties returned at the last election, and the
candidates and parties standing for this election. The winner of the
competition would be the person who predicted most accurately
which party would come to power, and with what majority. Calvinia
was a Nationalist stronghold and the seat of Dr. Malan himself, so
there could be no possible doubt about who would win Calvinia.

We ate spaghetti and argued amiably about the election; none
of us except Laurie considered that the Nationalists had a chance
of coming to power. "The most they can get is a few more seats."
"Forces of reaction be damned—you can't tell me people have forgotten the way the Nats cheered the Germans on during the war?"
"The United Party is moribund." Laurie drew the slippery strands
into his big loose mouth, drooping his eyes sagely. "You can't rely
solely on the popular appeal of Smuts. Like a poor film counting on
some idolized Face to put it over." "Well there you are, Laurie—
you fill in your entry predicting victory for the Nats. Dr. Malan our
Prime Minister. Win a hundred pounds." Laurie's fat face creased
into paunchy laughter. "Believe me I would, but somehow it seems
a bit disloyal."

Beneath the inconsequence of my part in the talk I was aware,
as on another level, of the hollowed-out feeling within my body, a
shaken newness hidden, yet like the trembling of one's hands when
they have been put to some delicate strained balance of muscle in
the performance of an unfamiliar skill. Somewhere I was withdrawn
in the consciousness of this, and I watched and listened, even
talked, from something of the still center of the cat, blinking out of
itself into a room, or pregnant women, who hold themselves secret
and contemplative. I found myself watching Joel and Paul closely;
Joel's face when Paul was talking, Joel's manner when he spoke to
Paul. And when the certainty came to me: Joel likes him—I knew
why I had been watching them. I had wanted Joel to like Paul. To
admire him, even. When Joel gave me the opportunity by offering
me a cigarette, he must have been puzzled by the depth of the smile
I felt come into my eyes for him; grateful, appealing, confessing—
the smile with which a woman presents her child, or her lover.

And so the strangely commonplace Sunday evening passed; I
even spoke to my mother on the telephone, a polite, quietly pleasant
conversation of inquiries and answers, and the promise that I would
be home for the week end after next, if not the next.

The odd, self-conscious unreality of facing other people after
making love with Paul passed so soon that I did not remember it
had ever been. In the busyness of our lives and the casual proximity
of John and Jenny our time alone together was limited and we grew

increasingly reckless in our passion. Of course, we had whole long
evenings together in Paul's flat, but there were many nights when
his work took him to meetings and he would come to the Marcuses'
to have coffee with me at eleven or twelve o'clock, and there were
also nights when both he and I had work to do. If I took my books
and went with him to his flat, we found that neither of us got anything done; we would lie on his bed in the dark, smoking and talking
and drifting into a delicious slow love-making that left us exhausted
and longing only to sleep where we lay. And then instead of sleeping, we would begin to make love all over again in order to stave
off the horrible time when we would have to get up and go into the
cold to take me home. The next day I would sit in a lecture theater
with my head lightening to sleep with the low sound of the professor's voice, and at lunchtime we would hear each other's voices,
faint and secret over the telephone, the clatter of a typewriter in the
offices of the municipal Native Affairs Department at his end, and
the enclosed echo of the public telephone booth at my end, somehow
emphasizing the laughing, tender sympathy we had for each other's
weariness.

So we would resolve that I must work at the Marcuses' flat. He
would bring his reports to write up or he would read or talk to John
and Jenny if they were in, and we should have the comfort of each
other's presence. But it was on these occasions that we found ourselves becoming more and more bold. The Marcuses would go to
bed eventually and I would feel the edge of the electric light wor-
rying my eyes like grit, and know that I was too tired to concentrate
any longer. Paul would sprawl in his chair yawning again and again
that quick young animal yawn, showing his teeth like a tiger weary
of the cage, and say to himself: I must go. I must go home. Then
we would rest on each other a moment in love and the desire for
sleep. And the desire for each other, a strength beyond our tiredness, a freshness beyond our day-depleted energy would suddenly
and desperately seize us, and with the fear that one of the Marcuses
might come in for a book or something forgotten, at any moment,
and the sweet inhibiting agony of withholding from each other those
intimately known particular cries with which each found his pleasure intensified by the knowledge of the pleasure of the other, we

made hasty and trembling love. Once the need came upon us irresistibly when the Marcuses had gone to have a bath, and we had
promised to have coffee ready for them when they came out. With
their voices a few yards away coming with the strip of light beneath
the bathroom door, we lay on the floor, unable to resist as the salmon
is unable to deny his death leap upstream. The inflamed bars of the
ugly radiator burned over our heads, we smelled the city-ground
dust of the carpet. Yet in our ignoring of the situation, with its threat
of sordidness and embarrassment instead of danger, there was an
element of the real, deep, dreadfully dignified moment of wild creatures, who accept their mating as compulsively and unconditionally
as their birth or death. We could not postpone our need of each
other for a more convenient place or a more socially acceptable time;
we had not reduced love to the status of an appointment for tea.
Although Paul was my first lover, and although, or perhaps because,
I had been brought up in the world of the Mine where all human
relationships were seen as social rather than personal, I had by some
miracle grown up woman enough to recognize this proudly. I regretted nothing that I did with Paul, suffered none of the timid
shames that sometimes come, despite reason and intellect, to women
who have rejected the nurturing of a sterile gentility. And in the
beginning of our relationship as lovers, I became aware, too, of the
merging, in my love, of aspects of Paul which in any other human
relationship would seem far removed from one another: my pleasure
in his body and the work he had chosen to do, his involvement with
the dreary, hidden life of the Africans, and his appetite for enjoy-
ment, for dancing and drinking and talk, became one, each neither
more precious nor even more intimate to me than the other.

Much later Paul was to say to me with hopelessness and fascination, as if he stared at something he could not see the end of:
"We're terribly involved with each other." And I was to say, to avert
his eyes and my own from it: "That sounds like Isa. The sort of
thing she says, all dilated pupils." But now, at the beginning, the
total involvement, the man, the lover, the purpose, was only delight,
a joy to be exclaimed over inside oneself.

The job that Paul did first interested then excited me. There was
nothing romantic about it, except that it was poorly paid, a vocation

rather than a profession. Yet it was the only kind of job, unless one was a priest working in a location mission, that could bring a white man deep into the life that went on behind the working faces of the Africans who surrounded us. Even a doctor working in a native hospital only touched the lives of his patients in one situation, that of hurt or illness. But as a welfare officer—first he had been a junior, now he was an assistant to the chief—Paul entered into the gamut of the Africans' lives. Of course, he knew them chiefly in trouble, seldom in joy, but as he explained, the damnably wonderful thing about them was the way they scaled down their standards of expectation so that no matter how wretched and unlivable their lives were, there was always the possibility of some whiff off the abundance of life bellying momentarily the sails of their spirit. A joke, a good pinch of snuff, even a promise you might not be able to keep, brought out the living eagerness that ugliness and dreary dispossession stifled interminably but could not kill.

At this time Paul was handling what was officially termed "Poor Relief"—the work of the department was divided into two sections, the other headed "Housing." The work that his section and in fact the whole department did was in principle the same as that done by similar municipal or government welfare organizations all over the world. Investigation into the homes of delinquent children, maintenance of deserted wives and families, some sort of succor for the extreme situations which breed out of poverty. All this is commonplace in America or Europe. Everywhere in big cities there is a human silt of misfortune, a percentage of waste that through weakness, disability and the inevitable pressure of urban life, is cast out by the city and yet by the city's guilt and conscience is kept alive. But in South Africa there is one difference; a difference so great that the whole conception of charity must be changed. The people among whom Paul worked were not the normal human wastage of a big industrial city, but a whole population, the entire black-skinned population on whose labor the city rested, forced to live in slums because there was nowhere else for them to live, too poor to maintain themselves decently because no matter what their energy, their skill, their labor was not allowed value above subsistence level. So he spent his days taking to this gigantic artificial pauperdom the pal-

liative measures designed by sociologists for the small percentage
of a city's poor.

He was intensely aware of this and sometimes the knowledge of
it, incontrovertible fact kicking away the sense of achievement from
beneath the dupe of a difficult day well managed, would throw him
into a mood of restless depression. —I noticed that with him, unlike
other people I knew, depression did not produce inertia; he would
want to go out, tackle things with a kind of anxiety and leave them
unfinished, constantly search for someone to talk to so that if you
were alone with him he exhausted you with his compulsiveness.
"What's the good of handing them out blankets when they need
votes—?" he'd say. "Edna and her crowd are right. I'm wasting my
time. Truly. One step away from the dear old ladies of the church,
distributing buttered buns and alms." At this I grew indignant. "We
can't all live historically, and leave it at that. Very comforting if we
could. What are you supposed to do, let them freeze or starve while
they're waiting for the millennium?"

"I'm an enemy of progress because I am helping to resign them
to their lot. Two-pound-ten a month pension and a delightful hessian
shelter, and you'll be so enchanted with your life that you'll prostrate
yourself before the white man forever."

"Well, I don't see why one can't do both—support their right to
emancipation and make their lives a bit more bearable in the meantime. That seems to me the most admirable thing anyone can do."
Paul laughed at my championing of him, but perhaps more than my
lover, or a credo, it was the personal myth by which I wanted to live
and which I had now embodied in him, that I was defending so
jealously.

Paul worked very hard and rarely within the limit of set hours.
The fact that there were no telephones in the native townships except in official offices, clinics and schools made it necessary for the
welfare workers to make all their visits to the people's homes, even
for the most trivial inquiry, personal ones, and he spent his mornings, at least, driving out on investigations. His life came to me as
a perpetual journey through the lives of others; snatches of their
personalities, their predicaments, came on his speech and the vividness of his face, and filled me with enthusiasm and the sense of

a closeness to life which I had never before known. The Mine was
unreal, a world which substituted rules for the pull and stress of
human conflict which are the true conditions of life; and in another
way, the University was unreal too: it gave one the respect for doubt,
the capacity for logical analysis, and the choice of ideas on which
this equipment could be used to decide one's own values—but all
this remained in one's hand, like a shining new instrument that has
not been put to its purpose. In my case I sometimes looked at its
self-evident efficiency (Miss Shaw has written an intelligent and
painstaking paper on the prosody of Gerard Manley Hopkins. This
examination of the sources of group conflicts is an excellent piece
of work, indicative of a grasp of her subject unusual in a student
. . .) and wondered what the purpose was. What Joel had said once
about belonging only to the crust, beneath which the real life lay,
came back to me. Paul was rooted in that life, in the rural, slow-
gestured past and, more important, the confused and mazelike city
life of the present.

He burst into the flat one afternoon at about three o'clock. I was
sitting at a space I had cleared for myself at the table piled with
Jenny's sewing, doing some work. He threw down his coat, came
over to me with the cold hands and light face of someone who is
stimulated by talking to people and driving through a city on a gray
afternoon. He put his hands to warm into the hollow of my neck
under my dress. "What's addling your little brain now?"

I looked down at the half-typed sheet, the notebook with its
scrawled points. Nineteenth-century English novelists. The kind of
paper that thousands of students have written before me, thousands
will write after me. The engraving of George Eliot with her massively
intelligent horse face and her two bunches of ringlets staring up
from an open book.

I felt stale and cramped, suddenly reminded of the woman who
sat in the window of the invisible mender's shop, crouched over old
stockings. I dismissed myself. "And where have you come from so
early?"

"Sophiatown. One of those erring husbands floored me this afternoon. I used all the classic arguments about responsibility and
duty to persuade him to come back to his wife—the poor thing can't

seem to keep him home for more than ten days at a stretch. He's one of those little men with wise monkey faces who make good craftsmen. He listened to me politely as if he understood it was my job and I had to get my piece over with. Then he said, producing something irrefutable, something we couldn't fail to agree on—'But she's so ugly. Tell me, how can a man live with such a face?' " He shook his head. "—And, my God, she is a damned ugly woman; I couldn't help feeling some sympathy for him."

"So what did you say?"

He sat down in a chair and pushed his fingers through his hair. "You're no oil painting yourself, I told him. —Couldn't say a damn thing. She *is* ugly. —And he roared with laughter. We both did. We sat in my office laughing like two men in a pub."

He laughed again at the thought of it, but I sat looking at my papers.

"Paul, what am I staying on at University for? Why don't I get a job—?"

"But, my dear girl, you're going to get a degree?" He knew what I meant, but he liked to test me.

I felt enormously disconsolate. Somehow Paul and the monkey-faced man laughing together in the office made me impatient with myself. "When I've got it, what'll I do? I don't want to teach. Any sort of academic life—I wouldn't like it. I've never had any desire to write. So what'll I be? A nicely educated young lady."

"Darling, why do you ask me? If you want to leave University, if you want to get a job, for Christ's sake why don't you? I can't stand you when you're timid and uncertain. Damn it all, you're not under Mummy's wing now, are you?"

"But I am. So long as I stay at University and they keep me, of course I am."

I went over to him and put my arms round his knees; he played with my hair, tugging it back behind my ears. "They're looking for a house again," I said, speaking of the Marcuses. "Jenny definitely pregnant?" "Almost certain." We looked at each other as if to say, how can people let these things happen. "That's the trouble with being married," he said. I smiled. "But it can happen to any of us." "Yes, but when you're married the social sanction makes you care-

less. People say they won't be, but they always are. You know . . .
what does it matter, after all, if something should go wrong, we are
married. . . . And there you are. Houses, families, necessity for
money and more money, all the things you want to do pushed off
into some vague future." We held each other close in our agreement
on this. The idea of domestic life came to me as a suction toward
the life of the Mine, a horror of cosy atrophy beckoning, and it was
becoming impossible for me to ignore the fact that even the marriage
of John and Jenny had some disquieting elements for me.

"Joel once suggested marriage as the career for me. I was
indignant."

"Did he? I wouldn't want a woman to make a career of me. If
being married turns into a career afterward, that's too bad. But I'd
want it to start off because whatever else she wanted to do, she
wanted to do it living with me."

I knew that I had not conveyed accurately what Joel had said
and meant, but the small injustice to his perception seemed unimportant. I closed my eyes and was conscious with a kind of pleasurable fear that the whole world had narrowed itself down
frighteningly into the possession of what I felt in my arms; my life
had settled on Paul. "That's what I want," I said. "Whatever else I
do, I want to do it living with you. The marriage part is incidental."
He dragged me up from the floor and kissed me as if I had something
in my mouth he wanted to take from me. We had one of those
moments of pure fascination in the absorption we had in each other.
He said to me, studying my face with what was almost exasperation,
"What is it in you? What are you, after all . . . ? I ask myself that
a million times. . . ." And he touched my face with a finger like a
feather, and suddenly took my head in his hands and squeezed hard,
as if he would crack a nut.

Later Jenny came back from a walk to the shop at the corner.
She had the baby with her in his little cart, where he sat propped
upright, his big head wavering in its knitted cap with the cat's ears.
As she wheeled him in she called sharply: "Throw something over
the machine, quick!" But his gums had bared in the aghast silent
preparation for a howl. She snatched him up and the scream came
out, face down in her neck. "He's terrified of the sewing machine,"

she said to Paul. It seemed to me that she never entered the room these days without calling out some warning or instruction—The window, please, there's a draft and he's cutting his lower teeth. John, for God's sake—those drawing pins. You *know* he puts everything into his mouth. Helen, put on a record with less brass, I think it makes him restless, it's too loud. . . .

Paul was gently whirring the handle of the machine. "Look, old fellow, listen to the lovely noise. . . ." But Jenny covered it again authoritatively. "No, he's too frightened. It must have some association for him we don't understand." And she repeated to Paul a theory from one of the books on child care in which she was increasingly absorbed. Then we went on to speak of the proposal to buy a house. Paul mentioned the house of an acquaintance at the office that possibly might be for sale. "It doesn't matter about it being old," she said, wiping the baby's unwilling face with a napkin. "We couldn't afford a new one, anyway. I've found that out in the week I've been round the agents. But how do the bedrooms face?" Paul had been there only once, and could not be sure. She stood listening to him with her head tilted seriously. "You see, children's bedrooms should face east, so that they get the sun when they wake up in the morning."

When John came in I said: "Paul's got a house for you in Parkcrest." Jenny and he looked at each other and her nose wrinkled— "Oh, is that where it is—"

"Why?"

"Well, we thought we'd like to stay on somewhere around Hillbrow—our friends are here, or most of them—and somehow all the progressive, less materialistic people seem to live here."

"Parkcrest belongs so solidly to the small bourgeois with his wife and his children. . . ." added John.

I began to laugh. It was not the kind of laughter that draws others warmly in, even if they do not know its cause. I laughed on my own and could hear my own laughter, a woman's high peal, coming down through the room the way one sometimes hears a laugh in a restaurant and turns to see where it comes from. Paul looked at me with the little bracket of a smile marking the corners of his mouth. "Hillbrow," I said, "full of dear old ladies living in boarding houses—

that's all—it's just the *idea* of Hillbrow being a Bloomsbury or Greenwich Village."

When John and Jenny were annoyed, they had a way of discounting the perpetrator of the annoyance by pretending that they were too much occupied in the conduct of their own affairs to notice unimportant comment. Now they both had their eyes fixed on some point in the room that ignored me, and he said, not as casually and irrelevantly as it might seem, "I asked Nathoo Ram for Thursday, Jen. And I've put off the von Berheims." "Oh, good. It'll be the girl's day off and that's always better for tempers all round."

"D'y'know, Paul," he said, with a careless laugh, "we run the risk of getting kicked out of this building every time Nathoo Ram comes? There's a clause in the lease that says no non-Europeans are allowed on the premises unless in the capacity of servants."

23 IT ALWAYS AMAZES ME to notice the disproportion of feeling to action which human beings show in their lives. In theory, there is an abstract value put on event which has little basis in reality. It is not the conscious changes made in their lives by men and women—a new job, a new town, a divorce—which really shape them, like the chapter headings in a biography, but a long, slow mutation of emotion, hidden, all-penetrative; something by which they may be so taken up that the practical outward changes of their lives in the world, noted with surprise, scandal or envy by others, pass almost unnoticed by themselves. This gives a shifting quality to the whole surface of life; decisions made with reason and the tongue may never be made valid by the heart—a woman may continue to love her husband when all her friends agree she was perfectly right to rid herself of such a worthless creature. And it also gives rise to those small mysteries which affront us when what we consider the appropriate emotions fail to appear in people: his friends are shocked by the passive acceptance of his wife's death by a man who cannot explain, for he scarcely knows it himself, that her presence has been dead to him for several years.

The changes of the next few months of my life came about almost absently. I passed through them like someone pushing a way unseeing through a crowd, her eyes already on the figure she knows is on the other side. I left the University with less emotion than I had sometimes felt over giving up a dress that I no longer wore; I saw my mother and father off at the station when they left for England with the mildly stimulated response to their excitement that one catches from even the most casual of holiday farewells, and that disappears the moment the train pulls out and you turn into a café where the measureless fascination of your own life waits over coffee.

Because they were preoccupied with the imminence of their "trip," as this crowning fulfillment of success, solidity and privilege was always referred to by Mine people, they were less upset by my leaving the University than they might have been. My father had for some time been drawn toward the trap of the parent who gives his child the education he himself endows with the mystical powers of what has been denied him: informed as he believed I must be with this power, must he not doubt all his opinions where they conflicted with mine? If I wanted to leave the University before getting my degree, might not the fostering independence of the University itself be proved in this . . . ?

My mother said: "Of course it's this man behind it. I've told you all girls are alike. It's a waste of money sending them to a University. As soon as some man comes along they forget all about their great keenness to study. I knew we'd be throwing our money out."

I had taken Paul home with me to the Mine once or twice, and although the Sunday with its elaborate dinner and lack of conversation was hardly a success (Paul was polite but endured the day by seeming not to be there, his tall freckled brow behind the newspaper, a boredom that agitated me expressed in the angle of his legs), my parents accepted him for what he sounded to be rather than what he was. The son of an old respected Natal family—the fact that the Clarks were wealthy was pleasant, but what really impressed my parents was that Paul's father was a Justice of the Peace and that "Natal" was in itself a guarantee of pure English blood and allegiance to England, the distinction of an eternal Colonialism they desired above all else. Like most parents on the Mine, they feared to find themselves with a son-in-law with an Afrikaans name; if it happened, they would say: "He's Afrikaans, you know, but very nice, so what does it matter?"—but the disappointment would never be swallowed. If one's daughter went so far as to marry a Jew, at least one would get the awe and sympathy with which people regard aberration.

But Paul could not have sounded more suitable, with his solid Anglo-Saxon background, and along with the suitability they naturally assumed the satisfactory pattern of his relationship with me. The young people were going about together pretty steadily—nowadays parents are not expected to ask, of course, but still, one sees. . . . When his position improves (or some such inevitable delay is over) there will be an engagement, a wedding (a big one with all the old residents of Atherton and the Mine? Or perhaps a quiet one with just His Family . . .). Anyway, Helen would be comfortably settled, and that was all one could ask.

If my father was disappointed because I had not graduated, and my mother felt that money had been wasted on me, there was at the same time consolation for them, generated by my mother, in these indications that I was proving myself no less, if no more, than any other daughter of their world. In my mother's softening toward me over the waste of my father's money—she judged only by official results and it did not occur to her that although I did not have a degree I might have benefited by my years at the University—I could detect a curious note of satisfaction in seeing me caught by what she believed was rightly the inescapable; the ceremonial of engagement, marriage, a "nice little home."

They were gone; my father with his bowling kit (he had at last given up tennis) and a letter of greeting from the Atherton Rotary Club to a Rotary Club in the south of England, my mother with the pigskin handbag presented by the ladies of the Mine. I was working temporarily in the bookshop that had employed me during vacations; Jenny and John had found a house at last, in the very suburb which they had scorned.

All this, though it affected its conduct from day to day, existed lightly on the perimeter of my life; nothing could touch me at this time but Paul. My love for him was at that extreme, exclusive, intensely selfish stage when nothing and nobody interested me unless connected with him. All the small pleasures I had enjoyed before were blocked out by the strong joy of him—the shop windows I had lingered before, the poetry I had murmured over, the half-heard conversations in busses—the immediacy of life streamed past me ignored: I was fixed only on him. Food was actually tasteless unless I ate with him, in music it seemed I heard the tenderness, the excitement and the sadness of our love-making. Like some surgical alteration to the structure of the brain that blocks out certain capacities of thought and action, passion paralyzed my responses to anything outside its own image.

Although Paul was gregarious by nature, we saw less and less of our friends. I did not want to share him with anyone, was largely oblivious of any company other than his own, and he was so caught up in his work and in me that there seemed to be little time to spare for others. When we went to a concert or a play we would be surprised to be reminded by friends met in the foyer that it was two or even three weeks since we had seen them. "Where have you been?" someone would say. And we would look vaguely apologetic, the air of two people who have gone to ground, lightly affronting the group by their lack of need of them, setting up the slight irritation of an envious curiosity. Sometimes they merely waved, faces turned toward us over the heads of the crowd in recognition of the separateness we had retired into. Once or twice it was Joel whose big dark head I saw (even from the back I always recognized him instantly in a crowd) and it did not seem strange that I should be content to smile and flutter my hand, and not make the effort to go up and talk to him, our old, deep, dependable understanding of no more claim than casual acquaintance before my preoccupation with Paul and myself.

Even the limited interest of my job did not trouble me. It was so far from the work demanding and transforming all my energies and imagination that I had hoped would present itself to me through the University that, had it had any real place in my life at the time, it would have filled me with frustration. But the days passed quickly

among the smell of books, and I earned enough money to keep
myself in Johannesburg. Paul's was the job into which I projected
all my pride and interest.

I was now typing the thesis to which I had so vehemently denied
I would give any time. I looked forward to the hour or two I spent
over it every evening after supper, watching the phrasing and the
punctuation as if it were a piece of literature. One evening when we
had had a little argument over syntax—How many times must I tell
you, he said, I don't want a ghost writer, I want a typist—and it
had ended in laughter and my getting my way, I said to him as I
picked up fresh carbon and paper: "You know when you first came
back from Rhodesia the Marcuses wanted me to offer to do this
for you."

He smiled, and said through teeth clenched on an empty pipe,
"And you didn't?"

"No. I said why the hell should I."

He stretched out his foot and gave me a prod on the thigh.
"Hoighty-toighty. Well, if you hadn't changed your mind eventually,
it certainly never would have got done." —In the lethargy which
sometimes comes up in reaction against a piece of trying work accomplished, he had let his thesis lie unpresented for four months,
simply because he could not bring himself to go to the trouble of
having a fair copy made of it.

I said as I typed: "They annoyed me by making a sort of privilege
out of it, like wiping the blackboard for teacher. They kept impress-
ing me, if you don't offer Isa will do it."

"Oh that," he said shortly. He leaned across to the table and
took up my pen, made an alteration on the sheet he was reading
over. "I suppose they lost no time in letting you know about that."

"About what?"

"Isa." He put the pen back. "They were always dead against it.
I don't know why. Some sort of antagonism they have against her.
They were right, of course, it was a mess and a mistake from the
beginning. But not for their reasons."

I had stopped typing and I kept reading along the lines of keys;
the letters, figures, hieroglyphics, a chip on the tail of the question
mark. I felt I was waiting for something to happen inside me. "Paul,

I didn't know about anything. I mean Isa. You've had an affair with her?"

He looked up; half-surprise, half-concern, with the suggestion of accusation that comes from disbelief. The intensity of the expression gave his face the vividness that was his greatest attraction. I saw him most pointedly, it seemed, as accident sometimes arranges things, at the particular angle which was my personal vision of him, the turn of his face that I could see with my eyes shut; that I can see still.

I thought of Isa, willed the sight of her, crinkling up her eyes at me over a glass, oddly haggard with her hair hanging round her like a little girl, precociously young with her hair drawn up off her long head as if it were painted on. "You slept with her?" I wanted to make it real to myself. Isa ugly toward the end of the evening when she had had a lot to drink and was tired. Isa making someone like Herby purr in the joke of her attention like a cat.

Paul merely made a little movement of culpability that distorted his mouth; lifted his hand swiftly, palm open, questioning.

Somewhere parenthetic to my quickening of concern I was faintly stirred, fascinated by this momentary flash of his existence simply as a man; not my beloved, flesh with ways of its own, a mind, particular, sometimes puzzling—the whole computation of personality of which the essence is that which is always left out, cannot be classified—but simply a living being shaped by its maleness.

"I knew she was fond of you. . . . You talk well together."

"Like a vaudeville act."

The terse casualness of the summing-up fell lightly between us. I looked at him.

And it came to me suddenly: I did not care. It mattered as little to me now as it did to him. The reaction, the revulsion I had waited for fearfully in myself was not there. I thought with a kind of pride of surrender to something painful and sweet in its dangerous completeness: Nothing matters. Nobody. Not even Isa.

I sat with my hands resting on the typewriter, looking at Paul.

"You look a little drunk," he said. "That's rotten brandy of John's. It kicks you in the back of the head about two hours after you've forgotten drinking it."

24 AT THE END OF 1949 I went to live with Paul in the flat
in Bruton Heights, Krause Street.

He had had a very bad infection of the throat during which I
had gone every day to stay with him, and sometimes spent the night
because it was difficult for me to get home alone after dark to
Parkcrest—where I had moved, with the Marcuses, to their house.
Then when the infection cleared, he had to have his tonsils removed,
and I went home with him from the nursing home.

I sent a message to the bookshop to say that I was ill. All day
long we were alone together in the hot bright little flat, Paul's pajamas that I had washed flapping on the balcony, our cigarette
smoke blue in the sunlight round the bed, the collection of newspapers, books and lozenges littering the sheets. Walking up the
street to the vegetable shop in the morning, I had no compunction
about my job, really would not have cared if someone had seen me.
In the shop I stood enjoying the little imposture of waiting among
all the other housewives, middle-aged women who weighed out their
own tomatoes—not too green, not too soft—and smart young women
who dangled a car key on the index finger and pointed, without
touching, at what they wanted. Back at the flat, Paul would mimic
for me the funny, charming speech of the Portuguese market gardeners who both grew the vegetables and ran the shop. I cooked our
food and read to him (he liked the sound of my voice reading something familiar, a translation of Stendhal, the poems of Donne) and
at twelve we would eat together, the tray between us on the bed.
Then I would push the windows as wide as they would go, and pull
the curtains. The summer day seemed to curl up asleep outside; we
would hear the sound of the native laborers' picks digging the foundations for a new block of flats on the other side of the street.

I lay down beside him (he had the warm puppy-smell of people
who are in bed) and with his arm hooked around my neck, he read,
very swiftly and silently, detective stories that, the moment I began
to follow the lines from the angle at which I lay, sent me off into a
kind of singing sleep, like the sound of cicadas rising in my head.
Sometimes we made love. I would tease him: "But you're supposed

to be a weak convalescent. If you're strong enough for this you should be working." "For some things," he would say in the hoarse closed whisper which was the only way he could speak, "you don't need your voice."

We would lie there quietly, spreading our limbs for coolness on the rumpled sheet. "Listen," he would say, "everyone's away. Everyone's working. The whole town's reckoning and arguing and persuading and measuring up and putting down. Only us." And there was a special pleasure in the sense of our desertion, our malingerers' possession of the hot quiet afternoon in the emptied building and the emptied street. We could still hear the picks, pitching dully and regularly into the earth.

When evening came—we could see nothing but the sky from where we sat, deepening green and now showing a star like a glistening drop of water, though the noise of homeward traffic beat and swirled below—he did not want me to go and I did not want to go. I would run down out into the street again to get a paper. We drank gin and lime juice to the mild intermingling of other people's radios, city equivalent of the cheeping of birds in the dusk. We did the crossword together in that desire to stretch one's concentration lazily—like making a muscle—that comes pleasurably from idleness. For half an hour, on the gay confidence of the gin, I felt entirely in command of the pots I set cooking, pans I set sizzling. Paul sat up in bed shelling peas. I shouted a running commentary to him from the kitchen as I cooked. And afterward he liked me to come to him smelling of talcum from the bath, my hair brushed out and the make-up washed off my face, and we lay together listening to records and hearing the roar of the traffic rise, far down, as other people went off to cinemas and visits. Quite late, because we talked so easily at night, circling out from the still center of ourselves to politics and death, the confidence with which we spoke of the uncertain future, the hesitancy with which we spoke of the certain past; gossip, impressions—we fell asleep, curled round each other like two cats in the narrow bed.

When we talked about the kind of life we should live together I would say: "I want to live with you in the greatest possible intimacy." I said it with a deep earnest satisfaction that was at the same time apprehensive, lying back on the pillow and looking at him. And I do not know that I knew exactly what it was that I meant; though I knew what it was that I did not mean. I did not want to belong to the women's camp while my husband belonged to the men's camp. I did not want to sit talking to women of things that "did not interest" men, while he sat with the men talking of things that "did not interest" women. I did not want him to be a scapegoat, hidden behind a newspaper: "I'll have to ask my husband," "I don't know what my husband will think"—as if he were a kind of human reference work, a statute book on which the state of the household internally and in relation to society was based. . . . When Paul questioned me, I could only pause, and then say, like another question, an obstinate question rather than an answer: ". . . This, I want this. It must be like this." I knew this warmth of physical intimacy—eating, bathing, sleeping, waking together—was not all of two human beings rooted in each other but free, yet it was all I had so far come to know of the state I imagined.

Paul delighted in it for itself; for him I think it was immediate and complete. There was a peculiar charm in loving a woman, a girl as young as I was, whose desire was to identify herself entirely with his being. Older women he had known had, I imagine, wanted to possess *him*; they took him to themselves. But I wanted to devote myself to him. He felt he owned me, and all the love and pleasure I could give him. It was a sort of young male's kingdom into which he had come into his own after being the darling page boy of the court. When I put into words the way we spent our time together, he was quite maddened; he kissed me and caressed me and worried at me in enchantment with the way I was made and the things that I said.

I never went back to the Marcuses'. When the week was up and we both descended into the world, like two children who have made a suburban room their secret tower, we could not live apart again. It was senseless to see each other in snatches, to lie at night the distance across the town away from each other, to eat and talk with others. All that was senseless; the only thing that was right and simple was to stay together. It is curious how moral censure never seems applicable to oneself. I would say of others: "Aren't they living together?—I heard he had some girl in his flat?" —But it never occurred to me that people might speak of Paul and me in the same casual tone, that I might be to them merely some girl who lived with a man. In any case we were as good as married; the marriage was a mere formality we had still to go through. We had wanted to marry at the end of the year, when we had saved a little money and could perhaps go to Europe. But now: "We'll get married when they come back," said Paul, speaking of my mother and father. "I want to shoot you down to Natal at Easter to show you to my people. We'll go for the long week end and then I can take you to the Drakensberg, and we'll climb."

My mother and father, writing to me from Devonshire of the "real English Christmas and New Year" they had spent with my father's stepsister, stood vaguely sentinel in my mind. I did not really think of them; yet they were there. I continued to write to them from the Marcuses' address. . . .

Paul could not understand my deceit with them. That I should not want them to know that we were living together, because the knowledge would shock them, he could perhaps admit; it was simply expedient. But that I should be ashamed of my deceit, that I should "pull a guilty face about it"—that annoyed him. "Are you ashamed of living with me?"

"How can you ask?"

"Then if you're not doing anything you're ashamed of, what are you feeling so bad about?"

I could not answer.

"You know what you remind me of? A little girl who has been told God is watching her all the time. And if she does something God thinks is naughty, he will know, no matter where she is, no matter how she tries to hide it. . . . Just look at you."

And I stood there, in the sudden descent of dismay that came with their letters; fingering the envelope, addressed in my father's rather beautiful hand (its sweeping flow always suggested some freer, other side of him I had never seen, as the sight of his bare knees, in tennis shorts, suggested to me as a child another existence outside the known one as my father). My mother would sit down and write her pile of letters in her large wavering hand, where the tails of the y's in one line looped through the crosses of the t's on the one below, and then my father would address the envelopes for her, consulting the little pigskin notebook where the addresses were all set down. . . .

"It seems so mean . . . ," I said, not wanting to annoy him. I saw so clearly in the light of his presence, the set of his head, the small impatient movement of his foot, the childish stupidity of my scruples, that let me lie and yet made me whimper over the lying.

He knew I was troubled but though he wanted to be sympathetic he could not conceal his boredom with the reason; it came through the smile he gave me now. "—Then tell them if it'll make you feel any better . . . ?" He put on his hat with the air of getting back to the real business of life, picked up his cigarettes and the car key. He was the only young man I knew who wore a hat, and somehow it was part of his sense of vitality, that well-worn but smart and expensive hat clapped unerringly on his head as he went out. It was typical of Paul that his careless love of good clothes was accepted unquestioningly by people like the Marcuses, who would have scorned the manifestation as hopelessly materialistic in anyone else. He came over to me and kissed me before he went, lifting me tightly off the ground although he was not particularly tall, and then setting me down again.

For him the consciousness of being answerable to one's parents for one's moral actions was something he could not conceive of in me, even something slightly ridiculous; for to him I was an adult woman, answerable only to her own integrity. When he had gone I felt ashamed and disgusted with myself for being less than this. I had the horrible feeling that the Mine had laid a hand on me again; Atherton had gleefully claimed me as one of its own, lacking the moral courage to be anything else.

I put the letters into the back of the kitchen drawer behind the string and corkscrews and a broken top (how had it got there?) and went out. The flat boy interrupted a conversation on the entrance steps to turn and greet me with a little grunt of friendly pleasure preceding and tailing off after his "Mad-*am* . . ."; he was a tiny, big-headed Basuto, wearing, like the clothes of an elder brother, the white cotton kitchen suit provided for the god-bodied great Zulu who had preceded him. I reaped the geniality engendered by long conversations in Sesuto with Paul. Over the road two white men in workmen's overalls watched me pass and, grinning, shouted something I did not hear because of the noise of the concrete mixer which two natives were feeding.

At the bus stop an enormously fat woman in black sat spread on the seat in the burning sun. She moved her feet a little, like a restless elephant. A woman with a shopping bag that bulged although it was empty, as though in exhaustion, joined us, jumped on and pawed at by a small boy. As I sat between them with my flimsy dress falling away from my bare legs and the scent of my own powder rising from my neck in the heat, I felt a sudden return of power. The pure arrogance of being young; free, risen every day from love, this was the long moment, limitless when you are living it, brief when it has passed or you have never had it, that was conferred upon me by the drab indifference of the women on either side.

Perhaps it is in moments like this, selfish as the laws of life itself, yet humble in the evidence of the flowerlike nature of human beings despite their brain and spirit, that happiness is sharpest. I know that it came to me then as sudden and delightful as a bird sheering up out of nowhere into the sky.

That summer was the second under Nationalist government. (The jokes of the Sunday afternoon when we had all talked over the election-forecast competition had, with the calm irony of event, become fact; Laurie was our prophet and not our clown.) As people always do when the unthinkable comes to pass, we had braced ourselves to the curious letdown of finding ourselves on the losing side, looking with a sense of unreality at the flat-faced, slit-mouthed Dr. Malan staring back from under the caption PRIME MINISTER, and had waited for calamity to come down.

Nothing happened. Of course nothing happened. We wanted a quick shock, over and done with, but what we were going to get was something much slower, surer, and more terrible: an apparent sameness in the conduct of our lives, long periods when there was nothing more to hurt us than hard words in Parliament and talk of the Republic which we had laughed at for years; and, recurrently, a mounting number of weary battles—apartheid in public transport and buildings, the ban on mixed marriages, the suppression of Communism bill, the language ordinance separating Afrikaans and English-speaking children in schools, the removal of colored voters from the common electoral roll and the setting aside of the Supreme Court judgment that made this act illegal—passionately debated in Parliament with the United Party and Labor Party forming the Opposition, inevitably lost to the Government before the first protest was spoken.

When the impact on individual, personal lives is not immediate and actual, political change does not affect the real happiness or unhappiness of people's lives, though they may protest that it does. If the change of government throws you into a concentration camp, then your preoccupation with politics will equal that you might normally have had with your wife's fidelity or your own health. But if your job is the same, your freedom of movement is the same, the outward appearance of your surroundings is the same, the heaviness lies only upon the extension of yourself which belongs to the world of abstract ideas, which, although it influences them through practical expression of moral convictions, loses, again and again, to the overwhelming tug of the warm and instinctual. The people I knew were "politically conscious" and as liberals or left-wing sympathizers they knew more thoroughly and perhaps felt more deeply than the United Party conservatives the reactionary shade into which the country had passed simply by fact of the Fascist Nationalists coming to power. Yet although they talked gloomily, I did not see in anyone's face the anxious concentration of concern I had seen come so quickly over the sickness of a child, or the haggard foreboding that kept pace with the disintegration of a love affair. In the private worlds where people secretly decide the success or failure of their attempt at life, the old battles made or broke; it was only very slowly, as the months and then the years went by, that the moral climate of guilt and fear and oppression chilled through to the bone, almost as if the real climate of the elements had changed, the sun had turned away from South Africa, bringing about actual personality changes that affected even the most intimate conduct of their lives.

In this Paul and I would probably have been much like the

others; but our circumstances were different. Because of the nature of his work, Paul had always been as daily, hourly conscious as of his own aliveness of the silent condemnation of the Africans; that accusing condemnation which others were varyingly aware of, like a distant gaze on their backs. He lived in the midst of it. His life was a reversal of the life of the average Johannesburg person. They went about their own affairs, in a white world, vaguely intruded upon by the knowledge that beyond the city where they had their offices and the tree-hidden suburbs where they lived, there was a scattered outcast city from which the emissaries came—cleaned up to approximate to the white man's standards of decency—and disappeared into again. He went about his affairs in a black world, in those townships (even the word was the white man's generality for something he had not seen—some were the rows of houses the word comfortably suggests, others were huddles of tin and sacking, junk heaps animated by human beings) dumped outside the city, and for him it was the clean, prosperous, handsome white world that existed on the edge of consciousness. He never drove back to it without a sense of incredulity that this city—these girls in fancy shoes coming from offices, the men reversing into parking bays with hump-necked skill—could cut itself so pitilessly in two and close its eyes so completely to half its life. Sometimes he found himself looking with something almost as hot as hate at the white people in the streets, seeing even the most unknowing of them as despots in their very ignorance of what was wrong and terrible where they walked; but at other times he would tell me how he suddenly had the sense of Johannesburg as a beleaguered city, ringed about by all those smoking, wretched encampments which she herself had created. . . .

Paul began to say things like this now. He had never said them before, and now, although he still laughed and derided what he called the "Hysterical-Histrionical Friends of the Downtrodden African," there were times when he seemed to struggle with a sense of drama? evil? that made him speak in spite of himself. At first I did not know what to make of it; I even felt half-amused, in a puzzled sort of way, at catching him out in the kind of highly colored fantasy of disgust from which he had so often brought me down to face the unpleasant facts at which my imagination had started up like a covey at the sound of a gun. But when I realized that these outbursts of his came not from the frightened shying away of a suddenly exacerbated sensibility, but out of a long working familiarity with the facing of ugly facts, I understood that something was changing in him.

The Africans had, of course, more to fear from the Nationalists than anybody. But they themselves felt that they had had so little to hope for under the Smuts Government that all the change had done was to substitute a negative despair for a positive one: lack of hope, for fear. The leaders said in the phrases leaders use, Now the velvet glove is off the iron hand, that's all . . . ; and the simple people who did not understand politics and could only understand the white animus against them if it was personified, as in their tribal days they had made power realizable in the carved image of an idol or a bunch of bones, shook their heads in apprehension of the "bad man" Malan. Paul told me how, in a way, the idea of Malan even became a comfort to them. If there was a shortage of meat: Malan doesn't think we need to eat, they said. If there was no house for a man and his family: Malan wants us to live like animals on the veld, said the woman. Over all that had been wrong, and would continue to be wrong in their lives—This Malan . . . , they said.

But though in that first year of the Nationalist rule little changed for them materially, and the combination of shockingly sordid living conditions, poverty, and a kind of deeply felt inarticulate horror of their own subjection before *everybody* who was not a native, that resulted in curious, mad, apparently irrelevant bursts of rebellion, arose out of the years of benevolent United Party rule, the very fact that the Nationalists sat up there in authority humiliated the natives. In Parliament cabinet ministers spoke of them as "Kaffirs." There was continual official talk about the preservation of the "purity of white races of South Africa" and the "sacred duty of the Afrikaner nation to keep itself unsullied." The Africans had always been kept outcast; now they began to feel it, to feel themselves outcast in their very features and voices. In their bewildered or hostile or mocking eyes there was the self-search for the sores the white man saw upon them. Even the black children, aping the passing of a white woman in the street beneath our flat, expressed unconsciously in their skinny jeering bravado the attitude: Well what can you expect of me? I'm black, aren't I?

Statutes and laws and pronouncements may pass over the heads of the people whom they concern, but shame does not need the medium of literacy. Humiliation goes dumbly home—a dog, a child too small to speak can sense it—and it sank right down through all the arid layers of African life in the city and entered the blood even of those who could not understand why they felt and acted as they did, or even knew that they felt or acted.

At this stage, when all that was done to implement the plans for apartheid—a carrying to the extremes of total segregation the division of the ordinary lives of white and black that had always existed, socially and economically—was little more than a tightening-up of discriminatory devices, it was often the way in which such things were done rather than the things themselves which was so offensive. When the Nationalists introduced the ban on mixed marriages and also made it punishable for white and black men and women to cohabit, there was something shameful in the manner in which the police hunted up their prosecutions, shining torches in upon the little room where an old colored woman lay asleep with the old white man with whom she had lived quietly for years; prying and spying upon what has always been the right of the poorest man to sleep in peace with his woman.

Other people read of these things in the newspaper, but Paul came face to face with such a happening. He had temporarily taken over Colored Poor Relief, which was administered separately from Native or Indian Poor Relief, when a couple was arrested in Vrededorp, a slum suburb of racial confusion. He knew the woman because it so happened that she had been to see him a few days previously about her brother, a slightly crazy old man for whom Paul was trying to get an old-age pension. The woman herself was one of those milky-eyed, still creatures, roused only to obedience and the cooking pot—more like a work-stunned old native woman than the shriller, more conscious colored. The man with whom she lived was very old, had never heard of the ban, and had lost touch many years before with the white race which he was defiling by lying in this creaking great bed of the poor with this bare-gummed creature whose slack skin had once been filled with a woman. —The people who lived in the room next door told Paul that when the police came she jumped out of the bed screaming and crawled beneath it. And when they tried to get her to come out, she kept screaming for her "Doek, my doek!" (the piece of cloth she wore round her head) and would not come out until someone had given it to her, and she had struggled to tie it on cramped under the sagging springs of the bed. The neighbors shrieked with laughter all over again at the telling of it.

"Can you imagine the two old things," said Paul shortly, "a torch shining on their faces. Opening their eyes into it like those poor damn fool hares that get transfixed by the lights of your car on a dark road."

Later he went to see the woman, because without the man (he had once been a railway worker and had some sort of pension) she was destitute and it seemed that Paul would have to try to get her a pension, too. She said to him: "What is wrong with this man? I stayed with two men before. The one ran away to Capetown. The other one died after thirteen years. Now this one is wrong?"

A kind of minor panic flew round among the colored people. Most of it was ridiculous and unfounded in danger, but its spark of actuality was the special distress and embarrassment that people feel when their sexual privacy is threatened, even by implication. People said to one another that they were afraid to go to sleep in the same room with their wives. The inevitable hooligans played the inevitable joke of climbing up to windows and waking people up by shining torches in their faces. One evening a colored clerk in Paul's office confided, half afraid he would be laughed at, half afraid what he said should be taken seriously, "I used to be so proud of my wife's European looks. You know she's quite often been taken for a white girl? Now I'm wondering—" He stopped, wanting the assurance of Paul's laughter that it was ridiculous to go on. And Paul laughed, but a moment later the thought forced itself up in the man again. "If anything like that happened to us, I'd do . . . I don't know what—" He had the pleading, tense expression of abstraction that anticipates the doctor's order for some too-intimate investigation. But of course Paul laughed again, and said to him, "For Christ's sake, Robert, you know you and your wife are both colored, there's nothing on earth to worry about. And anyway, they'll only do this a few times. Just to satisfy the predikants and the Cabinet ministers."

"Of course you can see a mile off his wife's a colored girl. Only two or three shades lighter than he is," Paul said to me. He smiled. "Out of a reversal of the very thing he fears now, he's liked to think her that much nearer the distinction of whiteness."

But later that same evening when we were sitting in a cinema, I had the feeling one learns to pick up so quickly from someone one loves, that his mind was not going along with the diversion of the film. He stirred in his seat now and then as people do when they come to the turning point of their own thoughts and then go back to the beginning all over again. Once he hesitated and then putting his mouth to my hair said: "The funny thing is, he's always seemed—you know, I could talk to him without any mumbo jumbo, the way people like us talk among ourselves." I nodded vehemently, my eyes still on the film, like a hostess who continues to give polite attention to her guests, while she tries to catch the gist of the urgent confidence someone is pressing upon her in whispers.

When we came out we were both in a rather passive mood— the film had turned out to be bad in a dulling way—and we drank our coffee comfortably, but without speaking much. Once we got home something that often happened suddenly happened again. The sheer pleasure of coming home together alone to sleep in the same bed, the same room, turned our passive mood inside out. Paul got into my bath with me and we fought and laughed and criticized each other's washing technique. In their desire to know each other minutely, lovers return quite seriously to those dull questions to which children give so much weight: Do you wash your face first or last? Do you stand up when you do your legs or sit down and hold them up out of the water? Paul finished his performance, when I was already drying myself, by disappearing head and all under the water in the way that he knew horrified me. He came up laughing and lay there, water streaming from his hair, all his body broken up into wavering and ripples, magnified and distorted. As I gave him a cigarette, Auden's line came to me, ". . . the bridegroom, lolling there, beautiful." We got into bed half-damp and made love so ecstatically and swiftly that I murmured something about ". . . only over too soon . . ." and at once Paul began to make love to me again. We lay there with my hand on him lax the way I liked to keep it after he had parted from my body, on the edge of making love a third time or going to sleep, each possibility as delightful as the other. Neither asleep nor making love, we lay there in the balance between the two, our eyes open, not speaking. The lights of cars we could not hear, turning the bend at the top of the hill, perhaps, traveled over us faintly, one after the other, a long pause, then another and another, slipping down the window and the wall and across the floor and over the bed—where each saw the other's face come up silvered and the peaks of the bedclothes like a fold of hills—then up the other wall and over the ceiling into darkness.

I took my hand away.

I took it away instinctively, in answer to some other withdrawal. Paul did not move, but with each wash of light I felt come into my mind through his own, the real pain and strangeness of that conversation with the man Robert, and even the jokes of the others. And I knew Paul was thinking of it; feeling for himself the impossibility of a white man understanding these things out of his own security.

Just as I went off to sleep I had one of those curious starts in my mind—the mental equivalent of the jump of a leg or an arm momentarily jerking your body back to wakefulness—that flips up a piece of past consciousness. I did not remember that incident of the Sunday afternoon I went with Joel to Macdonald's Kloof; for a moment I was *there*. The sun was down and the air smelled of dust and eucalyptus. I walked past the old Afrikaner packing up baskets and rugs. I called to Joel, Wait, there's something stuck to my shoe—and he picked up a little piece of twig and scraped at my heel. And the torn thing was there.

The only difference was that this time, unlike the real time that it happened, we were not safe from disgust. We got into the car full of shame and I kept my face turned away from Joel, although I seemed to see his face all the same, as you do in a dream. And perhaps it was here that it all really became a dream, and I was asleep.

25 I OFTEN ASK MYSELF now whether I was ever really happy at this time; and I find I must believe that I was. My measure of happiness so far—it changes all through life, like one's idea of what age is getting old—is the intensity of my identification with living; those periods when I have known myself to be crawling through summer and winter like a slug falling listlessly from leaf to leaf have been the seasons of misery. And by this standard I was happy, though perhaps it was the kind of happiness that you can stand only once, and when you are very young.

The revelation of being well loved in the body is an astounding experience. It carried me along, buffeting through everything else that weighed in on me or harassed me, even the practical worries attendant upon itself. And there is no experience that gives one a closer feeling of being in life; in fact it is like an explanation without words that turns an abstraction into possessed reality.

Then, too, not only was Paul the source of this joy, he was also at grips with the huge central problem of our country in our time, something that had oppressed me not only in my intellect since I had grown old enough to have a concept of man's freedom, but in my blood. What he could do was pitifully little and pitifully inadequate, but I was at that stage in idealism when the gesture was satisfying in itself. I believed then that the only way for a man to fulfill himself in South Africa was to pit himself against the oppression of the Africans. It did not matter in what way he did it; the thing was so sinister that there was hardly a job or profession where it was not implicit and the question did not come up, if not in so many words, a dozen times a day: Are you for them? Or will you add your weight against them, along with all the others? —And I believe this still, although I understand now the consequences of such a way of life, as I certainly did not do then; something that makes all the difference between one's right to hold such a belief, and one's unfitness to do so.

It seemed to me utterly satisfying that Paul should have chosen this job of his—hopelessly limited as it was by the whole framework in which it functioned—rather than some profession whose prizes

and successes were really only relevant to the world of Europe where
a man did not start off with the immediate advantage of a white skin.
The fact that he was so small and the thing he put himself against
so enormous and tangled gave me a peculiar pride in my love for
him. —It gave our relationship something of the quality that height-
ens the excitement of love during a war; I do not mean the quickened urge to mate in the threat of death, which you may feel whether
or no you believe in the war, but the more complicated sense of the
passionate integrity for what you both believe, in which your lover
exists in the midst of the heedless crashing hostility that comes from
both sides, sometimes his own as well as the enemy's.

Of course, I could never express to Paul this concept of himself.
He would have laughed it out of existence and have been exasperated with and even ashamed of me; he would not have said so, but
I should have felt he was thinking again: the Mine, the Mine, showing itself in the excessive reaction from a life without a single real
idea, to the extremes of romantic idealism. And I should have been
conscious again of the dowdy unsuitability of the way I wore some
of my convictions; like a woman accepted in fashionable circles who
sometimes gives away her forgotten provincialism in her choice of
hats.

But often, when I looked at Paul without his knowledge, a queer
swelling excitement came up in the back of my throat, I wanted to
grip tightly the arms of the chair I sat in: I had it all; there . . .

Most of the time Paul came home very late and very tired. Out
of the official work of the Department had grown a whole extension
of activity that almost doubled it; the impatience of people like Paul
with the inadequacy, sometimes the total unsuitability, of what the
Department offered the African townships made them try to supply
something of what was missing, out of themselves. It was impossible,
for anyone who saw the Africans as men and women with the same
wants and hopes as anyone else, to be satisfied to hand out food or
clothes or money to those who lacked the basic necessities, and
ignore all those other nagging and endless and less easily satisfied
needs that showed everywhere, in every street and every face. Nothing to do, nowhere to go, no hope of change. The young boys kicking
a stone along the gutter because they have no ball and know no

game. The schoolteachers and young clerks borrowing books from
the little library (a charity handout of the discarded books of white
people) and reading in the paper of the plays they can never see,
the concerts they can never hear.

Paul and a few other people in the Department helped with the
organization of discussion groups, supplied a portable player and
the loan of records for a music society; found journalists and lawyers
and actors to go out to the bare solemn rooms at the Community
Center to lecture. They commandeered bats and rackets from the
cupboards of their friends to give some purpose to the one or two
open pieces of ground that the Department listed on its reports under
"Sports Facilities." And they became expert at filling in applications
for Departmental funds in such a way as to avoid their narrow
stringency and stretch their validity to cover expenditure that was
officially "beyond the Department's scope." "But I'll wangle it somehow," I have often heard Paul say, telling me of some scheme for
which money or facilities were not available. He would narrow his
eyes and lift his chin while he thought what lie, what approach,
would be best. And though he laughed at his own craftiness that
had developed so efficiently out of necessity, there was in his eyes
at these times he afterward mocked a concentration of determination,
blank, grim, that he did not see.

One Friday night early in January we were coming home from a
Brains Trust which had been held in one of the native townships.
Gathered in the hall there had been the usual small group of subdued, expectant people; the air of awkwardness about them coming
from the lack of group consciousness, the unfamiliarity of identifying
himself with anyone that marks the intellectual who lives in a backward society and is accustomed to being the lone, the self-excluded.
The joy of finding themselves among their own kind could not come
to them as spontaneously as it did to the dancers of jive who filled
the hall on other nights. When I came in, I felt a pang of anxiousness
for the meagerness, the curious tameness of the whole show—something that, I knew by now, inexplicably vitiates efforts of this nature
just as it does those occasions of genteel patronage when white
people distribute prizes and shake their heads over the charm of
black babies, or the skill of black handiwork. Paul dashed across

the stage (six chairs were set out behind a long table, there was a
carafe and a glass at one end) and I thought in a burst of irritation,
Christ, why do they have to treat *him* as if he were a city councilor
deigning to be present—why can't they give him the due of thinking
him a man, like themselves.

But the people whom Paul had asked to sit on the "Trust" were
black as well as white, all interesting speakers and all public personalities in one way or another, and when the discussions got
started and the surface of the audience's solemn attention was broken up by the pleasure of interest, a buzz of murmur or dissent, and
often—for one or two of the speakers were really witty—by laughter,
audience and speakers forgot themselves in one another, and in this
perfectly natural relationship between human beings, the whole
thing became a success. It was obvious, too, that Paul's personality
had a lot to do with this. Here, as always among people, he had the
instinct of giving them what they wanted and then taking fresh stimulation from the giving. And then he had the advantage of being, in
himself, as perfectly at ease with both Africans and Europeans as
any white man could be in our time; he knew most of the audience,
the individual foible or special point of view, and when opinions
from the floor were called for, he could look out over the heads and
bring in a response by resting his eyes in a knowing, smiling, challenging way on the very person who would be likely to have strong
feelings on the subject under discussion. I watched him, sitting and
listening to the speakers between the times when he would have to
rise and sum up the "Trust's" opinion; his mouth opening a little
with a quick intake of breath now and then when some comment on
or disagreement with what was being said almost moved him to
interrupt, his body curled up like a spring, one leg over the other,
elbow in the palm of the hand of the arm that was tightly across his
chest, fingers of the other hand, that pushed against his cheek, twirl-
ing a strand of hair at his temple. Once he screwed up his eyes and
looked out quickly over the heads at me with the abstracted following air of someone who feels the attention of another like a reminder.
I had the queer moment of seeing him look at me for a second as
it must be when he looked at a stranger; and then he winked, the

purposefully lewd batting of an eyelid that he sometimes used in a
very different situation.

So coming home in the car I felt, over the slight uneasy excitement that the thought of the morning, nearer now, claimed me (my
parents had arrived back from Europe on Wednesday; I was going
to spend my first week end with them), animated by flashes of the
evening on the surface of my mind. I chattered about it; what this
one had said, how that one could possibly hold such-and-such an
opinion—but did not have much response from Paul. He leaned
forward a little as he drove, with a silencing movement. It was only
then that, quite taken up with my own talk, I felt he had not been
listening, or rather had been resisting what I said.

"—What is it—?"

He frowned. And after a moment when we both listened, I not
knowing for what: "It's nothing. That ticking again. Must be something in the mechanism of the clock, that vibrates at a certain
speed." He settled back and after a short silence the dusty bright
hall began to light up in my mind again. "It must be a hell of a
surprise to a man like Carter Belham to find himself answering
awkward questions on the methods of the press, to old Fube. And
Fube was at him and at him, with his, I'd like to ask you further,
and There's just one more point. . . . Did you see. Once or twice
Belham simply blustered. There just wasn't anything he could say."
My voice sank into my thoughts. Carter Belham, the big, brandy-
suave editor of one of the newspapers belonging to a powerful conservative group, nipped into discomfiture by the dry voice of the
native schoolteacher (the kind of "decent" scholarly African he was
accustomed to pleasing by calling him "Mister") asking if he could
tell him if any directive was given to newspapermen reporting affairs
affecting Africans? —The editor trying to turn the advantage to
himself by putting on that air of good-natured helplessness which is
intended to suggest the bulldog worried at by something small and
sharp-toothed: the bulldog restrained in his very possession of his
own invincible jaw. "I'll bet he would never have come if he'd known
it was going to be like that?"

But Paul seemed suddenly very tired and he let my talk drop.

In a little while he said, out of silence: "Half of them weren't there. Sipho and Fanyana and the others. The ones who count weren't there."

"Oh, I don't know. How can you say that—"

He lifted his hands off the wheel in a slight shrug. "You get all enthusiastic. The reign of the ear of corn." (He was referring to the line of a poem by Lorca that I liked—"a black boy to announce to the gold-minded whites the arrival of the reign of the ear of corn.") "But they don't come any more. And they're the ones who count, the ones who've really got something. Without them the others don't get anywhere, their ideas will remain where they were. It's always like that; there are a few who . . . you know, you see the same thing among ourselves, in a crowd like Isa's. The hangers-on and the boys whose heads move somewhere. The hangers-on can only go so far as the heads take them." He said after a moment: "Sipho would have asked some questions, all right. Belham and Dr. Lettica would have heard some calm cold logic from that black boy. . . . That look of making allowances for the poor inarticulate savage—the way Belham looked *encouraging* every time anyone black got up to speak —by God, that would have dropped off his red face as if Sipho'd suddenly taken a rabbit out of his own mouth. —Hell, if they'd been there. —I wanted a chap like Belham to see that his conception of the thinking African is out of date and third hand, bears as much relation to the real thing as a circus-trained ape to a man."

"But wasn't Sipho at the debate last week?"

"I've told you, they don't come any more." There was a growing movement, among the Africans, of non-co-operation with the whites. It had started with the policy of the Communists and the leaders of African Nationalism as a semiofficial affair, but now it was spreading and becoming something quite different: a kind of distaste, even in those Africans who had European friends with whom they could mix on decent dignified terms, for anything that was inspired or assisted by white people. Sipho was a friend of Paul's; it was he who (in his person and what he told) in the first place showed Paul the refinement of frustration that comes to the educated African. He had asked Paul to help him arrange lectures and music recitals for the small group of his own kind who were starved for some sort of diversion in a society where the only pleasures allowed to Africans were old Wild West films (specially chosen as suitable for the primitive mind), all-night jive sessions on what was imagined to be the Harlem pattern, and illicit drinking dens.

"Well, he's cutting off his nose to spite his face."

"He's right—he's perfectly right—" Paul's profile was closed against me. He spoke as if he were impatient with himself. "Anyone with any guts must do the same."

The ticking noise—which was not the running of the clock, for that had stopped at fourteen minutes to five some day long before I had even met Paul—was the only consciousness we shared for the rest of the way. It was somehow impossible for us to go on talking of Sipho because we sensed it would not really be talk of Sipho, but a dragging up and examination of what we had settled to live by: Paul in the job he did every day, I in the symbol I had made of him for myself. Shut off from each other by this, something else that was unshareable, but this time for different reasons, took me up and washed me that much further away from this loved person whose familiar head, like a beautiful shell from which the inhabiting creature is absent, was only a little higher than mine in the dark, and whose elbow, as he changed gear, touched against my arm unnoticed. A light sick nervousness for tomorrow flowed back to me from where it had been waiting. Anything connected with home always brought up with it the emotional reactions of childhood, so that if I thought of something pleasurable related to Atherton and my parents, I would not feel the mild, easy sense of the pleasant with which I would be impressed by a pleasure on the same level arising out of my adult, independent life, but the high-flown excitement with which a child invests the trivial. Now, when I was entirely independent of my parents and their mores, the thought of going home to Atherton tomorrow and explaining that I was living with Paul reduced me to the feeling of chilly hollowness, damp-palmed and with my stomach tightened inside me, that I had known the day before a music examination. The fact that I was ashamed of this feeling, and could refute it utterly over and over in my reason, did not shift it. It remained sitting there inside my body like some old genie, released by the word "Atherton" to possess me.

And I could not speak of it to Paul. It did not belong with our life and I did not want to show it to him. It could only show him a girl I might have been whom he could not have loved; whom he would never have bothered to know—whom, in fact, he would never have met.

From the corner of the car into which I had curled myself I looked at him, tightening and releasing the corner of his mouth at his thoughts. Of Sipho. Of the evening. If he thought about my silence at all, thinking it to be the same as his own. As we came through the town (people were winding out of the cinemas, breaking up like confused ants round the parked cars) an astonishing loneliness came out of me. I say came out of me because that was how I became aware of it: as the thin-drawn music of a street musician comes out of the noise of a street. You lift up your head as if all the clamor had been silence and this sound is the first you have heard for a long time.

In the lift I said to him: "What are you going to do tomorrow?" and he looked up and smiled and then looked inquiring for a moment and said: "—Oh, of course—! You won't be here. Well, then, I think I'll ring John in the morning and see if they'd like to see a picture. Have to be a late show."

"Why, what's happening in the afternoon?"

"I'm going to plant grass. Really. The new sports field at Jabavu."

We eyed each other in the distorting greenish light of the lift and we both laughed, as people do when they have not forgotten a quarrel. In the morning we woke very early and I began to talk as I could never resist doing when I knew he was awake, no matter what the time. He slid his thigh between mine and scratched my neck with his beard. "Hell, darling, why do you have to go for a whole week end?" I began to kiss him and caress him with a desire born of reluctance; of the empty excited nausea that was back with me again the moment I wakened, making my very presence there with him unreal. Yet there was the familiar miracle I could never take for granted—how, from sleeping so close together, when we wakened our bodies were always both at exactly the same temperature of gentle warmth, so that for a few drowsy minutes it was difficult to tell the touch of your own limbs, one against the other, from the touch of the other's.

The character of that warmth changed in him now.

I said dubiously—"I ought to get something." "Oh, damn." I loved the way he looked at me, glittering, demanding. At times like this when my whole body suddenly began to flow in desire for him, there was a moment of perfect tension, of balance before the terrifying slither down the sheer. And in that balance, the sight of a state that exists only between the here and now, and the measureless streaming of time from which we take up the little scoopfuls of here and now, I expressed my snatch at it, empty-aired, dissolving, in the wildly emotional compulsion to caress Paul's face and head, that, though passion and the knowledge of being wanted made joyful, had something in it of the way a woman falls upon the face of someone dead; seeking to possess what is beyond the reach of lips, the touch of hands.

We exist on so many levels at once.

At the same time I was aware of the faint smell of soap round Paul's ears; the ringing of an alarm clock in the flat below that came through in dull vibration, like a shudder; and the half-threat of fear that would come back to exact its due, almost superstitiously, for my practical carelessness.

26 I DID NOT SAY anything to my mother until Sunday afternoon.

I had intended to tell her quite simply and flatly as soon as I got home, but I went through the whole of Saturday and Saturday night and Sunday morning and Sunday lunch with the words in my mouth, while at the same time all the things I did say and the whole manner of behavior in which I let myself get more and more involved, made them more impossible to be spoken. On Saturday when I arrived there was the present-opening—they had brought me a great many, and they produced the really beautiful things (there was an Italian silk shawl of the kind I had always wanted, and a won-

derful hat made entirely of peacock feathers) and the hideous things
(a set of "souvenir" wall plaques of London, made out of pottery
molded in relief, a thistle brooch from Scotland with "Weel ye no
come back again?" engraved round it) with a puzzling impartiality
of triumph. Then at five o'clock there were "a few friends over a
drink" and I found myself bending about, in the "good" frock I had
fortunately brought with me, offering the plates of decorated biscuits
and hot sausage rolls I had helped my mother prepare earlier. The
arch tone of this gathering—the Cluffs, the Bellingans, the Compound Manager and his wife, and one or two other officials, who
were accustomed to keeping in mind the occasion of a "party" rather
than merely enjoying eating and drinking and company for their own
sake—extended to include me. I was being "welcomed back" too,
if only from Johannesburg; I had not been seen on the Mine during
the six months my parents were in Europe. When I was chaffed,
usually by the men who had "seen me grow up," I responded with
the same smile of deprecating my own sense of privilege that my
mother was showing, near me, as she chatted and answered questions about her holiday, conscious of the new clothes and the obviously English shoes at which she could feel the other woman
looking. Old Mrs. Cluff had her arm round me as she rose to go.
"She's grown into a lovely girl, Jess. —You were always my little
lass, weren't you? —That's right. I used to tell you, didn't I, Jess,
there's nothing like a daughter." And my mother—she had put on
weight in England, and had had her hair cut in a new way, so that
on the animation of two or three drinks, her face seemed to have
changed from the way it was when I was a child, rather than got
older—saw us suddenly in the relationship that the old lady created,
and paused in her high-pitched amiability to say with sudden emotion: "Yes, and I suppose I'll be losing her soon." The old lady
shook her head like one of those big benevolent figures that nod in
shop windows at Christmas. "A son's a son till he takes a wife, but
a daughter's a daughter all her life. . . ."

On Sunday morning I heard my mother up early and from the
called consultations with Anna between the other rooms of the house
and the kitchen, I knew that one of those total reorganizations of

cupboards which had always followed our return from a holiday ever since I could remember was in energetic progress. This time, because she had been away so long and brought back a fair number of new things, the upheaval was on a larger scale than usual; standing beside her, directed to put this there and hand her that, with my father looking on, I thought: She is making space in their life for the fact of having been to England.

My father had not put on any weight. Thin, but more bright-skinned than usual, whether from the cold in Europe or the heat of the latter half of the passage home, I did not know, he did not keep away from us in some reading or other occupation of his own, as he used to do, but hung about on the edge of my mother's activity. Once or twice he ventured a mild protest: "What are you doing with that, Jess?" —My mother ignored him and threw onto the pile of things to be discarded the old golf umbrella with the broken spoke. She had a peculiar venom, as if they were conscious enemies, for things which she suddenly decided had outlived their margin of possible usefulness, and were therefore occupying her cupboard unlawfully. "The whole lot'll do fine for the jumble sale. If they're still holding them the third Tuesday of every month, I won't have it cluttering up the garage too long." (It fascinated me to see how quickly and unthinkingly she was taking up the order of her life from the Mine again; the six months among other peoples, in other countries, sucked smoothly in, passed along and assimilated by the Mine like a lump, rather larger than usual, taken in by a snake.)

But mostly my father "fed" my mother as if they were partners in an act. "Wouldn't mind being there now, eh?"—he pointed his pipe at a little painted wooden gypsy caravan they had bought in St. Ives to give to Maureen Eliot's small boy. "Oh that creamed trout! And the view from our window . . . !" She shook her head as she sprinkled moth killer on a shelf of spare blankets. She twisted her head round to him. "Tell Helen about the fisherman who thought you had your own gold mine."

And my father told the story, taken up here and there and expanded by my mother, and then handed back to him again while she waited, smiling, for the well-known point—"Go on, you go on."

It seemed to me that in this unconscious pantomime of acting as a foil for each other, they oddly achieved a kind of intimacy that I had never seen between them before.

At lunch we had a bottle of red wine—because they thought I should like it, I knew. "—It may be cheap there," said my mother, "but you can't get a decent cup of tea anywhere in Italy." I drank it although I dislike red wine and I talked all the time I ate, about how hot it had been at Christmas, and the muddle-up there had been at the post office about a cable they had sent me before they left, and the way the piece of chiffon my mother wanted to know about had turned out when it was made up. I talked about the camping week end that Jenny and John and Paul and I had planned for what proved to be the wettest week end for five years . . . and, warming to it, my heart beating fast at the horrible homeliness of my duplicity, I told my mother that Jenny was expecting another baby, and . . . "Well, she's quite right. They're young people, and I suppose he's doing quite nicely now; they might as well have their family while they're young."

After lunch my father went to lie down. He said the wine had turned sour on his stomach, but he had that hazy pleasant look of wanting to drop down somewhere and doze that goes with wine that has agreed with one almost too well. My mother and I went to sit on the veranda, where it was cool. She was knitting; some special wool she had bought herself in Scotland. Her chatter died away, perhaps also because of the wine. I sat there with my heart beating up faster and faster. After a few minutes of sunny, warm silence she said to the bird dangling in his cage: "Chrr-ip, chrr-ip, eh? Chrr-ip!" and looked back to her knitting.

I said: "Mother, I should have told you I'm not living with the Marcuses any more, I'm living with Paul."

Her face suddenly came alive out of its content of food and relaxation. She looked at me with the quick intense suspicion of an adult hearing from the mouth of a child something it cannot possibly know.

Then her glance stumbled; it was like a nervous tic catching a face unaware.

"What do you mean?"

And while she spoke coldness hardened into her face, it became something I have never known in the face of anyone else, possibly because the face of no one else could make that impression on me: stern.

"I've been living with him in his flat ever since he was sick."

"You're living with a man, living with a man as if you were married to him." She stopped. "Living with this man and lying, writing letters and lying— What do you want? To end up on the street?"

I thought with a rising distress of panic, I knew she'd do this; it's ridiculous—she's making it a tragedy, terrible, world-come-down, hateful. She's twisting it up into hysteria. But she had done it already; I was in it, shaking before her horror of myself.

I said: "It's not like that. Don't be silly, we're going to get married anyway. People now—"

"Yes, they've got no respect for anything, you've got no respect for yourself. And what kind of a person is he, to behave like that with a girl from a decent home. . . . Women who must have a man to sleep with. Women who can't live without a man. A university education to live with a man. How can women be such filthy beasts?"

All the time she had never taken her eyes off me.

She began to weep, and I saw that now that she was older she cried like other women; it was no longer hard for her to cry, and so it no longer had any more meaning than the simple relief of other women's tears. I cannot explain the strong strain of peculiar joy that seized me, apparently so irrelevantly, as I understood this, so that I could say quite commandingly, "Don't cry, if Daddy hears you cry he'll be alarmed."

"I don't want to see you," she said, and already it seemed in her face that she no longer saw me, "I don't want you in this house again. You understand that?"

The peculiar joy swept into hatred. I hated her for leaving me, for blaming me, for making me care that she did. I trembled with hatred that for a moment made me want to laugh and weep and abuse; and that left me hot and cold at the escape of knowing that that was what she wanted: that that was how she wanted me to behave.

My father came in and the whole scene was gone through again, but in myself I was stubborn; it was over. I was sitting it out.

We even had tea before my father took me to the station. In silence as if someone had died. While we were sitting at the dining-room table drinking, the smell of the room when I bent over the table painting from my color box as a child came to me, immediate, complete, unaltered. The print-smell of the pile of English news-papers, the oil-smell of furniture polish, the cool dark fruit-smell from the dish on the sideboard; and the smell of ourselves, us three people, my father, my mother and me, with which everything in the house was impregnated like objects in a sandalwood box, and that, when I took out something from home in the atmosphere of the flat or the Marcuses' house, gave me the queer feeling of momentarily being aware of myself as a stranger.

27 AS SOON AS I got into the train I dropped back my head and closed my eyes: Paul. Paul; Paul. I know that I should have liked to have said the name aloud, but opposite me in the empty carriage was a very young Afrikaans girl with a daughter of four or five years old, curled and hatted and hung about with trin-kets, like her mother. Like her mother she was utterly composed, silent, absorbed in the trance of her Sunday best. She played with a little bangle engraved "Cecilia," and stared at me without curi-osity, as if she were measuring what I thought of her.

When the train jerked into motion I thought: Now; I shall soon be there. And my desire to say Paul's name, as the little girl had to feel the shape of her bangle, I turned into a little movement of a smile with my lips.

I scarcely opened my eyes again until we reached Johannesburg. In the peculiar bright confusion that comes down with the felty blood-darkness of one's eyelids, the clear images of the afternoon that had passed, the whole two days, were pushed away in a jumble, like the swept-up bits of a broken mirror. I hung to the thought of Paul that swelled, image, word and sound the way one's last conscious thought looms and expands before sleep or anesthesia. In that darkness he was my one reality. It seemed that he must be thousands of miles away, unattainable in yearning. I could not believe that in less than an hour I should be standing in an ordinary call box hearing his voice matter of fact and that I should see him walking down the platform looking for me. . . .

When we got to Johannesburg station I was trembling and sweating as I jumped down from the train and pushed my way through the people, murmuring nervous apologies and holding my head high and anxious. The telephone in the first box was dead and I rushed into the next one. It smelled bad and I dropped my handbag and parcels and week-end case on the dirty floor and lifted the receiver in anxiety. The dry, snoring sound came back. I dialed and could hear my own breathing, harsh in that small space.

The bell rang only once and in the middle of the second ring Paul answered it and I heard his hello. I don't know what I had expected, but even though the fact of its ringing on unanswered would have meant nothing more than that he was out at one of two or three places where I could easily have got him, I knew the moment I heard his voice that if there had been no answer the ringing of the telephone would have dropped me into a fearful despair. There was a second's shudder at what I might have felt and as my face crinkled in relief at the sound of his voice, I saw the magnifying line of tears lifted in my eyes. Through them the scratched walls of the call box came alive.

"For God's sake come and fetch me. Quick. I'm in an awful public telephone thing that smells."

"Well"—he was questioning the excitement in my voice—"well, so you're here. Why didn't you phone, may I ask?"

"I did. On Saturday. But you weren't there—"

"You knew I'd be at Jabavu."

"Yes—I forgot. And then I couldn't. —I can't explain now. I'll come to the front entrance. Eloff Street."

"No, come to the side."

"The baggage drive-in side? All right. . . . But be quick!"

I saw him. He seemed to grow along the street out of my watching. I dropped my things all over the seat and the floor of the car and pulled his head down in my arms and kissed him. It was all very awkward with my one knee on the seat and the end of my handbag sticking into my side. But I felt his warm mouth (I could taste fruit on it) and I dug my fingers into his linen jacket and I shut my eyes for a moment against those eyes and that high freckled forehead and that beautiful nose that I loved more than ever now that I knew its one secret fault, a displacement of the septum that at a certain angle spoiled its line. He pressed his hand tightly into my back, surprised but ready.

"You've been eating a naartje," I said.

We both saw him, lying on the bed dropping the curls of fruit skin on the floor.

"Cursing like hell because you didn't come home."

Quite suddenly we did not know what to say; he feeling the obligation of my smile, that smile of relief and wonder that holds your face with the intensity of a frown and that you are powerless to control.

So he drove us home to the flat rather fast and the great need to talk, to tell him, became curiously not urgent, but something that could rest in the surety that it could be told at any time; I did not want to speak at all. He swirled down into the basement garage and, in the gloom pungent of petrol, pulled me over to him and kissed me passionately. "Was it bad—? Me, too. . . ." I kissed him back in the dissimulation—not something you do not feel, but something that you do not feel at the particular time when perhaps the other does—that webs over the great spaces between the moments of identity which create love. And out of the knowledge, half guilt, half regret, that it had not been possible to miss him in this way during the week end, all the irritation and anger and resentment of the very things that had made it impossible, that pushed it out in the much stronger need of something else from him, burst up urgently in me again.

I said: "Oh, Paul, do you know what she said when I told her—"

He was leaning into the back of the car, where we had thrown the parcels. "Told her what? What's all this loot?"

"Told her about us. She said I was disgusting. She said: 'You're a filthy beast.' " The ring of my own voice came back from the low concrete girders of the dark place . . . thy beast.

There was a snort from the car. He slammed the door, looked over the parcels, laughing explosively. "Oh, Christ, no! Did she? Did she call you a Magdalen, Jezebel? Did she? Did she really—?"

His laughter came back, too, rings of sound thrown smaller and smaller until they closed in on my ears again. He jerked his chin over the parcels to urge me up the steps. "Come on, what's the matter with you—?"

He said, walking where I could feel him, just behind me up the dingy narrow flight: "Hell, that tickles me. . . . Didn't you want to laugh in her face?"

"Yes," I said.

I felt, like some secret horror walled up inside me, beating on the walls with cries that nobody but I should ever hear, the panic and anger of being under my mother's eyes. I saw her gaze hardening over me. . . . (The minute before, she had called to the bird, and the bird had answered her. . . .) Woman who . . . Filthy beasts.

I said, in that tone of laying something before the other which one uses when one no longer knows what one is saying will mean to him: "She says she doesn't want me in the house again."

"*Naturally*. Even the turn of phrase—not 'want you in the house'——Come here, beast"—he caught me by my hair and, putting his head round over my shoulder, kissed me clumsily, a little roughly, not quite finding my mouth in the semi-dark. Amused, he whispered to me some private little formula of endearment, the kind of thing that can only be spoken and never written down.

Tears came up in my eyes, and when we came to the light of the ground floor and the lift, I held my eyes very wide and glassy so that he should not see.

But already he was talking of something else, and as I put my things down in the flat, hesitantly touching at this and that, I roused myself to what he was saying—"So what did you do after that?" —

He had just said that the grass-planting had gone on until after six.

"Guess where I had supper?" The ridge of his nose was burned, he looked at me challenging, smiling.

I don't know why—out of weariness, out of depression, perhaps, it flew into my mind: "Isa's."

He laughed impatiently. "With Sipho."

"Oh? How did that happen?"

"He turned up at the field at about half-past five—just happened to be strolling by, of course. . . . Came straight over to talk to me, but we couldn't really talk there, so I went home with him."

"But isn't he against the field?"

Paul sat down in the big chair. He said with an air of grudging pride: "They're going to boycott the field. Nobody will use it. They held a meeting afterward—on the field. Sipho spoke damn well. And the colored man from Newclare I told you about. But I don't trust him, he's too glib, he's already picked up all the catch phrases of international politics. Inevitable rogue getting on the band wagon. But there were a lot of simple blokes in the crowd—good crowd— and they just blinked back at him the way they do. Sipho—I don't know how to explain it—he's got compassion, that's it, real compassion. He can afford to say simply what he feels because he really does feel. And you can't fool a crowd like that. They seemed to smell out the truth in him. Not that he isn't clever, too; but he does the dramatic thing instinctively, not calculating its effect. Like the field. The field just naturally handed to him the perfect example of the useless good will—the good old Christian kindness, the pat on the head to reconcile the dog to the kind master holding the chain (pretty good? that's Sipho's own)—that is no longer any good to the African. 'We don't want kindness, we must have freedom. . . .' " He fell into restless silence, his glance wavering from object to object in the room, composing an horizon of its own out of the shapes of my parcels (that peak contained the plaques of London); the drop to the floor where the shoes that I had kicked off lay; the jagged rise past the desk to the window. There was an irritation in him, waiting for me to say: so you were planting grass for the field one hour and applauding its boycott the next. . . .

Bewilderment and a sense of confusion close to fear came to me

so strongly that I stood there, unable to go through even the mechanical motions of hanging away my clothes, finding something for
supper. This feeling, like an overwhelming lethargy, seemed to come
from the room itself; all the ordinary things I had used, taken and
put down thoughtlessly in my happiness, filled me with depression.
The lamp, the faded quilt, the yellow cushion I had bought, the
Egyptian cotton hanging, the ebony mask from the Congo in whose
mouth there hung the flower I had stuck there last week, now dead,
dangling like a cigarette stub. Where is he? How will one half of
him spend his life working at what the other half opposes? How will
he do it? How can you do it? Where will *he* be himself, all the time?
The mask. The quilt. Calendar ringed in red (last month's date so
that I shall make no mistake this month). Stitched Egyptians with
their long cold eyes. Plant in pot that didn't let anything grow. Nothing has anything to do with anything else, I thought. How can he
do it. What will become of *him*, while he does . . .

And at the same time, my mother's mouth saying, Filthy beasts.
The living room with the cushions plumped and the curtains drawn
and the clock striking alone, like a sleeper speaking suddenly in a
dream.

Nothing fits, I repeated to myself. Ridiculous, one side; horrible,
hurtful, the other. But of course it was ridiculous. I could see my
mother and me in that scene now and of course it was ridiculous,
flinging about like puppets. Of course it was ridiculous. . . .

Paul said, with the attention of his eye, his mind sunk deeply
somewhere else: "What is in there, anyway."

I looked at the parcels. "Some things they brought me. Put them
on top of the bathroom cupboard." I felt I should never open them.

The next day I was walking out of a theater booking office during
my lunch hour when I came face to face with Joel Aaron: with a
little start of horror, as if Atherton, the Mine, my mother, had suddenly opened before me in the Johannesburg street. I covered this
recoil which even in the second that I knew it must be showing on
my face shamed me, by pretending an exaggerated surprise. —That
in itself was unconvincing, I realized as I feigned it, because why
should I find it a shock to meet someone whom I knew to be fre-

quently in town?—But one awkwardness leads to another, and I
could only say with an effusiveness which did not belong with Joel,
and did just exactly what I wished not to do: put him in the category
of a stranger: "What are you doing now? —Why don't I ever see
you!"

He stood there looking up and down my face as if he were
measuring it, faintly smiling. He was getting heavier in the shoulders; he wore the kind of jacket he had always worn, shabby or
merely nondescript, one could never decide. He said absently:
"Drawing houses."

"Joel! You graduated at the beginning of the month." Shame and
regret stunned me like a slap across the mouth. I did not know how
to express it. I stood there turning the tickets in my hand. He
shrugged, smiling.

"I should have been there. Oh, I wanted to come. . . ." But of
course the notice of the graduation ceremony had been in the papers. He knew and I knew that I had known about it.

I kept saying, ". . . Oh, how could I have . . . I wanted to, really
I *meant* to . . . I shouldn't have missed . . ."

He did not answer, but only went on smiling quietly, as if waiting
for me to finish.

My protests petered out into silence between us. People passing
jostled against our shoulders so that we seemed to be bobbing toward
and away from one another. At once he said over this: "How do you
like the work in the Welfare Department? Is it giving you some
satisfaction?"

"It's not much, you know. Nothing more than a typist really.
How did you know?"

"I was in the shop on Tuesday, and they told me you weren't
working there any more."

There was another silence. I pushed back a strand of hair that
kept blowing down over my eye with a gesture that, I suppose, to
someone who knew me well, was particularly my own: I have always
liked my hair tight and smooth. I saw his eyes travel with my hand;
come back to rest directly on my face again. I had the curious feeling
that I was apparently always to have with him, no matter what distance of time or commitment to others came between our meetings,

that he saw in me what no one else did, things, even ordinary, trivial, physical differences of which only I myself was aware. For instance, I felt now that he noticed that I had not penciled my eyebrows that morning (they were heavy, for a red-haired person, but too light in color) and that under his eyes I was tautening the muscle at the left side of my mouth that would show where I had got the faint line, from cheek to mouth, that I had surprised on my face lately.

"It really isn't much of a job at all . . . ," I said again.

"Paul's must be pretty damnable now, though," he said. It was a polite and sympathetic observation that anyone who read the papers and knew Paul might make. But again I had that feeling of the prescience of Joel; something disturbing, that I felt in some obscure way was a comfort, but that I was impelled to struggle against.

Now suddenly I was impatient to get away from him.

"With his temperament, it's likely to make him schizoid." I turned the question into the exaggeration of a joke. We went on to talk inconsequentially for a few moments. —He must promise to come and see us (he wrote down the telephone number on a cigarette box; I wrote his—he was sharing a flat with Rupert Sack—on the theater tickets). —That was a good play; he had seen it on Saturday night. His job was in the nature of marking time. . . . —Oh, he didn't quite know yet: maybe Rhodesia, after all. Maybe Europe, and lately he'd been thinking seriously about Israel. . . .

"Well—" I made the little shrugging gesture of collecting myself to go. "Yes . . ." He pushed the cigarette box into his pocket and touched me momentarily, so lightly it might have been by mistake, on the elbow.

As I turned, and he was already a little distance from me, I suddenly called back: "I was there yesterday. I spent the week end. . . ."

He nodded. "Been away, I know. . . . See them about again now I suppose." And he nodded again, deliberately, lingeringly, as if the nod were some message he must get to me silently over the distraction of the passing people.

So we both stood a moment arrested in the current of the pavement. And then he was gone and I turned quickly and hurried across the street walking fast in the kind of burst of release. The refrain went foolishly inside me: I don't want to think of the place, I don't want to be reminded of it.

But when the relief of fast movement was checked and I stood, panting a little, in the lift going up to my desk in the Welfare offices, remorse, the real pain of wanting back the chance to do something left undone, that I do not think I had ever felt in my life before, filled me with distress; distress maddening and sad in its uselessness. I should have gone to his graduation, how was it I did not go when I had wanted to go so much: now I felt so much how I had wanted to go. How could I have ignored this—*forgotten*. Yes, I had forgotten. Now I could not believe what was true: that I had forgotten. The thought of it, like awareness of a lapse of memory, an aberration of which you have no recollection; as if there is discovered to be another person in you who mysteriously wrests you from yourself and takes over, thrusting you back to yourself in confusion when the fancy takes it—the thought of it made me sick with dismay. I had the instinct to clutch, searching at my life, like a woman suddenly conscious of some infinitesimal lack of weight about her person that warns her that something has gone, dropped—perhaps only a hairpin, a button—but maybe a jewel, a precious letter.

As I sat down before my typewriter, I thought: It's as if I haven't slept, it's as if since after lunch yesterday until now has been one continuous day, without the divisions of a normal day, on and on. . . .

The line of patient natives waiting to see Paul when he would come in later in the afternoon turned the yellow-whites of their eyes on me, and away again.

28 SOMETIMES WHEN I came back to the flat earlier than Paul, I would go out onto the little balcony and sit balanced on the wall, my head against the partition which divided our flat from the one next door. Often I had not even troubled to wash or to put my things away; I simply came in, dropped to the bed what I was holding, and wandered out.

In the late summer, this was the best hour of the day. And the day usually had been a monotonous one; the offices in the old shadowy building which seemed, as you looked in, as cool as a dairy, were damply stuffy, the odor of old documents tightly stored by vanished tenants coming out in the heat like an invisible stain reappearing on a wall; and the reports I typed, the letters I wrote were the mechanical reproduction of someone else's record of rigidly circumscribed methods of dealing with certain recurrent situations. The calm repetition of the work that came to my desk every day brought alive for me Paul's flat statement that no case was ever finished, except by death. They came once, they will come again. The poverty of the Africans was a wheel to which they were tied; turn, and it will run its weight over them again. So the same letter, the same reports. And if you cut them free of the wheel, that will be the end of white civilization, said some. . . . Anyway, white civilization is doomed, said others. . . .

Perhaps my job was more useful than the one I had had selling novels to leisured women.

I sat on the edge of the balcony, shut out even from the flat. It was like being in a cage suspended from the invisible ceiling of the sky, and what went on in the sky was at my level. If I did not look down I could forget altogether the existence of the street, and the human perspective which is the perspective of the street, and to which, once your feet are on the ground, you are fixed. The new flats going up opposite had reached only the second floor and the building was not yet high enough to block out my sky, to present, like a juggling act, a layer of human activity, figures moving about among chairs, tables, enclosures of light, hundreds of feet up in the air. But the life of the sky, leisured, awesome in the swift changes from calm to storm that human beings can only understand emotionally, in terms of anger and love, beauty and ugliness;—the life of the sky, analogous only to the sea, usually so far above our heads that we have given it to the gods, was suddenly discovered to me. Clouds took the place of trees, and the light, breaking up space in suffusion or falling, falling, straight, sharp, swift, had an architecture of its own. Now and then a bird opened suddenly like a fan past my face. And the soft clouds moved plumped up on their flattened bases like the breasts of birds resting on water. Sometimes they piled into tableaux; held the last of the sun on their gleaming contours; dissolved, with something like lack of interest, into thinning wisps parted and re-parted to nothing against the air.

Often, in twenty minutes, I saw the whole of a summer storm, enacted for me but not involving me.

In a patch of dark suffusion over the outskirts of Johannesburg that I could not see, I could hear thunder prowling; now and then striking out at the sky with a vicious claw that drew lightning. Torn somewhere, the dark cloud slowly emptied itself of a queer dark ragged streak of rain that fell awkwardly, sideways, and did not not seem to reach down to the earth at all. It was difficult to believe that this was what was happening when I crossed the street some-times in a brassy, threatening light between city buildings, and sud-denly felt the warm wet drops splotching my arms. But from up here I saw the rain peter out, like a tap drizzling off as it is tightened. And soon there was only a lavender-gray haze where the storm had been, or where it moved off, a mixture of the benign and malignant, to come down again somewhere else.

If I had had to give a name to what I was doing when I sat out there alone and idle for half an hour, an hour, I suppose I should have said I was waiting for Paul. Yet I did not think of him. When I came out I shut the glass balcony door behind me; with a twitch of recollection, I might catch sight of my hands, carbon-grimed along the sides of the fingers. But I did not think of him, of his closed face haughty with irritableness, or talking with a burst of expan-siveness, swagger and exaggeration too tense to be funny, after two or three brandies had put a match to his weariness. I did not think of him; or of my father, from whom I had had a letter; or of my mother, from whom I had heard nothing and whose silence had become visual for me: her chin pressed back to her neck and her nostrils whitening; or the half-funny, half—I did not know quite what—difference between the picture of my life that they resented and were shocked by, and my life as it really seemed to be. Or the drifting gap between the way I myself believed I was living, and the way the days themselves passed. I did not think of any of this. The shuttle of my mind was still. In the unhuman context of the airscape there was nothing to set it going again, endlessly crossing this with that in terrible industry that had none of the anarchic freedom of confusion, but the inescapable determinism of a complicated pattern. Even my eyes moved slowly among the large movements of the clouds, that melted, merged, altered without the human quality of will without which people cannot change. If I felt anything at all (unconscious of the brick hard under my thighs and the building behind me, the body which by the differences in the desires and vanities in it gauges for one what the mind, which lives differently, does not always know: whether one is a child, young or old)—if I felt anything at all, it was something nearest to, but not the same as, the feeling that had closed softly down upon me as a child, when I had gone out under the fir trees or the gum plantation in the early morning or late afternoon, or when I had lain down suddenly in long uncut grass, and the physical change of discarding balance seemed to change me instantly and magically and everything was drained from my consciousness except the movement of blood in my head that made me believe I could feel the earth turning, and myself curved close against it, not falling off. . . .

When I heard the front door bang, at once very far off and narrowing to the immediate, somewhere behind me, I would swing my legs down, jump. He's here. For a moment, the glass door in front of me. My heart beat up slowly, as if with effort. For another moment, I did not open the door.

But the minute the door was flung carelessly, he stood there; —it was all right. It was as if I waited for someone who, O relief, had not come. And every day it was repeated, this anticipation like dread, that was instantly foolish and nonexistent once I saw him. For he was Paul, of course. It was as if this was something I had forgotten. Paul with his freckled brow—and see, the things we said, the ordinary, warm commonplace things. (Why don't they dust off your ears properly?—He runs his nail along the rim of his ear, where the barber has left a scattering of hair cuttings. I turn his head round as if I were looking at a vase. Well, at least it's not too short at the back this time. No, well, the usual man's away this week. Then why don't you change and always go to this one? Oh, I can't—their feelings are easily hurt. And I like him. He's gone to Ganzbaai to fish and it's only the second time he's seen the sea. When he was seventeen he went to Durban on a motorcycle.)

"What's the matter with your behind?" he noticed one evening.

I was rubbing where the wall had cut into my thigh and now the blood was pricking back. "Gone to sleep," was all I said. He went to the kitchen for a bottle of soda. I took it from him to open while I held it out the window, because he was bad at opening bottles and always let them fizzle out over the floor. "Hell, Helen, you're becoming a rotten wife. You might have put food on." He had seen the empty stove.

"I was tired."

"If *that* job tires you . . ." He smiled, sighing, pouring out our drinks.

I took my glass in silence.

"Oh, don't start, now, for Christ's sake," he said. "I can't even joke. If you're that bored, you can change it. The Department will go on without you. There probably isn't anything it couldn't go on without, that Department. It matters so little whether it goes on or not, and whether it goes forward or backward. . . . —You wanted it badly enough. You pestered me to get it for you, and I told you at the time—" He stopped, looking at me over his drink with annoyance that I felt was more at himself than at me.

Yet I said, watching the way he always sat, one shoe rolled over underneath the sprawl of his leg: "I'm not bored."

"Disappointed. Well, I'm sorry. I told you it'd be as dull as ditchwater. You might as well sit and knock out brewery orders. Sell ladies' underwear."

We said nothing.

His eyes traveled round the room for the ash tray which he expected not to be, and was not, there; he dropped two dead matches into the neck of the empty soda bottle. I stood against the window sill, taking my drink in regular gulps, like medicine.

At last he said suddenly, as if he was giving in to an insistent importunity he had refused to hear: "Oh, come on. Come here—"

And his voice was impatient, sullen and pleading, all at once. He
drew me down to him awkwardly, pulling at my arm, and we kissed
anxiously. When we kissed out of longing his mouth was warm and
firm, drawing me in softly; now he tried to impress the kiss upon
me so hard that it was not a kiss, but a distinct awareness of certain
separate things, his lips, the wetness of his saliva, the sharp edges
of his teeth. Yet his eyes were a little dazed, as when we had been
kissing in passion, although he looked at me keenly, almost suspi-
ciously, as if to dare the appearance of something he was watching
out for. Close to his face, I gazed at him unashamedly, watching
him watch me, and the alien quality of this moment between us, the
incongruity of it, a moment so detached, lonely and critical that it
had no place in the merging exchanges of love, surprised us both
in quick guilt at the same instant, as if one, resigning himself to his
own untrustworthiness with the regret because of the unquestioned
integrity of the other, went to steal a treasure known to both and
found the other in the act of stealing it. . . . He slid his hand over
the smooth material that covered my thigh, and smiled with the
corner of his mouth. "Pins and needles? Shame. Shame. . . . I'll
wake it up, this little rump. . . . These bloody Indians. I spent an
hour and a half trying to persuade a Diagonal Street fruit merchant
to let a colored family stay on in his house in Vrededorp. He's got
an eviction against them and they can't find anywhere else to go.
After seven years or so. Says he wants the place to turn it into
workrooms for his brother who's a tailor. *He* can't find anywhere."
He was looking at his hand on my thigh with close attention, his
eyelashes showing against his cheek, his nostrils drawn down toward
his mouth, the way an artist regards a composition assembled for a
painting. He pressed his fingers gently into the flesh, watching his
nails whiten, then slowly relax into pink again. "Quite true of course.
Where can an Indian get a shop? He was sorry, but family must
come first. If we can find his brother a shop . . . Swine. Wouldn't
give them even another month."

After a moment he shook his head and said: "See . . . ?"—
placing himself before himself and me.

I knew what he meant; how he had caught himself out, thinking,
almost by infection, the way that he fought all day against people

thinking. He was annoyed with the landlord because he was being hard and unreasonable: the fact that the man was an Indian had no bearing on the hardness or the unreasonableness.

I gently detached myself from him—I could never bring myself to move away from Paul's lightest caress abruptly; it was as if I feared always to break something that might never be made intact again—and went to the kitchen. Steak in the refrigerator, two tomatoes, half an avocado pear. Paul had balanced the pip on matchstick supports over a marmalade jar filled with water. The steak looked bright red, tough, long fibered. As I pounded it with the handle of the bread knife to soften it, I saw that the pip had already parted and let one pale string of root down into the water. Nearly half-past seven. You're a rotten wife, Helen.

As I cooked and all the small noises of cooking rose up around me in the little dark kitchen that smelled always of curry, I thought, It's funny, we hardly ever talk about marriage now. Neither of us has mentioned it for months. We were going to get married when my parents came back.

Yet I could not imagine it. Moving with mechanical deftness that was not without a certain pleasure in the doing of a number of simple things at once—turning the steak, freeing the eggs from the edge of the pan, keeping an eye on the toast—I said to myself, Feel it; just like this, yet you would be married. Another name; I smiled at this schoolgirl realization of it. The first thing it implies is some sort of common future. And that was what stopped me. I know how we are now, I can go into the next room and put my hands on Paul's shoulders, speak to him (and at this point I called out absently, Shall I lay the table, or put it on a tray? —No, it's too hot. On a tray. We can eat outside), but we seem to be living a kind of interim period. I caught my breath in a little gesture of distress to myself, for the difficulty of understanding this feeling that was more knowledge than feeling. How to explain this feeling of not having started; of something in oneself crying in excuse: Wait! We are nowhere, not ready, so many things to be settled, so many things taking our attention, swerving out lives this way and that. . . . Yet how can human beings wait? Wait to live until an atom bomb explodes, a government is overthrown, a white man knows a black man to be just such another as himself?

Then there would be no world. Human beings cannot wait for historical processes, I thought with dismay and anger. Then why must we. . . . But the cry comes out, a head lifted from the preoccupation of confusion—Wait! Please wait! Paul throws himself more and more violently into a job in which he believes less and less. So where does that lead? Where does that find a future? It has only a now; it cancels itself out.

It cancels itself out! —I was afraid of this thought I had stumbled on. I was appalled at the frame of it in words.

My mind sought to distract itself from the contemplation of our state; this place where we wished to stay in order to convince ourselves that so much that was in us and our circumstances was temporary, to be overthrown, and then . . .

He should give it up, I said resentfully. Give it up. Nobody can go on doing something he believes is fruitless. And now I felt like an angry child who wants to kick something, to kick something and spill over with angry tears.

Then what would he do? How live, then, with himself?

—Then he must accept what he does now for what it is. My job is this that and the other. It will not give a single African an education, a skilled job, a voice in the way his people are to be disposed of, or even the right to build a house for himself when he hasn't anywhere to live. But he can't go on struggling and arguing and conniving to give his job the scope it hasn't got, all day, and sneering at and deriding everything he's done, the moment he pauses.

I told myself, putting the plates and cutlery quickly on the tray: I will tell him this. The statement had the air of an ultimatum. I will tell him this. It was not a piece of advice; people so close to each other cannot give advice, any more than one can advise oneself.

And so we ate our supper, out on the little balcony. The fat clumsy moths fell against the lamp and taxied lamely between the plates. Paul searched up and down the theater page of the paper, irritable for somewhere to go. I ate slowly, and often paused; but my hand went out for my glass of water; I drank; went on eating.

He threw the paper aside. "Nothing—" —but already indifferent to whether he went out or not. The moon was not up yet and outside the dusty edges of the lamplight the summer night was thickly dark. We put out the lamp to get rid of the insects, and from where I sat, smoking, I saw down away to the left the still darker bulk of buildings, solid as mountains of rock, become fragile as shells, brittle and delicate towers of tracery as the lights went on, hollowing them out, chipping out rectangles and oblongs. Now if you had flicked them with your thumb and finger they would have given back the flat airy sound of fretwork infinitely fine and thin. If you leaned over and picked one up you would be startled by the lightness of it, like picking up a teaspoon made of tin. . . .

He said: "I saw Edna Schiller today."

"Did you?"

"She's not in the second batch, either, though Hugo is."

"I think she's disappointed. She gives me the impression of being distinctly peeved. She feels she's been done down." The bill for the suppression of Communism had been passed in Parliament, and several of the people we knew had been "named" and informed that they would be charged under the new act. Edna, who had lived on a fantasy of danger for so long, was now apparently to be denied this first real martyrdom: so far her name had not appeared on the lists. When I had spoken to her I could not help feeling that she regarded this omission as a real slight.

"You're developing a brand of venom all your own, you know. Polite and peculiarly nasty. And always for people like Edna. Perhaps it takes some courage to take the risk of turning out merely to look ridiculous," he said wearily.

The sudden defense of Edna was sheer perversity of mood; he had laughed about her a hundred times, joined with Isa in the baiting of Edna's secretive pomposity. But the silence into which his words sank said something quite different. After it was said, his last sentence echoed between us as a comment purely on himself. With it he had chosen to take my attitude toward Edna on himself; snatching up the amusement, the mild scorn in a compulsive determination to spare himself nothing. He was determined to make me feel that I had been ridiculing him. I was infuriated with the unfairness of the guilt he was making me feel; a guilt which he was inventing, for which I was not culpable, a piece of twisted interpretation for which he wanted me to give him the pleasure of my inflicting pain.

There was real enmity between us in the darkness. I was glad of the dark because I should not have wanted him to see my face as I felt it was and could not have made it otherwise, stiff with resistant anger, I would not even light another cigarette, although I wanted one, because I could not trust the light of a match, showing my face.

After a long time I burst out: "Why do we all live in a perpetual state of crisis? —'This is not my real life, of course, it's just the way we live now.' —But it's nonsense. We should all see it's non-sense. However you live day after day is your real life. You can't keep the substance of it intact meanwhile—like a child saving a sweet whole to be eaten under special conditions."

He was interested. He flickered out of his listless restlessness. "The times aren't good enough to merit the expenditure of our living. That sort of feeling, I suppose."

I said: "Isn't it idiotic? We know that life doesn't keep. Yet we all have the feeling that the present is something to be got over with, and *then* . . . How long have the Nats been in power? Nearly two years. So for two years now everyone who isn't a Nationalist has been going around in the kind of released state of disaster. Going around saying, Well, until this is over and we get them out again, or: Perhaps we won't stay to see what happens—what about going to Rhodesia? Or Kenya? —Even if they haven't the slightest inten-tion of going anywhere, it doesn't matter: the state of mind is the same. If you are waiting for something to alter, something to happen, if you possibly may be going to go away and live somewhere else, your whole life *now* becomes a state of suspension. It is like disaster: the same feeling of urgency, putting aside of normal incentives, making do temporarily with what you can. But the big thing about a disaster—"

"What exactly do you mean by disaster? Politically, the Nation-alist regime is a disaster all right."

"Not the way I mean. —A flood, say. Or an earthquake. The big thing about a disaster like that is that it passes. You *are* existing temporarily, you *will* begin to live again when it is over. But with us the state of mind of disaster is becoming permanent. At this rate it can go on for years. We could sit for twenty years, like flies paralyzed but not killed by a spider, so long as the Nats stay in power. An unfortunate interruption. Shelving this, shelving that, because 'things are so uncertain here,' 'we never know what will happen.' "

"There's an election every five years, you know. There's just a chance they might get thrown out."

I moved impatiently in my chair. "—Well five years, then. A year, ten months, if you like. It makes no difference. The state of mind's still fraud, a piece of self-delusion. This is our life and it is being lived out now the way we don't like it. This is not time out."

"Ah, that's true," he said slowly, "that's true." Then he said, in the quick tone of remembering a point he had wanted to question: "To go back a minute—the fly and spider business. —You talk as if everyone's resigned himself to Nat rule. And you know that's not so; you talk as if we weren't kicking like hell."

"Oh politically, yes. I grant that politically we're protesting madly. Even in ordinary private talk we're protesting. But you know that wasn't what I was talking about. It's inside. Inside ourselves in the—what's the word I want—the nonpolitical, the individual consciousness of ourselves in possession of our personal destiny: it's that which we've put aside, laid away in lavender; postponed."

I took a deep breath and we both laughed suddenly at my vehemence. I was roused by what I had been saying and I felt, for a few minutes, a glow, a relief of talk that was like the satisfaction of something accomplished.

But in a short while it faded.

That was all I had said. The relief, the satisfaction came to me spuriously, out of stimulation; they belonged to the conclusion of the saying of what I had not said. I had meant to say, but had not said.

29 I SUPPOSE THAT that night, like so many others, we went to bed and buried ourselves in each other in the silent, intense love-making that was all we had now. For it was as if where once we had had many different landscapes, many different meeting places; dreamy encounters in the sun, gentle meetings in a shade, the closeness and laughter and excitement of clinging together in a high and windy place—we had now only a strange deepening descent into steeped darkness, like a heavy silent river closing over our heads. We made love too often and I found that I kept my eyes closed tightly, even in the darkness. When it was over I would open them and lie there staring into the dark. When it was over; it ended now, with the ending of the act. So many nights I lay there, still, and noted my own lack of peace, my heavy possession of myself, with a mind as aridly wakeful as I sometimes had had when I was at the University, and had gone to bed after studying too late. Where was that mazy warmth, that lulling completeness, easy, already halfway over into sleep—the one real moment of freedom from self a human being knows? I told myself that love cannot be always the same; there are times when it is not so good as others. I even took comfort in my lack of experience, my youth, and told myself that perhaps it always changed after a time, was like that for everybody, and would change back again. . . .

And on other nights in the sharpness of my mind afterward I suddenly became aware of and seemed to see again my own greed for my satisfaction, which had just been enacted; I saw the way in which I had performed every caress, every intimacy with my will fixed savagely only on the attainment of that final physical crucifixion of pleasure. For that spasm I would have pierced Paul's flesh with my nails, forgotten his existence entirely in the determination to have him exact it from me; he, who gave it to me always so beautifully, without any thought from me except my love for him. I saw myself struggling like a beetle or an animal. A horror of myself came upon me; I was disgusted. I hated my inert, sated body, still now, like a drunken thing. And at the same time some other part of my mind started up in fear lest the whole of love-making, that fearful joy I felt with strong instinct I had already only won for myself against some threat which might have withheld it from me for ever, might be tainted with this disgust, and lost. I would turn to Paul and press my cheek against his back and put my hand up to feel the line of his hair, the outline of his gently breathing lips and the warm, beating surface of his neck, as if to assure myself that he was beautiful, desirable, that no shred of disgust could adhere here. . . .

Yet we made love too often, and while my mind said with dismay, We are not in this wholly, this is bullying something fragile that cannot stand it, like a well-trained animal my body ignored me and mechanically obeyed the summons. When I looked at Paul, reading or shaving or sitting beside me in the car, it was in disbelief; it could not be he; and at the same time a tacitly ignored collusion of guilt made a silence between us on another level than that of speech.

It did not help, either, this love-making. Whatever he hoped to wring out of it, and I, half-reluctant collaborator, must have half-hoped for, too, the tight-stretched fabric of that late summer only tautened and faded. Paul was bewilderingly difficult to live with. He had been put in charge of the housing section, a piece of office machinery which, nightmarelike, existed to administer something which literally did not exist, and all day long he heard the pleading, argument, cajolery, resentment of thousands of Africans desperate for homes—all quite useless; there were 1,100 houses for 20,000 families. "They try everything," he said. "It's as if they feel that if only they could find the way to outwit me, the secret, the magic word—there the house would be. When people persist in investing you with a certain power, you begin to believe after a while that you've really got it. . . . I have to keep in mind that there are *no* houses. . . ."

The shortage of housing for Africans was not, like the mild difficulties being encountered by white people looking for flats or houses, due to the interruption and material shortages of the war. No new houses for Africans had been built in Johannesburg for seventeen years. The old "locations," long ago filled to bursting point, simply went on overflowing onto the veld in squatters' en-

campments of scrap iron and mud. The government and local authority kept handing the responsibility for providing housing back
and forth to each other in horror; recently there had begun a move
to make the industrialists, whose expanding need for labor had
brought thousands of Africans to town, catch some of the weight.
This provided a third set of protests, a third shrug of shoulders, a
wider base for stalling and deadlock.

Paul went through the farce of his work and, at the same time,
doggedly made notes, collected facts, did what he called his own
"snooping" and obstinately presented reports, surveys and suggestions that he was always told were "very interesting." Very
interesting—and the councilors and the officials took them away
with that air of brave, sober, sad determination which had become
the face to be worn, like the special face people keep for funerals,
at the mention of African housing. And Paul knew that it was all a
waste of time, a waste of breath, a waste of their sincerity or their
false concern: no money would be found for sub-economic housing,
the Africans did not earn enough to afford economic housing, and
in any case, there was no part of the white city, east, west, north,
south, that would not raise an uproar at the proposal of a new African
township going up anywhere near its borders.

Then at night and at week ends he was involved with the African
Nationalists whose edict was non-co-operation, and who, sickened
with the neglect of their people under all governments and all intentions, good and bad, mistrusted and refuted even practical good
will. For them I saw him sitting over books and tracts about the
methods of passive resistance that Gandhi and Nehru had used
in India. For them he sent home for his law books and questioned
and requestioned Laurie over obscure legal points that he himself
did not understand. Twice already his activity with African Nationalists—all lumped together as "Communists" by the government
and the police, although the African radicals and rebels were of all
kinds: Communist, Nationalist, plain opportunist—had been gently
questioned by the head of his department. Employees of the Council's Native Affairs Department were, naturally, not allowed to in-
volve themselves in the Africans' internal politics.

In time, it was clear, Paul would lose his job. Perhaps that would not have mattered; perhaps, one could argue, it would be best. But I saw that it would matter, that far from being best, it would be disastrous to him, because he put himself as passionately into his job as he did into his unofficial work for the radical Africans. Equally, if he kept his job by giving up the other association, that would be disastrous, too. He would despise himself either way.

For Paul had made up his mind to do the impossible. I watched him and it was in his face and the way he walked and the way he performed the most trivial of daily actions. To make up one's mind to do the impossible as a gesture of defiance to a society that has blocked the outlet of one's energies in the attainable is a catharsis that may have some sour satisfaction. But Paul was not doing it like this. For him it was not a gesture; it was a way of life he had set for himself, a deliberate attempt to treat his own capacities in terms of a man who backs all the horses in a race, contending his hopes and his loyalties and his preferential partisanships one against the other. He cannot lose, and he cannot win. He scarcely knows any more what to hope for. It was more and more difficult to talk to Paul because whatever you said incensed or irritated him somewhere. If I railed, as I did, against the maddening futility of much of the Department's work, he would fly to defend it from what he sarcastically called the easy attack of ignorance; after all, he knew only too well its limited funds and its scope rigidly circumscribed by the policy of the country as a whole. If, after some uselessly reckless or stupid or arrogant piece of behavior on the part of Fanyana and his crowd, I criticized their lack of plain human consideration, he was angry because he knew them to be as pricked full of hurts every day as a bull inflamed by the picador's darts, and one small example of careless rudeness toward himself merely provided the instance that showed up the intact and unmarred surface of the white man's skin.

This calm analysis is clear and easy now. But the facts, before they were sorted in retrospect, were not clear or easy to live with. It did not seem like this to me then. My behavior toward Paul kept me in a spell of anxiety which never left me; I loved Paul and part of my loving him was my belief and pride in the work he had chosen: how was it possible, then, that the difficulties of this work, affecting him, should throw our relationship out of balance? What was the matter with me? Why couldn't I manage? Why couldn't I give him what he needed? —why, I didn't even *know* what it was, couldn't find out. . . . This situation, unimagined at the outset of our relationship, like most of the situations that arise to confound two people (I had sometimes looked at, fingered with a thrill of fear in my mind, the things which I believed happened to men and women: the lover grown fat and coarse-handed; divorce; the jealousy of a woman who is afraid of losing her man), was something for which I had no preparation, even by the precedence of others.

At first I clutched at anything I thought might hold together the torn and tearing garment of our relationship; but while I snatched the edges together with a comfort or a promise to myself in one place, the seams burst, the thread raveled out somewhere else. So in the end I did what so many other women, all through time, have done in situations beyond them. I became afraid to move inside that garment. It was torn in so many places, the seams strained so frailly everywhere, that it seemed that only by keeping quite still, scarcely breathing, would it hold together.

From somewhere a long way back, from the blood that came down to me from my mother perhaps; the blood which ran narrowly and which I hated because it had survived and always would survive by so doing, by draining off the real torrents which bear along human lives into neat ditches of domestic and social habit—from this blood came the instinct to go quiet; shut off the terrible expenditure of my main responses; take, trancelike, into the daily performance of commonplace the bewilderment, the failure. Because this blood was not all of me, but only a kind of instinctive female atavism, this does not mean that I was resigned, that I accepted. Only that my hands took over the command of themselves, taking into the action of pressing peas out of a pod, or moving a pawn on the chessboard (we had begun to play chess when we were alone together; ostensibly because I always had wanted to learn: when we played we did not have to talk), the fears, like an invasion of strangers, which now, never left me.

We saw a great deal of our friends again.

We went very often to the Marcuses, and to Laurie, and partic-

ularly to Isa Welsh, because there the same people always would
be leavened by new people; Isa liked to expose herself and her
friends to unfamiliar opinions and faces, the way people who cul-
tivate the body seek to expose themselves to the sun. We appeared
among them all as unremarked as a young couple who, after the
self-sufficiency of the engagement and honeymoon period, by the
habit of marriage are released again to seek diversion.

In Lourenço Marques Isa had met a young Italian pianist who
was about to do a concert tour of the Union, and who knew Moravia,
and she had him to stay for a week or two. He was a soft-fleshed
young man with the curious combination of a dark, sallow face and
very white plump hands, and he was obviously completely bemused
by her. She moved in his company with the air of pique and dissatisfaction which showed in her when she knew herself desired and
admired by someone who didn't interest her; I believe she felt it a
waste. She only wanted to talk to him about Moravia. At the same
time she had a young Indian couple, a trade representative and his
beautiful wife, who were not actually staying with her, but with
whom she was so enchanted that she kept making occasions, inviting
people to the flat to hear Arionte play, to eat a real Indian curry
prepared under the advice of the diplomat's lady, in order to be able
to have them there too.

"Aren't they beautiful—" She came up, ignoring with the authority of her enthusiasm her interruption of the conversation of Paul
and myself with Arionte and Jenny. "Really, they make the rest of
us look bilious. Oh, it's not that I'm just enamored of any color but
my own—there are millions of Indians more hideous than we're
monotonous. But they're just two lovely people, and their color happens to suit them perfectly . . . (—Have you talked to him?" she
asked Paul. "You must go and talk to him, he's got a mind as
incisive as a knife, a pearl-handled silver one—) like you, Jenny.
When you first came from England. Your color suited you perfectly."

"And don't you think it suits me any more?" said Jenny crossly,
although the rest of us were laughing. She had developed a touchiness toward all women who were not, like herself, somewhere in
the process of creating a family. She had made up her mind in this,
as in every other stage of her life, that the stage in which she hap-

pened to be involved was the only decent and worth-while way to
live. So at present, unless a woman was pregnant, suckling a child,
or pondering the psychological mysteries of toddlers, Jenny regarded
her with a mixture of irritation and self-righteousness.

"I've told you; it suits you admirably. But you haven't got it any
more. You've taken on the protective coloring of the country; can't
distinguish you from any other Johannesburger, today."

She was moving off (Isa never waits to see where the arrow falls,
whether it goes home or not. . . . —D'you notice?— Paul had once
said to me— I've never been able to decide whether it's callous or
vaguely honorable, in a chivalrous kind of way . . . ?) when she was
stopped by a young man who had come up behind her.

"I just walked in. Could have walked out again for all the notice
you take of me—" It was Charles Bessemer.

"Hullo, Charlie—ah, you smell nasty. Is it the perfume only
brave men dare wear?" She drew him round to us.

"Nuit de Gastrectomy," he said, sniffing at the cold smell of
ether which clung about his clothes.

"You still use the same old kind?" I said.

"Oh, *hul*-lo." He turned.

"You know Helen. . . . And this is her Paul. Jenny you know;
and this is Arionte, we don't call him by his surname because he
gets preferential treatment here, or because we can't say Guiseppe,
but because he's on the way to being a Solomon or a Schnabel—"

A kind of extra shininess came to the pianist's smooth forehead,
in place of the blush of pleasure impossible to anyone of his complexion. His shy quick look was the laying before of us of the fact:
you see? the wonderful way she is?

The "And this is her Paul" was one of Isa's little experimental
darts, tossed just for fun, in the course of more important preoccupations; I caught the faint quirk of the side of her mouth, like a
private wink to me, careless and not malicious, as she said it. It
was for Charles, who she knew had once been interested in me (Was
there a twitch? No? Well then, the thing just glanced harmlessly
off), and to tease Paul, who continually told her how disgraceful it
was that Tom had no designation other than "Isa's husband."

Charles thought a moment and then said to me unexpectedly:

"What happened to your friend from Mariastad?" —Isa was not really disappointed; she poured him a drink from the little stained table loaded with bottles, beside us.

"You mean Mary? I don't know really. She's teaching somewhere; I haven't seen her for ages."

"And you, too? —Teaching?"

Paul laughed as I said: "Do I look as if I am?"

Charles said, looking straight at me with his faint sharp smile: "You look like I always told you."

I said to the others: "He once said I looked prim. I was insulted."

Above Isa's murmur, "Quite right, quite right to be," he said firmly: "That wasn't all. She remembers the rest."

"I worked in a bookshop, and now 'I am an employee of the Johannesburg Non-European Affairs Department.'"

"Is it as bad as all that?" said Isa, suddenly putting on a social manner of concern.

"Indeed?" Charles rocked back on his heels, took his drink from her.

"Typist. Grade E, about. Salary scale, third from the bottom." I did not know quite what it was that made me talk like this; there was something in Isa's company that encouraged people to mock at themselves. In me it sounded rather feeble and a little silly. I said: "I'm going to chuck it up. I'm going to get out very soon."

"A job like that—you should be doing it for the love of it—" Charles had a way of fixing his look on you; that narrow, diagnostic look as difficult to avoid and as blank to meet as a squint.

"How you preach, Charles!" Isa was delighted with her disgust. "So bloody sanctimonious about other people's jobs. When you only cut people up because you love the cutting. So lucky suffering humanity needs to be cut up! —But really what made you get her a job like that, Paul, in the first place?"

"Well, I wanted to be where he was—"

"—And it's the only kind of thing I could get for her there. She's not trained." Paul completed my explanation.

There was a pause, so slight, so brief that I noticed it only because for a moment I heard the general noise of the room. "I see," said Isa.

And then I became acutely aware of the pause, which was already over, of the attention of the others, that was already turned from Paul and me in talk. . . . wanted to be where he was . . . The innocent way it had come to my tongue, blurting out the simple answer. And a minute before I had had their attention and their sympathy for the vehemence with which I had told them, I'm going to give it up, I'm going to get out soon.

Depression came over me and drew me back from the other people in the room, so that being incapable of being involved with any of them, I seemed to see all the several groups at once, to watch their mouths shaping talk and their faces and bodies supplementing and contradicting what they said. I felt a dull envy for Isa, taking the small pleasure of the triumphs of her tongue. I thought almost with longing of the struggles she must have given up to content herself with the substitute of these things; and I wished for a moment that I were clever enough to be able to ignore their unreality and emptiness, or that I was another kind of person, a person for whom they could ever have some meaning. In that room full of people whom I knew well enough to fear their curiosity, I wanted to cry. In a bus, in a train, among strangers I would have cried, as people sometimes have to, cannot always wait to be alone. But here I dared not, and so all these people, my friends, became enemies.

The Indian was talking to me about the dances of her country and bent her draped head over a book on Balinese dancing which Tom Welsh had laid in her lap; it sometimes happened at one of Isa's parties that some beautiful gentle woman suddenly drew Tom to her side and kept him there the whole evening. They talked very low and no one ever joined them or interrupted, no one ever knew what the long, absorbed conversation had been about. Only Isa would look up, worried, now and then, at the head of the woman, and say good night to her when she left with an extra, compensatory fervor; she felt that the poor woman had been bored.

Paul had had just enough brandy to key him up to his warmest charm; he wore it like a suit of clothes that has not been worn for a long time but fits as well as ever. His voice and Isa's flashed back and forth across the room. The "music hall turn" was on between them.

Arionte said: "I wish so to talk. I have been speaking English only one year now. . . ." And then he eyed me for a moment. "You say you like Mozart. Just now I play you . . . Some part the D Minor."

There was a relief in jealousy like a sudden scalding. It was something over which we could have an open argument. Paul said: "Helen you know this is ridiculous. What is it you really want to fight about?"

But I grew afraid.

I no longer wanted to touch that nervous mass which trembled between us.

But it seemed to me for the first time that he knew. Later in the dark he said in a loud wakeful voice: "We're terribly involved. Terribly involved with each other. . . ."

And I tweaked at the pretense of jealousy again: "*That* sounds like Isa. The sort of thing she says, all dilated pupils."

He said again, as if the thing was threshing itself about in his mind, showing, disappearing, ungraspable, distressing— "Involved . . . ?" I had no answer.

We quarreled again about Isa. I would pick up this petty weapon in my sense of weakness; a sudden spiral of irritation that blinded and smarted like a whirlwind; dying in a flurry of dust and dead leaves.

"I cannot understand why you do this." He had the exasperated look of an animal worried into anger. And when it had happened a number of times, goaded as I had goaded myself: "Yes, of course I like Isa! All the inadequacies she had as a lover are her virtues as a friend. Christ, she's a grown-up person! I can talk to her. Yes, I can talk to her and she doesn't expect me always to be consistent, every word that comes out of my mouth to fit into some idea she's got about me! Every time I say something I have to watch your face measuring it up; I've got to see your eyes change or the expression round your mouth fade—"

Then he, too, looking about for something to break the silences between us, instinctively felt for it, closed his hand round it. "I think you're hankering after your mother and father. All this moodiness comes from a part of you that hasn't grown up. You still wonder if you aren't being a naughty girl, and it amuses me." He stared at me obstinately, smiling. "It amuses me.

"Why are you such a damned hypocrite?" He pressed me.

Shortening the hem of an old skirt, or caught in the pause in which I sometimes lost the sense of what I was reading, nothing had been further from my thoughts than Atherton and my life there and my mother and father. In fact, the unvarying daily predictability of that life, in which the equal predictability of the life I had imagined had seemed just as assured, seemed as far from me as those curiously vivid anecdotes of babyhood which belong to pre-memory and that we have only come to know through being told by others.

Yet he had found, as intimacy cruelly makes it impossible not to do, the one spot in my secret assessment of myself that had once been inflamed, and that reddened in tender shame from time to time. I trembled in hurt at this confirmation of what I had feared in myself with humiliation and disappointment. When he saw the roused hostility in my face he must have felt as I did when I was possessed by a drive to torment him, and saw that I had succeeded: the whole challenge died out of him listlessly in a kind of defiant shame; it was not what he meant, what he wanted, after all. And it left a burned-out loneliness in the very center of one's love for the other.

I had said: "I want to live with you in the greatest possible intimacy." That was one of the things I had said so many times, with all the awkwardness in the shaping of the words that makes the things that lie deep and dominant in us so difficult to say.

I saw this thing turn, like a flower, once picked, turning petals into bright knives in your hand. And it was so much desired, so lovely, that your fingers will not loosen, and you have only disbelief that *this*, of all you have ever known, should have the possibility of pain. All the time, you are seeing the blood trickling a red answer slowly down your hand.

30 I LEFT THE WELFARE OFFICE at the end of April.

On the Wednesday of my last week there, my father telephoned me. I went to the telephone expecting the voice of John, with a message from Jenny about some book on antenatal exercises I had promised to get her at the bookshop where I had once worked, and I heard one of the bright, interchangeable voices of the Mine switchboard operators: "One moment. . . . Your call, Mr. Shaw, you're through. . . ."

Our conversation was not so much tense, as stilted with a kind of shyness. "I just wanted to know how you were, my dear. . . ."

"And you? Everything all right?"

"Oh, yes. Just as usual. —Well, I don't want to keep you from your work, Helen—"

"It's all right. As it happens this is my second last day. I'm changing my job."

"Oh?" He wanted to show me how little he wanted to criticize or upset me, my father who had started as office boy and ended up as Secretary in the same office on the same Mine, and for whom a change of job would have been almost as great a disturbance as the transmigration of his soul. "Have you found something that suits you better? That's very nice."

"Well, not yet. I've got one or two things in mind. The Belgian Consulate, for one. . . ." "That should be interesting; a chance to have contact with the wider world. Well, I hope you get it, my dear—"

I sat down to my desk again: the call scarcely had been an interruption at all.

An hour later I suddenly asked the girl at the switchboard to get me the Mine number. I heard my father hold back the surprise in his voice as, in his bewilderment with me, he suppressed any show of emotion in case it should be the wrong one in my eyes. "Daddy, do you think I could come home this week end? What do you think—"

"No, of course, Helen. It will be all right. Your mother won't say anything, I'm sure. Only don't say anything to her. Just let it be

as if nothing had happened. She'll be very glad." —he paused—
"Sometimes she's hasty. And afterward she can't—it's not in her
nature . . ."

"I know. Good, then. I won't phone her. You tell her and I'll
come. On Saturday. In the morning, most probably."

I told Paul that my father had telephoned me and that I was
going to Atherton at the week end. "Didn't I tell you?" he said.
" 'Never darken my doorstep again.' And how long is it—six
weeks?"

We were having lunch in the basement cafeteria round the corner from the offices, where the smoke and sizzling of hamburgers
thickened the noise of the crush, and the hands of the Indian waiters
flashed like conjurers' as they raced to serve too many people at
once.

I shrugged.

He flicked the two little marbles of butter, buried in a lettuce
leaf like pearls in an oyster, onto my roll, and leaned over and took
the butter dish belonging to the next table, where two fat young men
and an ogling girl were just rising. "Next they'll be asking tenderly
after me. I'll be coming along for the week end, too. And they'll be
secretly planning their grandchildren."

At home where a thousand times we were alone and the tension
between us urged it, there was a space cleared for it, it had never
been spoken. But now I said: "We'll never be married." It was
spoken quite simply and flatly, from some part of me that was not
aware of mutations of which his easy, half-flippant mood and the
restless, food-murky den were one.

He put his paper napkin down slowly under his hand. It was a
gesture halting everything. "Why do you say that?"

I said, far away, looking at him a long way across the crowded
little table: "Because it's so."

"But what makes you say that—" He had the little twitching
nervous smile of the onset of strong fear or anger. "You can't just
say it— Why? Why do you?"

"You know it," I said again.

His hands made a flurry of picking up a spoon and fork; faltered
beneath his gaze and mine and took up instead the teaspoon needed

to stir his coffee. He drank. "Mad," he said to himself, "things that come to you."

The waiter jerked his head for our attention as if he were putting it impatiently round a door. "Sweets, miss?"

"D'you feel like anything—"

"What about you? If you do, then."

"Well it's five past already, and you said you wanted to go down to the framer's. . . . We might as well go straight off." He stood up to let me edge past the table in front of him.

The paper napkin lay in a tight ball beside his plate.

I lay on the lawn at the side of our house under my bedroom window. The bottom of the jasmine hedge had thinned with age and through it I could see the front garden and the doves which flopped down, every now and then, in the dust and the red leaves blown from the Virginia creeper. Our house was shedding its shaggy summer coat; the leaves had turned bright and brittle, and there were patches where the brick showed under a light tracery of bare tendrils. The cement had worn away with years of rain, and the edges of the bricks were rounded, crumbling.

Under my head was one of the cushions from the veranda. Don't take one of the good ones; take an old one from the veranda. Yet who will ever wear out the good ones? What was the occasion for which everything had always been saved?

I lay letting my eyes follow the line of upended bricks that marked the border of the path and the crescents and circles of the flower beds; so had I followed them with my feet when I was a child, balancing myself against the mild sunny boredom of a summer afternoon. (Where had I read it: It is always summer when you remember childhood. . . .) The week end was already half over and it all had passed at the tempo of this midmorning. Soon my mother would call out (she knew she would not be clearly heard and so a minute or two after Anna would come slowly round the side of the house, coming right up to me and saying suddenly: The missus says tea, Miss Helen) just as she had called for breakfast this morning and dinner last night. The hours flowed in and out between the beacons of meals, and there was nothing else to divide up the day.

It had all been so easy in such a matter-of-fact, flaccid way, like the expected resistance of a muscle that is discovered to be atrophied. My mother, who never had the strength to give in, could always evade. She did it this time by creating an atmosphere of convalescence in the house; she treated my father and me, and even herself, as if we were all recovering, shaken, from an illness we did not speak about. We did not speak much at all, in fact; she made it seem as if this was to be expected when one must conserve one's strength.

So I lay on the lawn on Saturday afternoon, I lay on the lawn all Sunday morning. I don't believe I thought at all; just flicked over images in my mind, people and places I had not remembered for years blowing suddenly bright in the darkness behind my eyes the way the wind ruffles and arrests the pages of a picture book. Olwen; the dark settling on the shuffling children in the Atherton cinema on a Saturday afternoon; Mrs. Koch, her veined, elderly feet freed in the sand; myself, standing on the dining-room table while my mother evened the hem of a new dress; the Dufalettes I used to watch through the hedge, so that I could tell them apart more accurately by their feet than by their faces. I was not asleep but I preferred to keep my eyes closed. When they opened involuntarily it was as if something split; the light seared in; then I could see the angle of the house, the hedge, the garden; and, if I rolled half onto my back, on the perimeter of my sky the tops of some of the old fir trees which soughed about the Mine over the faint rough pant of the stamp batteries like the sea drowning the subterranean cries of its monsters. And, just seen behind the Dufalettes' chimney, the derrick of the shaft head itself. The house, the hedge, the garden, the shaft head: it all said: I am. But when I let my eyelids drop darkness again, nothing was; there were rents, tears, sudden fadings in the vividness of what I saw that proved the nonexistence of these faces, these places: harmless, by being past. Even a threatening image carried reassurance in its ephemerality; nothing more than a fist shaken in the distance by a hand that will never be near enough to strike again.

The evening before, I had spent what I suppose was an incredible evening at the house of the Compound Manager. D'you think this is all right? Or should I take off the flower? —My mother came into my room in the convention of seeking reassurance about her appearance, as she had done a thousand times before. She wore a green crepe dress with a string of pearls and an artificial tea rose, the outfit that, with well-defined variations, would be worn by every other Mine woman there. She smelled, as she always had done, of lavender water. (As a child this weak sweet scent had been a means of social discrimination for me; once when my mother had been puzzled by the identity of a woman who had called in her absence and left no name, and my mother had asked me to describe her, I had answered: She smelled like a nice lady.)

When she had gone out of my room, repinning the velvet rose, I looked at myself in the dressing-table mirror. I looked very different from my mother, though we were both tall, and I had her red hair. The forehead which she would have "softened" with a few curls I kept bare and prominent, the back hair which she would have cut and permanently waved, I had as long as it would grow, and wound round thickly into a sort of tight little crown. Yellow shantung dress with a peasant-style skirt, bodice tight to show off my breasts. Belt and heavy earrings made of copper medallions (we had tired of native beadwork, and it was beginning to appear among the artificial pearls and American costume jewelry in department stores). Un-rouged face, brilliantly painted lips. Short unpainted fingernails with the large heavy dark ring Paul had saved to have made for me by the German refugee. (But that's a man's ring, my mother had said, holding out a hand with fingernails of opaque mauvish-pink and her gold-and-diamond engagement ring which was always a little dimmed by the pastry dough that got stuck in the well at the back of the setting.)

The outfit, the face, that any one of the women I knew at Isa's or the Marcuses' might be wearing at this moment. I dragged the earrings down the lobes of my ears; unclasped the belt. But there was nothing else, in the old chocolate box full of jewelry which I took everywhere with me, that I could wear. Porcelain horses that were faultily made and wouldn't stay on my ears, silver gypsy hoops Isa had once given me; the native beadwork; round pink cabbage roses made of glued seashells which my mother had bought me from some woman who made them because her husband had abandoned her and she had even less talent for making a living any other way.

I put the copper medallions and the belt on again and went to the Compound Manager's.

There there were all the sweet things of my childhood that people like myself had lost taste for. —Usually we didn't eat at all but were offered gin or beer or brandy the moment we walked in, and went on having our glasses filled up until, if it was a party, a big hot dish of curry or canelloni came in with bottles of wine or, if it wasn't, coffee with confectioners' biscuits. But here, on the little gazelle-legged tables that had awed me long ago, little flowered dishes of chocolates, toffees and peppermint buttons were put out. At a quarter-to-ten sharp we were led into the dining room and were sat down to the big table from which a shower of painted gauze the size of a bedspread was whipped, baring cake stands and silver lattice baskets filled with cakes and cream-topped scones and tarts, all made by the hostess, like the wide glass plate of sandwiches (for the men, I remembered; one of the axioms of the Mine was that men don't care for sweet things), all precisely cut and decorated with streamers of lettuce and sprigs of parsley so well washed that here and there a drop of water still gleamed on the curly green. Most people drank two or three cups of tea from the thin, flowered cups which all matched (every Mine hostess had a "best" set that would enable her to serve a dozen or more without using odd cups) and it was not until eleven-fifteen and a quarter-of-an-hour before everyone would rise to go, countering the host's "But it's Sunday tomorrow . . ." with "We must have our beauty sleep . . . ," that a polished cabinet smelling of new green baize was opened and the men were offered whisky. They stood around sipping at cut-crystal glasses with a rose design, but the women were not offered anything. They drank only at sundowner time.

The discrimination was not obvious or awkward because the women had grouped themselves apart from the men all evening. I, of course, was with them, sitting on a small spindly chair: You're a young light one, Helen, we old ones with a middle-age spread need something more solid—and laughing they lowered their flowered or lace bulk into the deep soft chairs and the sofa. One or two took

out their knitting; the hostess had a decorated felt bag from which
came the fourth of a set of tapestry chair covers she was working.
The others exclaimed that they wished they'd brought their knitting,
or the hem of a child's dress that had to be done by hand. That
reminded another of a new way of hemming she had read about in
a magazine. Oh—someone else thought she'd read that—was it in
the *Ladies' Home Journal*? No, the other didn't get the *Ladies' Home
Journal*, it must be in some English magazine. "Well, I get all my
knitting patterns from *Good Needlework*," said another. And at once
they were all talking about the magazines and papers that they
"took"; I recognized the names of the neat stacks of thin threepenny
women's papers I had been given to amuse me on visits to their
houses fifteen years ago. "I've been a subscriber ever since we've
been on the Mine," old Mrs. Cluff was saying, her head nodding
agreement with each word she spoke. "What was that?" someone
asked. "*Home Chat*"—she turned smiling and nodding—"I've been
getting it for many years." "I remember," I said from my chair. "It
used to have Nurse Carrie's page in it. Excerpts from people's letters
were printed in italics, and then Nurse Carrie answered underneath
in ordinary print." They laughed indulgently—but I had got my first
inklings about sex from that genteel page, poring over it on the floor
of Mrs. Cluff's sitting room when I was eight or nine.

Sitting on the delicate chair, I heard again all the warm buzz of
talk that had surrounded my childhood. It was as comfortable as the
sound of bees; no clash of convictions, no passion, no asperity—
unless this last was on a scale so domestically close-knit and contemporary that I could not catch it. Their talk flowed over me, flowed
over me, all evening; one after the other, peppermint comfits dissolved in my mouth.

When at last we rose to leave, I spoke to the men for the first
time, although through the evening I had heard snatches of their
talk, drifting across the path of my wondering attention. Mine gossip,
it had been; and the shares they had been tipped off to buy in the
Group's newly opened Free State gold fields; and—hotly argued—
the selection of the team to represent the Mine at an inter-provincial
bowling tournament in Natal.

The Compound Manager said, drawing in his cheeks at the dryness of his last swallow of his whisky: "Helen . . . So . . . it's a long time since you've deserted us. You like the city, eh? I don't think you've been to see us since your parents went overseas—?"

"D'you know," I said, smiling, "the last time I remember being in your house? The morning of the strike. A Sunday morning, when the Compound boys had a strike over their food, and I came with Daddy to see. They were standing about all over the garden, and we came inside—into this room—and Mrs. Ockert was giving everybody tea."

"Oh, no!" he laughed, astonished. "—D'you hear that, Mab— Helen says the last time she was here was that time when we had the strike."

"But that's twelve—no, thirteen years ago," objected Mr. Bellingan.

"You were with us," I said. "I remember you were with us."

"Heavens, Helen, you must have been here a number of times after that!" All the gentlemen laughed round me.

"Well, that's the last time I remember!"

They all began to recollect the strike; like a performance of theatricals, taken earnestly at the time, that becomes amusing in the retelling. One had done this; the other had thought that. The Compound Manager put down his empty glass and, hands in his pockets, rocked on his heels, knowing, smiling, at a situation he had dealt with.

"Ah, but things were still done decently in those days," said the Reduction Officer. Old men, confronted with two world wars, jet aircraft and atom bombs, sometimes spoke like this of the Boer War, in which they had fought: the last gentlemanly war. "This kind of thing coming up on Monday—we didn't have that then. But of course the mine boys have always been the good old type of kraal native, not these cheeky devils from the town, don't know what they want themselves, half the time, except trouble."

And that was the one reference anyone there made to the May Day strike of African and colored workers which was only the duration of Sunday away from us.

When I went back to Johannesburg that Sunday evening I caught a fast train that did not stop at the Atherton Mine siding and so my

father had to drive me in to Atherton to the station. We went slowly
down the main street, arrested at every block by the traffic lights.
The town had changed a great deal since I was a child, slowly, of
course, and I had seen it changing, so that while it was happening
I had not seen the alteration of the whole structural face, but merely
the pulling down of this old building, the filling up of that vacant
square where the khaki weed used to grow and the dogs clustered
round a poor little vagrant bitch in season. But this evening I had
the shock of discovering that in my mind the idea of Atherton carried
with it a complete picture of the town the way it must have been
when I was nine or ten years old: it rose up in connotation like a
perfectly constructed model, accurate in every detail. And I saw that
now it really was nothing more than a model, because that town had
gone. The vacant lots blocked in in concrete, the old one-story shops
demolished; with them the town had gone. A department store was
all glass and striped awnings where two tattered flags, a pale Union
Jack and a pale Union flag, had waved above the old police bar-
racks. A new bank with gray Ionic columns and a bright steel grille
stood on the corner where my mother's grocer had been; the grocer
was now a limited company with a five-story building, delicatessen,
crockery and hardware departments, further down the street. As I
say, all this had happened gradually, but I saw it suddenly now; it
did not match the Atherton alive in the eye of my mind. In the
shadow of two buildings a tiny wood-and-iron cottage lived on; a
faint clue. Here at least, the one Atherton fitted over the other, and
in relation to this little house I could fade away the tall irregular
buildings, and place the vanished landmarks where I had looked or
lingered.

Sitting beside my father while he changed gears and drew away
as if the car were a live creature to be treated considerately, I felt
queerly that it was as impossible for me ever to walk in and out the
shops of this real Atherton as it was for me to walk again in the
small village that had gone.

On my lap I held the paper bag my mother had given me before
I left. "Half the fruitcake," she had said, and I knew that inside it
would be wrapped in a neat sheet of grease-proof paper, the kind
that had wrapped my school lunches. "No good my keeping it all,

there's no one to eat it. And if I give you the whole, it's the same thing, isn't it—" And she had stopped in cold embarrassment at her own voice, that had implied that I was alone, and so doing, had reminded both of us that I wasn't, that someone would be there to help me eat my mother's fruitcake. She had stiffened and answered with offended monosyllables the commonplaces, suitably removed from the subject, about which I went on talking to her. I suppose it was funny, really, and perhaps I should have been secretly amused. But I had only wanted to say to her—I don't know why—: Mother, I haven't changed. Look, this is me; you know me: just as I have always been, before I could walk and before I could speak and before I had loved a man and taken him into my body. And I thought, She will never recognize me, she will never know me again. Even if I could speak it would not alter it.

I said good-by to Daddy on the platform. There was a tranquillity in him, as if he were seeing his daughter off to school after a week end at home; there is the certainty that there will be many other week ends when she will be coming home. As I kissed his cool shaven cheek, the cheek of an aging man with little tendrils of broken vein under the thin skin, I had again the queer feeling I had had in the main street of Atherton. I would keep coming; but the way I came would never be coming back.

The train rocked into speed, clacked through the Mine siding without stopping. The tin shelter marked EUROPEANS ONLY, the fading shout of Mine natives jumping back exaggeratedly as we passed, the dark, ragged gum plantation that hid the Mine, the Recreation Hall, the rows of houses and my parents' house itself. A single dusty light burned already above the siding, although it was not yet dark.

There were a great many natives on all the stations, but that was nothing unusual for a Sunday night. Neither was the air of excitement, which one like myself, deaf to the meaning of the words, found in their voices. Sunday clothes, beer, and the still greater intoxication of leisure commonly accounted for that. At one of the larger stations I noticed several men wearing rosettes. The train jolted them away; the outcrop of the gold reef which ran along under the ground began to pass my window again: shaft heads, old untidy mine dumps with the cyanide weirdly hardened and fissured by years of rain, new dumps geometrically exact as the pyramids, towns like Atherton, brickfields, smoking locations, mines, clumps of native stores on the veld—the windows wired over for Sunday—another dump, another mine, another Atherton. Everywhere, gradually sparsened by the increase of human rubble, the cosmos which sprang up every autumn. Even when first I had started traveling to University, they had been a thick wake in the path of the train, in many places. Now they showed pink and white among the khaki weed which was stifling them out; when the train stopped at a small station I could smell it, rank on the cooling air and the smell of water. Below the station was one of the dams that chemical infiltration from the Mine colored mother-of-pearl, making, by incidental artifice and a strange reversal of the usual results of man's interference with nature, something beautiful that was not.

At this little station a newsbill stood against the wire fence, though apparently the paper boy had sold out his stock of papers and left. It was rucked up under the wire frame that held it to a board: STRIKE SITUATION: POLICE PREPARED FOR TOMORROW. Of course not—those were not rosettes: no wonder the men weren't dressed like a football team. Freedom Day badges. Yet I could not feel anything about the strike that was coming tomorrow, the strike that, the whole of the previous week in Johannesburg, we had talked of. Neither fear nor apprehension nor curiosity at the nearness of this threat—to ourselves? to the Africans themselves?—that would soon be here; soon now. Tomorrow something might get up on its feet that was being fed for such a moment every day. Nobody knew what it would be like, what it could do; this thing to the Africans a splendid creature of their own power, to the white men a monster of terror. Even people like Paul, Laurie, Isa, myself, had to say to ourselves: Maybe this will be the day when the patient hands will come down in blows, when our mouths will be stopped for the things we have not said.

But seeing the bill, the station, the dam, the cows which stood up to their knees in the painted water, begin to move past, none of that was real to me. I thought, The last time, the last time I came back from Atherton, I sat with my eyes closed all the way. I remembered how, the last time, I had kept my eyes closed to block out

the distance between myself and Paul, to get to him faster. I had
lain against the seat saying inside myself, Paul, Paul. I closed my
eyes again for a second to remember it.

But it was not there in the dark.

I sat like a person who is physically tired, letting the movement
of the train shudder my hand against the window ledge, letting the
landscape slide by under my eyes. I might have been looking down
upon it from a plane; it was so familiar, this repetition of mine, town,
dump and veld I had known so long, from so many journeys; and
so far away. As far from me as the first stars, seeming to catch the
light rather than give it off, like the turn of a woman's ring faintly
flashing a prismatic gleam.

31 NOTHING HAPPENED on Monday. I know. Not only because it was true in fact, the papers said so; but because
I felt in the anticlimactic calm of that day a kind of guilty reflection
of my own state. It seemed to me that the fact that nothing happened
justified my lack of interest, made it excusable.

It was my first day—I will not say of leisure, it was not that,
but of lack of work.

Paul had been out when I arrived back at the flat the evening
before. I had made myself some Russian tea and gone to bed (how
the Mine fed one to extinction, truly to extinction—all the blood
comfortably deflected from one's doubting brain to one's satisfied
stomach). Much later he had come home. The light was already out
and I listened to him moving softly about the room, not telling him
I was awake. When he slid into bed beside me I put out my hand
as one might do in sleep; he put his hand on my waist as one
comforts a child who stirs. I did not ask him where he had been.
Neither of us spoke. We lay, he with his meeting in some location
shack that I guessed he must have been to, I with the pleasantries
and best china cups of the Compound Manager's lounge, like people
who do some highly secret work and so even in intimacy are alone,
each with an aura unpenetrated and unquestioned by the other. At

last he put his hand up round my breast and shifted his body close
along the length of my back, the way he had slept always since our
first night together. Or perhaps, out of habit, and halfway to sleep,
I only thought I felt him there.

In the morning he did not say anything about where he had been.
As I trailed about in my dressing gown—since I did not have to go
out to work I had not bothered to dress—I thought how odd it was;
by pulling so hard the other way, one always seems to find oneself,
at some point or other, arrived at precisely that condition of life from
which one shied so violently. The women of the Mine, making a
virtue of what was really the comfortable expedient of the kitchen
and the workbasket, rather than accept the real, vital meaning of
living with a man. Jenny, this first woman I had ever known who
had kept her own identity, and left that of her husband uncrushed
—now so enamored of her reproductive processes that she habitu-
ally mouthed John's opinions rather than allow the interruption of
thinking out her own; had apparently shelved as thankfully as any
shopgirl leaving the cheese counter for the escape of marriage, the
stage designing in which she had once been so passionately interested; and preserved her radical views in suburban moth balls.

Here I was, back where they were, cooking a man's breakfast
and keeping my mouth shut. Not for the same reasons—but what
consolation was there in that? Turning the egg over because that's
the way he likes it, done on both sides. Even my hair, hanging
uncombed, seemed to confirm the picture. When we both worked—
and that was only last week—we had snatched our breakfast together, feeding each other like birds, at the kitchen table. But this
Monday morning, the first of May, I stood about while Paul sat down
and ate; plenty of time for me to breakfast.

It was a beautiful morning; the sun sloped down past the balcony. I went out and looked over. The buildings were pale in the
early light, the rising hum came from the city.

"Well, what d'you expect to see?" he said with a smile.

I stood at the side of the table, putting my hands down on it
awkwardly. "I don't know. . . . It seems just the same. There should
be *something*, I somehow feel." He went on eating, his gaze following
my words out the open glass doors, where he could see nothing but

the morning air. He doesn't talk to me about the strike any more, I thought, he doesn't tell me what he's thinking of what he knows and fears out of what he learned last night. He treats me as if it were something out of my ken; the week end at Atherton he hasn't asked me about has put it out of my ken. We never used to have things that were outside each other's ken.

"What are you going to do with yourself?" he said.

"Oh, I've got lots of little things," I said with the conviction of someone who has no idea how her time is to be made to pass. He ruffled my hair as he got up to get his hat and a cigarette: a father who cannot be expected to tell a child what he is going to do in the world this morning. "No—" I said, turning my cheek, "not on my mouth—I haven't cleaned my teeth yet."

He had no sooner gone than I flew out onto the balcony with a fastbeating heart; but there was the little car, coming out from under the building, turning into the street and away. He could not even see me.

When I turned back into the flat I found myself feeling almost self-conscious. I had never before been alone there in the morning; the room looked at me like a servant surprised by an employer in the performance of some work that is always done when the people of the house are out of the way. I saw the room, a disparate collection of inanimate objects, for the first time; in the normal course of my life with Paul it had been nothing but a background for our talk and activity, our sleep and our waking. It had handed things silently and I had taken them without thinking. Now it confronted me and I thought that not only was it like a slightly put-out servant, it was like a servant who didn't recognize my authority, anyway. This was Paul's room, these were Paul's things among which I had been living. In spite of the stockings on a chair, the jar of face cream beside the bed, the mask and the cushions, I had made no mark, no claim on this room. These things which were mine could be packed away just as a hotel room is cleared of the few personal belongings of each successive guest, remaining adequately equipped with all the necessary accouterments of a room and always retaining its own character.

I made the bed and stacked the dishes in the sink for the flat boy to wash (we had an arrangement with him) and bathed and dressed. I thought of slacks but that would have made it feel too much like Sunday, so I put on a dress instead, noting, as I always did when I fastened a belt, as if it were some relieved discovery that I must keep making, that I was young, that my shape was good. My hips are too narrow, but I'm tall and my breasts are nice. I wonder where I get them from? My father's side of the family? My mother has no breasts; as if she had forgotten about them. —For a moment I was completely absorbed in this timeless preoccupation. Shut up in this little room in a great city where factories were silent, shops were without messengers or cleaners, and the streets were suspicious of their normality, I contemplated something that would never change, that when it left me, would already be coming to life in others.

I took the tea and the slice of toast I had made myself out onto the balcony, perhaps to evade the room. Opposite, the half-finished block of flats was empty and silent; the builder, one of the prudent employers I had read about in the paper, must have told his employees not to come to work, because even the white workers were not there. I sat out on the tiny balcony half the morning, and later two little silent children with bare feet and shabby dungarees came to play on the builder's sand. Perhaps they came from the building in which I was sitting; I realized as I sat there that the tall shabby walls, the brown-painted corridors and the stale, boxed air of the lift did not have an existence solely about Paul and me, but were seen in the same function by a number of other people, all very different from us and one another, whose lives now signaled for recognition. There was the sound of a duster being shaken out on the balcony of the flat below, the bumbling rise and fall of a crooner's voice, and then the terse nasal barks, very loud, of a radio play recorded in America, coming from a window on the right. I heard a telephone ring for several minutes; stop, ring again, and then cut off abruptly.

The sun shone steadily on the two small boys: they had found a sifter now, and were busy piling it with sand, letting the sand run through, and then shoveling the same sand into it all over again. The flat boy came in, greeted my explanation of my presence with apparent pleasure at the idea of my being there, whatever the reason, and breathed a song to himself as he rubbed the floor, just as if he had been alone. And over to the left, Johannesburg opened its mouth in its usual muffled roar. I could detect no note of panic—in any case, had there been screams, the howls of the monster at last risen staggering to its feet, they would have been blocked out for me by the indestructible brisk cheeriness of the radio next door.

I said to the flat boy: "Did you hear if there was any trouble this morning in the locations?"

He sat back on his knees like an amiable zoo bear and laughed. It was a deep, phlegm-roughened laugh, because he smoked a lot —his pipe stuck out of the pocket of his "kitchen boy" suit even now. He said, with the tolerant grin at a blood sport which didn't interest him: "Nobody say. I didn't see nobody. But plenty boys come to town last night, sleep all night where they work." He lived with the other flat boys next to the boiler rooms on top of the building, leaning over the parapet on warm nights to twang his guitar above the concrete.

Another one of the good old-fashioned kind.

I tried to rouse myself to do something. Sitting on the balcony smoking in the sun, I thought, I *am* like an invalid: between the illness and the cure. Sitting weakly in the sun. It was the state of suspension I had spoken about so heatedly to Paul that night when I had wanted to tell him something else: what am I waiting for, why don't I go and phone up the Consulate, write a letter about that broadcasting research job? It seemed to me that the strike had something to do with my inertia: waiting for something to happen. (Can't do anything because you're waiting for this, that, or the other. —That state of suspension, today in its acute form.) Yet I knew that I was not even really thinking of the strike at all.

Toward lunchtime I telephoned the office. I don't know why I was surprised to find that Paul was there, the voice of the girl at the switchboard just as usual. "What's it like in town?" —My voice had the subdued, hesitant tone of someone tacitly atoning for a piece of shaming disregard; a woman who has ignored some indisposition of her husband's may speak in just that tone when next she sees him, and if he answers, as he will, as if her concern for him had been consistent, they can both successfully make her lapse nonexistent.

"Haven't you been out? It's all quiet. You know. The rural peace of Johannesburg—" I heard a man's muffled laugh: someone must be in the office with him.

"And at the busses this morning?" —We had expected trouble at the location bus and train termini, where we knew there would be pickets.

"Nothing, so far as we've heard."

"So if the police can keep their hands to themselves—" I felt awkward as if I were suggesting an aspirin.

"Yes, we must wait and see." There was a pause.

"—But they must be itching on their batons—" I tried again.

"I haven't been out in any of the townships yet today," he said shortly. "Did you phone the Consulate?"

"No. Perhaps this afternoon. If I don't fall asleep. You've no idea how odd it is, being in the flat in the morning."

"Of course I have—when I was sick? Don't you remember?" His voice chided me in a guarded intimacy, perhaps because of the presence of the other person. At once I revived, stung to naturalness: "Oh, but that was quite different. That's why I didn't even think of it."

"Look, I must go now, darling."

"Are you going to be late— Because if not—" I was eager.

"I can't say. I don't think so. Because there are a lot of things I should do this afternoon that I won't be able to. Oh, and Isa phoned; she wants us to eat there. So if I'm late I'll go straight there. If I'm not home by half-past five, say . . . And you can go up when you feel like it, she'll be home all afternoon, she said."

"Oh, *tonight*," I said.

"Why, we weren't doing anything?"

"No. All right." I'm not sure that I feel like Isa, I wanted to say.

I did fall asleep. I lay down on our bed with the blue quilt over my feet and thought: When I get up in about half an hour I'll phone her and tell her we can't come, I'd already made some other arrangement, and then I'll phone him and tell him. The sun, filtering through the net curtains, warmed the crown of my head through my hair; the woman next door had turned off the radio and a warm space of silence hung above the surge of traffic.

32 WHEN I AWOKE it was five o'clock. The sun, moved away from the room round to the west, had left five heavy drops of honey trembling on the wall below the ventilator brick. Opening my eyes on these I had the familiar confusion that follows a spell of sleep at an unaccustomed hour, felt all the rooms where I had slept rush past my mind before I could seize and steady myself into this one, and then jumped up with a sense of panic. I had the telephone receiver in my hand before I remembered whom I had to ring up and why.

Well, it was too late to put her off now. A little sick and dazed from getting up too quickly, the nausea transposed itself into a re-action against the thought of going to Isa's that evening. I thought: I'll phone Paul now and work out some way of getting out of it.

"He's left, I'm afraid. He went out about half an hour ago." It was a new voice; must be the girl who had taken my job.

"Have you any idea where he went?" I asked.

"Just a minute—" She was eager to please, in her newness. "Someone says he said he was going to the Community Center."

"Which one?"

"The Richardson."

"Thank you very much." I was just thinking, Now is the number 52-8529 or 92, when the telephone jangled under my hand. Instantly, I was sure it was Paul. Urgently I said: "Hullo—"

Laurie's mild, slow voice, the voice of a fat man, answered. "Helen—hullo . . ." We exchanged pleasantries, commented on the uneventful way the day had passed off. "Is your man there? I want a word in his ear."

"I was just about to phone him. He's at the Richardson Center."

"Oh, blast him. I want to speak to him right away."

"Well, why don't you phone him there?" I said. "I was going to."

"No, I can't," Laurie said, "I can't explain. . . . But I can't tell him what I want to tell, over the phone. I was going to come over to your flat, if he'd been home." He laughed. "Don't think I'm crazy."

For some reason, I felt vaguely embarrassed. "Well, I don't know what to suggest. I don't know when he'll be back. And if I can't get him before he leaves the Richardson, he'll go straight to Isa's. We're supposed to be eating there. —You could drop in there later, and see."

"No," he laughed again, a little irritated at having to keep up a mystery. "It'll be too late. Might be, even now, as he's already in the township. —Well I'll have to take a chance on saying what I have to say in some sort of guarded way over the phone. Give me the number, will you? And you don't mind waiting five minutes so that I can ring him first? I'll tell him to ring you, if you like."

"Yes, do that. The number's 52-8529." I was suddenly sure of this. We both rang off. I was tingling with a vaguely alarmed curiosity. But although he had made it clear that it was not from me, but from the telephone, that he was withholding an explanation of the message he wanted to give Paul, I, too, was irritated by the mystery. —He's getting like Edna and all the rest, creating for himself the importance of dark secrets. Paul won't thank him for it anyway; he'll laugh.

The telephone rang again almost immediately. "Look—" said Laurie, "there's no reply from the place." "Of course. The switchboard must be closed. Operator keeps ordinary office hours, there," I remembered. Laurie said: "D'you think he might still be there?"

"Very likely."

"Or he might be on his way home?"

I laughed. "Sound deduction!" But Laurie ignored it. "I think I'll take a chance and go out there," he said. "That's if I ever find the place."

"Oh, it's easy, you can't miss it. When you turn off the main road you keep turning to the left, three times, and then once right past the Apostolic Faith church, it's a funny little place with a silver-painted roof." I stopped myself suddenly. "Laurie, take me with you.

Please. Come and pick me up? I've been in all day and I've nothing to do till Paul comes. I wasn't going to Isa's anyway, that's what I want to talk to him about."

"Well, at least you know where this place is," he said. "—All right. If you really want to. But be ready. I'll be there in ten minutes."

Laurie's car was a long narrow English model, very beautifully cared-for. His fat body sat in it as incongruously as a sack of potatoes dumped in a boudoir. "Just give it a gentle tug," he said as I pulled the door in behind me; the door closed with an oiled click. I felt suddenly the pleasant relief of being out, anywhere at all, in the air and the moving streets, after the confines of the flat. "It's about Fanyana, of course," he apologetically confided at once, as if he was sure he was only confirming what I must have guessed. "I heard today on good authority that they're watching him. They have to be able to lay their hands on a few 'inciters to public violence' when they need 'em, to prove what an efficient police force they are. And Fanyana's one. He's only got to wiggle his little finger." Laurie demonstrated, moving free of the steering wheel a white, dry-skinned hand blotted with the brownish marks of some liver ailment. "If Paul's got any sense, he must keep away from him. It'd be a much more serious thing for Paul if he were arrested as the inciter of an inciter—" He laughed, moving his shoulders which overflowed the curved back of the seat. "You know how they are—they make up their minds you're an inciter, so you're an inciter— What can you do? You could have been teaching Fanyana how to embroider. . . . You're an inciter. So. Go and argue with them."

"Oh, but it's all right," I said, "nothing's happened. There haven't been any incidents to be blamed on anyone."

"No, but I think Paul shouldn't be seen even talking to Fanyana today."

I shrugged. "He's probably doing that now." I couldn't help feeling that Laurie was getting excited over something that would be no news to Paul; he knew that the police were interested in Fanyana, and had been for some time.

"By the way, d'you think they'll let us in?" Laurie asked.

"At the location? Oh, yes. They know me, I'll fix it." For a moment I had not realized what he meant; the strike had already taken on the character of an alarum that had never gone off, and the ban on the entry of Europeans to native townships which would certainly be included in police security methods seemed as nominal as had been the posters illustrating air-raid precautions in our country which had never known a raid. Yet the reminder gave a slight fillip to our little expedition. The fact that I felt Paul would consider Laurie's urgency a piece of dramatics added to this something of the pleasurable illusion of adventure with which children invest some unnecessary action by pretending to believe it vitally important. We were quite gay, and passing the Criterion Bar, Laurie said: "When we've collected Paul we'll come back and have a drink somewhere."

As we shed the city, dusk was falling.

"At dusk, reports of bloodshed and violence followed in rapid succession. At Orlando, Sophiatown, Alexandra, Moroka, Jabavu, White City, Mariastad. . . . It was the start of a night of terror after twenty-four hours' tension."

This was how it was described in the papers next day. While we were driving through the dusk that thickened like pollen about the street lights, the trains were going home, some in the direction we took, some toward other townships, carrying workers who had defied the strike and who were being escorted from work by the police to assure their safety. The stones that were to be thrown and were to draw back bullets were lying ready to hand in the unmade streets and the vacant lots filled with rubbish. The men were already restless in the streets, the voices of the women shrill before the dark houses. That was what we understood when we read about it.

That night, rioters stoned a police squad at Alexandra. The police fired into the mob. A bus queue shelter was demolished, coffee stalls overturned, shops looted and gutted, and a cinema burned to the ground. A crowd attacked the bus depot, and another police squad, hurrying to the scene, met with a road block and was stoned. The police got out of their cars and fired. At Orlando trains were stoned. On the Reef, at Brakpan, a thousand demonstrated outside the location, screaming and shouting, and were dispersed by a baton charge of a hundred police. At Atherton location, a large crowd defied the ban on public meetings, refused to disperse, and were charged by the police with fixed bayonets. Then the police fired, and three people were killed on the spot. Everywhere in the townships there were "disturbances" of one sort or another; stones were thrown. Stones were thrown, and one way or another, drew blood. Later that week, one of the Native Representatives (there were three and they were all Europeans) moved the adjournment of the Parliamentary debate then in session, so that the May Day riots could be discussed in the House. The leader of the Opposition, General Smuts, did not support the motion. Letters were published condemning the brutality of the police, praising them for courage, accusing them of incitement; hailing the dead rioters as martyrs, expressing satisfaction at the dispatch of dangerous hooligans, urging black and white to make "this tragic and bitter clash" a basis for the return to Christian tolerance. There was a report of how, over the week end, when the ban on public gatherings in African townships was already in force, a wedding party had been broken up by the police; a group of mourners, sitting in the small yard of a bereaved house after a funeral, as is the custom with Africans, were intruded upon by the police and ordered to go home. An elderly African who had been one of the group said: "They treat us like wild animals. Perhaps after all we can get nothing by peaceable means." Still later, a commission of inquiry set up to investigate the cause of the riots, said that the anti-police attitude of the Africans was due to liquor and pass raids on their homes in the early hours of the morning, and the treatment of native prisoners by young policemen. This attitude, the commission stated, was not racial—black and white policemen were equally hated, resulting in "a complete disregard of authority of any kind."

On that night, eighteen natives were killed, thirty wounded. Two of the dead had suffocated in the burning cinema, sixteen were shot by the police.

When Laurie and I got to the township entrance, there was no official in sight. Laurie slowed the car, swaying to the side of the sandy road which had no curb. "Do we go straight through?"

"No, we might get stopped farther on, and I want to be able to say we've got permission to be here." I knew the native policemen who did duty at the entrance; I might not know those whom we were likely to meet inside. Laurie hooted, a serene, smoothly accented bleat that was what one would have expected to come from a car like his, and the familiar, fat, light-colored police boy came out of the administrative building with a sort of slow-motion skipping movement, exaggerating his concern at being found absent from his post. He greeted me, grinning with excitement. "We're a bit out of order here today," he said, proud of his English. "May we go in?" I said. His eyes took up the reflection of the car lights, which, with the smokiness of the location atmosphere added to the gathering darkness, Laurie had suddenly found it necessary to switch on. "Well—you're from the Welfare, isn't it? Mr. Clark, he's nearly a resident here!"—he was delighted with his own humor. "Of course, we've got instructions, no Europeans, and so on. . . . But for you it's all right." "We're going straight to the Center, Mr. Clark's there waiting for us," I agreed, and he saluted us on.

It is always surprising to find how much darker an African township is at night; far darker than anywhere else where there are houses, and people are living. In a European quarter, even if there is a street where the lamps are sparse and most of the houses happen to be in darkness, there is a general lightening diffusion from all the other lights in the city, so that you forget how thick darkness really is. Already that thick dark was curling up and wrapping about the small low houses; lighted windows showed irregularly on either side like cigarette tips glowing. The first street we drove along seemed quieter than was usual at this hour, but when we turned left again into another street as dim and quiet, I noticed a paraffin-tin fire outside one of the houses. The cooking pot on it was boiling over and over, bubbling and streaming down into the coals. The house was closed and quite dark; a fan of red light from the fire wavered over it. Farther on there was a strange pale low light that seemed to breathe rather than burn. When we drew level, it was a candle alight behind a rag of curtain in another dark closed house. As I looked at it with a momentary pleasure—the light of a candle was something else one didn't really know—a corner of the rag was looped back by a very small black hand and the faces of two African children watched us go past.

When we came to the Apostolic Faith church, we seemed to have reached the normal evening location clamor, the rising, muffled blare of shouts, talk, yells and laughter which was faded and far off above the streets we had left.

And then we were in the heart of it. That is the only way I can describe it, the way I shall always remember it. Shocking, splitting, like the explosion of maniacal loudness that assaults you when you turn a radio volume full on by mistake. The awful heart of that endless shout which rises from the throat of a location at night.

Not thirty yards away a crowd was bellowing round a telephone booth, the only telephone booth in the whole township. They butted and screamed, the whole solid wall of their bodies—solid and writhing as a bank of fish in a net—caving forward. Seconds before I saw, before I understood, at the instant at which that *sound* smashed on our heads, I snatched at Laurie's arm with such clawing horror that the car swerved to the side and stalled. He turned on me, astonished. My roughness seemed to have startled him more than what was happening. "What are you doing, what are you doing?" he shouted, but his voice was faint against the din. Above the mass of the crowd things were waving, poles or bars, I shall never know, but heavy things that were being held upright with difficulty, drunkenly, and that fisted down on the little conical tin roof of the booth so that it tore and fell in like a piece of silver paper. The crowd seized on the booth as if it could be shaken into speech. A high-pitched yell sent them back; something that might have been a railway sleeper heaved into the air and then bricks and plaster gave way and fell into the bellowing. The telephone box with the receiver swinging flew out over heads. Part of the door—some of the glass panes must still have been unbroken because in the instant of its passage through the air, I saw a watery zigzag—broke up as it hit the wall of a house. And then a short man in big white shoes (I can see those shoes now, I could almost describe the shape, the rather pointed toes, though I know it seems impossible that I really could have seen them so clearly) shot out of the crowd and picked up the telephone. Yelling, he held it aloft like a head on a pike and he raced over to the small municipal building—it was the depot where milk was sold at special rates—and smashed it against the wall. An accolade of stones followed his action in horrible applause. The windows of the place smashed, the door was kicked in. At the same time one of the stones missed its mark and pricked the bubble of the only street light.

Laurie was sitting with his great heavy arm stretched out pressed back against me like a barrier, as if he were restraining me from jumping out of the car. Behind it I breathed like an animal that has been caught and is being held down for branding. I thought I should burst with horror. I do not think I was afraid, I had no room for fear because I was so mad with horror. Again I was overwhelmed by an emotion whose existence I had not ever thought about, every bursting blood vessel pushed full with a racing blood I had not counted in the emotional scope of my life. Everyone fears fear; but horror—that belongs to second-hand experience, through books and films.

Even while the darkness doused the crowd a new light came up, and with it an ecstatic shrill scream, a note out of the normal range of the human voice. The crowd drowned it hoarsely, cutting across it with rasping throats: the municipal office was burning. People were running past us all the time now, summoned by the success and passion of the flames. The firelight ran excitedly all over them. And I saw that the owner of the scream was a woman who stood out in the road apart, a woman with a hump that must be a baby tied on her back. She leaned forward with her hands on her thighs and sometimes the scream was only a contortion of her face, sometimes it jetted out against the massive bellowing. Other sounds, too, came in flashes of lucidity out of the confusion. The deep panting of the shapes which ran past us. I felt a cringed stiffening in Laurie's arm and the side of his body that was pressed against my side, every time this sound was flung to us—so personal as opposed to the anonymity of the bellowing, in passing. Laurie was afraid. He was not horrified, he was only terribly afraid. I do not mean that he was cowardly, but that he had been in a war, he knew what men were like, and it was not what was shown to be in them that affected him, but the practical calculation and fear of what this might threaten toward others. "All right. It's all right," I remember he kept saying. "All right. It's all right."

I don't know which way they came, whether it was from behind the crowd or from behind us—it is strange how in confusion a large, important happening, that you must have seen clearly, is sometimes impossible to remember, while a minute detail survives perfectly, like a tiny ornament left standing after an earthquake—but suddenly the police were there. They came like a tidal wave churning through the crowd. And the crowd smashed and boiled back against them. The woman was screaming without stopping now; I heard her distinctly. Stones hailed down. A man wriggled out of the turmoil of the crowd and darted waveringly across the road, pausing every now and then to snatch up a stone. I saw him clearly for a moment, isolated, his collection of stones held in the pouch he had made of the corner of his jacket, his face at the downward, intent angle of a child on a beach gathering shells. Just at that instant there was a kind of scuffle in the midst of the struggling mass of people; a shot cracked like a whip above their heads. There were more shots, shots and their echo, clearing a split second of silence in the space of the retort. The man with the stones looked up with a movement of surprise, as if someone had tapped him on the shoulder. Then he fell, the stones spilling before him. I knew I had never seen anyone fall like that before.

That was the last thing I saw. All that happened from that moment on—the police who came angrily to the car and questioned us, escorted us out of the location; the screams, the running, shouting, gaping people; the way Laurie tried and tried to start the car, the engine leaping into life and dying out again—all this was a dragging backward from the sight of the man in the road. I was pulled away with my eyes still fixed on the only thing that I saw: the man lying in the road. Perhaps they picked him up, perhaps they took him away, perhaps they trampled him where he lay; for me he will remain forever, quite still in the midst of them, lying in the road.

And that was all. The whole thing couldn't have taken more than fifteen minutes. We were out on the road back to the city, we were still in the big English car, we were unhurt. Not even the dust raised by the feet of the rioters or the flying ashes from the burning building had touched us, protected by the closed windows of the car. We drove straight to the nearest hotel, and sitting in a close, dingy bar lounge, with a dry old palm crackling in the draft every time the door opened, we smiled at each other with a ghastly strangeness, like people who have just been dragged up out of the water.

I suddenly began to shudder as I drank my brandy. I shuddered so violently that I could not swallow. "Violence"—the word burst upon my mind like a shell—"Violence." "Laurie, it's the most terrible thing in the whole world. Nothing, nothing like it. . . ." All at once I was terrified, I was chattering with fear.

"Come. I'll hold it for you, you drink." Laurie did not look at me, but kept his eyes lowered down his heavy face as he held the glass to my lips.

33 PAUL SPOKE ABOUT IT afterward as my "adventure." "Helen's adventure at the barricades," he called it. Laurie and I were in considerable demand at the homes of our friends; people saw to it that we were invited at the same time so that we both might be present when the tale was told; and told it always was. Laurie developed quite a technique in the telling; I got to know the exact points at which he would drop his voice, "throw away" an aside, pause, and place the emphasis of hesitancy on a particular sentence. After the first two or three times the progression of the story came to me to be the unvarying order of this delivery; it was his technique only that I heard. Had he related some other incident in its place, but raised and lowered, quickened and slowed his voice at the same intervals, I should not have noticed the difference.

One night when Paul said again something about Laurie's having told someone "your adventure," I said, after a little while: "I don't know why you always say that. —It wasn't. I feel as if I never was there at all. Only that I saw a man killed. And what was real about that was only the unreality." At the mention of a man killed, there came a look into Paul's face that made me feel, more than ever, isolated; even that real death, dropping on its victim before my eyes, seemed unreal to me because it was not my *idea* of death; even in the midst of a brutal reality, I was not involved, I remained lost, attached to the string of a vanished idea. I looked at Paul out of this lostness, like someone who is too far away to make himself heard and must rely on the mute appeal of his tense body. But he only nodded, as if to say: "That's reasonable enough"—feeling along the rim of his ear with absent fingers.

On the night of the riots he had not come home at all. The anxiety for him which had flooded into me after the relaxation into fear in the hotel lounge had not waited long for reassurance. When Laurie and I walked into the flat the telephone was ringing. It was Paul, speaking from the Mission School near the Richardson Center, and he had been ringing and ringing for me, at Isa's and at the flat. He was breathless, only his voice was there, and he did not give me time to explain. "Someone's hurt," he said, "There's been some trouble. I'm going along to Baragwanath."

He telephoned again later, from the Baragwanath Native Hospital, but he did not come in until nearly seven the next morning. It was raining softly. I got up when I heard him at the door, but he walked slowly, quietly, almost awkwardly past me, standing there in my thin rumpled nightgown, and lay down on the bed, where the covers were still flung back from where I had risen. After a moment he sat up, pulled off his shoes, and lay back again. His eyes closed, flickered, closed again. In his stillness, they would not be still.

I could not lie down on that bed. He was alone there. He said, putting his hand over his eyes: "I heard about you." He shook his head slowly. I stood there. After a while, I said: "Are you terribly tired . . . ?" His mouth looked weary, sulky, set; even under the haggardness of the beard which painted it with dirty shadows, his face had its peculiar beauty; it will have it always, I suppose, even when he is old.

"How did he get on?" I said, remembering.

"He's dead," said the voice from the bed. "He died at ten-to-six."

Paul had spent that night at the hospital with Sipho. Sometimes he sat beside his bed and sometimes he stood outside in the hospital corridor. Sipho had a bullet in his hip but he was dying from the fractured skull he had got when he fell; from the increasing pressure of blood that was flooding his brain and making his breathing slower and more porcine all night, until at last, it ceased altogether.

34 AT SEVEN O'CLOCK on Tuesday morning, long queues stood in the rain at every location bus terminus, waiting to go back to work. Within days, hours almost, the happening of the riots was absorbed into the life of the city again; the dead were buried, the wounded healed, and the hearings of those cases in which employers had arrested natives for striking went on in the abstract atmosphere of the courts. Paul pursued what he called the "lily-livered path" of the Department during his official working hours, worked (now that Sipho was dead) with Fanyana on the activities of the African Nationalists; and believed in the worth of neither. I do not think he could ever bring himself to forgive Fanyana for living while Sipho died; Fanyana who should have attracted violence because it was in him to mete it out; who was the opponent for a bullet, a man its own size—and Sipho, the man of peace, the disciple of Gandhi. But Sipho, without fear, in the knowledge of his own lack of threat toward anyone, had gone out to Alexandra on the night of May first, while Fanyana took care to stay at home. I think that the whole purpose of African Nationalism took on the twist of this incident, for Paul. He saw that in this incipient revolutionary movement, as in all others, the wrong people would die, the wrong people would be blamed, perhaps even the wrong people would inherit the reign of the ear of corn, when it came. Of course, he had accepted this always, in dialectic. What he did not know was that he had not accepted, and would never accept it in the real, the personal realm in which life is lived.

I stayed alone in the flat, most days. It was a beautiful May, that year, and though you could not see much sign of the lovely autumn that lingered, in the suburbs of the gardens farther out, and in the

Magaliesburg hills still farther, you could smell it in the air of the city. Up on the little balcony, I could smell it, that rich cool autumn. Most days I did not go out at all, and I got up later and later. I gave Paul breakfast in my dressing gown, and sometimes at ten o'clock I still was not dressed. I spent a great deal of time on the balcony, smoking and watching the building opposite going up, or not watching. Whether I looked or not, whether I saw or not, it went on getting itself finished. The white workmen shouted and twitted one another in a mixture of Afrikaans and English, as they worked; the Africans sang or laughed when they worked beside one another, were silent when they worked beside a white man, handing him up bricks to lay or mixing plaster for him to slap on. When the bell clanged for lunch hour, the scraping and hammering sounds stopped suddenly, and the voices were very clear, as if I were standing among them. The white men hung over the flat roof top, eating out of newspaper and drinking out of beer bottles from which the labels had been washed. One day one of them had a little mirror, which he used to flash the sun over into my face.

When the break was over the bell would clang again, and the white men would start shouting over the parapet to the Africans squatting below: "Come on, you bastards! Come on, what you think you doing down there!" And grumbling, sullen, laughing in unconscious imitation of the white men's raucous laughter, they would swarm up toward those grinning faces waiting, indolent and masterful.

I would go inside quickly, close the door, and lie down.

I slept a great deal. It did not seem to matter how late I got up; in the afternoon I would sleep again. And when I woke sometimes I would not bother to get up. Paul would come home and find me, still lying there. "Aren't you well?" he asked. But although I could not measure it, because I had no sense of well-being, I knew I was not ill. "Well, if you're sure . . . ," he said. "Oh, I'm not worried about *that!*" I understood suddenly what was in his mind. But although I reassured him at once, smiled even, the occurrence of the thought in his mind later began to take hold in my own. Suppose I am pregnant? Nothing had gone wrong, I had no known cause to fear this rather than any other month, and I had never feared before.

But now I began to be obsessed with the idea, to fear that by some devilish miracle it had happened, and for several days went about in that peculiar state of female dread which always had rather disgusted me in others. When a denial, irrefutable, unperturbed, the turn of a cycle, came from my body, and brought with it the immediate dissolution of the dread, I understood the nature of what I had felt. The dread of cheap little sensual innocents, who are afraid the casual eye that was attracted by them may "let them down"; the dread of women to whom love is an entertainment, like a visit to a cinema, and who do not want to be hampered in the pursuit of fresh entertainments.

The dread of an attachment to a man that can never be broken, by a woman who wants to be free of him.

The whole month went by and still I made no effort to find another job for myself. By the time I had telephoned the Consulate for an interview, they had already engaged someone else. Later on, tomorrow, next week—I told myself—I shall go and speak to the man Laurie mentioned. I shall go and see the woman publisher John suggested; the advertising man Paul used to know in the army. I did not even go into town more than once. And when I did, I did not seem to know how to fill the time, although sometimes, when I had been working, I had longed for a whole free day to shop and stroll about. Somehow the shops did not offer any connection with my life; I saw them as one glances at the things in the shop windows of a strange town in which one finds oneself with half an hour to spare between trains: this hat, this piece of flowered silk, this gadget for sharpening knives—they will not be seen on, or belong in the houses of, any people I know; I shall not be here long enough to need to sharpen knives, buy a new hat, or choose material for another season's dress.

So I stayed in the flat. As the traveler might decide for the station waiting room, after all. I find it difficult to remember how I passed the days, because I know I did so little to fill them. I don't think I even read, except the daily papers. I would open the papers and read the "Readers' Views" page and "Letters to The Editor": letters about the riots, which were still coming in, still being published. "What sort of a country are we building where the gaps between the white Haves and the black Have-nots are shamelessly widened every day? Those people who, out of fear for their own precious skins, made the greatest talk and fuss about the Rand riots three weeks ago have now comfortably settled back into safety of their homes again, perfectly content to close their eyes to the disgusting squalor, poverty and frustration that gave rise to the riots and which exist, unchanged. Do they ever stop to think how, with the approach of winter . . ." ". . . must urge a stricter police control of the locations. Could not some system be devised whereby both native men and women would carry identity, or residents', cards, which they would have to produce on entering a township? This would force hundreds of loafers and troublemakers to stay in their own homes at night, and get rid of a large shifting population that would then have to go back to the country. . . ." ". . . May I ask your correspondent how yet another card, pass, what-have-you, could be expected to be tolerated by a people already so restricted that they might as well be enemy aliens instead of being so indisputably an indigenous people in their own country that even Dr. Malan (supposing they were white instead of black, of course) would have to admit them to the first class of the pure-blood South African hierarchy?" The paper would blow about in the sun, slithering to the dusty corners of the balcony, and I would hear the voices of the workmen floating up from over the way: Hurry up, there, you bastard! Franz, you bastard, bring me the flat paint—d'you hear me—ahh, voetsak, go on, hurry up!—I never knew what the black men said back, when they talked among themselves in their own language; for that belonged to their own world, and I, I supposed—I must go along with the workmen.

The old sense of unreality would come down upon me again. A calm, listless loneliness, not the deep longing loneliness of night, but the loneliness of daylight and sunshine, in the midst of people; the loneliness that is a failure to connect. I would pick up, in my mind, Atherton, Paul, Johannesburg, my mother and father; Paul. Like objects taken out of a box, put back. But in the end there was only myself, watching everything, the street, the workmen, life below; a spectator.

This went on until the beginning of June. The autumn was suddenly gone; one morning the city came up out of the night as if it had been steeped in cold water: bright, clear, hard, it was winter. I walked out onto the balcony in a sweater, but I felt the air at my ears, and my hands were cold. I had been going to sew back the sleeve of my coat that had pulled away from the lining. I felt now it would be too chill to sit out there; there was a change. As I gathered up the coat and the cotton and scissors, I stopped, and saw that it was not only in the air. The building was finished. I had got so used to seeing the work going on over the way that it had existed in my mind as an end in itself. I had scarcely noticed that it was nearing completion, that it was no longer a framework gradually filling in with bricks and glass and paint, but a building, a place where people would live. Now it was finished. It blocked out much of the sky that I had sat and watched, some months back, after work in the evenings. It was quite finished, and the workmen were hauling down the material they had left on the roof. A lorry was being piled with the sand on the pavement, where the children had played.

The building was in front of me, five stories high, clean with fresh paint. On top, the chimney of the boiler room crooked a finger. A row of gleaming dustbins waited to be put into the kitchens. I thought, When I came here with Paul the first time that Sunday afternoon, they were just beginning the foundations, you could see right out over the hill, you could see the Magaliesburg.

And it came to me, quite simply, as if it had been there, all the time: I'll go to Europe. That's what I want. I'll go away. Like a sail filling with the wind, I felt a sense of aliveness, a sweeping relief.

The lorry rolled down into the street and drove away.

35 "NOTHING LEFT but all of Europe," said Isa, putting her small, sharp-looking hands to warm round the teapot. She had met me in town, on my way to go and say good-by to Jenny Marcus, and had turned me off into a tearoom. "It's a stage most of us get to. I wonder what the European equivalent is? Longing to get out to the wide open spaces, I suppose. Let us leave this damp and

overcrowded England and go where the sun shines and men are
men. Et cetera."

She gave one of her little jumpy shrugs and picked up the bill.
She pulled on her beautiful velvet coat, folded a scarf round her
little throat, where you could always see the pulses through the thin
skin; her head rose from her impressive clothes like the head of a
bird from its plumage. She smiled with an unashamed acceptance
of her own fascination, and said as if it followed out of my look:
"You don't have to worry about him and me. I've often meant to talk
to you about it, but I don't know . . . Now perhaps it doesn't matter.
—He'd never really want me because I'm too clever for him." She
laughed, raising her eyebrows and nodding her head to show me she
meant it and must admit it, as we walked toward the door. She paid
at the cashier's grille and the door swung us out into the street,
talking. "I'm too clever for him, and so I go in for debunking. I
debunk him all the time, out of irritation mostly, because he can't
debunk me. Isn't clever enough. If I could find a man who would
have the brains and the guts to debunk me . . ." She moved her
shoulders a little, under the flowing coat. "Because of this he
couldn't really love me, I mean it never could have been anything
but an affair, even before the advent of you. You're too clever for
him, too—not with your head," she added, as if she knew I couldn't
compare with her, "but in your emotions. I think you're one of those
women who have great talent for loving a man, but he's not whole
enough to have that love expended upon him. It's too weighty for
him. He likes to be all chopped up, a mass of contradictions, and
he wants to believe they're all right. He isn't enough of a central
personality to be able to accept the whole weight of a complete love:
it's integration, love is, and that's the antithesis of Paul. You frighten
him, I frighten him. Different ways, but all the same . . . And I
couldn't want him, not permanently. You need never have worried
about that. Not that I flatter myself you did."

We had reached her car and she unlocked the door for me. By
the time she had gone round to the driver's seat and got in beside
me, her attention had been attracted back, with the brooding inev-
itability of a magnet, to herself. She said: "South African men. You
can look and look. That's the terrible thing for a clever woman here.

She may find one who's her equal—just. But she won't find one who's cleverer than she is, who can outtalk, outthink, beat her at it." Her lips showed her teeth in a strange, lingering smile of pleasure that she abruptly dismissed, as one dismisses a daydream. "Unless he looks like something gestated in a bottle and brought up on ground book dust. But a real man; there's always some point at which you feel them cave in. . . . Tom, Paul, even Arnold. . . ." She waved a hand in dissatisfaction at her husband and her lovers. "A woman like me needs the world. Like a boxer who can't find any more opponents at home, he's met 'em all. Match me—outside— away. I'd soon have the nonsense knocked out of me, they'd show me my place." She turned to me, laughing.

I felt again the mixture of stirring antipathy and liking that I had always felt for Isa. I thought to myself, She's a flirt, even with women, though with women the game is played differently. But today I warmed to her in another way; as she spoke I came to understand something about her, and so to feel the sympathy and even pity that divests others of the sense of their superiority that hardens us toward them. It was true; she was too clever; too clever for her own maddening primitive womanly instincts, the desire to be dominated and to look up to a man as a god. Household god. I smiled. "No household gods. That's your trouble," I said. I had forgotten the hostility and sense of distaste, almost, that had made me close away from her when she calmly took up discussion of what was to me my private and personal life, making it, as other people's lives were, matter for social intercourse.

"Bloody little clay figurines," she said. "Very nice. Made out of Vaal River mud. —You know, I think I'll come in with you. I haven't seen the baby yet and you know how Jenny feels about things like that. Should I turn into Claim Street?"

She had offered to drive me to the Marcuses' house. "No, carry straight on, there's a shorter way. I'll show you."

"There was something I wanted to tell you—I'm damned if I can remember what it was," she said, pulling up at a robot. A man crossed the street before us, and she followed him with her eyes, as if he would remind her. He was young, with the dark, handsome animal surliness of some young Afrikaners and he looked back at her. She forgot that she had been trying to remember something, in the little game of holding this young male with her eyes. We shot forward as the lights changed; "Doesn't matter— You leave on Tuesday, you say? Train or plane?"

"No, Wednesday. Plane. I'm going East Coast, that's why I'm boarding the ship at Durban."

During the hour we spent at Jenny's house, we chattered about my plans; the job I had been promised in London; the things I must see, the people I must look up. "Don't forget Frederick at Sadler's Wells," warned Isa again. "I did have the address of the flat or whatever it is where he lives, but I can't find it. The best thing to do is to send him a note to Sadler's Wells." In my notebook I had a whole list of expatriate South Africans who were storming the theater, the ballet and the art studios with the talents which they believed had outgrown South Africa.

Before I left I dutifully asked if I could have a last look at the new baby, and was surprised when Jenny led us into the children's room and picked the little dangling creature nonchalantly out of his crib: when her first child was a baby, no one had been allowed to pick him up outside his specified play hours. But it appeared that she had changed her baby manual since then. This boy was being reared on the principle of what she called "the natural young animal"; he was hugged, carried about, and allowed to suckle at will, like a kitten. Jenny asked me whether I could find room in my luggage for a large photograph of him which she wanted to send to her mother in England. "Thanks, then. It won't take any room at all, really. You can put it flat on the bottom. It's being framed now, but I'll get John to drop it with you on Wednesday morning, on the way to work."

Isa was leaning over the baby, like a child looking down into a fishpool. She had two children of her own, but the special quality of children seemed to dawn on her only through the children of other people. "Ah, that's it. Now I remember—it was about Joel Aaron I wanted to tell you, Helen. He's going to Israel. You must look out for him when you get to Durban. He must be there already. I think he's sailing about the same time as you. On one of those Italian boats, though."

I turned to Isa with surprise, but while she was speaking, Gerald, Jenny's elder child, came skipping in the doorway and at once brought himself up short at the sight of visitors. Jenny was questioning Isa about Joel, but I heard no more of what they said. The little old toy the child had been carrying had dropped, and hung from his hand. It was the plush rabbit that had been hanging from Paul's hand the first day I saw him. Paul stood in the doorway of the Marcuses' flat and in one hand he held a bottle of wine, in the other he held this rabbit, hanging by the ears.

I think it was there and then that I parted from Paul; not later, when he kissed me with those hard, long kisses and pretended that this was a holiday on which I was going, a holiday from which I would come back. Certainly it was then that I wept, and had to move quickly over to kneel at the little boy's side, so that Jenny and Isa should not see the tears.

36 IN NO TIME at all when the plane comes out of the hills behind Durban, the green seems to melt and dissolve in a mist and then suddenly it is the sea, there below. It is the sea, greenish, like the grasslands, moving, like the grass beneath the wind.

As the engines cut out the air seems to cut out, too; a warm heat, liquid, fills your lungs. The plane comes down and there you are, the figure of yourself providing another facet for the brilliant, glittering, soaring light of sea level.

I left Johannesburg on a cold, dusty July morning. The grit at the airport blew against me sharp as rime. When I landed in Durban less than two hours later, it was summer. The old airport on the Snell Parade was still in use then, and the taxi that took me to my hotel passed smoothly between the green of the airport with its fringe of umbrella trees on one side and the sea deep green behind a low bank of bush on the other. The sea was very calm and it turned onto the beach in slow coils, clear as spun glass. The very sight of the sea in this mood does something to one's breathing; I began to breathe slowly and deeply, as if for months I had been wearing something tight that had now dropped away. And while I was being received into the big old cool hotel, while I signed the register and went up in the lift with the young Indian page whose dark forehead matched the polished panels, and wore, as if unable to forget the humidity of the summer months, a beading of sweat; while I hung a dress or two in the stiff old-fashioned wardrobe that smelled of cockroach repellent, and sat a moment in the soft, limp-smelling armchair, a kind of shaky happiness came over me. It was the kind of happiness that has little to do with one's mind.

A hotel, an airways service, have something in common with a hospital in that they reduce one's life to a program of needs, to which they minister. Handed a magazine at the start of a journey, summoned to dinner by a gong, this outer simplification of living tends to produce a corresponding inner one: Your life really does become simply that: a time for mild diversion, a time to eat, a time to sit on the chairs comfortably provided, and look at the sea, to which the hotel is thoughtfully turned. I thought that this mild assumption of one's needs would take care of me very well for the few days before my boat sailed.

When I had unpacked, and lunched, I walked down to the South Beach. It was not the fashionable beach—that was on the north side—and even so early in the afternoon, when most holiday people were having a siesta, there were family parties on the sand, the parents drowsing and the children, ignoring the seasons of the day, shrill and dripping. I took off my sandals and walked away up the beach toward the long arm of furzy green that curves round the entrance to the harbor; away to the right I could see cranes gesticulating above the hidden docks. I remembered my father, talking about the "bar." Out over the bar. That calm, heavy-looking stretch of water on which the little lighthouse looked down; what would it be like when the ship slid through it? And as I watched, a ship did just that, came past the conglomeration of waving steel antennae, left the escort of tugs spinning vaguely in her wash, and, breasting, busy, silent, was out. There was a bleat. It came perhaps from her. (A bleat like the hooter at the Mine.) Her profile of orange-striped black funnels and up-curving bows moved slowly against the green arm. I watched her, climbing up the sea to the horizon. And then she was a paper shape, a cutout, very clear, and apparently being pulled along like Lohengrin's swan in a theater, by strings off stage—straight along the straight line of the sea's horizon.

I came back slowly along the sand, and went up to the hotel for tea. Afterward I took a bus into the town (the plan of Durban is very simple and sensible: the visitors live in a long strip of hotels, spread for more than a mile along the beach front; the town lies immediately behind that, on either side of West Street which lifts up from the sea; the residents live behind that, up in the hills) and went to the shipping office. Again there was the calm assumption of one's needs. The young man across the mahogany counter showed me a plan of the ship: my cabin, here; my berth, this one. The ship would dock tomorrow and I must be on board by ten o'clock on Monday morning. Sailing time, four-thirty P.M. I wandered about the pleasant town, bought myself a cake of fine, hard, perfumed soap of an imported brand that was unobtainable in Johannesburg, and a green scarf to tie round my hair; it might be windy on deck. The afternoon was not too hot, and every now and then the usual city smell of petrol, stale sourness from bars, and stuffy sweetness from beauty parlors parted to a breath from the sea.

Back in my hotel room, I found some flowers on the bedside table.

The maid had put them in water for me, but she had left the cellophane wrapping and the card on my bed. On the card, a childish hand had copied out "WITH LOVE FROM BRUTON HEIGHTS, PAUL." They were florist's roses, long-stemmed, denuded of leaves and thorns, the petals of the long buds a little crushed and crepy, though still beautiful, like the eyelids of a lovely woman who is no longer really young. I loosened them in the vase, but they still looked as if they belonged in the foyer of a cinema. WITH LOVE FROM BRUTON HEIGHTS. What was that, a reminder, a claim? A sudden perverse desire to put a hand on something because it was no longer there; an impulse to test out whether it really had gone; irresistible, just to make sure? But the flowers, ordered by telegram, the card, written by the hand of the junior shop assistant, defeated everything, as gifts that have to be made through the paid agency of others do

always, impartially, whether the original intention was merely a social gesture, or a desperate symbol of the deepest feeling. These
flowers standing on the dressing table were somebody's work, carried
out unperturbed and mechanically. I was safe from them.

The life of the hotel swirled up round me; people were up and
down the corridors, in and out the lift; doors banged, bath water ran,
there was the ring of telephones and laughter in the rooms as people
dressed. In the dining room Indian waiters were in and out, up and
down; I saw myself, in the mirror walls, looking at the Buddhalike
headwaiter, red-sashed and watching above folded arms. People
drank coffee afterward in the lounge and on the wide veranda. A
ricksha boy came whooping past among the stream of cars, joggling
two small boys and waving his feathered head, like the tail of a
peacock put on in the wrong place, ". . . see one once in a blue
moon. And I believe the municipality isn't issuing any new licenses
to them, so they'll all be gone soon," someone at the next table was
saying disgustedly.

"Yes, it's true, they give you the idea that that's the normal form
of transport in Durban. It just shows you how much you can believe
about the travel posters you see of other countries. Come to beautiful
Austria . . ."

". . . kills them before they're forty. The strain on the heart."

And on the other side a family argument was going on between
a young girl and her mother. "You know what those beach things
are like. And this is a wonderful film, really, Mummy. I don't want
to hear the same old man singing that thing about Ireland. Or wherever it was,—They do, they do, they always have him."

"He had a trial gallop on the beach this morning. . . ."

"All right, tomorrow then. But you must get the desk to ring you
before seven. . . ."

They ebbed out, into the town and the cinema and the night
clubs. They trailed upstairs and trailed down again with wraps, ready
to drive out to roadhouses. I went to my room early, looking out at
the bobbing lights on the harbor for a moment before I got into the
big, soft, anonymous hotel bed. And the next morning I watched
them go, all the holiday-makers, down to the beach after breakfast,
with a kind of indulgence. A young man who had spoken to me in

the lift appeared in a shirt patterned with hula girls. "See you . . . ,"
he said, waving a towel toward the beach, and I smiled and shook
my head. He was so careless of the response he elicited (there were
hundreds of girls and no doubt he signaled to them all that he would
meet them on the beach) that he mistook my meaning and waved
back enthusiastically.

Just before lunch, I saw my ship come in. An old gentleman
stretched, yawned, put his paper down. "That must be the *Pretoria
Castle*," he said to his wife.

"What?"

He pointed to the horizon. "There. That grayish white thing. I
just saw in the paper that she's due in this morning."

"I haven't got my glasses," said his wife.

Although I wasn't going aboard until Monday, I decided that I
must go down to the docks after lunch to have a look at the ship.
In any case, it was as good a way as any of passing away the afternoon. I always had loved wandering about the docks, even as a child,
and now that I myself actually was going to sail away in one of the
ships, I felt I should find a whiff of the promise of the places I was
going to, as well as the fascination of those I probably should never
see. I found myself dressing up for this ship; I cleaned my white
shoes and put on a frock that suited me particularly well, and a big
linen hat. I even opened one of my suitcases and took out a pair of
new gloves (farewell present from Laurie).

I picked my way among the trucks and the coils of greasy rope
to the wharf where a harbor policeman had told me she was berthed.
And quite a long way before I reached her I could see her, a big
gray wall of a ship, parked as solidly as a building. Smaller ships
on either side looked too small for people to live in, by comparison.
Or alternatively, she looked too big to float. The companionway was
down, opening surprisingly into her towering gray side and showing,
inside this flap of ship, a wide stairway and a great bank of flowers
before a mirrored wall. But I was not allowed to go up; an official-
looking man in white explained that this was the period, directly
after the disembarkation of passengers, when they "gave her a spring
clean, and so on." He grinned in a matey fashion, and I could not
resist telling him—someone—that I should be a passenger myself,

in a day or two. "Then you'll have plenty of time to see her," he said, smiling indulgently. "But you can pop along tomorrow if you like. She'll be all open then."

I stood a moment, following the sweep of her, up, up. The huge anchor, hooked with vanity, like an ornament, on her side. Runnels of rust streaming down from it over the pale paint, like seaweed she had forgotten to flick off. Down between the edge of the dock on which I stood and the lower limits of the bulk of her, a foot or two of dirty water slapped, afloat with matchsticks and the shapeless, ugly humps of dead jellyfish, like the torn-out eyeballs of sea monsters. I wandered along, looking up at docks of ships on which men were at work, or sailors, with the disheveled, careless air of women discovered in curlers and slippers, hung over the rails in vest and pants, talking lazily to someone below and flicking cigarette butts into the domesticated water. I wished, now, I had asked what the name of Joel's ship was, and where he was staying until he embarked. Yet somehow I felt Isa wouldn't have known that, anyway. But it should be easy enough to find out about the ship, from the Lloyd-Triestino people. That was the Italian line, and there were only two ships, as far as I knew, on the route. Joel . . . It would be odd to see him again, here. I was not sure whether I wanted to; actually the whole idea seemed so improbable that I felt indifferent. At this point I stepped aside to avoid some sort of unpleasant-looking mess that had been spilled on the dock, and almost bumped into a man in a vaguely nautical outfit—tight serge pants and a polo-necked cotton jersey. We dodged back and forth before each other for a moment, and then he stopped, smiled, and gestured me past. We both mumbled, "Sorry!" and on impulse I said: "I wonder—d'you know if there's an Italian ship in now?" "You've just passed her. The *Ostia*. She's over there, beside the *Pretoria Castle*." He pointed back over my shoulder. I turned to look again at the squat white hen of a ship almost under the prow of the huge mail ship. So that was it. I walked back and had a look: *Ostia*—I had read the name when I passed before, but it had seemed to me vaguely Scandinavian; I did not connect it with Italy.

The smallness of the ship beside the *Pretoria Castle* fascinated me. A dumpy little thing, riddled with portholes and hung about with rickety-looking decks. Joel in this, I in the immense creature next door. The hen and the elephant. It seemed perfectly ridiculous; I saw us, firmly fixed, in Atherton, walking along under the pines in front of the Mine Recreation Hall.

The companionway was down, here, too. There was no one to stop me at the foot, so I went up, swaying slowly on my too-high heels. A uniformed man at the top watched me with a considering air, as if I were being given an audition for something. "May I come up?" I asked, already there. He looked at me broodingly. His eyes were so heavily liquid dark that he seemed to have difficulty in shifting the focus of his gaze. He shook his head. "Unless you know someone passenger. You must go to the office, get a card for permission." I was annoyed that he had let me climb up for nothing. "You mean from Lloyd-Triestino? But where is the office?" He told me the name of the street. "Look," I said, as if I had not understood properly, "but I do know someone—" There was a chance that Joel's name might be on the passenger list, even if he was not yet aboard, and if it was not, then I should know that either he had sailed already, or was going on a later ship. In any case, I might as well take a chance: I was curious to look over this fat little *Ostia*.

The man took me to the purser's cabin, down a step from the deck into a dim stuffy passage, into a biscuit tin of a room crammed with a vast desk. He consulted with the man behind it, over a passenger list, and at last said in English, "Ah-ron. Mister J. Ah-ron. Is second class, number 197," and ushering me back into the passage, left me to the ship. I did not know whether he meant that Joel was already aboard, or whether he was merely confirming the fact that the name I had told him was, indeed, on the passenger list. As I stumbled about the curious, narrow intricacies of the ship's internal disposition, I thought it less and less likely that Joel was aboard; no one else seemed to be; at least no one who looked as if he might be a passenger, although in one or two of the cabins into which I peeped, I saw a sort of homely disorder, as if people recently had lain on the bunks. But the whole ship seemed to be in a state of semidesertion, hazy untidiness. It was dark and unbearably stuffy, and a smell of cooking faithfully followed all the convolutions, stairs, doors, hatches and barriers of the various classes, of which there was a bewildering number. I knocked against an insect spray and a broom, picked my way round pieces of canvas-covered baggage, and once found myself brought up short in the darkest, smallest lavatory I had ever seen. Outside in the comparatively brightly lit passage —one bleary globe burned in the ceiling—there was a notice suggesting that passengers should wear a woolen band round the stomach, as a precaution against stomach troubles prevalent in East African ports.

I went from first to third class and back to first again, quite inexplicably, but on the way I saw a dining room decorated with sporting painted dolphins to distract the passengers' attention from the scrubbed wooden boards at which they were evidently to sit, and a lounge furnished with brocade settees, a little yellow marble fountain in the form of a bird gargling into a shell, some potted ferns, a dais with a white piano and some music stands, and a neat little bar at which a solitary man sat, working out something on a piece of paper. A fat woman (she must have been a stewardess) smiled "Scusi" as we edged past each other into another passage and I found at last that I was suddenly in the second-class section. All the cabins seemed to be empty and the doors were open, except one, which was closed, and from behind which there came a low growling and a high-pitched giggle. The door of 197 was open, too, at the same angle as all the others, but I put my head in, just to see what Joel's particular cabin was like. He was lying there on the bunk and the sight of him, Joel, unmistakable, real, gave me a ridiculous start of fright.

He got up in slow astonishment. Frowning, he said: "No. Helen?" We collided with each other in the tiny space and we kissed, quite simply, as if we had always done it, for the first time in our lives. I never could have imagined I should be so happy to see him. And because it was Joel, I could say it to him: "I never could have believed it would be so wonderful to find you here. You don't know how glad I am. I don't know myself how glad I am." He was standing back from me, looking at me and shaking his head, smiling. "I can't imagine why you're here. . . . I don't know what you're doing here."

I felt excited, soaring. The whole excitement of the fact of my

going away, the loneness, the strangeness, suddenly made me drunk,
like a potent liquor that requires certain conditions before it begins
to show its effects. I boasted about my progress over the ship and
puzzled and amused him by references to the woolen band I hoped
he was wearing round his belly, and though he was eager to ask, he
was content to wait for an explanation of my presence. He sat down
on the edge of his bunk as if it were all a little too much for him,
and listened to me.—There it was again, instantly, the way it always
had been; nobody ever listened to me quite the way Joel did. Some
part of me noted this even while I was chattering; he sat there with
his knees spread and a little tuft of dark hair showing through his
half-buttoned shirt, his broad dark face resting its gaze on me. He
loves to hear me talk. So I talk better. I have more to say, it comes
out of me more succinct and livelier.

I was so animated now that I did not sit down, and as I moved
about the tiny cabin, I had to steady my big hat with one hand. He
smiled at this, very slowly, gently, not to offend, the warmth of the
smile bringing a glow to his face which was sunburned too dark,
and giving to his eyes, by contrast, a clear liquid lightness which
seemed to take color, from the line of green water showing through
the porthole. (His cabin was not on the dock side of the ship, but
faced across the harbor.) I broke off as if to consider myself in his
eyes. "Very elegant," he said, smiling. We both laughed. "But a bit
too garden party," I admitted. "—No, don't take it off. We're not
going to stay in this little pen. I'll try and dress up to match and
then perhaps you'll consent to be seen in the town with me."

"Joel," I said, "I'm going to England."

"Ah, of course, that explains it. You're going to be presented in
that hat. Miss Helen Shaw, one of the South African debutantes
seen leaving Buckingham Palace after the presentation to the King
and Queen yesterday afternoon. She is the daughter of Mr. George
Shaw, for many years an official of the Albion-African Group.

"So you're going to England."

"Yes."

"When?"

I gestured with my head. "In the one next door. The *Pretoria
Castle*. Sails on Monday."

"Mine sails Saturday. What's today, Thursday? —Come on, Helen, you don't want to hang about here, do you? I can hardly offer to show you over the *Ostia*, you've seen her from port to starboard, bow to prow. Let's go and have some tea."

Now I sat down on the bunk and watched him, while he scooped the trickle of cold water from the tap over his face, found a stiff, starched towel with *Ostia* embroidered in red along the border, put on a tie and a linen jacket that was hanging behind the door. "Who told you I'd be here?" "Well, Isa, in a way. She said you were going to Israel in an Italian ship." And talking we went along the passages and up out into the sun of the deck in no time at all, now that I had someone to show me the way. The officer at the top of the companionway watched us go down, as moodily as he had seen me come up.

As we turned onto the dock, Joel said to me: "You are alone, here—Helen?" And I said, my face hidden by the hat: "Oh, yes, quite alone."

We spent an afternoon of happy inconsequence. Our long easy intimacy in the past, unconnected—because we had seen each other so rarely and then not at all, during the past eighteen months—with that period of my life which lay so perilously close behind me; the pleasant anonymity of a background strange to both; the complete severance of the present from the burden of the future, because, for both of us, a journey intervened—made us gay. We sat drinking tea in the curiously decorous atmosphere of the tearoom of a Durban department store, and then we walked slowly, and with many stops to look at things—I remember a bookshop, a florist's window magnificently splotched with poinsettias, a native curio shop hung with masks from the Congo, and Zulu shields—all the way down West Street to the sea, and the Marine Parade, where my hotel was. We discussed each other's plans, mine for England and Europe, his for Israel, but in a purely practical fashion; we did not touch upon reasons or motives, his or mine.

When we sat on the hotel veranda drinking beer to cool ourselves, I said to him: "Stay and have dinner with me. Just as you are. There's no need to go back to the ship." But he wanted to shower and change, and he insisted on going. We got the Indian page to call a taxi for him, and he promised to be back within an hour. I leaned on the still-warm stone of the balustrade, calling after him: "Be quick, if you're a resident you can get whisky between six and eight!" —and smiled, because I knew (it was a trait that puzzled me often in young Jews, who all exhibited in some form or another the loneliness of a rejected people, and who, of all people, one should think would be glad of the comradely bolster of alcohol) that he did not care whether he drank water or whisky, and since he knew neither the pleasure nor the need of it, probably did not know, either, that at that time it was under import control and extremely difficult to get.

Because I was to have a visitor, I was at once no longer a stranger to the hotel. I told the maître d'hôtel I should be wanting a table for two, and I bathed and dressed quickly.

But while I was putting the finishing touches to my dress I realized something that put an edge of self-consciousness on my pleasure. I was assuming a right to Joel's time and attention which would follow from a similar claim on his behalf for mine in the normal course of our lives in Johannesburg. But this had not been so. We had not seen each other; I had let him drop out of my life when it suited me—now when it suited me to take him back into it again, I calmly did so. I remembered the acute shame that had swept over me that day outside the theater booking office, when I had met him and realized that I had forgotten his graduation.

When he came into the lounge where I was sitting waiting for him, I was subdued. He came the length of the room between tables and flowers and people with the air of quiet, steady warmth about which he did not know and which was peculiarly his; he is the only person I have ever known who was entirely without self-consciousness, when he entered a room he saw only the person for whom he was making, did not feel, as people like Paul and I did, the eyes of others like vibrating tendrils.

I smiled and patted the chair beside me, and he sank into it with a little flourish of relief, but I saw in his face that he sensed the drop in my mood. Pouring soda into our drinks, he said: "And why are you looking at me so reproachfully?"

"Am I? Well, I don't mean to. Thank you—" I took my glass from him. And when I had made the gesture of taking a sip, I said: "At least, the reproach wasn't meant for you. Joel, I've been thinking, while I was upstairs—"

"Yes, Helen," he prompted me, gently attentive. He was sitting back with his glass in his hand, in no hurry to drink.

For a moment I looked back into his inquiring eyes in discomfiture. "I've got an awful nerve. I greeted you this afternoon as if nothing had ever happened. I mean here I am, taking up your time as if it belonged to me. Just as if nothing had ever happened. I realized it suddenly while I was dressing—here I am, gaily dressing because you're coming to eat with me—" (As I spoke I seemed to see in his eyes the recognition of the odd little verbal taboos which had overlaid my own way of expressing myself, and of which, perhaps, I should never be able to rid myself now, though the desire for emulation which had led me to assume them had lost its gods; in the circles of John and Jenny the middle-class indulgence of a regular nightly meal cooked and served by a servant was given the romantic aestheticism of wine and garlic salad in a Left Bank café and the decent frugality of a workman's bread and cheese by the simple expedient of never saying "come to dinner" but "come and eat with us.")

"Not that I wasn't pleased." —I made another start. "That's the whole thing. Because I was pleased. I realized that I have no right to be. In fact, it's an awful cheek. I haven't seen you for months and months and it was all my fault that I haven't, I know. I've greeted you at a concert as if you were someone I'd met casually somewhere. I didn't come to your graduation and I fumbled for words like a fool when I met you in the street. . . . And when I meet you this afternoon I've got the cool nerve to assume I'll be treated as if nothing has happened."

He had been looking at me quite seriously, as if he were listening to an anecdote about two other people, but now he smiled. "And you were." —He made a last attempt to keep up the casual surface intimacy of the afternoon. There was a moment when I might have taken up the cue of an easy, slangy, social patter; have said, using the old privileges of arch femininity which have become the frank

gambits of sex: "Then I'm forgiven?" And if I had, we might have
passed the following two days together using each other as pure
distraction, have danced and drunk and perhaps slept together like
cut flowers blooming in water—no one, not even ourselves, need
have noticed that the stems were severed, that there was no plant
beneath from whose root and dirt and drought we had taken shape,
and from which, still, all growth must come.

But I said: "I had a dreadful feeling that morning I met you in
front of the theater. I've never forgotten it."

He said very slowly: "Why?" And he tasted his drink.

"When I left you, I got into a sort of panic. I can't explain it. I
saw how I had wanted to go to your graduation, I really had wanted
to very badly, and yet I didn't. There was nothing to stop me. But
I didn't go. I forgot. It seemed to me that some other person had
forgotten. Myself—but some other person. And I felt I didn't know
who I was—bewildered. Of course you didn't know, but I'd had a
ghastly scene in Atherton with my mother the Sunday before. Over
Paul. Over living with Paul. And all the time coming back to Johannesburg in the train, I had managed to fight the-the *feeling* of
this scene—the things it made me feel, I mean—with the thought
that the person who felt these things was no longer me; the real me
was the one with Paul. I was flying back to her. And when I got
back and found that for Paul this really *was so*—he discounted my
Atherton self—he laughed at the scene as if it had been something
that couldn't have touched me—I understood at once that it had.
That creature in Atherton shouting at her mother was me. It all
switched round horribly, and the person who lived with Paul only
thought she was real. I slept and pushed it away, the way one does,
and then meeting you like that the next day started it all up again,
only worse. There was another twist. How can I put it? I subdivided
again. I saw this smiling, nodding, gaping, oblivious creature talking
to you, apologizing with insulting graciousness for something that
couldn't be apologized for. Something that had nothing whatever to
do with her. It belonged to the person she had supplanted. That's
the only word for it. Supplanted, that's what I felt. And then *that*
person seemed to me to be *me*, a creature come to life again with

such distress at what had been done and left undone in her name."

When once you have spoken like this there is no ending. Sitting forward on my chair in the hotel lounge with my hand tightly round the base of my glass, I did not know for a moment what I had begun by talking about; knew only that everything that was heaving up in my mind, apparently disparate, unconnected by chronology or subject, was relevant to and belonged indisputably with it.

When Joel spoke it was unexpected. "It was a tossup with me whether I'd speak to you or not that day," he said. The pinkish light of the room swimming with talk hooded his eyes. Now that he was older, I saw that they resembled his mother's, that remote old woman coming to life only when she was serving or preparing food for others, that old woman sitting in the corner with her shabby shoes crossed, watching me. "When I saw you I was angry. I suddenly wanted to tell you to go to hell."

There was a twinge of hurt in me at his words. They were casual enough in themselves; a natural reaction from hurt or irritation which would have brought a confessedly sympathetic smile from me, spoken by anyone else. But it was as if, for that moment in the street months ago, Joel had looked for something common, ordinary, blunted by use on everybody and anybody, with which to strike me, to show me by the choice of weapon rather than the blow the extent of my worth.

"I was angry. I was hurt . . . I suppose that's why. And you stood there all smiles, effusive, looking just as you always did." He paused, bent a match in two and fizzed his whisky and soda. We were both seeing me again, standing on the pavement in Commissioner Street, tilting my head at him. "But as you kept on standing about and playing with those theater tickets you had, I noticed something about your face—I don't know what it was, really. You seemed to be—put together too consciously. Does that sound silly?" He looked at me, seeing me now, not then. "I didn't want to say it any more."

There was a moment's pause, and we both drank. "You had your hair drawn back then," he said, and I knew he was remembering the piece that had blown down against my lips, and that I had kept pushing away. Somewhere inside me this was handed to me as a slip of paper on which is written a word of power; but the chastening of a minute or two before kept me humble.

Looking round at the people about us who were rising to go into dinner, I had a moment of dark illumination, far from Durban and the pleasant anticipatory buzz and the hushing of the night sea outside. I said fearfully: "I don't know what would have happened then, if you *had*. Told me to go to hell, I mean. Cast me off."

"Why?" he said.

I looked for words. "I think I should have screamed. Oh, I don't mean then and there, in the street. But inside myself. I should have lost control."

Later we stood on the jetty, leaning over the rail. Under the planks beneath our feet, we could feel the sea flinging its weight again and again. But it was too dark to see the water; a night without a moon. Looking back, there was the bright claw of Durban, reaching into the black. I could smell the hissing water down below, prickling up air to my cheeks like the sizzling of soda water.

"How do they feel about it?" I said, speaking of Joel's parents and of what he had just admitted, that in Israel he would be more likely to be planting potatoes than designing buildings.

"They wouldn't be too happy, if they realized it, I think. They would think it a waste—"

I smiled down to the dark sea. "A waste."

"—But, fortunately, they don't realize it. The idea of Israel dazzles out everything else. They see me going home."

I said after a minute: "You know, Joel, I think you might have gone anyway. Even if you hadn't been a Jew."

He looked round at me in the dark though I couldn't see his face. "Yes, maybe. —I suppose that's true."

"D'you remember what you said once, about belonging only to the crust in South Africa."

He laughed softly. "That Sunday outing."

The sea, drawing back its immensity of waters like a great sigh, poised a moment of silence.

As it burst forward, I began to speak again. "I don't feel even that any more. Even that night in the township—at the time it was terrible and immediate and I was *there*, in the thick of it. But afterward the worst thing about it for me was the fact that I was *in* it was only by physical accident. It happened around me, not to me. Even the death of a man; behind a wall of glass. . . ." The water lapped back at me, took my words away. "I envy you. A new country. Oh, I know it's poor, hard, but a *beginning*. Here there's only the chaos of a disintegration. And where do people like us belong. Not with the whites screaming to hang onto white supremacy. Not with the blacks—they don't want us. So where? To land up like Paul with a leg and an arm nailed to each side? Oh, I envy you, Joel. And I envy you your Jewishness."

At this he made a little noise of astonishment. "Why that, for God's sake?"

"Because now I'm homeless and you're not. The wandering Jew role's reversed. South Africa's a battleground; you can't belong on a battleground. So the accident of your Jewish birth gives you the excuse of belonging somewhere else."

Joel had turned his back to the rail and was leaning on his elbows. In the dark I could feel him looking at me, I felt he was looking somewhere other than my outward self, he saw penetratingly, with a kind of powerful instinct, where light was not needed. So he said, without a trace of irrelevancy: "Your people. You've finished with them, for good?"

"Oh, yes. I see that. . . . And yet when I went back there, that last time, I found a kind of comfort in those old ladies with their knitting and those men all comfortably notched on the official scale. Like letting the moss slide over your head in a stagnant pool. It's terrible to find yourself reduced to taking comfort from the thing you despise."

"Despise is a hard word," he said.

"Yes, I know. John and Jenny and Isa"—I avoided the inclusion of Paul's name. "But I shouldn't put the blame on them. Anyway, I can't ever go back to the thing I cast off in favor of what they had to offer—Atherton makes me shudder. But you, it beats me how you've done it. You've lived just as you wished, you do as you must, and you've managed to hang on and hurt nobody. And yet your people are as far from your kind of life as mine are from mine—if I can be said to have a kind of life. . . ."

Joel said, in a tone of voice I had heard from him before, long ago: "Helen, they did seem pretty impossible to you, didn't they? —My mother and father."

There was a second's hesitation before I answered. "Yes," I said. "Impossible for you."

"You mean the store and the things that make up their life and the way they look?"

"Yes-yes, I suppose so. I have to admit that's what I really mean. You're so different. Money is their standard. —No, that's not it— Money is their civilization."

"And what do you think mine is?"

"Yours isn't anything so ready-made. I should say it was the full exercise of human faculties."

"Good, good," he said, of the phrase. And then in a wary, half-bantering, questioning voice: "The good life . . . eh?"

"The good life," I said. "Don't say that. The good life."

"You thought Jenny and John and the others had it. Now you think I have."

"I don't say you've achieved it. But I believe you know what it is."

"Don't you?"

"Not any more. I'm not sure. Anyway, I know what it isn't. It isn't the hypocrisy of considering that something has been done to right wrongs because you yourself act as if they have been righted. The color bar isn't down because you've invited an Indian to dinner; you haven't struck a blow for the working classes because, like Jenny Marcus, you don't wear a hat." —I laughed with him. "Oh, yes, it's true. I think for me that was the beginning of the end, with the Marcuses. Jenny actually told it to me. John wouldn't let her wear a hat, because the bourgeoise women do.—That was the choice I'd made for myself. The life of honesty and imagination and courage."

"The full exercise of human faculties."

"Yes. I've got all the phrases, haven't I? But the things I've fobbed off on myself, under those names . . . Whatever I think about seems to bring me back to that dead native in the location: the good life and the thing that's actually lived, the idea of death and the actuality of the man potted down so quietly in all that racket. . . . There's the same hiatus there. Joel"—it was getting cold now, in a rising wind off the water, and my hands were stiff in the pockets of my coat—"why does it trouble me so much, this awful feeling I have of being at a remove from everything?"

He did not answer.

"Even over the riots. Paul and I had talked about the strike. It was something that belonged right in our lives, it wasn't a piece we'd read in the papers or a mild interest justifying someone's pretensions to liberalism. But that Monday I felt nothing at all; really nothing. No concern, scarcely any interest. All I thought about was Paul and the week end in Atherton."

Joel said: "D'you remember Brabantio? —Neither my place, nor aught I heard of business hath rais'd me from my bed; nor doth the general care take hold on me; for my particular grief is of so floodgate and overbearing nature, that it engluts and swallows other sorrows, and it is still itself."

The wind blew away the words and I had to ask him to repeat it.

"And what do you mean by that? What I think about myself— that in the end I'm too small-minded to have the capacity to feel for anything outside the sticky mess of my own sordid little emotions?"

"Only that it's a simple human fallibility to put one's own affairs—specially love affairs—first. In fact, it's one of the things that helps to ensure the survival of the human race. —You always set yourself such a terribly high standard, Helen, that's the trouble. You're such a snob, when it comes to emotion. Only the loftiest, the purest, will do for you. Sometimes I've thought that it's a kind of laziness, really. If you embrace something that seems to embody all this idealism, you feel you yourself have achieved the loftiest, the purest, the most real." —He felt that his choice of adjectives had missed the dual goal of my aspirations and added the two last with emphasis.

I said, rather painfully: "My own high-falutin' version of Jenny's little flirtation with the hat." I looked down again at the water, which I could not see. I seemed to be talking to a voice out of the darkness; Joel was so still and dim beside me, and the sharp salt wind stiffened my cheeks. Of course it was Paul whom he meant. Or whom, out of their truth, the words made him mean. But I did not want to bring Paul out into this exchange of thoughts in the dark. An odd loyalty (to what it would be disloyal to put the thought of him into words, I did not know; there are blind loyalties of the blood which are slow to conform to changes in the mind and emotions) made me keep silent. The wind seemed to ruffle the lights on the shore, so that they glittered once, as I looked, like scales. "I'm cold," I said, and as we turned to walk back to the land, "Joel, you were never taken in by the John and Jenny crowd. Were you? And yet you spent a great deal of time with them. Well, they were your friends—it was you who took me there. But you didn't swallow it all, the way I did. Yet I think you wanted just as much as I did"—I italicized it half-sadly, half-mockingly—" 'the good life.' "

"Oh, yes, I want it," he said. "Just as much. Too much, Helen, to expect to find it, first shot, just like that."

I went in front of him down the wooden steps back onto the promenade. "Joel"—I rounded on him with a sudden accusing dis-covery, curious—"why didn't you ever warn me about them—tell me. You could have told me." I paused as if to coax him. "I might even have listened." We were under the looped lights of the prom-enade now, and met with each other's faces. He hesitated a moment beneath a lamppost, checking our progress, so that we must have looked like two people who pause to decide on their direction. "No . . . ," he said, looking at me rather hard. His eyes were in the shadow of his brows, but I saw his cheeks move, as if he screwed up his eyes against a harsh light. "No. Not now. Perhaps some other time. It's a long story."

I laughed. "But there isn't much other time. It's Thursday night—pretty late Thursday night, too, I should imagine—and the *Ostia* sails on Saturday."

The next morning he arrived at the hotel soon after breakfast. He had walked all the way from the docks, because it was such a lovely day, and he was carrying a small parcel. Inside it was a carved ebony head I had admired in the window of the native curio shop the day before. "It's from the Congo, they told me," he said, as I set it down with delight amid the string and paper on one of the hotel veranda tables. "Joel, it's beautiful! I love it!" And he was as much pleased at my pleasure.

There is something about the spontaneous exchange of a gift that creates a special kind of ease between people; that Friday morning in Durban it seemed part of the general freshness and good temper of the day. We sat on the veranda with the rich and lazy assumption of the whole day before us. The waves lifted their shining backs and paused a moment, fixed in their own reflections, before rolling evenly to the sand; the whole sea glittered and hung, alive and beautiful behind the cars and busses and the clipped green spaces of the Marine Parade. I stretched out over the balustrade and twisted my neck up to the tall buildings which seemed to disappear, toward the top, in the bright air. "Makes you *dizzy*."

He came and hung out, too. "Terrific sweep of horizontal"—his hand went out over the sea—"contrasted with sheer vertical. Makes you really see what modern architecture is getting at."

"Or what the sea is getting at!" We both laughed. "Shall we go to the beach?" I said, wiggling my toes in my sandals.

"Which beach?"

"North or South, as you like."

He opened his eyes, which he had shut for a moment against the sun. "How would you like to go to a real beach, all to yourself, along the Coast?"

"Oh, I wish we could. To Amanzimtoti or somewhere. Would a train be an awful fag? —I'd like to?"

"Would you really? Good. Because I've got a surprise."

I laughed. "Another one?"

He sat forward, enjoying my curiosity. "A car," he said.

"But how?"

"I remembered a friend of Max's. I telephoned him, I talked nicely to him. Oh, it's a very smart car. He calls it a 'cabriolet'— know what that is?" We both giggled our ignorance. "Anyway, it'll be here at ten. He's sending it along with his driver. Then it's ours. We can go out for the whole morning, the day, if you want to."

To anyone else I should have burst out gaily: Joel, you darling. But somehow, even now, I could not show a flippant affection toward him. I said instead, standing up: "Joel, there isn't *anything* I'd rather do today. I'll fly and get ready." Perhaps this was worse, because it seemed to embarrass him. "Be careful you don't lose that toe," he said reflectively, as I moved off. —The little toe of my left foot always slipped the thin strap on those particular sandals.

The car was a new Citroën. We were disappointed because the hood didn't come down, but, as Joel put it, we gave ourselves the illusion of an open car by "opening all the windows and driving very fast with our eyes closed." We drove out along the South Coast road past Congella where we could see, away below, ships clustered against the wharves like leaves drifted to the sides of a pond. We came up through the sugar cane to the cliff that rounds above the sea just before the village of Amanzimtoti, we hooted our way through the litter of shops, fruit stalls and Indian children which impinges upon the narrow road near Isipingo, and we drove along the dipping and rising sea road in long patches of warm silence, broken, now—it seemed—by the sight of a little yellow beach, now by desultory talk. All semblance of city life dropped behind us. Each tiny village, in the faces of the holiday children or the slow walk of the retired residents to the post office or the general store, proclaimed the pace of the sea and the green bush. The cane sang with our speed as we passed; the sea drowned our voices where it broke on rocks. There was a hotel above a deserted beach where we had lunch, and men and women came tramping in from the golf course which belonged to the place, the fairways buried among sugar cane as if a barber had run his clippers through the long waving green. We bathed on another beach that was not a "place" at all, and drank ugly red minerals that dyed our tongues, at a village near by, because we were burningly thirsty and the village had nothing else to offer.

As usual, when people are enjoying having no fixed destination, this nameless beach was the one which pleased us most, and we

were sorry we had not come to it earlier. "Whatever happened to
Ludi Koch?" Joel asked suddenly, while we lay there.

"Got a store, the last I heard, somewhere near where they lived
before." I rolled over. "Were you thinking of Ludi Koch, now?" I
smiled, curiously, indicating the setting.

"Funny, I suppose the combination of you and this, put it into
my mind. What you'd told me, I mean."

I giggled and began smoothing the dry sand off my legs, with
pleasure; I could feel, like a secret flaw, the bristle of the reddish-
fair hairs which I depilated. "Love in the sun." I laughed at myself
at this distance, remembering for the time nothing of the pain, the
intensity; perhaps I was even boasting a little. I think we dozed a
while, after that. I woke because a fly was tickling its way along my
leg; at least, that was what it felt like: I brushed at it, but there was
nothing there but more sand. Joel's eyes fluttered open but for the
moment he was still asleep; I do not think he knew I was there.
And then I saw from the movement of his mouth as he swallowed
that he was awake, and looking up at the sky. What was he thinking,
this closed and bone-familiar being breathing beside me? Was he
really there at all, can a person be said to be present to one when
it is to be only for a few days, a time so short it could be computed
in hours, and human beings are apprehended only in flashes, over
a long evenness of years. I don't remember Ludi, I thought tran-
quilly. Perhaps I shall again at another time; but I don't now. The
tranquillity trod firmly down on it: I don't think of Paul. What I do
remember, I don't think of.

Joel was looking away, up into the sky, seeing nothing. *That
time* when I opened my eyes, I thought, he was looking at me and
I was sure he had been looking at me a long time.—I watched him
a moment longer, but he was not aware of it.

So I rolled back onto the sand, and lay there, in the warmth of
it. I was aware in my mouth of the want of a cigarette and in my
hand, of the movement that would touch Joel's arm and get it for
me. At this point he said: "Cigarette?" and while still I had not
moved, it was coming to me. "I was asleep," he said. I felt myself
smiling at him indulgently. He yawned with the daze—"What was

I saying, before?" I smiled again and shook my head, as if to say "Nothing. No matter." "Talk must have been in my dream," he said.

"I'm so happy where I am," I said.

When we were driving back to Durban I found myself doing a curious thing. "I was looking at you when you were asleep just now," I lied deliberately. "I was thinking how much like your mother you are, just around the eyes." He murmured some casual, politely questioning assent—"Yes?" or "Really . . . ?"; but I think he understood perhaps better than I did myself, that I was trying to say I feared I might have hurt him by some of the things I had said the night before; and that I accepted him, humbly, wholly.

We went to dance that night. In the pleasant, spurious, sentimental atmosphere of a night club that had so little to do with Joel Aaron, I talked to him as I have never talked to any living being: as I have talked to this pen and this paper. Perhaps more truthfully, for here I have myself to contend with, and Joel took away from me the burden of my ego, just as Paul had once lifted from me the burden of my sex.

I remember some of the things we talked of: Joel saying, "It's not only your own failure with Paul you're running away from, it's also what you conceive to be Paul's failure with himself. It's what I spoke of yesterday; you can't bear anything to be less than the creation you've made of it in your mind."

And at some point, myself saying, "In a way, it seems right that one shouldn't be happy in South Africa, the way things are here. It seems to me to be that as well; a kind of guilt that although you may come to a compromise with your own personal life, you can't compromise about the larger things ringed outside it. It's like—like having a picnic in a beautiful graveyard where the people are buried alive under your feet. I always think locations are like that: dreary, smoking hells out of Dante, peopled with live men and women. — I can't stand any more of it. If I can't be in it, I want to be free of it. Let it be enough for me to contend with myself."

He did not answer, and what I said seemed to stand in the air, with a guilty defiance. And it seemed to take point, if not quite the way I should have wished it, from the warm sham twilight of the night club; outside this tepid and muted-lit enclosure, where the weird and useless aspects of civilization, like the extra fins on effete tropical fish, were kept alive under special conditions, there was the beautiful city cleaned and fed and planted by the Indians who orig-inally had been imported as indentured laborers, and were hated; and the natives, who had been there before the white men, and were feared. And outside the city were some of the worst slums in the world, where all these people who were another color lived; and beyond that the reserves, where an old order of life had died, and a new order presented a slammed door; and beyond that still, the gold mines which had made the white man rich and the black man wretched.

We danced easily in this bubble blown up precariously, even a little sadly, above the reality. He said, smiling down at me: "Those University dances we used to go to weren't ever much of a success, were they?"

"Well, we only went to one, I think. —I wonder why? —I always felt so stiff with you. Not exactly physically, I mean. You always became *so serious*."

"I know. So did you, I felt. Not in anything you said—"

"No, I know. That's what I meant. —A kind of solemnity in the body."

"In the presence of your body, that is. I used to watch you with other people, and marvel at how calmly they took your weight and presence." He looked at me and smiled.

"And now it's so easy. I suppose we're older."

When the music trailed off and we were making our way back to the dim little sofa, I said chattily: "Joel, do you really think it might have been because you are a Jew and I'm a Gentile?" The idea of this distinction, at this stage in my life, made me laugh a little. He nodded, pouring me a drink. "Of course."

"But we were so close. Such good friends."

"Not close," he said, "just good friends. You were closer to Danny McLeod, who danced with his cheek on your hair the first time he met you."

"Did he?" I laughed with mock indignation. "I don't remember him. —Anyway that's not fair; just because he had a Scottish name and you know my mother's Scotch—"

"Still—"

"You thought at the time that that was Danny what's-'is-name's advantage—*I* thought you weren't attracted to me. I think I was a little hurt. No—disappointed."

He handed me my drink. He watched me a moment, his mouth curved in what was not quite a smile, gentle, but a little wry.

"Yes, I suppose I was a fool. What I feared would offend"—he stopped and made an appealing gesture of confession—"was exactly what was needed."

"I wanted to be loved," I admitted, still feeling it in the nature of confession, half-ashamed, because it was to Joel that it was being made. "I wanted to be touched and kissed as well as talked to. D'you think that was bad?"

"Bad," he said. "Bad. What would the Isa Welsh intelligentsia have to say if they heard you say a thing like that?" But when our laughter died away, he said: "Often and often, I used to feel, now I'm going to kiss her, now I'm going to lift up that hair and kiss the nape of her neck— Many times; but I never did."

"That's just exactly what I felt. Sometimes I felt myself making you want to kiss me, and then I'd stop myself, because I was afraid. I had the idea it would never be the same again. . . . So"—I suddenly became a little embarrassed, and was flippant to cover it— "other people kissed me."

He said seriously: "You had to be kissed."

I looked at him steadily across the table. "Yes."

"When I took you home," he said, "I knew it. When I went to your home. I try to explain it to myself; I think I can, now. The difference of nationality—between us—as it existed in the minds and emotions of our parents, mind, not as we conceived it—was a kind of unconscious taboo. Friendship was all right, it took place in the mind, in the interchange of speech and the world; but touch, an embrace between you and me—emotional contact reaches back into the family. It's very old, very deep, very senseless; and harder than you think, to overcome."

I said to him when we were dancing again: "What an odd place to talk like this in. Is it just a sort of softening in the maudlin atmosphere, d'you think, and we're letting down our hair and we'll be sorry?"

"No," he said, "it's because we aren't anywhere, Helen, you and I. There's a time, before people go away, when although they still walk and talk among familiar things in a familiar way, they have already left. The ship has sailed, for you. You've left it all behind you already, all the things you want and fear and have thrust away from you."

A kind of light sadness came over me, and translated itself into the terms of the shadowy, swaying place. It found expression in the small hoarse voice of the girl who sang with a melancholy intonation borrowed, like her accent, from America; in the smoke-wreathed privacy of the half-dark; and in the warm body of Joel, embodied all that I should put my arms about in leave-taking.

I felt I should apologize for it and said to him: "I think I do feel a little maudlin, after all."

37 THE YELLOW MARBLE BIRD had a dribble of real water running from his beak. A band was playing on the dais. The yellow brocade settees were completely hidden by people; people sitting on the cushions and on the arms, people clustering round those who were sitting. The little bar was lively with people, and the Italian stewards raced briskly round.

The whole ship was like a stage-set where the lights and the curtain have at last gone up.

Joel and I had two little seats crammed against the bar on one side, and the side of the dais where the white piano was, on the other. The band played, unheeded, and over and over again, "Darling, Je Vous Aime Beaucoup" and a rather peculiar version of "Sarie Marais." Joel said something, but I could not hear. "What's that?" He leaned over. "I said I understand that they double up as stewards, when they're not playing." I nodded, smiling, smiling. The

atmosphere was curiously like that of a large midday wedding re-
ception, where you are dazed by the heat and the crowd in their
best clothes, the pageantry of the wedding retinue, which somehow
seems to belong under electric light rather than the sun, and the
intoxication of champagne drunk at a time when other people are
banging hammers and pushing pens.

I leaned across and shouted: "It's hard to believe that this is
something the ship experiences over and over again, year in and
year out. It seems to take it as such an occasion." He nodded
fiercely, and shrugged at the impossibility of conversation. But a
minute or two later some people got up from a group of chairs near
the door and we pushed our way quickly toward them. We sat down
promptly and those chairs we were not occupying were immediately
whirled away over our heads with eager apologies. The band and
the talk were no longer deafening; we were beside the doorway and
could see the deck and feel the sharp heat of the day outside, instead of the stuffiness of perfume and wine. The four people whose
table we had taken were being photographed against the rails by a
press photographer. We watched them compose the instant at which
they would be fixed in the social pages of the paper tomorrow, a
Durban businessman and his family, the wife in her new hat and
floral silk dress, chosen, no doubt by the daughters, the daughters
holding their hats—one small and feathered, the other large and
white—against the wind, with gloved hands. Just as the camera
clicked the one could not resist, and did what she must always have
been disciplining herself not to do: smiled too broadly and gave her
too-prominent teeth a victory.

"What time is it?" I asked. "Another hour, still," Joel said. He
had a way of smiling at me, reassuringly, every time he felt me
looking at him, as if I were the one who was about to sail, nervously
excited at the departure.

"I'm rehearsing for Monday," I said.

"But you'll have the other role, then," he said. "It's easier to go
than to be left behind. Shall we have another drink?"

"I don't think so. . . . I'm slightly dizzy already—the glare more
than anything, I think. —You know that really does fit exception-
ally." He moved his shoulders in the new linen jacket we had chosen

for him in the town earlier in the morning; it is extraordinary how difficult it is to find something to do in the hour or two before a leave-taking.

I said to him, leaning forward on my elbows on the table: "I keep getting a feeling of urgency. My mind races. I'm afraid there are so many things I want to say to you that I'll only discover when you're gone. Don't you always feel like that when you're saying good-by to someone?"

"What things?"

I smiled and sank back. "When you ask me, I don't know. I'm just sure that when you're gone . . ."

"Write them to me."

"Yes, I know." But I could not rid myself of this acute consciousness of time; time, which was like a growing volume of sound in my ears; and would cease. Every movement in the people who crowded the lounge and passed and repassed across the deck, every time a man swallowed from his glass, or a woman turned to touch the cheek of a child, gestured time that length further on. Joel fetched two more glasses of gin and lime for us and then we sauntered aimlessly about the deck, where everyone stood about as we did, and groups burst into small explosions of excited laughter. The sun and the gin seemed to clash in my head; we made quite thankfully for the lounge again, and found a seat for ourselves.

"And yet it seems much longer?" I appealed. He nodded consideringly. "—You couldn't credit it's really only two days since Thursday?"

He smiled. "Timeless, I told you. Because we aren't anywhere."

"Oh, there is something," I said, remembering. To ask him something, anything, would still this feeling I had of being unable to shape questions that were vital to *myself*, that would, in some way I could not articulate or understand, help me to read my bearings if the desire to drift on a current should prove more confining than freedom of choice. "When I asked you, the other night, why you didn't try to give me some sort of inkling of the disillusion I was heading for with John and Jenny and the others—you said you'd tell me another time."

The casual piece of curiosity—what did it matter, now, when that part of my life which it affected was past, lived through; it had scarcely more importance than the idle disinterment of a lost summer: what did you really do (one may ask) that week you were so keen to come to the mountains, and then made some feeble excuse that obviously wasn't true, anyway? —This casual piece of curiosity dropped stillness over Joel's broad, browned face, shiny with the heat. His eyes, pebbles deep in a stream, moved. To escape them, or give them escape, I followed quickly the shape of his head, and saw, like a wire of light against the black, one white hair. It followed the exact curve of the others, away from the forehead across toward the crown. "Oh, that," he said. "You know about that."

I looked at him.

"We were talking about it last night. Or part of it. Two things could have happened to you, once in that set. You could have been entirely taken in by them, for the rest of your life. Or you could have seen through them, and been hurt and disappointed, as you were. If the first had happened, I don't think I'd ever have forgiven myself for introducing you to them." He paused and looked at my hands, drawing my attention to the fact that I had spread them, like starfish, on the table. "Very selfish of me. But the second— I couldn't warn you about them because I loved you." He spread his own hand to match mine, as if he were giving me credit for a certain background knowledge before passing on to the further points in a discussion. "You know that. I loved you very much and I didn't think, for reasons we discussed last night, it could ever come to anything. So I couldn't offer you any—disinterested advice, Helen. How could you have believed me? How could I have believed myself? How could it have seemed, perhaps even been, anything but a desire to keep you for myself."

I sat looking at him across the table and my eyes slowly filled with tears. I felt it happen, and he saw it, the pinkening of blood, the brightening of the pupil, the brimming I could not control.

He said, gently, still looking at me: "But you've known always, Helen." And after a pause, "There's nothing to be surprised about."

But he could not possibly know what was going through my mind. I said to myself, It's the heat, the excitement, the drink and the stirring awareness of the occasion. Everyone here feels it in some way or another, that is why they laugh so much, are too talkative,

or keep touching and fussing at their clothes. People only rise to
the surface of their lives when there is to be change, a threat. You
only say: I'm alive, when you see death. You only say: I'm here,
when you're about to go. But I could not calm the trembling that
astonished me all through my body; I felt for a moment that my
whole consciousness, resting since I was born, on one side, had
suddenly turned over, like a great stone on the bed of the sea, and
shown an unknown world, a shining unseen surface, different, different utterly, alive with waving weeds and startled creatures pul-
sating on the coral.

I could not speak at all for a moment and then I burst out
suddenly in a taut and trembling voice: "There's a white hair. I've
just seen it, let me take it out." And I leaned over and plucked it,
bending his head with my other hand.

Soon there was a warning bell; a further wave of discreet gaiety
took the ship. The band swung into a song which was taken up,
somewhere in the room, by a phrase from a throbbing Italian voice.
Joel and I talked and laughed as fast as the rest; a telegram boy
raced up the gangway with a last-minute batch of telegrams. One
was from me to Joel (I had thought it would not be delivered to his
cabin until after the boat had sailed) and with amusement we tore
it open and read it together. The officer with the brooding eyes,
moving crisply now, kept coming into the lounge and looking over
the heads of the crowd toward the bar, like a host discreetly indicating to the servants that the dispensation of refreshments should
cease; it was time for the guests to be going.

A voice echoed over a loud-speaker system, enunciating with
great precision: "Will all nonpassengers please leave the ship. *Tutti
i non passeggeri sono pregati di lasciare la nave.*"

The groups began to disintegrate, these pulled away from those;
it appeared that the woman in the elaborately veiled hat, carrying a
pigskin cosmetic case, was not a passenger, whereas the girl in gray
trousers and a pink head-scarf was. We kissed, and found, with the
rest, that we had said good-by too soon; a kind of pause settled on
the passengers, staying behind, the visitors getting up to go. Then
the voice urged again: "*Tutti i non passeggeri sono pregati di lasciare
la nave.*" A bell clanged. There is something about the knell of a

bell; it is as old and as universal in its summons as a battle cry. We stood at the rail watching the people go down the companionway. Joel had his hand on the nape of my neck, just under the hair, where it was a little damp. I did not want to be the last to leave the ship, so in a little while we embraced again, holding each other hand by the shoulders, and I left him and made my way down behind a woman who kept looking back at someone she had left on the deck, and a man who pulled her gently toward the dock below. The companionway was not very steady and I had to watch the placing of my feet as the dock came up to meet me.

And then I was standing on the dock and there was Joel, up there, watching me. He had taken out a cigarette while I was going down, and now it was in his hand, the thin waver of smoke passing before his face, I waved and felt foolish. He smiled back, never taking his eyes off me; I could see his hands so clearly, I remember, rather broad and the fingers spread on the white rail. A man was unhooking the companionway. It swayed off, the people on the dock backed, it was wheeled away. The ship was free, Joel leaned over and shouted: "Is it four o'clock?" And I ran to the edge of the dock and yelled back: "Yes. Don't forget."—That was the hour at which the *Pretoria Castle* would sail on Monday. I looked down again to steady my balance. There was a long curl of orange peel, swaying on the dirty water. As I looked the water slowly began to widen. I stepped backward, back to the protection of the waving crowd, from whom a long murmur had come.

More and more water washed up between the dock and the ship. The people hanging over the rails had the look in their faces of children who feel a slide giving way beneath them. There were fluttering hands, calls. It was a long moment, very hot, twelve o'clock on a Durban dock.

And then it hapened to the ship; she was no longer something breaking away from the land, a part of the life of the people standing watching her go. The water glittered up, foreshortening her, and she was just another ship seen from the hotel verandas on the beach front, flecked with colors and movement that must be unimagined people, saying unimagined things in an unimaginable, unheard pursuance of life.

I took a taxi back to the hotel, and when I got there, I saw the *Ostia* once more, a squat white shape, slowly pulling the horizon over her head.

38 PERHAPS THIS STORY should end there. Perhaps all the thoughts that came to me alone in the hotel that long afternoon were inevitable; perhaps they were not even the truths they seemed then to be, but were merely one of those flashes generated by the stress of an unfamiliar emotional experience on a mind already keyed-up, like a fire springing from the friction of two sticks. Perhaps I could never have loved Joel, anywhere but on a ship due to sail in an hour; no matter how much I wanted to. I have learned since that sometimes the things we want most are impossible for us. You may long to come home, yet wander forever.

But I thought that afternoon that perhaps I had always loved him, always wanted him, and merely made do, with others. With him, I believed, I might have achieved the synthesis of most of the things in which I believed. Of lovers and friends, he seemed the only one who had not discarded everything and found nothing. Unlike me, he loved his parents enough to accept their deep differences from him, and so he had not suffered the guilt of breaking the unreasoning ties of the blood. He had not placed upon any relationship with human beings the burden of the proof of an ideal. And now, he had the purpose and the hope of realizing a concrete expression of his creative urge, in doing his work in a society which in itself was the live process of emergence, instead of decay. All this came to me in shock and turbulence, not the way I have written it here, but in a thousand disconnected images, in the piecing together of a thousand things said and felt and half-remembered.

Yet I believe that although no part of one's life can be said to come to an end except in death, nothing can be said to be a beginning but birth, life flows and checks itself, overlaps, flows again; and it is in these pauses that a story is taken up, in these pauses that there comes the place at which it is inevitable to set it down.

And for this, my story, it seems to me that place comes not on the afternoon on which Joel sailed, but a little later, a matter of hours, in fact.

I must have been very tired that night and, my mind throbbing with exhaustion, had fallen asleep early and slept deeply. I woke to hear soft rain; to smell it. I lay quite still a minute and then I got up and went over to the open window. It was, I suppose, about midnight, and although there were still cars on the Marine Parade, they were muted by the rain and their feelers of light were mistily dowsed. The sea was entirely gone behind the rain. As I stood there, putting my hands out into the surprising warmth of it, I heard a faint sound beneath its own soft sounding, and I thought it was the ringing of my own ears. But it came nearer, clearer, and it was the drowned jingle of a tambourine against small sad voices. I saw in the street below the huddled figures of some little native minstrels, singing as they padded along in the rain. The song was a popular dance tune of a few years before, "Paper Doll," but they made it infinitely mournful, infinitely longing. I stood there quite still, for a minute or more. I shall never forget how I felt. A feeling of extraordinary calm possessed me; I felt I could stand there in full possession of this great calmness forever. It did not seem to me that it would ever go.

My mind was working with great practicalness, and I thought to myself: Now it's all right. I'm not practicing any sort of self-deception any longer. And I'm not running away. Whatever it was I was running away from—the risk of love? the guilt of being white? the danger of putting ideals into practice?—I'm not running away from now because I know I'm coming back here.

I was twenty-four and my hands were trembling with the strong satisfaction of having accepted disillusion as a beginning rather than an end: the last and most enduring illusion; the phoenix illusion that makes life always possible.

For a long time after I had lain down in my bed again, I could hear the native children, still singing and shaking their tambourine as they were washed away, fainter and fainter, into the soft rain and the dark.